To Stacey

Best

Tama Janowitz

# The
# Male
# Cross-Dresser
# Support
# Group

Also by Tama Janowitz

American Dad
Slaves of New York
A Cannibal in Manhattan

# THE
# MALE
# CROSS-DRESSER
# SUPPORT
# GROUP

## TAMA JANOWITZ

CROWN PUBLISHERS, INC.

NEW YORK

With much thanks and gratitude to Betty A. Prashker, David Groff, Amanda Urban, Gwyneth Cravens, Phyllis Janowitz, and Susan Magrino.

Copyright © 1992 by Tama Janowitz

Published by Crown Publishers, Inc., 201 East 50th Street, New York, New York 10022. Member of the Crown Publishing Group.

CROWN is a trademark of Crown Publishers, Inc.

Manufactured in the United States of America

Library of Congress Cataloging-in-Publication Data
Janowitz, Tama.
    The Male cross-dresser support group / by Tama Janowitz.—1st
ed.
    I. Title.
PS3560.A535M35     1992
813'.54—dc20
                                                                    91-39305
                                                                    CIP

ISBN 0-517-58698-3

10  9  8  7  6  5  4  3  2

Design by Leonard Henderson

*To Tim Hunt*

## The Dump

*There always is a fire now*
*and where the ashes have grown cold*
*Lover Boy and I walk quietly*
*around the beer cans tires and broken clocks*
*thrown like potlatch gifts of praise.*
*This year is good. The rats are fatter now,*
*and sit more quietly upon their pink behinds*
*when once they trembled at our lightest step.*
*Where are you now I wonder.*
*Do you remember when at night we'd run*
*and hide when police cars would approach*
*their headlights brilliant in the dark dark night.*
*Thank God the year is almost over,*
*and the promenade will end,*
*and I finally will forget you,*
*and the winter dark will come*
*and the fires will burn brightly*
*in the dark.*

—Phyllis Janowitz
1966

1

ALL DAY SUNDAY I LAY AROUND IN MY dirty sweatpants and shirt until finally I decided to go to the store. Normally I made an attempt to put on some makeup, to avoid public contempt, which I wasn't imagining. People really did give me strange looks, and some even burst into laughter. It wasn't that I cared, but when I went out I wanted to avoid mockery. This time I didn't bother. There was a man standing in front of the building. He had a bicycle with a basket containing a little white dog. When he saw me, a strange expression came over his face, as if he had just lost a filling.

"Excuse me," he said. "Do you know any apartments in this area?" His question was innocuous. Yet I had an idea he had been waiting for me. I was a bit suspicious. He was too handsome, a St. Tropez type with fawn-colored hair, a crisp white shirt, corky tan, and vaguely foreign accent.

"I think there was somebody in the building moving out," I said. "There's a terrace, too, which would be nice for your dog."

"Bubbela," he said.

"What?" I said.

"Bubbela," he said. "That's the dog's name. I call him Bubbie. It's Jewish for Little Grandmother. My name's Alby, by the way."

"I'm Pamela Trowel," I said. Now I was sorry I hadn't fixed myself up. I thought of my eyes, without mascara and shadow—small reddish berries with glutinous pulp. And how my mouth was gray as a curled snail, topped with thin, black, glandular hairs.

"I travel a lot," Alby said. "But I really like this neighborhood, and I wanted to find a place for when I'm in town."

"What field are you in?" I said.

"I'm a cinematographer," he said. "Listen, is there a chance you're free later? For dinner or a drink?"

I hesitated. "Well, we could have a drink," I said at last. "I, uh, I could tell you about the neighborhood, and stuff. Where should we meet?"

"I'll pick you up," he said.

I fixed myself up, which took a while: red lipstick, white powder, black short skirt, high heels. After a while I looked out the door. Alby was standing with his bicycle, holding the little white dog. I grinned to myself, imagining the look of delight on his face when he saw me looking so much better.

"What did you *do* to yourself?" he said in a shocked voice.

"I got dressed," I said, annoyed. "When you saw me before, I was just running out to the store."

"You looked better before," he said. "Now you look terrible. Geez."

I scurried to keep up with him as he started to walk. "Your little dog is so cute," I said in what I hoped was a placating tone. "Is it a poodle?"

"I don't know," he said. "I found Bubbie on the street, in San Juan, when he was a puppy. The veterinarian, he say he have distemper and put him to sleep, but I nurse him back to health. He comes everywhere with me." He put Bubbie down on the sidewalk to show me how the dog still had stiff legs. "Walk, Bubbie," he said. The dog was almost completely catatonic, more of a stuffed toy, really, with button eyes. He tried to follow Alby, but it seemed like his batteries were low, and he had an unnatural, zombie gait.

A block or so away was a bar; Alby chained his bike in front and smuggled the dog in under his jacket. Bubbie made no protest whatsoever, and promptly passed out under Alby's stool on the floor. The room reeked of sour beer and the high pitch of sugary, spilled Coca-Cola gone bad. The place was nearly empty, but Alby liked it, he said, because they showed the ballgames on TV. Two screens broadcast the Mets. "You like baseball?" he said. He was a baseball fan. In the mornings, on weekends, he played for a softball team in the park. "When I saw you, earlier in the day, I wanted to invite you to watch me play. But if you came the way you look now, my friends would laugh at me. Where are your glasses?"

"I'm wearing contact lenses now," I muttered. This whole business was backward; it was when I *didn't* wear makeup that people laughed.

"Why you do this to yourself?"

I squirmed on my bar stool, trying to ignore his question. "Where are you from, Alby?" I said.

He gave me a disgusted stare. "Why you ask this?"

This stopped me, momentarily. "I—I'd like to get to know you a little," I said. "It's called a conversation."

He shrugged. "I grew up in da Bronx," he said. His accent suddenly became a sort of ghetto Marlon Brando. His parents were French, he said—although it took some questioning to drag this from him—but he had grown up in the Bronx. He was the only white child in the area. When pressed, it seemed he hadn't worked in several years. How he survived, his income, where he lived—he grew more and more uncomfortable at being asked any questions. "I'm trying to watch the game on TV," he said when I wondered aloud why he didn't want to talk to me. During a commercial he conceded that he would answer my questions just this once, since it was our first date.

"So what kind of apartment are you looking for?" I said, hoping this was a less sensitive subject. There was no response. I got up to leave. The game wasn't half over. It was strange, because I really had the feeling—when I saw him outside my door—that he had deliberately materialized there, just for me. "Where you going?" he said.

"I'm going home," I said. "I'm tired."

"I'll walk you," he said, puzzled. He stood and stuffed Bubbela back under his coat. "You don't have to go straight home, do you?" he said. "Bubbie needs a walk. Come with me just for a minute to the little park, to give Bubbie some exercise."

The park was just up the street from my apartment. We walked slowly while Alby wheeled his bike. In the early evening gloom he leaned his bike against a broken lamppost and took my hand, abruptly pressing it against his penis, which he had slyly taken out of his fly. It gave me a bit of a jolt. It went down halfway to his knees, of the thickness of an infant's arm and half-erect. "I want you to be my girlfriend," he said.

"Look, I have to go," I said.

"Why can't I come in your house?" he said.

"I don't know you," I said.

"We can just cuddle, we don't have to do nothing. It's been a long time since I was with a woman. I'm forty-two years old, but I been saving myself, for someone like you."

Without thinking I shoved his organ back in his pants and neatly zipped it up. "Bye-bye," I said and started to walk home.

He followed me, talking in an angry tone. "You leading me on," he said. "You don't have to play no games with me."

"Good night," I said. "Good-bye." I shut the door. I could hear him kicking his bike into the street and then retrieving it. His parents, he had said earlier, had escaped France during the war. They fled to Argentina before making their way to the States. Was he mentally retarded? A drug dealer? His clothes were clean, and reasonably, casually fashionable. It was my own fault for thinking I could open my door and find a knight on a shining bike waiting to rescue me from my basement existence. My mother had always encouraged me to look upon life in New York as an adventure. It was, sort of—only now this creep knew where I lived. But I was fairly certain he wouldn't come back again, not after I had so blatantly rejected him.

Still, I felt agitated. I hadn't eaten, either. I waited until I was sure he had gone, and then I went out to get a slice of pizza. There was no one ahead of me on line. The usual three men were shoveling pies topped with canned, spongy mushrooms and pink, curled discs of pepperoni in and out of the ovens. I took a tray and put a plastic fork and knife on it. "Hello," said the man who liked me. "How are you?" He had one gold tooth and a mustache, tawny skin and black wavy hair. He considered himself very attractive—he was attractive—but I couldn't stand the way he looked at me, with an air that indicated he pitied me but was still willing to show me a good time. The other men exchanged imperceptible winks and nods.

I went to Genero's fairly frequently, and once allowed myself to be drawn into a conversation with gold-tooth after a longer than usual absence. "Where you been?" he said.

"Oh, uh, I've been busy," I said.

"You have vacation?" he said. "I go on vacation soon. Home to see my family."

"Where are you from?" I said.

"Afghanistan," he said. "I work hard, send money."

A great light and joy came into his eyes every time he saw me after that, causing me to recoil with dismay. All I wanted was to read my book and eat a piece of pizza in peace, and—though probably I was overreacting—I thought it was only a matter of time before he took his break and came over to join me while I ate. That I was no longer friendly wounded him greatly; there was pride in his blood, his gold tooth bore testament to that, and now it was up to me to reestablish relations, which I couldn't bring myself to do. "A slice of spinach-mushroom," I said, "Hassim." He was wearing a white plastic name tag. This was something new.

"Spinach-mushroom!" he shouted to the man next to him. Already his face had fallen, that I had let another opportunity go by for ending the cold war. He gave me a cool stare. *In my country,* I could tell he was thinking, *a woman such as you, past her prime, would be worthless.* I opened a book and looked down while the pizza heated. It was awful, being able to read people's thoughts, at least some of the time. This wasn't at all supernatural. Many people, however, thought very loudly. The day before I passed an elderly woman, in a brown, fake-fur coat—in the middle of summer—with a cane, she could barely move, and when I got close the woman stopped, and, giving me a sharp glance, she thought, *Go ahead, honey, look at me all you like but in fifty years you'll be the same as me!*

"Spinach-mushroom!" Hassim snarled again. The other man, dwarfish, with a leaden, Aztec face, took a slice from the oven and passed it over to me on a piece of foil. I got a Pepsi, carried my tray over to a table, and sat down. I looked at the slab of pizza, leathery, coated with red flux, embedded on its bier of crumpled metallic aluminum. The cafeteria was nearly empty, too late in the day for the high-school students who came after class, and too early for those eating dinner. A burly man mumbled in a nearly inaudible voice the recent facts of his wrongful arrest to a woman smoking a pale-lilac-colored cigarette, end tipped with gold paper.

I cut off a piece of pizza with the plastic knife and fork. The tines of the fork bent backward as I tried to carry the bite up to my mouth. A dot of grease glistened in the center. My mouth tasted like horseradish steeped in milk; I no longer had an appetite.

Across the room a woman bellowed, "Abdhul, stop kicking my seat!" She had a dome-shaped head and face the color of yellow chalk; after yelling about the seat she belched loudly. The man who was out on bail turned to stare in the middle of his sentence. She weighed at least several hundred pounds, her features, small and mealy, were embedded in flesh: and somehow, wrestled improbably around her head, was a violent, tropical scarf, ends tied up in knots like a squid or starfish.

None of this would have been particularly unusual except that the woman was surrounded by a group of kids under the age of ten or twelve. There was a large square box before her on the table and from time to time she opened the lid and took a bite of some farinaceous substance—anyway, half the time her mouth was open and whatever she was chewing was white and oatmealish. The children watched her eat in silence. "Abdhul, stop kicking the seat!" she said again, and gave one of the kids a halfhearted slap across the ear.

It was some time before I realized that what the woman was eating was fried chicken, possibly some kind of fried chicken patties and this . . . must have come from some other restaurant; Genero's didn't serve fried chicken and in fact it was in a take-out box. The children—I counted quickly, there were five—were not, apparently, to be given any food. They watched the woman's hand descending into the box and then up to her mouth, fingers wiping her chin. It seemed mean and sad, yet such sights were common enough in the city. I hesitated to get involved, and anyway, what could I do? Perhaps the woman was merely the baby-sitter, the children were such a wide range of colors and so close in age it seemed impossible they could all be hers . . . maybe for her this was merely a snack, and the children would all return home later for hot suppers, appetites unspoiled.

It was a mistake to stare so intently at her. Surely I had lived in New York long enough to learn something. I didn't think she noticed me, one of her big eyes seemed to go off in a different direction, but "What the fuck are y-ooouu looking at?" she suddenly bellowed, and I was reminded of a big moose with velvet-coated trunk or a grayish hippopotamus, huge pink mouth edged with stubby molars. The boys sat like trained pups, maybe she wasn't even talking to me, but I looked away. "I tole you, Calabash, to shut the fuck up or you're going to get me in a lot of trouble!" she said. I hadn't heard any of the children make a sound. She hunched over the take-out box and plopped another tidbit of food into her mouth with a smack. Even if I hadn't already lost my appetite it would have been hard to eat with those caiman faces, rapacious and patient, waiting for food. I took a swill of the sugary soda and scraped a bit of wax from the cup with my front teeth. Behind the counter the men had collected in a knot and stood muttering to each other. Finally Hassim left and went over to the turbaned woman. "Hey, lady, you leave now," he said.

She turned in her seat and bucked like an animal tormented by flies. "Leave me a-lone," she said. I plucked a mushroom from the edge of my slice. Ominous mushroom, tasting of life in a can or science laboratory. I had borne witness to such lives, anyway similar ones, many times. All around me the city streets churned with creatures of the elemental variety. The homeless and insane chanted the babble of the collective unconscious. I had seen a drunken and violent man tip over an entire block of garbage cans, spewing rotting meat, snot-filled Kleenex. In front of an expensive restaurant on my block late at night a woman stood with a three-year-old child begging for change. At a twenty-four-hour drugstore a man dressed as a clown, handing out advertising circulars announcing discount prices, burst into tears at the moment I passed, and I saw a pool of urine collect on the pavement at his feet, running out from under the billowing red-and-yellow harlequin trousers. Half the time I didn't know whether I was awake or asleep, these were fragments of dreams.

"You eat food here you buy, no' food you bring," Hassim said. But he took a step back as he spoke. Another man came out from behind the counter and stood nearby.

"Go a-way," the woman said. "I'm not bo-thering you." Hassim and the other man walked away to hold a conference. "Now look what you've done," the woman told the boys. "Maurice, stop kicking the seat or I'll slap the shit out of y-oou."

It was too much. Whose side was I on, and in any event what could I do? Poor Hassim, with his trembling, Kurdish pride, perhaps he had been left in charge of the restaurant, it was obviously breaking his spirit to have to work in this sweaty, garlicky pizza joint when he should have been out . . . prancing up some austere mountain on a tassled horse, scimitar between his teeth, now to be reduced to a shrivel before this gelatinous heap of a woman—*where he came from no woman would ever have raised her voice to him!*—and I could see him muster some kind of warrior rage, his gold tooth glinted from his curled-back upper lip, he would not touch her himself. "Lady, I call police!" he said.

"Beee qui-et," the woman said, though she didn't look at him and something was diffused. After all, she wasn't really bothering anyone, the cafeteria was almost empty. There was no reason why she couldn't have been left alone to eat, and maybe she would have . . . except for the presence of the hungry boys.

Though it appeared she was completely uncomprehending, she got up to leave, one last plop of chicken into her mouth, which she swilled down with a wash of orange soda from a can. She was nearly embedded between the chair cemented to the floor and the table. . . . The little boys rose without being told, and without thinking I stood and carried the slice of pizza over and gave it to one of them. "Do you want this?" I said. "I haven't eaten any of it."

He snatched it from my hands in a way that reminded me of a monkey owned by a cousin of mine in high school, a squirrel monkey with a worried face kept in a cage in the basement. Once I had given this monkey a silver bell—anyway, I had offered it to the monkey, through the bars of the cage. He snatched it from between my fingers with a guilty expression and then tucked it up under his arm as if it were going to be taken from him at any second. . . .

The boy—I saw now he was wearing a pale pastel sweatshirt, eggy purple—took the slice and without saying anything began to tear off hunks and put them into his mouth. The woman yanked his arm sharply, but the pizza didn't fall from his grasp. I backed away. Then they left, the woman bawling near the door, "Now look what you've done, I told you kids to be quiet."

Hassim gave me a weak smile from across the room, as if hoping for my approval. "This lady, she crazy," he said to the room at large. The woman who had been smoking the lilac cigarette made a glaucous clicking sound with her tongue. "Terrible," she said. "She didn't give those boys anything to eat. Some people—!"

The man nodded. "So my lawyer said, 'No problem, plead guilty and you'll get a suspended sentence, I know the judge.' So the judge gave me seven years. I was set up, from beginning to end. So I . . ."

I got up and carried my tray over to the disposal without listening to the rest of what he was saying. The trays stacked on top, chocolate-colored plastic, were flecked and greasy; probably they didn't even bother to wash them but just carried them back to the start of the cafeteria line. The swinging door to the garbage container flapped hungrily as I shoved my nearly full cup of soda inside. It didn't seem right to throw liquids in there, but I didn't see any other spot to leave it. Hassim had returned to his position behind the counter. "Bye-bye," I said, picking up one of the free local newspapers that were stacked in a pile by the door. But Hassim averted his glance.

The paper was an Upper West Side give-away; I got so engrossed in the cover story I stopped in front of Genero's to read it. The article was about a woman who lived only two blocks away from me, newly married, who had gone on her honeymoon with her husband to stay in a lighthouse on some Scottish island with a lot of cliffs. The first afternoon they had a little picnic, on the bluff, and during the meal her husband began to choke, he stood up, and the woman, wanting to dislodge the food, gave him a slap on the back and he toppled over the edge. I found it fascinating that the woman, who had to return home alone from her honeymoon, lived only two blocks away from my apartment. Maybe I should look her up and befriend her. . . . Because I was so engrossed in the article I didn't see the little kid, the one I had given the slice to, standing next to me by the front door. He gave my arm a tug. "Hi there," I said stupidly. "Where's all your friends?"

He didn't answer. Maybe he wanted money; I rummaged around in my bag, looking for change, and came up with a dollar. My pocketbook was filled with what I considered to be an indescribable amount of filth. I had the habit of collecting cents-off coupons from the Sunday papers for products I would never purchase or use. Various detergents and scrubs that even when marked down fifteen or twenty cents were far more expensive than the generic brands. Ratty bits of paper, old lottery tickets, half-eaten pieces of gum. Still, there seemed to be no sense in cleaning out or reorganizing my bag, when I knew I would only stuff it up again within days. I should have shoved the entire contents into the garbage container, if for no other reason than to listen to the pail's groans of dismay when it realized it was not being fed some delightful crusts of food.

I handed the dollar to the kid, who didn't say anything, and I walked away. Even though it was twilight the street still blistered with heat. The sidewalk and tarmac were like the feverish skin of some hospital patient over which the people walked like ants. "Bye-bye," I called to the kid, who looked down. I noticed he wasn't wearing any shoes. Perhaps he had come from some Caribbean island, where children ran barefoot, but it certainly didn't seem to be a good idea here in the city. Clumps of foamy spit dotted the ground and sticky trickles of urine, human and canine, trailed from building to curb in sparkling mountain streams. Didn't his mother—or whoever—know that tuberculosis had been on the rise?

There were other diseases too, and things like spirochetes that could bore their way up through the skin on the soles of the feet, where they would enter the body and cause . . . heartworm? Although maybe this was something that happened only in tropical countries. I was not that good on medical facts, but still I knew healthwise to go barefoot was not a good move.

Anyway, I had given the kid a piece of pizza, I had given him a dollar, and the stores were already closed. It was too late for me to take him somewhere and buy him a pair of shoes. And for all I knew the kid was richer than me. I had once had a friend, who had sort of . . . adopted a homeless family in the park, and after a few months, when they told her they had finally found an apartment, she offered them her air conditioner (the homeless girl had asthma) and an old futon to sleep on she had hardly ever used. "Oh, good," the woman told her. "We can use it in our country home." It turned out, that when the family told her they had finally found an apartment, what they meant was, they had found a *new* apartment. A bigger one.

I started to walk home. I had certain plans in mind, the first being that I would stop at a delicatessen en route and buy an onion roll: this delicatessen had baked goods, one of which was a particular roll with buttery flakes of pastry absolutely stuffed with pale shreds of onion. Then I could eat this, the next morning, for breakfast. A cold bath, paying the bills, watching TV, and bed were some of the other plans I had in mind. But when I got out of the delicatessen I saw the kid standing there. He must have followed me from Genero's down the street. "Bye-bye," I said again.

A block or so later I half turned around. The kid was still there, fifty paces behind. He stopped when I did. "What are you doing?" I said. He didn't answer. I shook my head and went on. I did not care to have this child follow me and find out where I lived. He looked short—maybe nine or ten, though having no experience with children I couldn't be certain of his age—but it was entirely possible he belonged to some sort of poisonous gang, who would lie in wait for me at my door and cosh me with pokers or whatever equipment juvenile delinquents were using these days. My building had no doorman, and my basement apartment, which hated me, would no doubt offer me no protection of any kind.

A block more and I looked back and he was still there. This truncated dwarf with citron-colored skin. "Go away!" I said. A tall man was walking his dog, a tiny hairy animal with lolling tongue and cataract-covered eyes, and both looked at me sharply. The child in the distance gave a nervous grimace but when I started to walk again he did too. Perhaps rather than lead him straight to my door I should keep walking until he grew tired and went away. Still I did not like to be bullied into feeling afraid to go home. I even went so far as to take a few steps in his direction and give him a stern, ferocious stare that caused him to look away and stop, though when I resumed walking he continued, unbowed, along my path . . . it was a free country after all, although not, I had always assumed, for nine-year-olds.

The streetlights came on, harnessing the greasy leaves of the trees, dessicated in the yellowish glare, and I was momentarily distracted. A few poor wilted London plane trees, blighted by some disease; stubs of young gingkos, newly planted that spring; a flowering pear tree, trunk bashed and hatcheted by some backing-up car—they were all stuffed into tiny slots in the pavement, in the gray, rock-hard soil. The summer had withered them, the little rain there had been had trickled over their roots and flung itself into the gutter without providing any nourishment. It was a sorry sight, the desperation of the city trees. They had struggled so bravely to breathe in the carbon-monoxide-laden air . . .

In front of my building I stopped. He was now only twenty paces behind. "Go away, kid," I said. "Where's your mother? Go home." I jabbed my key into the lock of the metal security gate outside my front door. The child took a few steps backward and then stood still. "What is, ah, what's your name?" I said in a rather stuttering voice. I paused waiting for him to say something; when he didn't speak I finished opening the gate, closed it behind me, opened the front door, and went in.

The air conditioner had given up producing any cold air. I jiggled the knob and it moaned, a chain-saw sound. I put my face in front of it and unbuttoned the top buttons of my shirt, huddling for cold. After a minute or so it occurred to me to look out the window; there was only one, located up high by the ceiling. I stood on the couch and peered out. He was still there, crouched on the top step, waiting. There was a patient yet strangely happy expression on his face, like that of some Peruvian laborer munching coca leaves. Though he must have seen me, I quickly ducked down. There was a rich layer of dirt on the sill, nearly thick enough to begin planting seeds. Then I lowered the crumpled metal blinds and turned off the lights.

At two in the morning I woke with a jolt. The bedroom opened onto a tiny cement yard (I was the only person with access) that was divided in back by a fence from the building on the next block. A woman was shrilling, "Sylvester! Sylvester!"

Sylvester was an evil black-and-white cat who roamed at large, highly territorial—he had even crept into my apartment, one afternoon when I left the back door open, and sprayed a suitcase in the bottom of my closet. I didn't catch him in the act but the suitcase (upon my discovery after a week-long search for the source of the smell) was permanently ruined. I wondered if Alby, my own personal lunatic, was waiting outside. A lower whimpering sound came from just beyond the door. I could call the police, although it would be hard to say just what crime had been committed—that I had met a man in front of my house, agreed to go with him for a drink, and that he had then, in the dark, taken his penis out? I guess it *was* a crime, but was it worth it to try and prosecute? It seemed too demented. Maybe it was just a stray dog outside, or some derelict: on several occasions I had surprised men urinating down my stairwell. I remembered the first time it happened, when I saw a person's legs in the window and thought someone was delivering a package, and so I went to the door and opened it. The man was so startled he ran off down the street, piss dripping down his legs. The next time it happened, the guy wasn't even perturbed; I yelled, "Hey, what are you doing!" (though this was perfectly obvious) and he casually shook himself and walked away. I had to pour a bucket of hot water into the area at the bottom of the steps (there was a drainage outlet there, for the rain that dripped down) but even so, the smell didn't go away for quite some time.

Or maybe it was thieves hiding their stolen merchandise. This, too, happened all the time. Among the things I had found on leaving for work:

a bag containing six pairs of brand-new men's Jockey shorts, size 34; two large jars of Taster's Choice, caffeinated and decaf; two pairs of worn, rather cheap women's shoes; and a very nice briefcase belonging to Jeff Slonim of Paramus, New Jersey, and full of his work papers. It took me most of one day to track him down; his car had been broken into.

Now I assumed there was either a man urinating out there, or Alby had returned, but I felt fairly safe, because even when my front door was open there was still the old-fashioned iron gate, curlicued and rusty, that provided a barrier through which I could see.

I fumbled by the bed for my glasses and got up, putting on an old pink chenille bathrobe I kept on a hook by the door. My eyes were half shut from sleep, I didn't bother to switch on the lights but fumbled my way down the hall. In the kitchen I took a bucket from under the sink and filled it up with lukewarm tap water. I envisioned flinging the water up the steps at whoever was there, through the metal-grid gate, although if I had been thinking more clearly it might have occurred to me that most of the water would probably splash back onto me; but if it was a urinator this would teach him a lesson, or at least scare him off, and if it was the lurking Alby I could explain, from my position of relative safety, that I had thought he was a derelict and if he didn't leave I would call the police.

Some of the water dripped over my bare feet as I lugged the bucket through the living room to the front door. Not bravery on my part, only a fine fury at having been woken from sleep, though who knew what I might find on the other side when I opened the door: a man standing with a loaded gun, or the acrid heap of a plop of excrement.

I opened the door, holding the bucket by its sagging handle, and without looking grabbed the bottom of the pail with my other hand and gave the contents a toss. At least half hit the wall and gate and came flying back at me, warm and wet and reeking of old Spic and Span—some gritty green crystals remained in the bottom of the pail. "Damn," I said. Then I looked up.

I had thrown the water over the kid who followed me home from Genero's earlier that evening. He hadn't gone away, he was still there. He was hunched over on a step, down a bit from street level, a drooping bundle trying, I suppose, to sleep. Now he had been violently jolted by half a bucket of the soapy stuff. His eyes blinked fearfully, luminous and puffed. He rubbed some soap from one fringed lid.

These details and more were illuminated by the forty-watt bulb that burned above his head. The eggy sweatshirt streaked with water and sweat. The skin on his face, that pale bright amber. His rostrate hair, black filaments. "God damn it," I said, "What are you doing here?"

He said nothing, but, letting out an involuntary whimper, shook himself doggishly. Then he gave me a grin. "For God's sake," I said. "Is anybody else out there?" I opened the metal door and peered around up over his shoulder. The portion of the street that I could see was empty. It was light under the street lamps, still hot; sour plops of rain began to fall. I grabbed the kid by his wrist and pulled him down into the doorway. "You can come in for one second," I said. "Until you get dry. Because it's my fault." I felt embalmed and depressed. What a sordid existence. I held on to him by his wrist and shut both doors behind us, flicking on the light.

In the center of the living room I let go of his arm. He looked younger than I had expected. He might have been attractive, except that his grin, which still hadn't gone away, split his face into a goofy Bozo clown, crinkled up his eyes, revealed his yellow teeth.

"What's your name?" I said. The smile went away but he said nothing. "Look, I don't have to do this," I said. "I have to work in the morning. For all I know you—you're going to come back here with your little friends and rob me." His mouth pursed, there were the beginnings of a faint mustache above his lip, though maybe it was just old food. There was a rancid odor about him, too, of garbage, garlic, potato chips, the ancient tallow of fast food.

I grabbed a towel from the bathroom and spread it over the couch. "You sit there," I said. He didn't move. I took him by the arm and pushed him back on the couch. "Sit down," I said. "Take off your shirt." He made a whimpering sound and clutched his hands around his shoulders.

"All right, all right," I said. "I was just going to give you something dry to wear."

I went into the kitchen and opened the refrigerator. Rice Krispies, a bag of prechopped cabbage to make instant coleslaw, a jar of antique olives. I had once had a dog who liked to eat salad. First thing in the morning, she insisted on having a peeled carrot, or some lettuce—since then I always kept a bag of green things around. I had been well-trained by that dog. I still felt her loss (she had been fourteen when she died, I had had her since she was just a pup a few months old) although she was spoiled, demanding, and needed constant attention.

"You like cereal?" I called. He didn't answer, but I put some cereal into a bowl and poured milk over it. In a paper bag by the toaster was a banana I had forgotten about; a little intoxicated fruit fly flew out, and I peeled the fruit and cut off the bad bits and sliced the rest into the bowl. Maybe he was thirsty—though there seemed to be no point in asking him—and I got down a mug that was covered with balloons and printed I LOVE YOU (a nightmarish birthday present though I could not remember who had given it to me or when) and I poured some more milk into it.

Then I thought better of this; I put it into a pan on the stove to warm and from the freezer I took a can of cocoa, which I think I had used only once, and I dumped some of this into the milk with some sugar. A little cocoa dust floated to the top and I stirred it around. I carried both things out to him. He was perched rigid on the edge of the towel, looking straight ahead and making a low humming sound.

"Here," I said. "Cocoa and cereal." I went back to get a spoon and a napkin. "Let me know if the cocoa isn't sweet enough." He didn't touch either one but sat still looking blankly ahead. "Rice Krispies!" I said. "You know, snap, crackle, pop." I mimed eating it with the spoon. "Mmmm," I said. "See? Good."

This was idiotic. "Fine," I said. "So you're not hungry. Maybe that piece of pizza filled you up, huh?" I took a sip of cocoa to make sure it wasn't too hot and then held the mug up to his lips. It might as well have not been there; he didn't even make any effort to push it away. "All right, then," I said and put down the mug. "In that case, I'll help you get cleaned up and dried off, and then we can . . . then you can go."

If I could at least figure out where he lived, I'd find a taxi, pay the driver, and put him in. "Come on," I said. "Let's go. Into the bathroom." I stood up but he didn't move.

Finally I grabbed his grimy wrist and pulled him along. I turned on the bathroom light and gave him a little shove in front of the sink. "Wash your face," I said. The walls were covered in places with a horrid yellow slime— some sticky glue or varnish from when the walls had been papered?—and tufted with strands of my own hair. They must have blown away when I brushed it and attached themselves to the yellow ooze. There was a hole in the ceiling by the corner of the shower that dripped with water from the upstairs neighbor. I grabbed a washcloth and, running it under water, smeared it over his face. "See?" I said. "Now *you* do it. You'll feel better, all cleaned up. I'm going to go find you something to wear."

There was nothing I could do about his pants, but I grabbed a baggy white T-shirt on which was printed a picture of a giant scorpion. I went back into the bathroom, carrying this and a shrunken black sweatshirt; he still hadn't moved, the tap ran and the washcloth hung limply in his right hand. "I don't know why I'm bothering," I said.

I took the washcloth out of his hand and pulled his stained sweatshirt off him. He made a feeble noise of protest, but the sweatshirt was already up over his head. "God, you stink," I said. What the hell, I decided, and

I pulled his pants down. He wriggled frantically, but I got them around his ankles and picked him up and out of them.

I turned on the shower, to what I imagined was a suitably lukewarm temperature. The shower head was attached to a sort of hose thing, and I took it down off the wall and let it spray at tub-level. "Now for the underpants," I said. He had on a filthy pair of Jockey shorts, but he wriggled so much and let out a thin, high-pitched scream, that I gave up. "Keep them on, for all I care," I said, and I picked him up and put him in the tub. He didn't wriggle but seemed to deliberately be making himself weigh as much as possible. Black puddles collected around his feet where they touched the tub.

He let out a low keening sound as I directed the shower head stream onto him. Surely this was some bizarre sadistic trait I had not previously noted within myself, that need to lure prepubescent children into the bath at three in the morning. It hardly appeared even to me to be a good deed.

With my free hand I smeared a green, scented bar of soap across his sunken chest. It was broccoli soap, one of a collection of vegetable soaps I had purchased for forty-nine cents apiece at the nearby discount job-lot store. In my cabinet I had the tomato, string-bean, eggplant, and cauliflower soaps as well. Apart from the variety in color they had no vegetative qualities, but I was fond of the hard little bars, printed on each box with a picture of the vegetable and listing its attributes. Each type had a distinct, earthy, slightly rotten odor. Once a woman standing next to me on the subway had commented on my scent admiringly. "Beefsteak tomato," I told her. She gave me a bewildered look.

The kid now squinched up his eyes, though I was careful not to get the broccoli in his face. As long as I had gone this far I decided to pour a little shampoo over his head and gave it a rub, feeling slightly disgusted at the greasy sebum beneath my fingers. With the application of water his hair lost its metallic, crunchy texture.

"Fine," I said, giving him a final spray. "See? All done." I put down the shower hose, pointing it toward the wall, grabbed a thin towel from where it was lying on the top of the shower stall, and wrapped him up in it. It covered him completely.

Of his own accord he climbed out the side of the tub. "Your pants are all wet," I said, turning the shower on myself with my back to him—I still had on my bathrobe, which I opened slightly in front. "I won't see, if you take them off under the towel. Then you can put on that T-shirt lying on the floor."

By the time I had rinsed myself and the tub and turned off the water he had put on the T-shirt and wrapped the wet towel around his waist. At least there appeared to be some comprehension of the English language on his part. The drawing of the scorpion clung to his chest and bullet-shaped, hunched shoulders. "You didn't even dry yourself off," I said.

The faucet in the tub still dripped, and I turned around and bent over to try to get it to stop. Maybe it just needed a new washer; a perpetual wet syrup trailed down and each time, though I tried to use all my force to turn the cold tap all the way to the right, it didn't stop. The tub was covered with a thin layer of grayish cells—some crucial enamel had been worn away, and whatever was underneath had the habit of attracting dirt that stuck and had to be scrubbed off with Comet. A little nest of hairs had collected at the drain, along with a gray woodlouse or doodlebug that lay on its back like a tiny prehistoric monster. There was no postponing the inevitable. I got out of the tub, wrapping my robe tightly around my waist. "Put your pants back on," I said. "Your sweatpants."

He gave me an anxious, greyhound look and pulled his pants up underneath the towel. His hand reached down for some sort of adjustment. I pushed him out of the bathroom. "Now you're going to tell me where you live and we can find a taxi to take you home," I said. "Somebody's probably frantic about you."

He took a step backward. His feet left little wet spots on the floor and his toenails were yellow and curly, the feet of an old man. I grabbed his wet shoulders and gave him a shake. "Answer me!" I said. "I'm not responsible for this!"

He closed his eyes and his body went limp and he began to slump from my grasp. I let go. "All right, all right, I'm sorry," I said. "I didn't mean to touch you."

I went into the living room and sat on the couch, bent over with my damp hair in my hands. After a pause he followed me in and stood in the center of the room. Involuntarily I gave him a rabbity smile. In the over-sized scorpion T-shirt, his mealy parched head to which the sparse hairs were plastered, his citron, perhaps jaundiced skin, he resembled some demonic sprite who had crept out from behind the plaster of my angry apartment. "Deaf-mute?" I said. Still, he obviously wasn't deaf. "Know any sign language? Want some paper to print a message?" His eyes were solemn, tired, his underlip drooped.

"All right," I said, rattling on to myself. "I have no desire to be arrested by the police and go to jail for kidnapping a child." I went down the hall and got a sheet out of the linen closet. The closet was jammed with crumpled blankets, mismatched pillowcases, ripped sheets of varying sizes in blue-and-yellow stripes and florid bouquets.

I carried the sheet back to the sofa and draped it over the front and back, then folded the back down to double. "You can sleep on this," I said. "In the morning you're out of here. When I go to work you'll go back to where you came from and don't bug me anymore. I'm too tired to go on with this bullshit at the moment." I gestured to the couch. "Lie down," I said. "Get in."

He went over to the sofa and I lifted up the top half of the sheet until he lay down. Then I covered him up and went back to my bedroom.

After a pause I got up. "Do you have to go to the bathroom?" I said. "Before you sleep? You want to do something?"

He made a sound that I assumed indicated yes.

I took his hand and led him back to the bathroom, opened the door, flicked on the light, and pointed to the toilet. "There," I said. "You can leave the light on, if you're afraid. Good night."

I went back to bed and tried to sleep. I didn't hear any noise coming from the bathroom. Finally I got up, knocked on the door and opened it. He was still standing where I had left him.

"For God's sake," I said. "This is really, you know, too much. I don't want to hurt your feelings, but there must be something wrong with you." I took his hand and led him back to the couch I had prepared as his bed. "In the morning, that's it, buddy," I said. "Good-bye and good luck."

I slept through the alarm and when I woke up it was nearly ten. He was still lying on the couch, face up. I put on the coffee and made us each a bowl of cereal, talking out loud while doing so. It was strangely pleasant, in a way, not to wake up alone.

"I hope you slept all right and that this morning you remember where it is you live," I said. "You're probably deeply traumatized. Was that woman you were with in the pizza parlor your mother? I'm making us both some Rice Krispies before you go," I said. A faint fur rippling in the bottom of the kitchen sink caught my attention. I had tried everything on the fur but still it returned. Windex, Fantastik, Lestoil—even bleach, but the fur, daily, sprouted up from its little Carlsbad Cavern, the drainpipe of the kitchen sink. It resembled the first down of a baby bunny, but with an evil, alien quality. If I did not keep scouring it and trying new poisons on it, it would sprout to fill the sink and eventually the entire room.

It was of this fur I chattered while I poured the milk over the tiny hollow beads of extruded rice. The Krispies floated up in the two black bowls, exploding like the cells in a pair of expirating lungs. Some bits jostled over the edge as I carried the cereal, a bowl in each hand, out into the living room. I put the bowls down on the draped coffee table (I had covered this cheap table with a sort of floral dress: the skirt hung to the floor and collected dust knots) and pulled up the narrow blind of the lone window at the top of the room. A thin gasp of daylight coursed downward and in. "Looks like another scorcher," I said cheerfully, feeling moronic.

The child sat up without prompting and a tannic smell permeated the air. Christ, the kid had wet the humpy sofa, my elephant. The sofa was not a terrific one, but it had a certain stalwart nature, pedantic legs and gray wrinkled hide of old brocade silk that I had grown fond of. The sofa was one of my few allies in the apartment; I had found it up where my mother lived, had it re-covered and shipped at no little expense to the city. The front ends and side were covered with brass upholstery tacks in a particularly soothing, hypnotic pattern. Now the sofa had been humiliated and betrayed, I sensed its antagonism directed at me. "Eat your cereal, kid, and get out," I said.

To my surprise he picked up the bowl and began to eat, his tongue and upper lip curling anteaterishly over the fragmentary morsels in the spoon. I noticed that at some time during the night he must have drunk most of the cold cocoa. A rich sediment of brown plastered the sides and bottom of the mug.

When he had slurped up the last of the cereal I stood and opened the door. "There you go," I said. There were a couple of dollars in change in a bowl by the door and I swept it up. "Here's some money," I said. "If you won't talk to me, there's nothing I can do to help. But if you're really lost—ask any policeman."

He got up and walked to the door. "Thank you very much," he said, before heading from the gloom into the light.

At work there were four messages and a stack of mail for me on Debbie's desk. Amber MacPherson was already on the phone. Her back was to the door; she had a habit of walking while talking on the phone, like a chained, mangy lioness at the end of a frazzled cord. Once while waiting to talk to her (she made me stand outside her door until she finished her call) I had clocked the length of time it took her to make one complete circuit or back-and-forth route; she averaged seven seconds coming and going. Perhaps it was her form of exercise. I tried now to get into my office before she circled around and saw me.

There was a call from the printer's—an inquiry about the color registration for an advertisement depicting a deer and a hunter wearing camouflage clothes, I imagined, which from the beginning seemed off-color; Mr. Parker from the Ithaca Gun company had called; a message (Debbie's handwriting was round and childish, she dotted the i's with circles, light-hearted and offensive) telling me a *man* (her underlining) had called but wouldn't leave his name or number but said he'd call back; and a note from Daniel Loomis asking if, when I got a chance, I would come into his office.

The magazine was called *Hunter's World* and specialized in articles on the latest hunting equipment, rifles, and remote game reserves open to sportsmen at a cost. I had been selling ads there for several years. When I first began work the publisher, Daniel Loomis, who had hired me, assured me that the job would be what I made of it. But the magazine had been in his family for forty-odd years and Daniel, a limp, benign man in his late thirties, obviously had no interest in any expansion; he was content to arrive each morning and go to his office at the end of the corridor on the same floor that had been leased by the magazine for the last thirty years, where he would shut the door and be unavailable until he stepped out for lunch. It was only the unexpected death of the editor-in-chief, Bill Burke, who had a heart attack in Kenya the summer after I arrived, that forced Daniel to hire a new editor.

My boss, Amber MacPherson, barely tolerated me. The week after her arrival I went to her with a suggestion that I approach the company manufacturing Wetland Socks to see if they could be persuaded to advertise. "Listen, my friend," Amber said. "You have fifteen regular pages of advertising a month. If you want to expand, feel free to do so with the personal ads in the back." She took a Diet Pepsi from one of her drawers but didn't offer me one. Of course she must have known there was no money in the classified ads. "You have an easy job here, rock the boat and you'll be out on your ass on the street, and frankly, I don't see who's going to hire you, coming from *Hunter's World.*"

Once I had eaten at an Ethiopian restaurant and the waiter brought over a huge pancake, nearly three feet in diameter, which he laid across the table; the edges of the pancake—I suppose it was some sort of bread—were to be used as a scoop for the food, it was both soggy and tasteless, and there was something about Amber . . . that reminded me of this bread. If it were possible to tear off the edges of her face or a plump finger or two then this was how she would have tasted. Anyway, she said a few more things and dismissed me. It was then I began to wonder if the magazine wasn't a front for . . . something, I didn't know what, a tax write-off? It dawned on me

I had been there for nearly two years and during that time I had only seen Daniel Loomis when he entered and left his office, we had scarcely exchanged two words; before his death Bill Burke had been away most of the time on mysterious trips that I assumed were subsidized hunting excursions; and since Amber's arrival she was constantly occupied with affairs that couldn't possibly have been connected with the magazine. The phone in front rarely rang, no writers ever appeared, all the articles were commissioned or submitted by mail, and apart from Debbie—the receptionist—myself, and Daniel, there was no one else who came in to work. The art direction and layouts were all done at the printer's in Ohio. It had vaguely occurred to me before that this was unusual. In fact, it seemed there was little reason for the existence of the New York offices at all.

After Amber's lecture I went down the hall to collect the office keys from Debbie's desk—the keys to the women's room were among them. The toilet was in the hall and had, some time back, been installed with a lock when one of my predecessors, working late at night, had been critically injured. She was found the next morning covered with blood, her head smashed numerous times against the tiled wall, though I didn't hear this story until some time after I had been working. The toilets had apparently been designed in the expectation of great hordes of workers. There were six stalls and five sinks; half the light bulbs were missing and those that were left flickered erratically in the dim room, its floor and walls covered with yellowed ceramic tiles.

As I passed Amber's office I could see Daniel Loomis's back, his slumped shoulders. He was blocking Amber's view out into the hall. ". . . completely ignorant," Amber was saying. "She hasn't brought in any new advertising revenues, and believe me, Daniel, take a look at *Rifle and Gun* if you want to see ad pages in a book. Now, I was thinking—my cousin Sandra has just graduated from Vassar, and . . ."

I hurried down the hall before she could catch sight of me and accuse me of eavesdropping. My office had once had a window with a view, but some years back another office building had been built next door, some ten feet away; now my window looked directly out onto a brick wall and over a narrow passage, twelve stories down. There didn't seem to be any access into this well, and over the years a layer of office garbage, several feet deep, had collected at the bottom, foam coffee cups, mimeograph and Xerox copies, wrappers from sandwiches, indestructible nonbiodegradable effluvia that would no doubt still be lying there twenty-five thousand years from now.

I heard a whuffle behind my back. "Oh, Pamela, there you are,"

Amber said. "I was just coming to look for you. Do you have a moment to talk?" She turned and I followed her down the hall, the mail still in hand. I had never noticed before how her legs were curiously knee-less, as if each had been hewn out of one solid piece of trunk. I could see the top of her head as I walked behind. Her hair was lemony-red, thick, and organized into an elaborate pompadour topknot like a topiary yew. Perhaps, looking in the mirror, she believed herself to resemble an elegant poodle. I felt some momentary compassion, listening to her wheezy gait as she padded heavily down the hall. Probably with each step her thighs stuck together with sweat. In her office Amber gestured for me to sit; the guest chair was covered in matted grassy fabric, along one arm a seam had split and dried-out foam bulged into the air. I put the letters on the edge of her desk and began plucking, half-consciously, at the intestinal innards while Amber sat with her profile to me. The weakness—near lack of chin—I found moving, and I thought of a younger, chinless Amber, giggling with schoolfriends before she learned that the way to get ahead in this world was to trample on those weaker than herself.

"Pamela," she said, "I want to tell you a story."

Here it comes, I thought, and it's my fault for not taking my life into my own hands long ago, I gave the arm of the chair a little pluck, and white, dried spores flew into the air. "Do you mind not pulling the stuffing out of my chair completely?" she said irritably.

"Sorry," I said.

"Years ago, shortly after my divorce—my first husband was an alcoholic, but from a very good family—I took a trip with his cousin to visit some friends who rented a castle in the north of Scotland. I don't know if you know Lady Graham-Stewart"—she looked at me while I shook my head—"but she had decided to rent out the castle that summer, while she was staying in Montego Bay. Actually, I was speaking to her on the phone last night, we hadn't talked in such a long time and I was interested in finding out if she wanted to rent again, some other friends of mine were looking for a place, and I said, if they were interested in shooting, during grouse season, or even just to walk along the moors, I couldn't think of anything more beautiful than Ardsley in the fall. Do you know Rupert Vernon?" This time she didn't even bother to wait for my negative response. "Oh, God, Rupert, Rupert. You really don't know anyone, do you? I'm surprised you haven't run into him, you go out—to all these clubs—and he's out all the time. Fiftyish, drinks a lot, is working on a book about being held hostage in Syria or Jordan?"

She seemed disgusted when I again shook my head. "Oh, I'm sure you know him. He wrote that book about the nurse who was a murderer with the twenty-million-dollar trust fund. It came out a couple of years ago. Betsy, Betsy . . . Friedlander, or Freudlich, some vaguely Jewish name, although she wasn't Jewish. She grew up in Texas, went to Miss Porter's, but then, for whatever reason, she decided not to go to college but become a nurse. It was a marvelous book; you really must read it. She's been in prison—they found her guilty of injecting, oh, I don't know, seventeen people, but frankly, I think they should let her out. It really doesn't seem right, does it?"

"No, not really," I mumbled.

Her tone turned vicious. "Oh, come on, Pamela, don't be ridiculous." Her line rang and she picked it up, still scowling. "Pimmi!" she said. "I've been trying to get you all morning. Listen, I want you to add four more on for the dinner this evening. . . . What? . . . I know I only said eleven, but there're certain people who are *important*. Anyway, there's only a hundred coming for cocktails, so I don't think—hold on one second." She covered the phone and waved me out impatiently with one plump hand. "On your way back from lunch, will you pick me up a blueberry yogurt and a pack of Merits. I'm not going to have time to go out today. We'll finish this later."

That was three dollars and twenty-five cents for which I would never be reimbursed. I grabbed my mail and went back down the hall to Daniel Loomis's office, but he had already left for lunch. I started going through my desk drawers. If I was going to be fired I wanted to find out how much stuff I had and how many boxes I would need to cart it home. . . . A stack of pale raspberry candies had melted through their wrapper and formed a clear pink pool on the bottom of the top drawer. A Swingline stapler, armored and waiting for a refill, lay on its side. A packet of white address labels, a small sewing kit with tangled thread, seven thumbtacks, a blue ribbon, a dried-out marking pen. An old birthday card from my accountant, decorated with a picture of a voluptuous female bee, stinger poised above an apple blossom and reading, "Have the Sweetest B-Day Ever!" Inside he had signed it, Yours Sincerely Art, and added a note reminding me to make my appointment early.

A pinhead-size cockroach trotted over Art's signature and with a nonchalant air made its way to a crack in the bottom side of the drawer. It frightened me to think of how many loose skin cells, flakes of dander and other discarded parts of my body this insect consumed during its activities at night. That something so small made its livelihood out of me—without my permission—was something to consider. By the time this roach reached its full size, it would be just as much a part of me as one of my own fingers or toes. Were I to smash it, it would be like hammering my own toe unto death.

This type of thinking would lead nowhere. I decided to go out to lunch, making as much of my time left here at the magazine as I could. Amber's voice carried down the hall, needling its way into my skin. ". . . he stepped out to see another doctor just now. The first doctor said—and this is strictly confidential, Pimmi, I haven't told anyone but you, and if this gets out . . . Oh, yes, I know. That's what you always say. Anyway, the first doctor said—and I agree, I think he's probably right—that he has M.S. You know, he fell down, last Christmas, in Aspen, and he was unable . . . No, he couldn't get back up. Just walking down the street! He wasn't even skiing! . . ."

There was a pause. "Just a second, let me shut the door, in case *somebody* is listening out there." I could hear her shut the door. I knew as soon as she got back on the phone, her animal pacing would resume, as if it were necessary to walk back and forth in order to make her voice travel across the telephone lines. I got a stack of mail out from its metal bin to take to the post office. Who knew how or why this had come about, but there were no stamps anywhere in the office—at least not for me. The Pitney Bowes machine she kept behind lock and key; any request on my part to use this resulted in a lecture or brusque promise that she would get it out later.

Somehow I slammed my fingers into the drawer as I shut it. I was trying to pretend I wasn't completely shattered, but in fact I was. My movements were unstable, precarious; I felt like a paper bag when the carton of milk leaks. The bottom had fallen out. I was to be fired, then. I had been at the magazine for three years; there was a minuscule amount in my pension fund, I would no longer have health insurance and I sincerely doubted there was any other book in town where I could get a position as director of advertising. Before coming to *Hunter's World* I had been one of a group of advertising reps; magazines such as *Vogue* or *Cosmo* already had established departments, and I doubted that any of their advertising directors (who received large commissions based not only on those ads they themselves brought in but a percentage of everyone else's) had any plans to leave. In any event, coming from *Hunter's World* would probably not earn me any high points. I tried to block my thoughts.

The streets were dripping with anguished humidity, recycled, over-heated air that was simply transferred from one pair of lungs to the next, with each person contributing a donation of saliva and moisture. Surely this should have united the workers on their lunch break into one connected tribe, as bees know one another by taste and smell, but there was an atmosphere of rage on the pavement.

In this area near 34th Street there were far too many people, shops filled with tawdry merchandise, hawkers of Ethiopian incense, illicit wristwatches, and flimsy bangles of pressed gold tin. There were days when—perhaps due to the atmosphere, or lack of sunspots—traffic seemed to flow smoothly on the streets, people smiled and apologized, but today was not one of them. The bees were wingless, marched with heads drooping, elbows poised to jab. Mollusks of phlegm dotted the pavement. The workers here meted out an existence under fluorescent lights, long windowless hours, in rubber gloves and face masks behind whirring whippets of equipment, as dental hygienists and sewing-machine operators, and cashiers ringing up toilet paper and hair spray.

The post office was cool and cavernous. A line of people stood behind a rope on posts, a digital sign said the waiting time was approximately ten minutes. I went to the end of the line, but just then a woman shoved her way in front of me, carrying a package. If she wanted to go ahead of me, I wasn't going to argue, although I couldn't help but stare. She was tiny, and on closer inspection it was hard to tell if she was male or female: she had no breasts or waist, and the features of her face, too, were absolutely flat, only a short stump of nose held up her glasses, as if she were a two-dimensional cutout. Her hair had been dyed orange and was tufted as if it were some grassy plant indigenous to a remote desert. She turned—or he, though in the end I felt she was female—and touched my arm. "You hold my package?" she said. "I must—" She pointed at the pay fax machine located on the far wall.

"Okay," I said. The package was small, tied with string, and marked in a labored, foreign handwriting, in a language indecipherable to me.

Already the wait was much longer than ten minutes. My fingers ached from where I had shut them into the drawer and I realized abruptly I was too weak to continue standing on line. Two policemen came in the door; it appeared they were looking for something, someone—they stood at the far side of the room staring intently at the people in line. They had baffled, meaty faces, perhaps a bit short by police standards, or at least by those depicted in the movies.

The room was growing black around the edges, a few floaters came into my eyes. *I'll have lunch now,* I thought, *I'm weakened,* and I started to look for the woman, to return her package, but she was nowhere in sight. Then an inspector in postal garb appeared from nowhere and made a tour of the line. He was burly, huge, with a head that had been shaved clean, and a curly, ligneous mustache. The policemen shuffled in the corner. "Lady," he said, and stopped. "That package—they're not going to accept it."

"It's not mine," I said.

Suddenly he bellowed. "I'm trying to speed things up here, people! If you got any packages, tied up with string—that's no good! You got masking tape—no good! Only regulation official post-office strapping tape is permitted! Only three staples per Jiffy mailer!"

"It's not my package!" I said. Gingerly I held it in my hand, who knew what microbes and bacteria the paper was crawling with. In my weakened state I felt too dizzy to even hold on to it properly—where the woman had gone, I didn't know. I would come back and mail it for her another time.

Near the door, just as my legs were giving out from under me a man hoisted me back onto my feet. In his free arm he held a little white dog with dead button eyes. It was Alby. I could almost have sworn, in the moment that my legs were collapsing, that before grabbing my arm he had quickly unzipped his fly, permitting the rosy round head of his dick to peep through just as my eyes reached the level of his waist. This must have been only a hallucination; surely he wouldn't stoop to this level with the police standing so close by. No, it was only my own sordid sexual imagination.

He held me up by one arm and helped me out into the stale air. "Low blood sugar," he said firmly, kindly. "Come on, I'll buy you some orange juice. Did you have lunch yet? Can you make it across the street, or should I get a cab?"

There was no objective reality. That was what life had taught me thus far. Maybe I had misinterpreted entirely the events that had taken place the other night. After all, I had dated many men in this city (though not for quite some time) but all of my dates and relationships had been a disaster. Was I supposed to believe that it was my warped interpretation? These thoughts and more came to me as Alby led me across the street, the limp dog still under his arm, the stranger's package in my hand. The gooey tar of the street stuck to my shoes, I could feel the tips of my heels sinking in with every step. We didn't speak. I was relieved at that moment to be rescued by anyone at all. "How've you been?" I muttered at last when we were safely across Eighth Avenue and he hadn't pushed me in front of a car. Alby gave me a disgusted, peculiar little smile. Oh, I loathed him, but at that moment felt myself drifting, my cells merging into his in my weakness, creating a thunderous goo . . . what did it matter after all, my intense dislike for him, when he was the only one there to hold me up off the ground?

He led me into a restaurant in the middle of the block. Just as we were going in the door he stuffed the dog into a nylon satchel; only the disembodied head peeped through, any waitress, or the manager, looking in our direction, would have seen what appeared to be a plush poodle-toy. He pushed the bag beneath a table and eased me into a chair. Then he sat beside me. "I—" I said.

"Don't speak," he said. He gestured to the waitress. "Could you bring her some orange juice, right away? And the menu." I had thought of him speaking in a kind of ghetto gangster style; but now he had reverted to the intangible French/Italian/Spanish mélange accent he had used when I first met him outside my front door. "I was meaning to call you," he said with a guilty whinny. "But I been busy."

"That's okay," I said, nodding.

"You know, I say to myself, what you bothering for, man? This girl, she think she, like, something special, you know? Like, she hurt my feelings, when I be very open and honest wit' her."

I hadn't the vaguest idea of what he was going on about. The room was swimming and when the waitress brought over my glass of orange juice I drank it in one gulp, the glib ice cubes chinking across my teeth. Instantly I was stronger and my first thought after the glucose raced along my veins was how to get away from him. From across the room Alby must have appeared quite handsome and presentable—dressed in a crisp white shirt with French cuffs, despite the heat, a sultry aura of some expensive male cologne—but inside the man's body was the mind and voice of a fifteen-year-old.

"I see my friends when I play ball, I go, like, I seen this girl, she nothing special, but I think she the one for me. They tell me, like, Alby, that's good, man, we been waiting for you to say this ting." This *ting?* Had he now fallen into some Jamaican speech pattern? And the way he kept using *like* in his sentences—why did people do this? Was it some defense mechanism, flung and interspersed here and there that meant *please don't question or attack me for what I'm saying, because I'm not really saying what I'm saying at all, I'm only saying something* like *what I claim to be saying?* In which case the use of the word *like* was being used to mean *similar to.* In other words, I didn't exactly tell my friends that I met this girl, but I said something similar.

Or perhaps the use of the word *like* was merely filler, signifying nothing. It was nothing more than a low-calorie white paste used to glue words together. All I knew was that it sounded simply moronic.

"See, like, I didn't want to tell you this before when we were first together," Alby said, sliding closer to me. He took my hand in his and spoke in a low voice. "My parents excape from Germany before the war and we went to live in Paraguay. Anyway, like, this didn't work out, so we moved to Brooklyn. I was the only white kid in the neighborhood."

"You told me something like this before," I murmured, though it sounded only vaguely familiar and for the life of me I couldn't remember the details of whatever he had said that first time we met.

He looked annoyed. "I have this friend, a Colombian dude, and he was into drugs, though not me, man. Anyway, he, like, very rich, you know, from the business, and then, last year he—phffft!" He continued to rapidly massage my hand, but with his free hand he made a slicing gesture across his neck. "He have no family, like, he an orphan, but he have a will: he lef' me his farm, in Colombia, four hundred hectares. Oh, it beautiful. That's where I getting ready to go jus' now."

"That must be, ah, nice," I said. I tried to disengage my hand to turn the pages of the menu, but he wouldn't release it. I was forced to use my left. It was your standard slightly upscale coffee-shop fare—the chef's salad (already I envisioned the tasteless green lettuce, the tasteless cubes of yellow cheese, the tasteless chunks of pink ham, etc.); the tuna sandwich (this would be a vaguely fishy blend of mayonnaise held together with a tiny amount of tuna binder); the hamburger deluxe (a large bland patty of meat on an airy bun intended to represent bread). There was no food left in the modern world, it was all food substitutes, brightly hued representations of meals dimly remembered, handed down through generations.

I suddenly got interested in what he was saying. ". . . takes three days through the jungle to get there; it's just below the mountains, at the top of where, like, the Amazon basin begins. Nobody live there but the Indians: these very good, old-fashioned people. Very safe, everybody live in communities and know each other. To get around, they have the beautiful horse called the Pasofino—brought over, like, by the conquistadors. They have a very smooth gait, this horse, smooth as glass; anyone can ride this horse. And here, a horse like that, costs ten thousand dollars! But there, you go to another farm, you say, like, I want to buy a horse, they sell you for one hundred dollars."

I wanted to go there. It became clear to me: this was to be my escape. I could marry him and move to the top of the Amazon basin. "How's the weather, Alby?" I said.

"Seventy-five degrees, year round. It's beautiful. No bugs, neither."

"Wow," I said. His gentle stroking of my hand, under the table, had rendered it curiously submissive; it was so soothing, I suddenly understood what it felt like to be a lobster or a chicken being hypnotized. Tiny flutters of pleasure were being released in the back of my head. Yet . . . obviously something was not right. Something other than his sturdy fingers was being used to massage my palm. It dawned on me that some time while he was chatting he had unbuttoned his fly and taken out his penis . . . unless he had six fingers and I simply hadn't noticed previously. The end of his penis was hard, round, and hot; it was a lot silkier than the rough skin of his fingers.

"Oh, for God's sake!" I said, trying to yank my hand free. But with his other hand he caught my wrist and held it down. I glanced under the table, over at his lap, but he had thrown a napkin over the entire affair, it was impossible to see.

"Please," he said, "this won't take a minute. Nobody looking. Don't make me suffer this way. I'm not an animal."

What kind of signals must I be giving off, to be treated in this fashion? "Let go of my hand," I said, "or I'll start to scream." Yet one half of me was strangely tranquil, even indifferent.

At the other tables (the restaurant was half empty) customers devoured bacon-and-spinach salads, bowls of oozing frozen yogurt topped with strawberry sauce and chunks of peanuts; nobody seemed to notice what was going on. He was now clasping my hand beneath his and forcing it up and down, in a highly professional fashion. His brow was furrowed with concentration, and when the waitress passed by asking if we were ready to order he managed to say with remarkable presence, "Not quite. Come back in a minute or two."

I suppose I felt sorry for him, particularly at his comment about animal suffering. Anyway, I hardly had a choice, unless I wanted to make a scene.

He wiped off my hand, and, bringing it to his lips gave it a little kiss. My hand, then, had been raped; who knew what post-traumatic shock it would later experience . . . I didn't mind so much, once it was over, to sit and chat and order something to eat. But my hand wanted to get away from him. I got up and walked out of the restaurant. I suppose he lingered to pay for his coffee and my o.j., but after a few minutes he caught up.

"Look, I'm sorry," he said. His accent had once again shifted, he had dropped whatever business he was into before, and now his voice was no different from mine.

"Just leave me alone," I said, walking faster. *Oh God,* I thought hopelessly, *why couldn't I have been born a tree?* I might have had a chance at happiness then, in the rich humus of some silent forest, cool leaves brushing the air, a long life at the subverbal level, connected to the other trees but alone . . . this, of course, was ridiculous.

"Can I see you again?" he said. There was a strangely pleased quality to his voice and facial expression. As usual, I had attracted the strangest variety of pervert. "I couldn't help myself," he pleaded. "I don't know what came over me."

I tried to ignore him, but finally something got the better of me. "I bet your parents would be very ashamed," I said.

"Oh, my parents," he said cheerfully. "They don't know what the hell's going on."

"Good-bye," I said in what I hoped was a firm voice, in front of my office building.

"I'll call you later on!" he said before I went in the door.

All afternoon I was strangely aroused and this made me disgusted with myself. If I couldn't be a tree then at least I might have been born a man: men's bodies and their minds were obviously completely unconnected. Now I looked at my hand in loathing and disgust. I went to the front desk to find Debbie. "You wouldn't believe what happened to me during lunch today," I started to say, but gave up. Her face, a round bubble decorated with lip gloss and mascara, looked at me brainlessly; how pleasurable that must be, to have no thoughts. She was flipping through a copy of *Bride's* magazine, although as far as I knew there was no potential bridegroom or fiancé in her life. She sniffed. "Amber's out for the afternoon," she said, apparently oblivious to the fact that I had begun and finished a story in one incomplete sentence. "But Daniel said, when you come back, you should go in to see him. What's that smell?"

I looked at the unmailed package still in my hand. "Were there any other calls for me, during lunch?" I said.

She shifted through a pile of pink slips. "There was one," she said. "But I can't find it right now." It was obvious she had taken some kind of course in receptionist behavior. How was it that she knew all the rules of stereotypical feminine activity. But that was a sexist way of thinking, I thought, as I walked down the hall to Daniel Loomis's office. Still, in all my probing, over the months, I could not find one element to render Debbie more than a two-dimensional cartoon character. It occurred to me that *I* would certainly not want to be a cartoon character—although more and more it seemed there were a lot of them out there. A lot of people in the world today seemed to base their personalities on things they had read in magazines and seen on TV, and Debbie was surely an example of this. Of course, the way she put together all her various attributes made her unique: the shell-pink lipstick and matching nail polish; her daily commute from Long Island City, where she shared an apartment with Bobette, a very

attractive transvestite (once Debbie had invited me to watch Bobette perform—he/she lip-synced to torch songs of the twenties and thirties in an
East Village nightclub); her dates with Carl, a friend of her brother's from
high school. She was only mildly interested in Carl, who worked on the
floor of the stock exchange, running paper back and forth. Some weekends
she went to her parents' house in Rockville, and while there she would
borrow the family car and go to the beach, or to the shopping mall in
Hempstead with a girlfriend.

Put together, all these various bits of information did make Debbie
sound like an individual person. But the point was, unless she suddenly
decided to move to a remote village in Spain, *there was nothing unusual about
her*. She was just a Debbie, like so many other hundreds and millions of
Debbies, Jennifers, and Tiffanys, all based on the same model.

If she moved to a village in Spain, then naturally she would, to the local
Spanish people, seem quite different, but of course she would never move
to this remote village—that was not what Debbies did.

"I bought these earrings at lunch," she said. I turned around and
stopped; she was holding up two dangling objects still attached to their
plastic backing, faux silver hearts and moons embedded with glass faces.

"Nice," I said politely. "Where'd you get them?" I thought she was
going to tell me they came from one of those newsstands on the street; most
of them sold this kind of junky stuff on racks, from Hong Kong and Taiwan.

"Macy's," she said, "On sale for forty-nine ninety-five." Already she
was removing the fake gold reptile heads from one ear, her long fingernails
clattering against one another like crab claws, in order to be able to put on
the new pair. Forty-nine ninety-five! It was impossible to believe. Where
did Debbie's money come from? She couldn't have earned much more than
three hundred dollars a week—how could she spend her money on such
garbage, vastly overpriced and already out of fashion? Similar earrings of real
silver and gemstone had been displayed in the window of Tiffany's several
years earlier; I suppose two years was the minimum amount of time it took
for Hong Kong to manufacture a knock-off. The originals were something
like eight thousand dollars—what would be considered "fun" jewelry at
Tiffany's.

My mother had recently sent me a photograph, clipped from her local
newspaper, in which a group of people walking through a railway station
had been photographed by some new, experimental camera. And about a
third of the people in the room had a mysterious halo circling their heads,
when photographed by this new device. The newspaper caption explained
that the people with halos over their heads were aliens. Some effort had

been made to trace these people, but none had been found. There was no record of their existence. Naturally the local paper in the small town where my mother lived was a little desperate for news—but mysteriously, this story was not widely reprinted. The point was not that a third of the population on earth or at least in the United States was aliens, but were the aliens the ones like Debbie who fit in perfectly—or those of us who just weren't quite right?

I was still carrying around the greasy packet that the woman had given me in the post office. I really must have been in a daze. It wasn't like me to almost faint in the post office and give a man a hand job in an upscale coffee shop. I went back to my office and flung the package in the bottom drawer, way in the back, hoping to block the smell. Anything to delay taking those final steps down the hall to Daniel's office. I assumed Amber skipped out for the afternoon, so that Daniel could fire me and she needn't face me herself.

What was to become of me? Much as I hated my job, I wasn't prepared for any major change. How much easier things would have been to simply drift along for a few more years, until I thought of something else I wanted or was capable of doing.

I applied some powder and lipstick to my face. It wasn't such a bad face, after all, unless there was another face around to compare it to. That was the tragedy of the thing—until there was a more attractive face situated beside my own, mine was perfectly acceptable.

I knocked on the frosted glass beside Daniel's door. "Come in, come in," he said with a slight frown. If only I had been Daniel Loomis! Wealthy, no worries—it didn't even matter that as a human being he was practically invisible. He was a man, after all, and a man, as long as he had no overwhelming physical deformities, held all the cards of life up his sleeve, particularly if he had money and position. "I, uh—" he said after a pause.

During that time I stood without speaking and watched his brow furrow into wrinkles in worried-rodent fashion. Far be it from me to assist him in making it easy for him to fire me! "You know, I, uh—" he said. Just then his telephone began to ring and he let it ring quite a few times while he talked. "I was wondering, Pamela, for some time, if you would have the time, for us to have a talk." He spoke more quickly as the phone continued to ring. "And I was wondering, this evening, if you were free, say around six, we could have a drink together, around six?" He picked up the phone and held his hand over the receiver.

"Ah, sure," I said. The pathetic mouse, why didn't he just fire me and get it over with? "And should I come back here to pick you up?"

He nodded. "By the way, don't mention this to Amber," he said before taking the call. I couldn't stop staring at him before I realized I was being rude.

There were a great many mice at the subway station where I got the train to work each morning. I don't know what they lived on—once there was a partially eaten cob of corn someone had flung down on the tracks, and certainly there was plenty of drinking water, albeit sporadic—the grate to the street was directly above the tracks and when it rained there were always pools of water—but otherwise there was only the occasionally oily wrapper from sandwiches and wads of gum.

Still, there was apparently enough food for the mice to breed and reproduce; none of the mice seemed starved, their coats were sleek and naturally mouse-brown, and they ranged in size from tiny, tiny mice the size of a thumbnail to fully mature kiwi fruit, complete with bright eyes and quivering noses.

Watching them dart in and out from crevices under the tracks and the sides of the walls while waiting for the train provided a lot of pleasure, too; moments before the train arrived in the station the mice could somehow sense its arrival, perhaps from the vibrations, and even the youngest looked up alertly and darted into its hidden nest.

My God, what was the point of thinking all the time! The only reason I had thought of this was because of the mouselike expression on Daniel Loomis's face. His beady brown eyes, his quivering, slightly red-tipped nose (now that I thought about it, this nose always had a moist, raw look) his mole-colored hair and half-size teeth—from everything I had learned about history, human beings had shown no signs of evolution, physical or spiritual, since the days of the ancient Greeks.

From various tidbits learned from the newspapers (and Debbie), I knew that Daniel Loomis's father had four hundred million dollars, and that Daniel was an only child. For probably less than he spent in dinners in restaurants each week, I could have lived happily for months if not a year. Meanwhile I had been irritated with having to buy Amber a pack of cigarettes and a yogurt for which I knew I would never be reimbursed . . . and lucky I had forgotten, too—she wasn't even coming back to the office today!

Nothing much happened during the rest of the afternoon. At six o'clock prompt Daniel came into my office, looking strangely cheerful and shy. "I thought, uh, if you didn't mind, we'd go up to my house," he said. "The housekeeper's on vacation, and nobody's there, but it'll be very cool and quiet—unless you'd rather just go someplace around here? Actually, a friend of a friend is having a book publishing party not far away—she's just written a book on being a dominatrix . . ."

"Your house is fine," I said. "Is it very far?"

"Oh, uh, we can get a taxi," he said. "I don't keep a car and driver just now," he added apologetically as we walked down the hall. "I'm very, very sorry about all of this."

What did he mean, he was *very, very sorry*? Why didn't he just come out with the bad news? In the elevator he huddled against the back wall, as far away from me as possible, as if he were frightened. I honestly couldn't think of anything to say, and he made me think of a miserable rat caught in the middle of a highway in a rainstorm. My bag was quite heavy; I had grabbed the junk from my closet so that after I was fired I would only have to make another trip or two to collect all my stuff. I had just taken loose odds and ends: an umbrella missing a spoke, a pair of sneakers I forgot to bring home one night, a bottle of clear nail polish for stocking runs, and my mail, which I put in my pocket. I'd read it later, and, if there was anything important, I supposed I could notify my successor.

Against my feeble protests Daniel insisted on taking the pink plastic handbag from my arms. I almost pointed out that he was much tinier—and therefore probably weaker—than I had thought, but stopped myself in time. Probably he was around five six or seven, but he had seemed larger than this until I stood next to him. We stood side by side in uncomfortable silence. "What did you mean, you're very, very sorry about all of this?" I blurted at last.

"That the elevator was taking so long!" he squeaked. Honestly, why did I have to go all the way uptown to his luxurious accommodations simply in order to have him tell me at length what was wrong with me and why he was forced to let me go? I wanted at that moment to tell him to wait for a few days until I got hold of my mother—he could fire me through her. There was an old family tradition, among the women in my family, whenever one of us wanted to quit a job we got our mother to do it. Maybe the same could be done for being fired.

Actually, this dated back only two generations. In high school, I had a job after school and at nights, folding shirts in a nearby discount department store. I was very bad at folding shirts and no matter how many times I was taught the correct way to fold a shirt they never looked very neat or organized after I folded them. Hour after hour I stood folding the cheap polyester men's shirts and arranging them according to size. As soon as I folded a bunch, a customer came over and took each one out, held it up, and then put it down, unfolded. I was not skilled enough at folding shirts to be promoted to cash register work, a step up. Eventually, after many months, I had earned $125, and I made my mother call up my supervisor—pretending to be me—and tell them I wasn't going to be coming back to work.

This was because I was afraid I was going to be yelled at. As it turned out, my mother didn't mind having to call up and quit my job, because years before, age sixteen, she had made *her* mother call and quit her typing job.

I could feel my blood literally boiling in my veins. Must I be burdened with this lifelong genetic defect of fear? Fire me, fire me, but there was no need to drag me through the ordure of it all. Never had I been so close to acting out the need to strangle another human being. He was tiny, we were alone in the elevator and probably in the building . . . it was summer, a Friday afternoon, everyone else had already left the building. . . .

All I had to do was press the UP button, strangle him, drag his body out and leave it in the twenty-fourth-floor hallway. "Mr. Loomis," I started to say, when he let out a yelp.

"Aaaagghh," he said, and cringed. "Sorry. Sorry. I'm a little nervous. That's all."

"Nervous?" I snapped. "Go ahead. Say it."

"Oh, gee," he said. He looked stricken, his skin the color of badly blanched celery. "I have a crush on you; I guess you've noticed. What can I say? Are you . . ."—he grimaced winsomely—". . . angry with me?"

"What?" I said.

We were both silent. The elevator completed its descent and the two of us bumped into one another in our haste to make it out the door. "Sorry," I muttered.

"Sorry," he said.

He had a crush on *me?* Why? The thing was, if not for his money, he would have made a lousy rich person.

Looking back, it occurs to me that my life has always been one of missed opportunities. I let things happen to me, because I never had the belief that it was possible for me to go out and make things happen. I just waited for things to come along, and during the in-between periods I was in a state of inanimate suspension. Milk, eggs, English muffins—I was lucky if I could activate myself for long enough to remember what it was I had to buy at the store.

My philosophy was such that I believed all it took to get ahead in this world, or at least have an exciting life, were: 1) connections, such as a father in the movie business, or inherited wealth, 2) great looks and physical attractiveness, i.e., large breasts and blond hair, or 3) talent. Gifted in none of these areas, how or why could I begin to bother?

I didn't even have a charming personality—if I had at least had that, others might have come to me and confided in me their interesting life stories.

My parents—I can't blame them for any of this: after all, everyone has parents, this goes back for many generations, if I were to blame my parents then they might as well blame theirs, and so on back to the dawn of man—were divorced when I was at an early age, and though this is a highly common occurrence, on me it had the same effect as a tree being severely pruned back as a sapling, and unfortunately in my case all I sent up after this were a variety of weak shoots.

In the cab ride Daniel said nervously that he usually left the office early in order to be able to watch his twins, two years old, eat dinner. Archie and Alice were not oversize for their age, but they were incredible eaters.

He had thought that his housekeeper was taking meat from the butcher's and selling it on the side or giving it to her family (his meat bills were so phenomenal) until that time, when, getting home early by accident he had watched his twins devour three lamb chops apiece. "And they weren't small lamb chops either," he said with a half-twitch. "Huge, pink, thick, juicy lamb chops, fresh peas and mashed potatoes."

I couldn't remember ever having had a huge, pink, thick, juicy lamb chop. As a child, living with my mother and brothers, on rare occasions as a special treat we had been given a thin, greasy, gristly lamb chop. But that was all. Just imagine, two years old and already eating lamb chops that I had only seen in photographs! "Your children . . . must be very oversize," I said.

"Oh no!" he said. "No, they're normal, for their age. But I never thought, until I accidentally stumbled into the nursery when the house-keeper was giving them dinner, that I would enjoy watching them eat so much. Actually, two of the lamb chops were for me. I was planning to eat the lamb chops. But there were none left." He looked weak and exhausted at having told me this tale. I supposed, really, it was rather sweet; such love and delight flooded his eyes at the recollection of the number of lamb chops his children were able to consume.

Finally we pulled up at the door of what I guessed was his house. It was one of those old limestone townhouses that line some genteel East Side streets. The inside, at least the lobby, had been decorated to resemble a Roman mausoleum or senator's home.

Large marble busts were planted atop pedestal columns; in between were funeral urns topped with giant exotic fresh flowers. The floor was

black and white stone checkerboard squares, covered with a silk rug of
entwined lions. The bottom of the wall was paneled in what must have
been the original dark oak; but along the top half trompe-l'oeil Pompeiian
landscapes had been reproduced in rich shades of red, green, and dark blue.

Next we passed through a sort of Louis XV sitting room; well, I don't
know if it was Louis the XV or something else, but this was a sort of formal
room with fussy brocade chairs, little tables strewn with photographs in
silver frames, crystal tchotchkes, everything in unbearably precise order
. . . the four sofas facing one another in pairs, the armchairs big and small
at just such an angle, all with the spindly legs of spiders. Maybe this room
was thirty or forty feet long, but it had been decorated, though perhaps not
deliberately, to make whoever sat there feel inferior and uncomfortable.

To my relief we walked straight through this room, through a series of
doors, up a curving stone stairs (this might have been removed from a castle)
and into a tiny prison cell with leaded glass windows, stuffed with heavy
black leather furniture and walls lined with books and an elaborate stereo
system. "This is my room," Daniel said, flinging himself onto a chair and
then getting up again to open a liquor cabinet and wet bar recessed into a
wall. "Actually, it was supposed to be the game room, but it's become my
room. It's the only room in the house I'm comfortable in. Although I do
like the swimming pool and the garden. My wife and her mother spent a
year and a half decorating the place."

"Lovely," I said.

"Do you want a drink? There's everything here but the champagne,
but I can run down to the kitchen and get some." He darted across the
room and flicked a number of buttons on the stereo system. "You like
flamenco?" he said as a man began to bawl in Spanish, a throbbing song of
despair or violence.

"And where's your wife?" I said at last over the noise. "And your
children? Are they here?"

"What's that?" he said. "No, no—they've gone away for a few weeks,
to Newport."

"You have a house there?" I said.

"Yes, yes, I grew up there as a child during the summer." He threw
himself down on a little leather ottoman by my feet and looked up at me
with a pleading dachshund air. "You see, you probably think I'm an idiot.
It was just this afternoon when it hit me. It dawned on me that I couldn't
go on without seeing your smile when you passed me in the hall. Do you
think I'm ridiculous?"

"Maybe a little," I said. "Is there . . . something to drink?"

"Oh, I forgot!" He was gone for an interminable time. Maybe he had to use the toilet first; it seemed impossible that the kitchen, or wherever drinks were kept, was so far away. While I was waiting I remembered my mail from work in my pocket and I began rummaging through it. There was an invitation from Amber to her cocktail party this very evening. That was something of a shock; not the fact that she hadn't invited me to the dinner party, which I knew was taking place after the cocktails, but that she had invited me to any part of the party at all. It was handwritten on big, stiff card paper, in a powdery envelope, the sort that might cost five bucks each at Tiffany's. So that was what she had wanted to tell me this morning, and in my paranoia I had misconstrued the whole thing! I looked at my watch; it was only just gone seven, I still could get over there. Why wasn't Daniel attending? Maybe he didn't believe in mixing business, but I wanted to go. I thought about finding my way back to the front, collecting my pink smelly handbag, but it seemed too rude without saying good-bye. So I went down the hall to the bathroom. It was almost the size of my living room, complete with a wooden toilet-throne. It really was a throne, the toilet was set atop a platform and it took four or five steps to get up to it, made out of shiny gold tile.

I mounted the steps to pee. It was embarrassing to be seated so high up; the walls were all mirrors, I was reflected half a dozen times perched on the regal pot. What if some of those mirrors were two-way? Boy, would that be a sick situation; for all I knew he had crept around to view, waiting for the moment when I had to go and use the facilities.

With such thoughts in mind it took me a long time to go. It was my fault for thinking that urinating was a private affair. After all, people did not feel it was necessary to eat in private; no, for eating there was no shame, in fact, it was an activity people commonly participated in together, to hoist particles of food up to their open maws and plunge it in. Simply by virtue of the fact that this opening was at the top end of the body made it permissible for this to be done in public. But urinating and defecating, those were things one liked to do alone. If things had been otherwise, the toilet itself might have been placed anywhere in the home—in the center of Daniel's stuffy sitting room, for example.

Finally my brain was able to give the correct command to go, and I urinated. My hands of their own accord were rummaging around for the paper. Perhaps it was carefully hidden in a carved Regency toilet paper box. But there was no sign of it behind or above. No toilet paper! Oh, for a female this was ghastly, to be unable to dry.

It had happened before, and then one solution was to stumble, pants at half-mast, over to the sink for a quick rinse, via the hands, so that at least one was not dripping with one's own urine, although still damp. But in this case I did not see how I was to make it down the four or five steps that led from the toilet; in any event, who had designed such a demonic toilet? Hadn't people who lived here ever come home drunk? If they had, they would know that the last thing one wanted at 3 A.M. was to topple from a four-foot-high toilet seat half naked.

I sent my hands out on one last search-and-find mission. I fumbled behind my back along the top of the ancestral throne; there was a flat area up there, wood with a knob, no doubt this lifted off so that the plumbing could be gotten to in the event that it needed repairs. To my relief my hand found a big wad of crumpled paper, slightly damp, which I carried down and used on my person.

Perhaps the maid had been dusting and forgotten this wad back there. Certainly it was not my first choice for toilet paper—I preferred mine unused. But under the circumstances I was happy with my find. Wipe and flush, that was my strategy. It was vaguely in the back of my mind to spend some time thinking about Daniel Loomis's "crush" on me, to use his word. But so far I had staved off such thoughts. So he had a crush on me; I found this hard to believe. He was married, anyway, and he was rich; this left us nothing in common.

I had a quick peep in the cabinet underneath the gold sink to see if there was any paper there, but it was empty. If there was any toilet paper in this house, the housekeeper must keep it in some filing cabinet labeled **T**. I ran my hands under the tap. Even though I had turned on the warm water, it was icy cold. Rich people were strange.

Suddenly I had a hideous idea. What if Daniel, during his lengthy absence from the room, had come into this bathroom with the sole purpose of masturbating, and used the remains of the roll of toilet paper to wipe up his joyful moment? Meanwhile I, coming in very soon after, had found and utilized this same piece of toilet paper to wipe the female portion of my anatomy? It was too unbelievable to contemplate.

I went back to the room. Daniel was waiting for me to open the bottle of champagne.

"I have a phobia about champagne corks," he said sheepishly. "When I was a child, my father opened a bottle and the cork hit me just above the eye. See that missing part of my eyebrow?" There was a little scar, nearly invisible, and I nodded. "I love champagne—I mean, I always make sure we have a few cases of Cristal in the house—but my hands shake too much to open it. Usually the housekeeper or Virginia opens the bottles. Do you mind?"

Actually I had never opened a bottle of champagne by myself before, although there had been a few occasions when I witnessed this event and had even sampled this magic elixir. It would be possible for me at this point to have drifted into a reverie of the poverty of my youth, but I was far too nervous at having to now pretend that I was accustomed to such things. "Generally, ah, someone else does it!" I said brightly as he passed me the chilled bottle.

"Just pry up those little bits and keep twisting it," he said. "But point it away from me!" This last was stated with a great deal of alarm as I aimed the weapon toward his face.

Unfortunately at this moment it occurred to me that, if my fantasy about his masturbation on the piece of toilet paper were true, he might very well have impregnated me. All it would take would be one healthy sperm, prancing on the edge of the paper I had used to wipe myself, to find its way up my vaginal canal, in a desperate search for a velvet home. But was such a thing possible?

I resolved to call my father, a gynecologist, at the earliest opportunity, and put it to him. I would phrase the question in such a way that he wouldn't suspect it could have anything to do with me. "Dad," I would say, "if a man masturbated on a piece of toilet paper, and then discarded it, and then a woman . . . went into this same bathroom, picked up the toilet paper . . . and only a few minutes had elapsed . . . and then used it to wipe herself after urinating . . . could it be possible for a sperm to live and impregnate her?"

I spoke to my father but rarely. He had been the head of a gynecology/ women's health clinic at a rural hospital, before divorcing, giving up the full-time practice of medicine, and marrying a wealthy woman who raised horses. He had never had to pay my mother much in the way of alimony, and for a time she worked in a cafeteria as a dietician. Since then it had been my mother's dream that my brothers and I might better our positions in society.

Until now, opening the bottle of champagne in Daniel Loomis's study, there had been not even a glimpse into a better world. At that moment the cork shot out and clipped him a good one on his right ear. "Ow!" he said, leaping up and performing a happy dance on one foot. The nerves of ear were perhaps connected somehow to the nerves of leg, in some marionette-like fashion; this was another question I vowed to remember to ask my father.

"Sorry," I said. "Oh, gee, I'm really sorry." I ran and grabbed his ear and began polishing it. He let out a shrill whimper of what I interpreted as pain. "Does it hurt?" I asked helpfully, massaging or rather twisting his ear involuntarily back and forth.

He had changed the record or tape to some kind of whiny Arab belly-dancing pop music, and even though he kept saying, "No, I'm okay, I'm fine," and was trying to hop away from my grip, I couldn't seem to let go of his ear, and in time to the music the two of us wriggled across the room, me in hot pursuit of his slithering attempt to escape. Finally the feeble command from my brain to my hand to let go reached its destination and I stopped my massaging and sat down in an armchair, the neck of the bottle of champagne still in my other hand.

After a pause he approached me warily. "I'll just pour us some of that champagne, if you're ready," he said. His little ear had turned a bright red.

"Sorry," I muttered again, handing him the champagne, some of which bubbled out the top end. "By the way, you're out of toilet paper in the bathroom."

The rest of his face flushed, leaving only the one ear a different color. So I was correct, then, in my interpretation of what had happened while he was alone in the bathroom. Men were so peculiar. The women's movement had not helped matters either; the male sex drive had been thwarted when women took over the job of openly pursuing the opposite sex.

Once it had been possible for men to think sexual thoughts and chase women around sofas. The minute the women stopped running, turned in their tracks, and stepped forward to meet the men as equal partners, the men let out a shriek and fled in panic. Mere chattel was not supposed to behave in this fashion. I envisioned the time would come when men would lie weak and helpless as toads and we women would have to coax them into a semblance of manliness. Even now there were articles appearing in magazines advocating that women return to their pre 1950s condition of housewifery. "Listen," I said. "Why don't you do an article for the magazine on women who rape men at gunpoint? I bet a lot of *Hunter's World* readers would be interested."

"What?" Daniel said. He knitted his brow as he poured a glass of champagne and drank it practically in one gulp. "Are you—kidding? That's a terrible idea. Frightening." He looked pensive as he sipped the dregs from his glass and rubbed his ear, staring at me intently, as if we were engaged in a conversation. Had I said something that he was internally debating? But as far as I was concerned no words had emerged from my mouth. "I guess I better be going," I mumbled at last.

"Oh, no!" he said. "Then I'll be all alone . . . I'm afraid."

"Have to work in the morning, you know," I said. This statement would give him the opportunity to fire me; it was now up to him.

A dull look came into his eyes. "I had so wanted to show you my collection of Ming vases," he said. "And ewers. Do you think I could see you again?"

"Oh, sure," I said, grabbing the foul pink bag as I went out. "I'd love to."

He stood wistfully on the top step. "Really?" he said eagerly. "So it doesn't bother you, the fact that I'm married and . . . my other problem, I mean?" I wanted very much to feel sorry for him. And in some way I did; he was so shriveled, wringing his hands together on his own front step, wrinkling his furry brow—he obviously had been the victim of some kind of experiment, of the cruelest sort, for what else could have traumatized him into collecting Chinese porcelain? Here was a suffering being. And yet, behind him was the huge townhouse; it was hard for me to put myself in his shoes, even though they were practically the same size as my own feet. He took a step toward me. "I don't know what's wrong with me," he said earnestly. "I'm so dreadfully unhappy."

"Oh, what a shame," I said. I really didn't know what else to say. I supposed it was more than likely that rich people were just as unhappy as poor ones; the only difference was that poor people thought all it would take to be happy was to be rich.

But there was something about a rich unhappy person that made a poor one want to smack him in the face. His weekly bill from the florist's was probably as much as my weekly salary, tuberoses and tulips all twisted and overheated so that they would grow out of pots at the wrong time of year. Six of my bathrooms could have fit into one of his. While I was going home to my Kraft Macaroni and Cheese every night, when I had the strength to make it, he was being served the rich people's food: crisp, tiny grouse with lingonberries, tiny white eels and the livers of unusual and rare animals, things normal people never even got to see. It really brought out commu-nist tendencies in me, that I could have screwed things up so badly by not marrying somebody rich or winning the lottery.

He stood before me looking like a wee bairn—or maybe it was the Finnish word for little troll I was thinking of—and all at once I felt that I was able to read his mind and gaze deep inside him, where I saw that really he would have been happier if he had been born a girl. Maybe he wasn't conscious of it, but I felt bad for being so critical of him just because he was rich and unhappy. After all, a person poorer than myself, such as a homeless woman with five or six kids, might think that if only she were me, with a two-room apartment and a job, then she would be happy. To my surprise when his curled little hand, in appearance a great deal older than the rest of his body, reached forward to gingerly shake my hand good-bye, I leaned toward him and kissed him on his pasty lips.

His yellow eyes lit up like pools of butter on the bottom of the frying pan, and he let out an elfin chortle. "Hey," he said. "Hey!"

"Oh, gee." I got embarrassed. Two glasses of champagne, that was all I had had, and all it took for a demonic, aggressive being, needing exercising, to be released within. "Sorry."

"Oh, no," he said. "Don't be sorry. Don't be sorry. I can't tell you, you've made me so happy. Nobody's ever done that to me before. A spontaneous gesture like that. And I'm so unhappy, I've been so unhappy, but now I feel—happy! Would you feel ashamed to see me again?"

I hoped I had the correct apartment for Amber's cocktail party. It had happened to me once that, meeting a friend at a party, I sat in an apartment chatting with a few people for twenty minutes before mumbling, "Gee, where's Patty? It's not like her to be late."

"Patty?" they said. "Who's Patty?" It was then that, glancing at the paper on which I had written the information, I realized I was at the wrong address. This party of Amber's was taking place in what I would call a luxurious penthouse. From the twenty-sixth floor there was quite a view of the homeless people below. I didn't see anybody that I knew, not even Amber, and I felt uneasy. At one time I had believed that at a cocktail party the correct behavior was to join up with a group of strangers who were chatting, introduce oneself, and they would then ease you into the general conversation. Who knows where I had obtained this bizarre notion. Could it have been from the warped mind of Dear Abby or some other advice columnist? *The Emily Post Book of Etiquette* circa 1953? All I knew was that in the past, whenever I had attempted this outlandish behavior, I was met with general snorts of disbelief and pitying, scornful glances. Rather than make some dreadful error now, I scuttled through the crowd over to the couch, where I sat down and gazed around the room. Whoever lived here had to be some sort of rich Egyptologist. There was a very large Sphinx carved in sleek black stone, and behind glass cases various hawk- and vulture-headed figures and a large wooden sarcophagus that could only have been real.

Sitting next to me on the couch was a very large man with porcine features, hunched over what appeared to be a bowl of caviar. He spooned quantities onto a spongy pancake, and popping it into his mouth let out a slurp. I couldn't help but stare at his face; a dab of sour cream remained on his nose. He was handsome, in a soft, boyish, decadent manner, the way a big, soft bag of money might be appealing. He had nice little deep-set eyes, too, which seemed to say BOY GENIUS in neon: Either I was hallucinating, or once again I was picking up on someone's innermost thoughts. He sort of reminded me of a young Orson Welles, or maybe Fatty Arbuckle. He was too busy devouring the caviar to notice me, but then I remembered a book that my mother had recently mailed to me, *How to Win Friends and Influence People*. Even though the book had been written in 1936 and the pages were falling out and it smelled musty and decayed, that book still contained good advice, which came back to me now. "Don't be argumentative . . . make compliments . . . draw the other person out . . ."

"Is this Amber MacPherson's party?" I said.

"What's that?" the man said, and took out a cigar from his breast pocket, which he rolled between two stumpy fingers in a somewhat lascivious manner. "Ah, yes, yes," he said in a grand voice, as if he had made up his mind to acknowledge me. "Amber MacPherson. Amber waves of grain." He shook, either with silent laughter, or without it. "I'm Bronson Newman, by the way," he added. "Care for a cigar?"

It was hardly an original gesture, to offer a woman a cigar, but I decided I was being too judgmental again. "I'm Pamela Trowel," I said, extending my hand and leaning forward to try and gaze into the silver bowl. "Is there any caviar left?"

"What's that?" Bronson said.

"Tell me, what do you do?" I said.

"I'm an art director," he said. "My father was a very prominent figure in the nineteen sixties."

"Oh?" I said. "Who was he?"

"I really can't tell you," Bronson said.

"Well, was he a member of organized crime?" I said. "Or some sort of counterculture hero?"

Bronson smiled wanly. "Most of the time my father was traveling. I grew up in Greenwich Village. You know, in many ways I always felt it was up to me to make good the family name. I went to Yale; I was a Marshall Scholar at Oxford. But I have a brother, Moe, who's in and out of mental hospitals, and a sister who's gay. Not that I feel there's anything wrong with this, she's my sister, but that sort of leaves things up to me—to be normal."

Just then I saw Amber approaching across the room. "Hi, Amber!" I said.

"Bronc!" Amber said. He stood and they embraced. Then she scowled at me. "What are you doing here, Pamela?"

"You—you invited me," I said.

"No, I didn't," Amber said. "You're crashing."

"I'm not crashing!" I said. I rummaged around. "Look, here's the invitation. It was with my mail."

"It's not addressed to you," Amber said. "You picked it up off my desk." Just then someone who must have been important came into the room because she grabbed Bronson by the arm. "Bronc, I want you to come and meet—" she started to say before a crowd surrounded her and swept her off to one side.

"Do you want to get out of here?" Bronc said. I nodded.

"It was awfully nice of you to escort me out," I said when we were on the street. How could I have been so stupid as to think Amber would have invited me to her party? I remembered two occasions on which I thought she was being friendly: once she asked me to meet her for a drink at ten o'clock one night and I waited and waited and she never showed up. As I didn't have her home phone number, which was unlisted, I couldn't call to find out what had happened. The next day at work she said the reason she hadn't been there was that she was tired and changed her mind about meeting me. But couldn't she have at least called the bar, asked the bartender to find me, so I didn't wait around like a moron? And one other time, when I first started working, she asked me out to dinner, and since I had so little money and the restaurant was expensive all I ordered was a salad and a glass of wine, but she ordered two martinis with olives and many glasses of wine and she had the crab cakes and then the calves' liver with pommes frites and then dessert, the seven-layer chocolate raspberry cake, and coffee and a sambuca, and when the bill came she said it was too much trouble to figure out who owed what and that we should both just split it, and I was too cowed to tell her—she was my boss after all—no. And so this meal cost me a small fortune, and I hadn't even eaten, although Amber had already inherited tons and tons of money because her father was allegedly a contractor who had built some crummy highway.

"What about a drink?" Bronc said. There was a tawdry bar on the corner, where it turned out Bronc was something of a regular. He knew about a certain obscure brand of Russian vodka the bartender kept behind the bar, not out on display, that tasted like lighter fluid. "Tell me," Bronc said, "are you Jewish?"

"Just what are you insinuating?" I said. I was a little on edge.

"I'm not insinuating anything," he said.

"Oh, yes you are," I said. "Are *you* Jewish? Or are you a *Christian.*"

"I'm not either!" he said triumphantly. "I'm a follower of the Dalai Lama." Apparently nowadays Buddhism was a sign of extreme success; in this city almost any time a person became a famous movie star or writer or had rich parents they became Buddhists and spent all their spare time flying to New Mexico or Hollywood, chanting to get more money and talking about reincarnation in a superior fashion. "Tell me, Bronc, were you ever married?" I said brilliantly after a few more gulps.

"Yes," he said.

"And now you're divorced? Did you have kids?"

"No . . ." he said slowly and a strange look crossed his face. "My wife . . . killed herself."

"Ah," I said.

"Since then, you know . . . I haven't really been involved in any real relationships. . . . In fact, I haven't slept with anybody in three years."

Surely all this was a positive sign, that he was confiding in me must mean something. "And you—you're surrounded, you must be, by the most beautiful women who are also . . . very aggressive," I said as the bartender, without any indication on Bronc's part, brought over two more glasses of vodka in thick, short icy glasses. "And you don't want to sleep with them?"

He nodded seriously. "I'm glad you asked me," he said. Under the influence I was startled to realize how much his face resembled that of a young beef calf. Big brown eyes, square jaw, a trifle stupid yet sweet; perhaps my mother was right, it was time for me to meet someone with a three-hundred-thousand-dollar-a-year income and settle down after all. It wasn't necessarily important to either of us that the man I married was Jewish, but it was an additional plus. After all, for five thousand years (or however many) my particular ancestral line had consisted of nothing but Jewish people (except for the occasional Cossack rapist) who met and reproduced with other Jewish people, forming Jewish children (religious or not), and it would be a shame if I had to be the one to screw up and break the chain letter.

"My best friend, Lee," Bronc was saying, "is the head of an ad agency—we're old friends from Andover and went to Yale together—and naturally Lee knows all the models, he's always introducing them to me or I meet them on shoots and, I don't want to sound immodest, but a lot of them . . . are very interested in me."

"Models—they're beautiful," I said encouragingly. "You don't want to sleep with them?"

"When I see them, I want to, excuse me, fuck them," he said in a tone intended I imagine to reassure me. I waited for him to make some point but he said nothing more.

"So do you?" I asked at last.

"No," he said. "No. I prefer just to fuck them in my head. That way, I don't have to get involved."

"Maybe that's due to your wife's suicide," I muttered. "And Amber?"

"Oh, she's just a friend," he said, looking around. The bartender brought over more vodka. There seemed to be a sort of loud roaring in my ears; the effect of this alcoholic beverage was remarkable. "Ever been to the Fabulous House of Hot Peep?" he asked.

"No," I said.

"Oh, me and Lee go there a lot. It's really fun—the sort of place most people don't know about. I'll take you there, sometime," he said.

What a camaraderie we had developed between us, in such a short time; I felt somehow . . . unfemale, yet not male either. It was just pleasant to be two people talking. "Great," I said.

"You know," he said, "I think it's terrific, getting to talk to you. I've never said these things, that I've often thought about . . ." He gazed at me with a look that seemed to say he could easily imagine me tied down to a bed with my legs spread while he inserted large objects such as miniature baseball bats or Coca-Cola bottles into my vagina. Probably more than one woman would find this to be a turn-on, in that it was quite a standard female fantasy to be rendered powerless in a sexual situation and therefore not have to take responsibility. "Do you want to go someplace else?" he said. "Or, have you had enough?"

"Sure," I said. "Let's go someplace else." I looked down at my watch; it was scarcely after 9 P.M. All I wanted to do was distract myself from my problems. If I could find a real boyfriend at the same time, even better. If only Daniel Loomis hadn't been married! That was why I had to try and replace him with someone else.

Bronc's car, a fairly new BMW, was badly smashed along one side, and the strips of trim had been peeled off one of the doors. The interior was filled with filth and junk, broken stereo tapes, sand and seashells, paper cups from fast-food chains, and a few old beer bottles. He drove across town, explaining that the car had been stolen so many times he no longer bothered to have it repaired. Once it had cost him six thousand dollars to have the car towed from a swamp where it had been abandoned in Jersey. That was the kind of guy he was, money meant nothing to him. "I got twenty thousand dollars in parking tickets this year, too," he said, almost proudly.

Meanwhile he pulled a flask of vodka out of the glove compartment, slurped, and passed it over to me. "Did you, ah, used to go out with Amber?" I said, taking a slug.

"With Amber?" Bronc said, pulling up onto the sidewalk and turning off the engine. "Amber MacPherson?" I assumed that tone in his voice was one of wriggling contempt, and that we were on the same side together. "Tell me," he said, "what do you think of her?"

"Oh, God," I said. I was trying to remain noncommittal, at the same time let him know I was in agreement.

He left the car on the sidewalk and I followed behind, where he paid five dollars for each of us to go into a place called the Fabulous House of Hot Peep. I supposed, momentarily, that this was some new Manhattan trend; there were always new trends in New York, and this one didn't surprise me. It was unsophisticated to act shocked, that much I knew. Even my ex-friend Patty had once gone to a peep house, in the company of a tiny African transvestite, possibly a pygmy, who she had met at the International House at Columbia University while attending summer school there.

In a way I was even quite fascinated to be going in: there were so many places in New York that as a woman one felt uncomfortable attending; I just hoped that Bronc didn't take all his dates here, and that to him I was somebody special.

It did seem as if he had been here before, though. "Come on," he said. There was a big neon sign off to the right that said HOT MOVIE WORLD and we walked past a row of little cubicles with doors; he grabbed my arm and pulled me into a room that was empty.

I suppose each room was designed for one person only, but we crammed inside. He had to keep putting quarters into a machine; two women and a pig were displayed walking down a beach, but no matter how many quarters he put into the machine, no sex took place.

Jammed together in the tiny booth with the dark curtain, I felt certain something momentarily was about to take place: a kiss, or some passionate embrace. Surely in other darkened rooms men had not brought women on dates. Bronc stayed as far away from me as possible and inserted another quarter; now the two women and the pig were taking a little dip in the ocean, the women had on bathing suits, they splashed water at one another. "Is this it?" I said. "Don't you think there's something wrong? Aren't they supposed to be having sex?" The pig had a happy smile upon his face and looked slightly sunburned; well, naturally, a pig would need sun block, if he were going to walk on the beach.

Bronc stared intently at the screen. "You might have a point," he muttered at last, swaying drunkenly against me. It was something of a relief, that nothing was happening of a sexual nature in the film—more and more I was thinking of becoming a vegetarian. Probably somewhere out there pigs and women were willing to have sex with one another because they were desperate for money, but it was too pitiful to contemplate. It dawned on me that there was a certain sense of anticipation in the air; Bronc was waiting for me to do something! Well, there was nothing for it then: I wrapped one arm around Bronc's face and tilted up my head for Bronc to kiss me. He let out a little scream, but conditions were so crowded that my pulling on his neck forced him to bend down. Briefly his mouth latched onto mine, as if two jellyfish had bumped into each other in the middle of the South Pacific. "I'll drive you home," he said.

He pulled his car up onto the sidewalk in front of my building, leaned over, unlocked my door, and practically pushed me out onto the street. "Well, ah—" I said.

"Listen," he said, "I was kind of—not telling you the truth before, about Amber. We're friends . . . very good friends. But I think . . . we could be friends too, that is, if you don't mention to anyone, that we're friends. I'd really like you to meet my brother."

"From the mental hospital?"

"He's fine now," Bronc said irritably. "Actually, he's only my half-brother. He's going to be very rich. But the thing is, I would certainly hope that . . . nothing that took place this evening was ever repeated. You know, don't talk about it." Out of the corner of my eye I saw a tiny figure hunched bitterly on my doorstep.

"Sure!" I said, hoping Bronc didn't see. "I won't mention it! It can be our little secret!" I leapt back from the car door—luckily Bronc was in such a hurry to get away he drove off before I had even properly slammed the door.

"You can't come in," I said, going down the stairs past the kid and putting the key in my front gate lock. The kid looked frightened. My God, was I cruel. Because this was a little, little boy, and it wasn't natural, for a child to just come along and . . . attach himself to an address. The child must have been desperate, and there I was, shoving past him and closing the door in his face, just about. Surely he couldn't have been wandering the streets since I pushed him out? Already this morning seemed ages ago, a lifetime even. All kinds of decadent and depraved events had happened to me, in thoughts and deeds. While he—what had he been doing all that time? Should I call the police, or some kind of child welfare office? But it seemed meaner to hand him over to the arms of the law than to just let him get on with his life.

I turned on the lights and took a can of tunafish out of the cabinet. To sit, with a bowl of tunafish, mixed with mayonnaise, maybe a little pickle relish, onions, a few thin slices of crispy carrots, in front of the TV set, aspirin, then a hot bath (provided there was even enough hot water—the taps had a way of running hot for only half a tub before dwindling into icy rivulets), that was my idea of a pleasant evening. Just as I was attempting to peel back the top of the can with the opener, the telephone rang. "I tried to call you before," my mother said, "but you were out."

"I just got in," I said.

"How are you?"

"I don't want to say," I said. "I'm speechless. You talk."

"Oh," my mother said. "Well, it doesn't look like your father is going to pay me any more alimony. A month ago I got a letter from him saying that as he is now three-fourths retired, he feels he can no longer pay me two hundred and fifty dollars a month. I wrote him back, saying that *I, too,* would like to retire. What kind of reason is that, for not wanting to pay me anymore?"

"I can't believe, twenty years later, this is still going on," I said. It occurred to me that even now, whatever else had happened since, my parents' divorce was still one of the biggest events of my life.

"I'd like to kill him," my mother said.

"Let me ask you this," I said, putting down the can and the opener. A little tuna juice spilled over the crummy table. "Were you planning to divorce Dad before his arrest when everything came out? Or were things okay, before that?"

There was a pause. "What do you think?" my mother said.

"I don't know," I said.

"I've been trying to brainwash you for years to think your own thoughts!" my mother said.

"Well, I don't," I said. "I think yours."

"Same thing," she said. "Perhaps we would have gotten divorced anyway. The truth was, I think now, I must have had my suspicions about his so-called fertility clinic, but I pretended not to know. After all, so many of the babies I would see in town looked just like him! And your father's looks were—are—very distinctive. That nose—it just wasn't common, especially on a baby. But I don't think he met Angela until he was waiting for the trial in jail. Apparently it's not all that uncommon: men in jail being pursued by women, I mean. It was Angela who came up with the bail money, after all; people were surprised, not that the bail was set so high, but that a doctor couldn't come up with it. But you have to remember your father always spent very freely, we were in debt up to our necks with the cost of building the clinic, and your father looked upon the few months in prison as a little rest. He was working on a book, he said. Of course, I see now that the reason he didn't mind was that he didn't want to bump into all those women and their husbands who thought the test-tube babies were actually theirs. Remember the neighbor?"*

It was a subject my mother might have discussed happily for hours, but one that I was weary of, at least to a degree; I only brought it up because I knew it was something that entertained her. "Now let me tell you what happened to me," I said. "Last night, some kid, a little kid, followed me home, and I told him to go away, but in the middle of the night I found him sitting outside, and so I took him in, because I had thrown a lot of water all over him. And so I sent him away in the morning. Only now"—I looked around and whispered in a hissing voice—"I just got home, and he's still there!"

"How old is he?" my mother said.

"I don't know. He doesn't talk. Nine, maybe. Six. I can't tell ages. I hardly ever see any little kids. And in my own head I'm only eighteen. That's why it's a shock to look in the mirror and see a middle-aged person who resembles a prostitute."

"If you're middle-aged, then I'm old," my mother said. "And that can't be. Take him inside."

"The kid?"

"Yes," she said. "Keep him. It would be nice, to have a child. I'll take him, if you don't want him."

"Seriously?" I said.

"Why not? Unless you want to have your own baby. You could go to one of those sperm banks."

"Aw, Ma, think!" I said. "You know that's not possible. What would my chances be? Not just Mitchell—but any one of Dad's kids would be well over twenty by now. And any one of them could have sold their sperm to one of the banks, and I might . . ." I didn't finish the sentence but crammed some of the little flakes of tunafish into my mouth in an attempt to gain temporary control of my flare-up of rage.

This was not the first time my mother had suggested this. Sex with men directly could be dangerous, leading to disease fatal or otherwise; also men

---

*The neighbor, Angela's best friend, had mysteriously become pregnant shortly after her husband left her. The child was known as "The Little Saint" (the woman's name was St. Clair) but my mother and I knew the real truth.

by nature were rotten, and as soon as they had sex with you were more than likely to drop you completely, or become obscene or unpleasant. My father was only one example of this. However, she was surely aware that for a number of years Mitchell, my youngest brother, had been putting himself through medical school in part by selling his sperm. This made me apprehensive about going to a sperm bank. I would not want to bear my brother's child, although some years back I had dated a guy who spoke fondly of his incestuous relations with his sister. His name was Emerson Crawford the Third, and he drove a Corvette. He decided to befriend me, although he was a wealthy freshman and I was a senior majoring in Oriental religion, before Oriental became a politically inappropriate word. I should have taken Emerson when I had the chance, before they erased my transcript: in retrospect, it was obvious I reminded him of his sister and could have landed him and even married him if I had been willing to go along with the charade . . . at the time I was very impressed with his purchase of a stuffed mongoose fighting a cobra, before stuffed specimens became offensive. He had bought it at a local antique store for two hundred dollars, enough to last me the entire semester. Once he took me out for a lobster dinner. Since then I had moved to New York, where I could scarcely get a man to speak to me. The men in this city—they really had it made.

My head now suddenly and abruptly expanded, swollen and taut, to the size of a hot air balloon, and then shrank violently to grapefruit size. What a magical and golden evening it had seemed such a short time ago: but now I wanted to die. "I think I may have to kill myself," I said.

"What did you do?" my mother said.

"I went home with my boss," I said, "for a drink, and when I said good-bye—I kissed him." There was a pause while my mother thought. "After I left, I went to a cocktail party, hosted by Amber MacPherson, my other boss. I found the invitation in my pocket. Only when I got there, she told me I wasn't invited. And so I left with a man, who took me to a bar, and I drank a lot of vodka, and then I went with him to a sex booth, where I kissed him."

My mother was still thinking. "This is the modern age," she said at last. "I think, what you did—that's terrific! Because now, a woman can kiss a man, and that's fine. I mean, that's not a big deal, is it, to kiss your boss? And what did the other guy expect, taking you to a sex booth."

"Oh, Ma," I said.

"What's your problem?" she said. "Did he push you away?"

"Yes," I said. "And he made a little sound—like a scream." There was a silence on the other end. I couldn't explain to her the depths of my despair, especially when probably I was going to feel worse in the morning. It was one thing to pretend things had changed for women; but in fact they hadn't. To take the aggressive, masculine role: this was traumatic. It was the men who had changed, not the women.

"In the old days," my mother said in a puzzled voice, "if you had a date, with a man, he would pick you up at your door. Everything seemed polite. Then, as soon as you got into his car, he would drive around the block, unzip his fly, and put your hand on it. It was unbelievable!"

"There's still a few of those left," I said. "I went out with one at lunch. My problem is, there's something wrong with the times we're living in."

"If you had a child, you'd be forced to think about someone beside yourself," my mother said. "For the next forty or fifty years, you'd have to worry about someone else, until finally you died. Get married. Have a child."

"The one thing I learned from Dad, was that I better be able to support myself, because nobody else in this world is going to do it. And I think, in many ways, this was a good thing he taught me. I believe all people should support themselves, male or female. But at the same time—"

"It would be nice to have a rich man to support you," my mother said.

"Exactly."

"I agree with both halves of your sentence," my mother said.

"One half of the sentence was yours," I pointed out.

Such were my darkest and most hideous thoughts. Was it my fault? Probably. Stuck at the end of the twentieth century, when everyone went around saying women were equal to men and no one admitted to the silent subtext—that the only real status for women was to align themselves with a rich and famous man. Even women who had made it on their own— famous blond rock stars, or TV journalists, or supreme court judges—were frankly viewed with contempt, albeit fascination.

My mother reassured me from an early age that I was destined for greatness; this maybe was a mistake, since it had left me with a feeling of failure.

From outside the front door a thin, high choirboy voice began to sing in an unusual caterwaul, or maybe it was a chant. Even my mother could hear it long distance through the phone. "What's that?" she said finally.

"I think it's that kid," I said. "Maybe he's torturing a cat."

"I guess you better go look," she said. "Let me know what happens."

So I went out to the front steps and invited him in. It was much easier for me to take charge of things after I had been told what to do. "What are you, hungry?" I said.

He nodded and looked embarrassed at having been caught in the middle of singing; it really was quite sweet, a small boy, singing away and thinking himself alone. It reminded me of Ralph, my middle younger brother, age five or six, singing, "Oh, my chicka-biddy, biddy, biddy bee," in a high soprano voice.

"Okay," I told him. "You come in, and I'll make us some tunafish, but only if you promise to talk."

He followed me down the stairs. "If you take anything, or break anything, I'll break your fingers," I said. After that he stood by the door and didn't come any farther inside. "Just kidding," I said.

He rubbed his groin and shifted from foot to foot. "Miss," he said, "can I use your bathroom?"

"You know where it is," I said. By the time he came back I had found some bread in the freezer and was toasting it. Something smelled faintly garbagy—perhaps a whiff of stale air wafting from the freezer, where food decayed at a slow rate. "Now," I said, carrying the bowl of tunafish into the living room. "First of all, tell me your name."

"Abdhul," he said.

"Abdhul what?" I said. He closed his mouth and refused to speak. "I told you, if you came in, you would have to talk," I said. He didn't answer. "Where's your mother and brothers?" I said.

"I don't know," he said.

"When did you last see them?" He shrugged. I didn't want to harass him too much; maybe he was paralyzed with fright. Or maybe he had amnesia. "Was it in the pizza place?" I said, trying to stay calm. "The other day? Have you seen them since then?"

"Nope," he said.

"Do you know where you live?" His eyes, pale tiger's-stone color, gazed past me serenely. I had no idea how old he was—for all I knew he could have been a thirty-five-year-old mentally handicapped midget. "Do you live in an apartment?" I said. "A shelter? What about—the park?" There was some slight flickering in his face at this, mysterious and inarticulate. There was a park a few blocks away. I supposed it was possible, if they came from some temporary shelter, that the lunatic—his mother?—took them to sleep in the park during the summer. Still, it seemed farfetched; surely the police or some social worker would have spotted a woman with five children living out of doors and taken them from her. "Is that where you always live? In the park?" He didn't answer. "Okay—after we eat the tunafish, we can go look for them."

I finished mixing up the tunafish. It was a terrible thing, to eat tunafish, even though I knew this brand did not kill dolphins to get them. Even so, a tunafish probably had some brains and feelings, and a life of his or her own. Just the other day, I had found in the supermarket a package of six large clams, wrapped in plastic, that were on sale at the end of the day for two dollars. I took them home to make soup. I was slightly nervous about clam poisoning, but I cooked four of them in a tiny pot for a long time, even after they had already opened; after all, as far as I was concerned, these clams were long deceased. I chopped them up to make soup, but as soon as I took a bite of the soup, a mouthful, I felt slightly ill, imagining that I was being clam-poisoned, although I wasn't sure what would happen to me or how long it would take.

I was thankful I hadn't used all of the clams. I had left the others in the sink, and a while later, when I was rinsing the dish, I picked up the other clam, and it . . . sort of grunted, in my hand! It was still alive, and it had opened slightly at being placed in cold water, and then, when I touched it, it shut up in alarm! I felt just terrible; it had never occurred to me that these clams could still be alive when I boiled them. I put the two remaining clams in a pot and added some sea-salt seasoned with herbs. I knew the clams would be soothed by basking in the salt water, only what was I supposed to do with them now? Was there any point in taking them over to the Hudson River and throwing them in? Weren't they supposed to be in sand, or mud flats, or something. In the end, in despair, I tossed them in with the trash the next day. The death of a clam, for which I was responsible. It was a tragedy for which I knew I was going to have to pay.

"Listen, Abdhul," I told the kid after we had eaten the tunafish. "We're going over to the park, nearby, and see if we can find your mother and your brothers."

"She's not my mother," he said.

This silenced me for a minute. "Ah," I said. "But she's in charge of you, right?" He had a convenient way of not answering when it suited him. "Come on, let's go," I said. "Before it gets any later." I grabbed my keys and pushed him out the door in front of me.

Riverside Park was only a few blocks away. There was an old highway exit ramp, blocked off, and underneath, illuminated in the lamplight, various people had taken up residence, with cardboard boxes, broken lawn chairs, metal pots placed over rubbish fires—it was relatively protected when it rained. I was afraid to actually walk under the exit ramp, however—it curved around behind an embankment; there was no telling what kind of psychotic was waiting in lurk.

"Is any of this familiar to you?" I asked Abdhul. If it was, he made no indication; I thought in any event I would have seen or heard some sign of a woman with five children—four, now—although, as I say, we didn't go all the way back around the curve of the ramp. The park was huge, it ran all the way from 72nd Street to the north, and there were a million places she could have been, if in fact this was even the park she stayed in. "What's her name?" I said.

"Brenda," Abdhul said.

"Would you tell me, if any of this looks familiar?" I said, and I yelled, "Brenda! Brenda, are you back there?"

"Oh, she wouldn't answer," he said.

"Why don't you lead me to where you think she might be," I said.

For maybe an hour I followed Abdhul through the tunnel that led down to the Hudson, up to the 79th Street boat basin, into empty playgrounds and through bushy overgrown footpaths. When it got later I realized he didn't have any idea of where he was taking me. It was like following an eager dog on a leash, a bloodhound who had been commanded to search and find, but who didn't have the slightest idea of what it was looking for.

I turned and started walking out of the park; he seemed ready to run on, but after a pause he crept up and followed behind me. I thought of taking a look in the pizza parlor where I had first seen him; maybe this Brenda and the others were waiting there, in case he showed up.

But peering through the glass front, into the brightly lit interior beyond, it was obvious she wasn't there, alone or with the other kids. I saw, out of the corner of my eye, that Hassim had seen me; he stopped stretching a white slab of dough and stood, quivering and delicate, waiting for me to come in.

"Nope, not there," I said to Abdhul, and took his arm to lead him across the street. "Let's go into the grocery store while I think of what to do." Maybe nobody would notice he was barefoot.

The supermarket was right across the street. I walked down the rows, wielding a shopping cart, faster and faster, tossing one item after the next into the basket, followed by Abdhul. I suppose I was thinking that if I kept at it long enough, this child would grow bored and somehow disappear. And, at the same time, if he was going to stay, then he would need food.

It didn't even matter what I threw into the shopping cart, what a lucky country it was to live in, where there was so much food, endless quantities, not like, say, Ethiopia or Russia, where there were probably only a few supermarkets and these had empty shelves. But it didn't matter, because no matter what item I purchased, I knew that when I got it home, took it out, and put it on a plate, it wouldn't taste like a goddamn thing. There were slabs of mozzarella cheese, prewrapped, and this would taste like a chewy sponge, and the rice puffs, these would taste like tiny chewy sponges, and the cherry tomatoes, so plump and red, would taste the same as the strawberries, flavorless, flavorless.

And there was something else, too: that little plastic basket of cherry tomatoes, prewrapped in cellophane, not only would they not taste like anything, but half of them would be rotten. That was how they made their money, these places—anything they had to sell that was fresh, they would prewrap it, and tell their help to put the rotten pieces underneath.

Oh, they were skilled at wrapping their rotten food: chicken, for example, which came sealed on little foam trays, all yellow and puckered, plump and tasty—when you got this chicken home and unwrapped it, phew, what a stench! There was nothing for it but to wash it off and drench it in some sugar-syrup barbecue sauce.

Or another favorite trick was to sell what appeared to be a bit of steak, or some plump chop—and then, when one got it out of the wrapper and into the fry pan, it was revealed that the back side was nothing but grease. Grease, a bit of fat and gristle, and even if this trick had not been performed, the meat would have tasted like nothing much anyway.

"Now, listen to me closely," I told Abdhul when we got to the aisle that sold wrappings, plastic baggies, and paper goods. "Here we have a famous brand of plastic wrap. Fifty feet, two twenty-nine. Now, in my pocket I have a coupon, good for this particular brand, that will give us twenty-five cents off. But, examining the merchandise carefully, we see that we can buy seventy-five feet of the store brand of plastic wrap for a dollar fifteen less than the more famous brand. Which should we buy?"

I wasn't going to give him time to answer; perhaps he wasn't listening anyway. "Store brand," he muttered.

"Yes!" I said. "If we buy the store brand, it's much cheaper, even though we have a coupon good for a quarter off. But there's one problem: the store brand has been carefully designed so that it adheres to itself, and there's no way to tear off a full piece. After only a few times of using the plastic wrap, the whole thing is completely tangled."

"Put it in the freezer," he said.

"What?" I said.

"If you put it in the freezer it doesn't get stuck together," he said.

"Oh," I said. "But then, I'll probably forget where I've put it. So we're going to buy the more expensive brand—besides, the box is nicer."

"Very good," Abdhul said.

I gave him a look. Was he saying this just in order to flatter me? But no, that was impossible to believe. If there was one thing I had learned, men never gave compliments unless they really meant it sincerely. Women and girls might make compliments that were lies, yes. A man, never; he did not have the wits about him to do so. "One of the biggest differences between men and women," I said, "is that a woman will ask a question, such as 'What is a line out, in baseball?' without being in the slightest bit interested, simply in order to be polite, and at the same time draw out whoever she's talking to. But a man wouldn't do this."

"Never?" Abdhul said.

"Oh, one or two, perhaps, there's an exception to every rule, but even in the case of these men who have learned the skill of asking a question simply to be polite, they give themselves away almost immediately by *not bothering to listen to the answer.*"

"I see," said Abdhul. When we got to the checkout line I told him if he wanted he could run back and pick out a box of cookies.

The wait on line was interminable. Apparently some item of the person in front of me wasn't marked with the price; the cashier disappeared in order to find out what it cost, and it was five or ten minutes before she returned. The same thing happened when she rang up our purchases. "Just relax, Pamela," Abdhul said.

"How *old* are you, anyway?" I said, knowing he wouldn't answer. By the time we got back to the apartment and Abdhul helped me put away the groceries I was exhausted. "Well, I don't know what to do with you now," I said. "Luckily tomorrow's Saturday, and I'll have time to figure something out. I guess you can sleep on the couch again; if I call the police, it'll take them an hour to come, and then who knows where they'll take you. We might as well wait until morning." Really, it would be entirely impractical for me to consider keeping him. I knew nothing about kids and they frankly made me uncomfortable. I supposed if I had had my own I would have felt differently about him or her; carrying it around inside your own body for nine months probably gave a person the opportunity to get used to the idea. I had never felt any longing to have a baby. I found a floral nightgown for Abdhul and I put it on over his head. "See, in many ways I was among the first to grow up in the modern age," I said, pulling off his pants. "From the time I was eight years old, my father smoked marijuana on a daily basis. My parents, who started off with the expectation of being a normal family—in those days the father worked, the mothers stayed home with the children, people saved for their retirement and hoped to move to a bigger house with a pastoral atmosphere—completely fell apart, as did so many other families when the late nineteen sixties came along."

"How old are *you*, anyway?" Abdhul said.

"That's of no import," I said. "Anyway, after my father began to smoke marijuana, I never saw him again. By that I mean he was no longer the same person; in fact, he could barely remember my name or who I was. He was, however, fonder of my younger brothers, because there were still some behavioral anachronisms left over from the old days—that boys could hammer nails and fix cars, and these were activities men of all ages could do together and not have to talk. You see, what happened was, everything was supposed to be overturned, but they only overturned half the things. Take you, for example: do you know how you came to be in . . . foster care?"

He looked rather adorable in the nightgown: it came down below his feet, covered with large yellow and pink roses. It reminded me of the days when I had forced my younger brothers to dress up in my dresses; luckily this hadn't had any effect on their later sexual orientation, at least as far as I knew. In retrospect it was curious that neither parent commented on the hours my brothers spent in drag. "I was kidnapped," Abdhul said.

"What?" I said.

"I was kidnapped," Abdhul said. "A long time ago. That's what Brenda told me."

2

**B**UT I DON'T WANT YOU TO GO OUT," Abdhul whimpered.

"It's just a cocktail party," I said. "I'll only be gone for a little while. There's lasagna, you can heat it up. And also peas, frozen peas, for a balanced meal."

"I'm too young to stay by myself," he said. Maybe he had a point. But obviously he was used to spending hours, even days, on his own. Probably by leaving him at home alone I was breaking the law. "Who invited you, anyway?" he said.

"Daniel Loomis," I said.

"Oh yeah?" Abdhul said. "He's married, right? How come his wife doesn't go with him to these things?"

"Rich people don't have regular relationships," I said. "She travels a lot, and she either takes the nanny and the children with her, or she leaves the nanny and kids at home. Apparently she and Daniel don't even sleep together, although Daniel says she doesn't have any boyfriends, which seems a bit farfetched to me, considering that since they've been married he's had several affairs, except for Madonna. She almost slept with him before she became famous but didn't."

Abdhul snorted contemptuously and went back to watching TV. I started to get dressed. Luckily Daniel had given me a bag of clothing his wife was planning to give to charity. I started to pull things out of the bag. By wearing his wife's clothes I hoped I would fit in to the sort of event Daniel attended, although I had never really seen anyone wearing this sort of thing. There was a blouse—maybe it was a vest?—that was a sort of tight corset lacing up the front, with a rubber shell that covered my chest. In trying it on, it appeared my choice was to either not tie up the corset strings tightly, in which case bits of flesh protruded, or strap the whole thing together. "Abdhul, help me tie up these strings," I said.

"What the hell is that?" Abdhul said.

"Wait, you haven't seen the whole ensemble yet," I said, holding up Daniel's wife's old skirt. It was obvious it would never fit unless I put on a pair of contortionist's pantyhose, the kind that women wear to flatten their stomachs—control top, I believe they're called. Once I had squeezed myself into the skirt I saw that, to make matters worse, the corset had a little flounce that came down around my hips, over the top of the skirt, contributing to my sensation that I was a ponderous hippopotamus or perhaps a hunched vulture with curved beak. Then finally I forced my feet into her shoes—there were a few pairs she was apparently throwing out. The ones I selected for this evening were ruby velvet, very high heeled and cleverly designed in such a way that it was impossible to do more than shuffle along at a minute pace unless I wanted to topple over. "How do I look?" I said.

Abdhul looked away from the TV set for a brief instant. "Ha!" he said with a chortle. "You look weird!"

"Thanks a lot," I said. Because I was so tightly bound, and I was nervous, naturally I began to perspire, only there was no way for the sweat to evaporate inside the rubber frontispiece, which was sticking to my skin like a Band-Aid.

Oh, I was wretched and out-of-place, in the room with the pink-custard floor and the young and brilliant Manhattan set. The party was being held in a restaurant that had been in vogue with the rich for many years; on the walls were badly painted murals of monkeys, dressed in baroque garb, engaged in various pseudohuman courtship rituals. I pretended to stare at the paintings while secretly looking around the room for Daniel. They reminded me of that tragic story from the Arabian nights where two women, or maybe they were girls, ran screaming out of the woods, pursued by two baboons, and the worthy travelers—who happened to be passing by at just that minute—assumed the girls were being sexually molested, slaughtered the baboons, and watched as the two girls burst into tears at the death of their lovers.

Where was Daniel? Had he invited me to this place just to humiliate me and prove to me once and for all that I would never fit into this world? The women in the place were dressed in wispy chiffon garments, sequined minidresses, and elaborate beaded jackets, breasts firmly strapped up near shoulder level. Attractive? Were they ever! They paced the room with restless sexuality, parading between the few pitiful specimens of men, and these women had packaged themselves so well that the bits of conversation I kept overhearing were all about: the Forgery of Cycladic Art; the Marketing of Mineral Waters; the Latest Arab Author in Translation; and constant repetition of a recent magazine article about the kinky sex habits of the president. There wasn't a single conversation I might have contributed to. Constant waiters circled with trays of stuffed mushroom heads and little heaps of caviar plonked onto pancakes. If only I had worked for a fashion magazine, instead of a hunting book, then I might have acquired a taste for champagne (which to me always tasted like a little dishwashing liquid in a glass of soda water) instead of beer.

Finally I saw Daniel across the room, and I stumbled toward him. His wife really must have had tiny feet. I decided I'd better not try to move and leaned against a chair, waiting, until he came over to me. Even at a distance I could see his watery eyes, the color of dirty ice cubes made from puddles, with their curious pupils the size of pinpricks, which gave him a strange intensity. "How wonderful that you could come," he said, taking my hand with a sort of bland detachment.

"What's this a party for, anyway?" I said.

"Oh, it's a benefit; I'm on the board of a small theater, which produces plays written by homeless and underprivileged youth," he said. I couldn't help but notice that even though all the women were so singularly beautiful, the men were either very gray and stout, or dressed in brilliant pink and blue waistcoats and smiling at each other. What had happened to the men in this city? Maybe the Russians or some other country were putting something in the water that caused them to look so dissolute. The other interesting thing was that everyone in the room had the same tiny nose, and each tiny nose had two little flaring nostrils. I wondered if they hadn't all had nose jobs and used the same surgeon. I was certain I wasn't imagining it: each person seemed to have a larger, invisible nose, like a superimposed "before" photograph, as if they were haunted by the deceased remains of the portion of the nose they had amputated. I had read about how people who had had a leg amputated continued to have a "ghost" leg, one that itched and often gave them pain although it was no longer there. Perhaps the same was true of people who had nose jobs, and they felt an uncontrollable urge to blow and scratch and pick what was no longer.

Just then a woman approached dressed in a lavender-and-lime-green suit, who Daniel introduced as Pimmi Stimples. Judging from the melting expression on her face, she was obviously in love with him. I was mesmerized, and at the same time horrified, because looking at her was like looking at an improved version of myself. She was the same as me, only better. Put it this way: her nose was smaller, her eyes larger and more widely set, her jaw stronger, her cheekbones more pronounced, her expression friendlier and more intelligent, her hair shinier, and so on and so forth. It was a shock, and even a blow to the system: what right did she have, to throw up herself like this before me, making a mockery of everything I stood for? I just couldn't understand why Daniel would express interest in me, when there was Pimmi Stimples. Couldn't he see I was badly in want of electrolysis?

I could feel myself descending into a sort of vegetative state, which had happened to me on occasion before. This was a sort of condition somewhere between vegetable and meditation; my mind fled the corporeal body, leaving it to stagger around without even any small talk to make it seem normal. Apparently under certain conditions I was capable of producing a natural Valium, in much the same way as it is said that runners and athletes produce endorphins. "Daniel, I think I better be going," I said.

"Oh, no!" Daniel said, suddenly tripping over his wife's shoes and nearly knocking me into a waiter carrying a tray of champagne-filled glasses. "Please don't leave, not yet!" When we had regained our balance he put his arm around my waist and together we tottered across the room. It seemed to be a bit odd—wasn't he worried about our intimacy getting back to his wife?—but when we were repositioned in the opposite corner he whispered, "I really want you to stay and meet my psychiatrist. He's a great friend; I've invited him here. I go to him five days a week, and I've told him all about us." I must have looked desperate; he added, quickly, "See? He's coming over here, right now." A grinning creature biting his nails approached. "Martin, this is Pamela. Pamela, Martin Feurey." Dr. Feurey reached over, I guess to shake my hand, only I was holding a glass of champagne, into which he limply inserted his fingers. "Yikes!" he said, yanking them out. "Sorry! I didn't see. But my hands are clean." He was in his early forties, but dressed in a blue suit with sleeves that were too short (perhaps it was an old discard of Daniel's?) with his curiously unlined skin the texture of an octopus, head crowned with silvery ringlets, all in all he resembled Harpo Marx or a pudge-faced cherub. From his lapel pocket he removed a drink-stirrer, which he rapidly twirled. "I'm trying to quit smoking," he said. "So, uh, as a distraction I usually hold this swizzle stick. So now, I, uh, I'm smoking *and* playing with my drink-stirrer."

"Ah," I said.

"Anyway, this afternoon, I was seeing a patient, down at the clinic, and he was lying on the couch, while I was sitting in the chair, clutching, my, uh, you know, drink-stirrer. So just as he was telling me he was impotent,

I got so nervous that the drink-stirrer flew out of my hands, across the room, and stabbed him right between the eyes!"

"Martin used to be a fashion designer," Daniel said, as if that explained everything. "I produced a movie, a few years back, and Martin did the costumes. I think he designed that dress you're wearing."

"But you don't anymore?" I said.

"No, I gave it up," Martin said. "I decided to go back to school, and I just finished last year. This is my first year as a psychiatrist. Unfortunately my apartment is only one room, so I usually make home visits."

"What if your patients don't have room in their apartment?" I said.

"Then I have to meet them in a bar. I don't really have very many patients, though. I'm trying to attract them."

"It must be kind of hard for you to acquire patients if when you meet them at cocktail parties you stick your hand in their drink," I said.

"Say, I have an idea," Daniel said. "Why don't you go and see Martin, Pamela? You know, the health-insurance program at work will pay for it."

"Good idea," Martin said.

"Mmmm," I said, noncommittally. But perhaps, I thought, it wouldn't be a bad thing to do. I could hardly call myself problem-free; in any event, it would give me a chance to talk about Abdhul. Thus far, no one other than my mother knew he was with me, and perhaps Martin would have some good suggestions or advice for raising a boy, even if he was from all appearances a nut case.

"I'll come over to your house, tomorrow night, and we can see if this is something you want to pursue. Say, six o'clock? I should warn you, though, that I'm usually late."

"That's something I've been trying to work on with Martin," Daniel said.

"No . . ." I said. "Not my apartment. It—it's too small."

"I see," Martin said. There was a certain pleased tone of discovery to his voice, as if by refusing him entrance to my apartment he had learned something personal about me. The two men stood looking at me. "I tell you what," I said at last. "We could meet at that bar . . ." I tried to remember the place where I had been with Bronc. "The Pony Bar and Grill."

"Good, very good," Martin said.

"Say, six o'clock?" I said.

"Let's make it seven," Martin said.

"I have to go," I told Daniel. "But thanks for the party."

"You're going?" Daniel said. "Don't you want to come out to dinner? With me and Martin?"

"I can't," I said, thinking of Abdhul at home.

"Then I'll walk you to a cab," Daniel said.

"Nice to meet you," I told Martin. Daniel slipped his sorry paw into mine as I headed out to the lobby. In the frosted mirrors, illuminated by sultry recessed pink lighting, it was touching how drab and tiny Daniel appeared next to my large, gooselike self. What did he want with me, anyway? The ridiculous flounce of his wife's former dress rippled around my hips in degrading fashion. Was she—his wife—into some form of humiliating masochism, to have worn such a style in the first place? "It makes me so happy to see you," Daniel mumbled as he jammed himself into the revolving door alongside me. "Shall I find you a cab at the corner?"

"I think there's a bus stop on the corner," I said.

"Oh no, grab a cab," he said.

" 'S expensive," I said.

"Here, here," he said, pressing some crumpled bills into my hand and flagging a taxi to a stop.

"Bye-bye," I said, flinging myself quickly in the back in order to not have to go through the good-bye rituals of human beings—or at least to avoid Daniel's pleading look for me to give him a good-bye kiss.

The cabdriver took off without noticing that Daniel was still in the process of slamming the passenger door; I watched him being thrown, or jumping, backward. That was the sort of person Daniel was, always out of touch with the physical world. Now that we had spent some time together, and I was less frightened of him, I saw that he was the sort who was constantly tripping over things or blindly stabbing himself in the eye with a pencil, eraser-end, or would crush his genitalia into the sharp end of his desk, all the while gazing at me with his earnest rodent eyes. It did endear him to me, for a man to be so uncoordinated was a terrible burden, stemming no doubt from some dreadful childhood trauma—maybe moles- tation by a Swiss nanny? I allowed my mind to wander before it occurred to me that the cabdriver hadn't yet asked me where it was I wanted to go, nor had I given him instructions.

He drove down the block at time-trial pace and I had to hang on to the strap above the window simply in order to avoid being flung across the seat. Finally at a light he slid open the Plexiglas that separated the front seat from back and when he turned his face with a half leer in my direction, I was amazed to see that his nose was neatly bisected, although still connected by a covering of skin tissue, so that the tip was pointing of its own accord in

two opposite directions. "I'm going to Seventy-ninth just off Broadway,"
I said. "Can you go through the park?"

"What park?" he said.

"Central Park," I said, a little disturbed.

"Was that your boyfriend?" he said.

"No . . ." I said.

"Is that right? I saw him giving you some money, though."

"He's my boss," I said.

"Oh yeah?" the driver said. "So you're single?"

It now appeared we were heading downtown—the wrong direction.
The cab was veering wildly from the right side of the avenue to the left. I
leaned forward to try and read his name from the taxi-driver license registration hanging above the glove compartment. John Terzacarlo, that was the
name printed on the laminated ticket. An overwhelming sensation of depression and fatigue crept over me. One of these days I was surely going to
be arrested. It had been three weeks since Abdhul moved in. By now,
certainly, there was no reason for me not to have notified the police, or
called the Child Bureau of Health and Welfare . . . Oh, monstrous beast that
was myself—there was no justifying my actions. I could see clearly the
prison that awaited, a gleeful heap of soiled gray stone, its iron gates an open
mouth anticipating my arrival. Abdhul's family would appear to reclaim
him, reporters would attend my trial, once incarcerated I would write a
book about my experience only to have the wretched boy's parents sue for
any royalties and movie-rights money. Perhaps with a skillful lawyer—
although I didn't see how I could afford anyone really topnotch—it might
be possible I had only harbored the child as a noble deed or gesture while
I attempted to find his true heritage.

"Listen, Mr. Terzacarlo," I said, rousing myself from my reverie. "Did
you hear the address I gave you?" He repeated it in a slow and deliberate
voice. "But you're going in the wrong direction," I said.

"No problem," he said. "I do numerology, by the way. Tell me
something: what date were you born?"

"April twelfth," I said reluctantly.

"You're a three!" he said. "You have a lot of willpower." When we
stopped at the next light he asked if he could take a look at my palm. I held
up my hand, which he grasped in his own, gently stroking it. "Wow," he
said. "You know, I do palm reading too. Your career line is really looking
great. You have a lot of good things coming up. Tell me something, do you
exercise?"

"No," I said.

"Ah," he said. "I teach yoga. Let me see something—slide over into the middle of the seat." I slid over. "Now cross your legs," he said.

When we stopped at the traffic light he reached back over the seat and gave my thigh a firm squeeze. "Not bad!" he said. "You have great muscle tone, for someone who doesn't exercise." He slid his hand farther up my thigh and squeezed again. "Not bad at all."

I was starting to feel slightly apprehensive. John Terzacarlo was ranting in the front, telling me about his sister, who was a writer—she wrote letters to men's magazines—and by now we were down on 14th Street, so far from where I had told him to go that there was no way I could possibly justify it in my head. "Just let me out here," I said in what I hoped was a forceful voice. "I have to get home to my kid."

"I want to wish you all the happiness in the world," he said. "I really mean that." If only the lights would change to red, I could jump out when the car stopped; but no such luck, we churned along over the craters and potholes of the decayed street. Just the other day, I saw in the paper, an entire section of a street collapsed and a car fell eight or ten feet, severely injuring the passenger and driver. At least though if this happened now I might possibly attract the attention of a policeman, because it was obvious John Terzacarlo had some fiendish plan in whatever was left of his mind. Now he headed for the dark confines of the meat market district. This was the area directly across Ninth Avenue: meat hooks decorated the front façades of buildings. There were few street lamps here, and in the murk men gallantly dressed in pink fluorescent hot pants and garter belts plied their trade.

I unrolled my window, hoping to yell for assistance, and was met with the thick fragrance of decayed meat, old blood, the sour smell of death. I searched my handbag in a valiant effort to find a weapon. If I had even a metal nail file I could have speared it into the soft tissue of John Terzacarlo's ear. But all that was in the little purse was a lipstick, a compact, a bank card, and house keys. Nor were there any loose or discarded weapons on the floor of the cab.

In any event, John had by now closed the Plexiglas window between front- and backseat, and if I had had a weapon I would have had to shove it through the little money box and then bend my hand around at an abrupt left angle—was there such a thing as a left angle? I had only heard of right angles—and no doubt he would easily have twisted my wrist and taken my gun, scissors, or knife from me.

So it was I must face my own death, then. What would become of Abdhul, amnesiac and helpless, lying at home on my queen-size bed, purchased from the previous occupants of the apartment (later I discovered not only had I been overcharged, but it was impossible to remove it from the apartment—it had come in originally through the back entrance, before further construction on the next building made such maneuverings impossible, and therefore I could have bought it for practically no money by threatening to charge the previous tenants to remove it). And my mother—how would she get on without me, we who were best friends, although from different age groups and spoke nearly every day on the phone, even though when I saw her in person I was never very nice to her?

John now turned onto the West Side Highway, entering from Christopher Street. When the car slowed around the corner, this perhaps was my chance to jump out. But my chance at ejaculation was over in a flash; the car now sped up the highway, the lights continued to be in his favor, and at a NO U-TURN sign he U-turned, headed back down the highway and at what appeared to be an illegal exit leading to a vast sanitation plant or garbage depository he pulled the car off the highway and into a waterfront parking lot.

Thank God there were plenty of other cars in the lot, I thought; I could see heads nearby bobbing up and down through the front windows of the automobiles. I fumbled with the lock and started to open the door. A heavy whiff of fishy air swirled around my head—apparently it was an off-day for the river. Across the Hudson on the New Jersey side the words MAXWELL HOUSE COFFEE flashed neon red, reflecting across the oily green broth. I started to swing my legs out the door.

I didn't know exactly what I was going to do. Obviously I couldn't run in Daniel's wife's high heels, the woman must have had her feet bound at birth; and the idea of knocking on the window of one of the other cars, dressed as I was in the rubber/velvet corset gear didn't exactly appeal to me either. Things would be awful if I were mistaken for a man; my plea for help would probably be misinterpreted as a cry for sexual attention.

Before I could get on my feet, John Terzacarlo got out of his seat and had come around to my side of the car. "Listen, John, don't hurt me," I said. "I know your name and I don't want to have to report you to the Commissioner of Taxi Drivers."

I noticed in his hand he was holding a sort of old-fashioned bat, like the billy club my grandfather, a former employee of the Bureau of Motor Vehicles before his death, had kept in a drawer on his side of the bed. Apparently what I said to John—about reporting him—must have antagonized him. Abruptly he gave a little cackle, then he threw himself to the ground on his knees, and grabbing my left ankle in his hand began to plant wet, fervent kisses, or possibly they were licks—I couldn't actually see his mouth with his head hunched over—on top of my foot. Even though Daniel's wife's shoes were too small for me, I didn't want to see them ruined with someone's saliva. I knew they had come from a very expensive store, and if I ever got tired of them my mother or one of her friends would be very happy to receive them.

With my right foot I kicked John in the groin as hard as I could. This made me feel terrible. The poor man doubled over, sitting down heavily on the pavement, and clutched his crotch. Rather than wait to make sure he was incapacitated, I got up and walked past him, through the parking lot and toward the highway.

He was moaning but still seemed unable to get up. "What about the fare?" he yelled after me between groans. *Why should I have to pay a fare in the wrong direction,* I thought, *even though it would probably now come out of his tips.* I wasn't exactly sure how the taxi system operated, but most drivers didn't own their own cars but had to give the sum total of the meter readings to the medallion owner.

The word *medallions* always made me think of small, round, expensive steaks, which in this case took on the connotation of testicles. Probably I had injured John's. I pictured them, shriveled and gray, inside his slovenly pants, pants covered with the juice from greasy hamburgers and coffee and other fast-food items he picked up during his night's driving and ate en route. Here his testicles had been sitting quietly inside his trousers, minding their own business, and now, to receive a sudden, abrupt blow with the pointed toe of a high-heeled shoe, how they must have scampered and screamed in silent, hurt despair! Exactly like rotten figs, left for too long in a plastic carton at the store and covered with demure fruit flies.

In some way this was a revelation, because it dawned on me how stupid I had always been. There were many references in literature to the sensuality of figs; in D. H. Lawrence, for example, figs were always referred to as the most sensual of fruits, and I had always thought this was because figs were very moist and tasty—a ripe, fresh fig, I mean, not dried. But now, I understood for the first time, that Lawrence thought figs were sensual because they resembled testicles. And though I did not know what a sliced-open testicle looked like, a fresh fig, inside the thin, brown skin, had another layer of white creamy flesh and then inside this a pink, seeded, heavy tissue region. Figs, testicles, figs, testicles, figs, testicles, figs.

By now, walking quite quickly, I had reached the highway, and, waiting for a break between cars, made my way across and to the uptown side. I only prayed a taxi would come along before John got himself back on his feet and into his car and came after me; luck was on my side, because even though taxis that were free rarely took the highway, one came along at just that moment. I flagged it down and got in.

The driver didn't speak English, but he drove straight up the West Side, and because my apartment was so close to the highway it cost me less than even a direct route would have from the restaurant. After I paid him I had three dollars left from the money Daniel Loomis had slipped into my palm and was pleased to have come away from the evening with a profit.

It was wonderful to return to the sanctity of my own home. "Hi," I yelled, opening the door. "I'm home!"

"Hi!" Abdhul said from the bedroom. "How was it?"

"You wouldn't believe what just happened to me," I said, going down the hall. Oh, he was sweet, lying weakly propped up against my dirty pillows—I had to remember to wash the sheets and cases eventually—eyes puffy and large-pupiled from too much TV. I kicked off my shoes and got next to him in bed. "What are you watching?" I said, and bent over to sniff his clover child's breath while he sidled sideways on his bottom to cozy up next to me. He really was very affectionate.

"Aw, it's some dumb-ass show about a woman who shot her kids," he said.

"Why?" I said.

"To get her boyfriend to like her!" he said.

"No good?" I said.

"Naw," he said. "Stupid. So, what happened?" He snaked his scrawny arm in around mine.

"Did you eat dinner?" I said. "Did you find what I left you in the fridge? Were you eating popcorn?" The bed had a strangely crunchy texture; I pulled a few unpopped kernels out from under me.

"Just now," he said defiantly. "I ate the other stuff, before."

"And did you warm it up?"

"No," he said. "I just ate it."

I wasn't exactly certain of his age, but even nine years old was maybe too young to leave a child alone at home to fix his own dinner. I probably should have explained how to turn on the oven. "This weekend we'll buy a microwave and then you can heat up food by yourself," I said guiltily. "Did you eat the peas?" He ignored me, his eyes glazed as he stared at the TV. "I thought you said the show was no good! And where'd you get the popcorn?"

"Bought it," he said, pointing to an empty bag, cheese-flavor, on the floor.

"Well, you shouldn't eat all this junk in bed," I said with a sigh. Something was all wrong with my behavior. I was like a mockery, a parody, of what I dimly remembered as being a mother. I had to remind myself that even though Ralph, Mitchell, and I had basically been left on our own as children, Abdhul was not yet trained in this fashion. "Anyway," I said, "I got a taxi, after this party, and the guy was a complete nut case; I gave him our address, but he took off in the complete wrong direction, he drove all the way downtown, jumped out in a parking lot, and started to lick my feet."

"You took a taxi both ways?" Abdhul said vaguely.

"Daniel gave me the money. Maybe I shouldn't have accepted. I just can't believe this man—that he could be driving a taxi, when he was so insane! This friend of Daniel's is a psychiatrist, and I'm going to go to see him, because the health insurance from work will cover it. I mean, I'm going to ask him, am I doing something wrong? How come I attract the nut cases?"

"You're putting out the wrong kind of vibrations, Pamela, that must attract it."

"How do you know?" I said defensively. "I'm not doing anything!" Still, I was secretly pleased that even at his age he was so bossy and authoritative; it was one more shred of evidence that men were just born that way. "That does it," I said. "Here come the spiders!" I made my hand wriggle over to him and crawl up his shirt, then up his neck, into his small ears and over his eyes and mouth while he squirmed and shrieked, until finally he wrestled me off.

It was the highlight of my day. His velvet skin, as soft as the tanned hide of a jacket made from unborn deer or fetal pig, his boyish, innocent odor, that of new meadow grass in spring and capped with the stale sugars of bubble-gum, fermented orange pop or some other soft drink, the heavy salts of popcorn bagged with artificial cheese, the stickiness of his dirty face and chin where layers of his various afternoon and evening feeds had so richly caked and dried, the alluvium of childhood—oh, I knew what I was doing was wrong, he was not mine after all, three weeks had gone by and I had made no attempt to enroll him in school or search out whence he had come. His little limbs flailed; he crowed and giggled; I would take him to the park on Saturday and sign him up for a boys' baseball team I had seen practicing with a youthful counselor. Nothing else at present seemed very important in my life; perhaps it never had.

"Okay, that's enough," I said, when his laugh began to reach a near-hysterical pitch. "Let's go take your bath."

"No, let's have the spider some more!" he bellowed.

"Geez, you hurt my ear!" I said. "Don't shout right at me."

Enough maudlin goo. I pulled him up by the arm; went into the bathroom, and began to run the water; told him to undress and pick out some bubble bath (I had bought him three varieties: a bottle in the shape of a robot with disgusting mercurochrome-red strawberry-scented liquid, a Mr. Bubble box of white powder, and a small tin of pearlescent marbles that, tossed in the tub, melted and produced a thin white spume) while I went into the kitchen and tried to organize things for the next morning.

Luckily it was still summer. No registration papers or vaccination shots were required to send a child to a nearby daycamp. What I would do, when fall came, I was not yet certain. The box of whole-wheat all-natural sugar-frosted flakes I placed on the living room table; opened a can of Mandarin orange segments and placed a few in a bowl with some of their liquid, then put it back in the refrigerator so it would be fresh in the morning to give him for breakfast before I left for work and he for camp.

These orange segments had been a part of my childhood, during the years before my parents' divorce: each day a bowl awaited me on the kitchen table, syrupy, each segment composed of a myriad number of tinier segments that burst in the mouth. Geisha brand was still canning their Mandarin oranges after all these years. Living in the rural countryside during the winter months that was the only fruit my mother was able to obtain. Back then we did not have huge supermarkets, and the local grocery store, visited only once a week, generally held only a few wrinkled apples. Apples, oranges, bananas, and canned Mandarin oranges, those were the fruits of my childhood. Since moving to Manhattan I had sampled many new things, among them green kiwis, cherimoyas, tamarinds, Persian melons, and tasty cinnamon-flavored fat pink bananas. Each time I felt amazement similar to what the ancient Aztecs, or maybe it was the Mayans, must have experienced on first sampling oranges—or the conquistadors, who first got to taste chocolate. Yes, life was good when a person could taste new varieties of fruits from foreign lands well into maturity.

For myself I put coffee in the percolator, laid out my clothes, and arranged a sliced bagel alongside the toaster. It was all evidence that I was becoming a responsible adult. Before Abdhul's arrival I had flung myself from bed each morning, and, snatching wrinkled clothes from the closet, grabbed a croissant from the croissant shop on my way into work. Responsible adults did not eat croissants, high in butterfat and with low nutritional content.

Before the tub could overflow I went and turned off the water. During my absence Abdhul had poured what must have been half the box of Mr. Bubble into the water. "Get undressed and climb in," I said. I liked to assist him from time to time with his bath, but—though it was ten thirty or so, I knew no one would call me at this hour—the phone rang. "Pamela!" a voice shrieked through the hammerheaded receiver. "Is that really you? This is your poor old grandmother!"

"How are you, Grandma?" I said. I wondered if I should tell her that she was now a great-grandmother.

"When I sit here, after some time," she said, "I get to thinking to myself, gee, I really am kind of a brave person, to be sitting here all alone, with a family that is so distant, and it would cheer me up a great deal to be able to speak to my granddaughter. Of course, it would be nicer if I didn't have to call you—or even if you were to send me a little note, telling me all about your life and your innermost, most private thoughts. Because a person, at my age, can get to feeling, what is the point?"

"At any age, Grandma," I said.

"Of course, I tell myself, the reason I don't hear from my granddaughter is that she is a very popular person. I imagine you have many boyfriends."

"No, Grandma, I'm not seeing anyone just now."

"It makes me very worried. Because sometimes I think to myself, isn't it a shame that my granddaughter is not a very happy person, and I would hate to think that you are depressed. More than anything I would like us to be close, so that you could tell me your innermost thoughts."

"Well, I—" I said.

"I remember when you were just a tiny child, you used to be so sweet and sensitive then, and I wonder: what happened? It seems to me that maybe your parents' divorce must have had tragic effects on you. Because when you were five years old, I remember you turned to me, and I was crying at that time, as I was about to leave after a visit, since your mother felt it was time I go. And you said, 'Don't cry, Grandma.' And I thought, what a perceptive and sensitive child, to notice that her grandma was crying."

I could hear a sound coming from the bathroom that sounded like a tidal wave. Even though I thought I had turned off the water, probably Abdhul had turned it back on, or else he was unloading it onto the floor with the old plastic mop-bucket he insisted on taking in there with him. "Listen, Grandma, I have to go," I said.

"Oh," my grandmother said coyly. "You're not alone."

"No, that's not it," I said. "The bathtub is—"

"All I can say, is that I hope he's a nice young man, or a person that can appreciate you."

I hung up and raced down the hall. I should have told her. It was a disappointment to her that I hadn't done better in life, or at least married and had kids. After all, a quarter of her genes were mine . . . Still, the way things worked in my family, it was just as well I hadn't confided anything: she might have called the police. Luckily having a kid around meant there was less time to brood over my behavior.

He had swilled half the contents of the tub onto the floor. "You're lucky we live in the basement, buddy," I said. Also the water was a peculiar yellowish hue. "Why is the water that weird puce color?" I said, flinging all the towels onto the ground to mop up the mess.

Every single towel I owned was a different color from the next, and most had frayed edges—lime-green, reptile-brown, American flag. A towel was a towel after all, though some day I would perhaps be the sort of person who had matching, thick towels of varying sizes. Probably Daniel Loomis's wife had matching towels from some expensive linen shop. Probably most of the United States had matching towels. Even the poorest people probably went out to the store and used a credit card to select a number of matching towels for their bathroom.

That was how we did things, here in the United States. Every single magazine on sale at the checkout counter advocated matching towels. One half of me also wanted towels that were all the same color, or complementary colors. But the other half of me believed it was a sign of spiritual evolution not to throw away old towels but continue to use them. The only purpose of a towel was to dry excess water from the corporeal body. And the towels were one of the few gifts I had ever received from my father. Many, many years before, my grandmother—the one I had just finished speaking to—bought various mismatched towels on sale at a department store, and then gave them to my father as a present. Then my father did use the towels for many years, until I graduated from college and moved in to my first apartment. As I was the firstborn, it was to me he gave the old towels. At the time I had done my best to be grateful. If ever I were to reach a pure and true inner gratitude, perhaps I would be evolved enough to throw the old towels away and buy new ones.

The faster I mopped the floor, the faster Abdhul splashed the water out of the top. "Whee!" he said, "the ship is sinking!"

"What did you do, pee in the water?" I said. "Nobody could pee that much. A beautiful color, puce."

"Puce is pink, not yellow," Abdhul said.

"What are you talking about?" I said. "Puce is yellow, a sort of yellow color."

"Look it up," Abdhul said. It must have been that the warm water was loosening some sort of old glue between the tiles. The floor wasn't just wet and yellow, it was the consistency of old maple syrup.

"Don't argue with me," I said. "Quit splashing or I'm going to have to do something to injure you. If I wanted a kid, I would have had one. There's no stigma attached to having an illegitimate child today. In fact, many men are turned on by pregnant women, and some are looking for a ready-made family." I wiped off his nose with a still-dry corner of one of the towels. A glob of goo stuck to the edge. I tossed him a runny stick of soap. "Make sure you rub it all over, and then I'll come back and rinse you off," I said.

I took the wet towels and threw them into the hamper. Then I went and opened the dictionary to *P*. He was right. Puce was not yellow, but a pink somewhat similar to cranberry. How could that be? My God, it was like suddenly learning that the color orange, which one had always known to be a color somewhere between red and yellow, was not orange after all, but purple. I went back into the bathroom with a dry towel. He was dandling the buttery soap between two fingers, inspecting it as if it were some alien organism, and had obviously not done a thing about cleaning himself.

I lunged forward to take it from him so I could rub him down and get the whole bathtime over with, and fell nearly flat on my face. The old tiled floor was now covered with a thick, cretaceous jelly; apparently when the varnish or tile cement or whatever it was had dissolved, it had freed this gel, which swelled up with the moisture, bulged out from under the tiles, a clear viscous matter that now buckled the vinyl floor squares and as I watched nearly doubled in size. "Look what you did!" I yelled. "Do you know how much it's going to cost me to get some plumber or somebody over here to repair the floor? Huh? Answer me!"

The corners of his mouth trembled and turned down. "I don't want to stay here anymore!" he said. "You hurt my feelings." My own mouth sagged and tears came into my eyes.

"I'm sorry," I said. "Don't pay me any attention. I didn't mean to hurt your feelings." His lips quivered and he didn't answer. "Anyway, you were right," I said. "Puce is pink, not yellow. How do you know about the different colors? You must have artistic tendencies." I took the shower head down on its hose, let the water out of the tub, and rinsed him off. "Please don't be mad at me," I said. "Let's be friends again."

When he was squeaky I hoisted him onto his feet and wrapped him up in my terrycloth robe. Luckily he did not have a sulky nature, or else his memory was very short-term. "Shit, what's all this?" he said when he got out of the tub. The gelatinous life-form on the floor had by now nearly quadrupled in size.

"I don't know," I said. "But I can't deal with it now. Let's just leave it and go to sleep. Maybe it will have gone away by morning."

"I have to take a poop," he said.

"Now?" I said. "You have to do it now? Why did you wait until now? You just had a bath. And anyway, you're supposed to get up and do that in the morning." He shrugged. "All right, all right," I said, shutting the door behind me. "I'll go make up your bed." I went into the living room to adjust his sheets on the couch. I was sorry that I was behaving so badly. Perhaps I was due to get my period. It seemed I was always due to get my period, or else I was just having it. Even a female dog only got her period twice a year. I was loath to admit that because of this monthly surge of hormones a woman could not be president of the United States. After all, men had their steady supply of testosterone, that made them want to set off firecrackers, burn ants under magnifying glasses, and drink beer in the company of other men at baseball games. Even a woman with the most violent groundswell of monthly hormones was more connected to reality than any man, however—although I would not be able to offer concrete proof at this particular moment.

I tucked the sheets around the edges of the couch and plumped up the pillows. "Hurry up and brush your teeth," I yelled.

Half the time Abdhul knew little more than a newborn infant. Maybe he was younger than nine; perhaps he was only six. He didn't seem to know, and I had had no experience with children, except to hold a girl-friend's ten-week-old infant that immediately burst into tears, so I handed it back. Who knew what kids were really like today, unless you owned one? On TV they all seemed as old and as wise as if they were tiny Elizabethans, trained and dressed to be shrunken adults. I suppose a doctor or a dentist could have given me a better idea of approximately how old Abdhul was; anyway, I knew that a veterinarian could tell the age of an adopted dog, so I assumed the same was true of children. But so far I hadn't had a chance to make appointments for him, another sign of my neglectful behavior. He had some sort of awful skin rash on his left leg, a pink, oozing, vaguely tropical patch which, though I tried to treat it myself with over-the-counter topical antibiotic cream, didn't go away. There were all kinds of weird skin fungi that people picked up in New York—this same girlfriend with the baby, for example, had been to Bangkok where she got a sort of traveling fungus, that would travel around from time to time on various parts of her body, and all she had to do was rub against a tree, I guessed, and this skin fungus from Bangkok would be spread to an innocent passerby who touched the tree while they walked their dog, and from them it might spread when they carried out their bag of garbage and a homeless person stooped to fondle the bag and open it.

Also Abdhul's teeth were in terrible condition—I'm not certain if he had ever brushed his teeth on a regular basis—covered with yellow plaque, a few were missing, though whether this meant he was younger than nine and losing his baby teeth or that they were simply rotten I didn't know. I had tried to question him about his life with Brenda and the other boys, but although he was now very talkative, this was one subject on which he refused to speak.

While I was waiting for him to finish in the bathroom I lay down on the couch. The rubber sheet I had bought to cover it crinkled rudely beneath the sheets. I must have been exhausted, because I nodded off, thinking of what a terrible person I was. Who else would be so unkind to her own grandmother? Here she had grown up in impoverished circumstances and had to work from the age of fourteen in a sweatshop in Manhattan, stitching oilcloth onto umbrellas. It wasn't her fault that all three of her husbands had died under mysterious circumstances and that her own son, her only child, had had to almost retire from the practice of medicine after the awful trial. It probably wasn't her fault either that after my parents' divorce she was so busy remarrying and burying her husbands that eight or ten years went by without her seeing any of her grandchildren. Now, close to ninety years old and in good condition, she wanted to be friends again; but how could I go down to visit her with Abdhul when she had deliberately selected a retirement center in Florida where no children were allowed, not even to visit, and though her last husband had enough money—before his death—to purchase a two-bedroom apartment, she had decided against this, so that any visitor had to sleep on a musty old fold-out couch in her already overcrowded living room.

Still, she was a real extrovert, and there was a lot I could have learned from her. If she waited for a bus, she was certain to strike up a conversation with the person waiting next to her, and this was admirable, and explained why she had so many friends. Men were crazy about her; she was one of the only women of the fourteen thousand old people in the community to acquire a new boyfriend, because the truth was, in a retirement center there were a few elderly couples who were married, but the rest of the men were dead.

Even though I had never actually met my grandmother's boyfriend, my father had told me that he was very nice. Morris Grabinowitz drove my grandmother around, he took her to the post office and the shopping malls (my grandmother no longer drove or kept a car since she backed over Merton—that was husband number two—in the driveway) and even though, according to my father, my grandmother frequently berated and bossed Morris Grabinowitz so much he swore he would have nothing more to do with her, *he always came back in the end.*

Maybe I should go down there and take a few lessons from her, in seducing a man—at the same time she could meet Abdhul, and I could drive the two of them to Disney World or some alligator farm or other tourist attraction. There had to be some way for me to evolve spiritually as a person. It was thinking thoughts similar to these that I fell asleep.

I woke several hours later and got up and went to my own bed, where Abdhul lay tangled in the sheets, whimpering softly. I didn't wake him but lying beside him dozed off again.

The morning was hot and sticky, even with the air conditioner on all night. I turned it off and opened the back door. Life had become nearly ritualistic by now. I gave him a clean T-shirt and a pair of my magenta shorts with a string-tie waist (one of these days I would have to take him shopping) and was just getting ready myself when the telephone rang. It was my mother. "How are you?" she said. It was unusual for her to call this early in the day.

"I'm all right," I said. "Grandma Vi called last night, and I was mean to her."

"That's because she's not in her right mind," my mother said. "And just because she's crazy, doesn't mean you have to act sane. Anyway, the only reason I'm calling is because I received another upsetting letter from your father. Your father is a gonif, a thief, a manipulator, and he reminds me of Lee Harvey Oswald."

"Lee Harvey Oswald?" I said.

"In some ways, yes. Tell me, how's Abdhul?"

I paused in order to swat a huge plump fly with a request for money from an organization that owned a sloop that sailed up and down the Hudson River. If I sent them twenty-five dollars, I could be part-owner of the sloop, which was concerned with the polluted conditions of the Hudson and would do its best to promote the cause. Through a program of advocacy the sloop was working to make the river fishable once more, although I could not read the rest of the brochure due to the corpse of the fly. Was it some kind of mutant? It was so ripe, so juicy, and not very quick on its wings. Actually, now that I looked around I saw the place was swarming with flies—could they all have come inside in the moment I opened the back door?—and there was a foul, eggy smell in the air. Tiny specks of fly feces decorated the tabletop where I kept the telephone. Why didn't some scientist work on breeding edible flies? It would certainly be an assistance to Third World countries where there were food shortages. Flies could live almost anyplace; in fact, the more impoverished, the healthier the flies. There could be fly soup, sun-dried flies, fly stew.

Some kind of commotion was happening at the front door; the doorbell was long out of order, and so I had placed a sign in the window telling people to bang on the glass for assistance. "Hello?" my mother said. "Are you there?"

"Just a minute," I said, "There's somebody at the door."

"Will you be safe?" my mother said. "I'll hold on. Don't let anybody in."

I got up and opened the front door. Luckily I was separated from the street by the metal security gate. A burly woman was standing with a file folder in her hand. "Excuse me," she said. "Is this the psychiatric center?"

"No," I said, and went back in. "Listen, I have to go," I told my mother. "I have to drop Abdhul off at camp, and there's something growing on the bathroom floor that I don't know what to do about."

"What is it?" my mother said.

"It's like a gelatin," I said. "I don't think it's expanded since last night, but I think it's alive."

"Be careful if you use a cleaning solution on it," my mother said. "You know it's dangerous to mix compounds. Never mix bleach and Ajax, for example."

"Really?" I said. "What happens?"

"It produces a poisonous gas," my mother said.

"Is there anything else? I'll call you later on."

"No," my mother said. "I just wanted to be the first to let you know: I'm going to kill your father."

The Ethical Society where Abdhul went to camp was located in a massive fascist structure built in the thirties that took up nearly a square city block. By accident, walking to the park one day with Abdhul, I had seen an advertisement for daycamp—there were special, extended hours for working parents, the rates were low, and after Abdhul had settled in I gave him the keys so that if I was going to be late he could walk the few blocks home and let himself in.

I took him inside the front door and left him with a crowd of other kids and their departing mothers. There was a pool in the basement of the building; some days they swam, other days they were taken by bus to the beach or a parkland, or they molded clay in the basement to resemble food such as pizza, eggs, and hamburgers—the art teacher was an admirer of Claes Oldenburg. There was also some emphasis on ethics, although I had no idea what ethics they were. Still, it hardly mattered: any ethics, I supposed, were better than none, as long as they were consistent.

The other mothers appeared to be a filthy lot of Upper West Side former hippies; anyway, a number of them had long gray hair, old Indian print skirts, and expensive jewelry. It was my suspicion that they were all from a similar background of would-be intellectuals, the daughters of entertainment lawyers and psychiatrists; they had gone to Barnard and Radcliffe, postponed having children until their thirties, and attended all the latest theater. Certainly I had nothing in common with them, although I had chatted briefly with a woman named Judith and another named Penny Merriwether.

The director of the program, a kindly, bearded man with a limp—one leg was shorter than the other and he wore a sort of built-up shoe to compensate—came over just as I was telling Abdhul good-bye. "Will you be coming back later to pick up Abdhul?" he said.

"I could," I said. "Why?"

"I wondered if I could have a quick word with you," Ralph said.

"We could talk now, if it's quick," I said. Just then a little girl with a homely face and a look that seemed to indicate she had been told frequently that she was very beautiful came over and pulled on Ralph's arm. "Ralph, Ralph," she said. "Carrie and Veronica are putting their tongues in each other's mouth. And they're charging money to watch."

"How much?" Ralph said with a thoughtful expression. He cleared his nose nervously; I had noticed before that he was one of those people with a frequent nose-clearing tic, similar to the whuffle made by a seal after devouring a mackerel. "I think it'll be easier if we chat later," he said. "Most of the kids will have gone by then."

I thought I would be the only one to arrive so early at work. Debbie usually got there at ten, Amber MacPherson frequently even later. With Daniel Loomis there was no predicting, although since we had become friendly he sometimes showed up before lunch and then invited me into his office for a cup of coffee. It was a relief to have an ally at work. Amber seemed to be harassing me less, though I did wonder if this wasn't because she was busy plotting or scheming some monstrous plan of humiliation for me.

Lately I had been the one to unlock the place, but this morning someone had gotten in before me. The lights were off in the hall; I flicked them on. Old fluorescent lighting, so antiquated that it made a sound as if something were being fried before flickering on and then off and then on again. I crept very slowly down the hall and into my office. Even though the lights were off, there she was, Amber, rummaging through my desk drawers. I must have startled her, because she let out a sort of squeak. All at once I felt sorry for her, with her fat-lady wheeze. She wasn't so very fat, and she probably wasn't even that much older than me, but I felt sorry for her, and that was my mistake. Never feel sorry for your enemies, or try to put yourself in their shoes, because as soon as you do that, you're practically on their side, and since *they're* on their side too, that makes two of you against yourself.

She wasn't at all embarrassed, after her initial shock. "You should be careful," I said, "all alone in the office. Whenever I come in early, I keep the front door locked. There was that terrible bathroom episode, remember."

She didn't even bother to explain what she was doing. Probably if I had questioned her, she would have claimed to be looking for staples. I would have to put a few mousetraps around; of course, I would probably forget where I had put them, and they would spring on myself.

"You're in nice and early, for a change," she said. She was dressed today in another of her bizarre costumes; something sleeveless, from which protruded her plump arms: it had little frills around each armpit, then came up in a sort of mock turtleneck. Her heavy chest was heaped with big oily pearls that I knew were genuine. "Well, it's a good thing you're here early," she said. "Because I wanted you to be involved. Virginia Loomis is coming in at ten for a meeting, and I thought you'd want to be there."

"Virginia Loomis?" I said. "Daniel's wife?" What if she recognizes her shoes, I wanted to say, her shoes, which I was wearing and which Daniel had smuggled out of her closet, from a bag of things she intended to give to charity?

"That's right." A slight smirk crossed Amber's face and one of her tiny chins wiggled. I don't want to seem cruel, that was simply how she looked, but I should have been more careful with my thoughts because she bristled suspiciously. "I have to leave early today because I have a fitting for my fall wardrobe." She named a designer best known for outfitting the drab wives of ex-presidents. Twice a year she went to the designer's studio, or whatever it was called, and picked out all her clothing. Even though she was so mean to me, there was something I sort of admired about her. I practically had to beg her for my paycheck every two weeks—she was the one who signed all the checks—and she usually arranged to be out of the office, or out of checks, whenever it was time for mine. She thought nothing of telling me to go and buy her something, but never remembered to pay me back. And yet, as I say, I did like her. Her supreme confidence, her authoritative demeanor, her security of her place in the world—if only I could have had just a little bit of what was hers! "I've never met Virginia," I said.

"You haven't?" Amber said. "Actually, we're related; she's a second or third cousin: she grew up near me in Tuxedo Park. I don't know if you knew, years ago I was having an affair with Daniel—but I thought I'd mention that now, before Virginia gets here. You see, we're practically a family, Pamela, apart from you. Do you have a boyfriend yet?"

"No," I said, and turned on the light. Her tiny eyes glinted at me and blinked, the skin around her eyes was puffy and swollen and yet there was a certain Rubenesque beauty about her, her lank, reddish-blond hair and thunderous figure.

"Oh, what a shame," she said. "If I had realized, after all this time, that you *still* didn't have a boyfriend, I would have invited you to lunch the other day; I had lunch with the cutest professional football player! What a hunk—and smart, too! He would have been perfect for you if only you had met him."

"Why were you having lunch with a football player?" I said.

"I'm thinking of running him on the cover."

"On the cover?" I repeated.

"During the off-season he breeds hunting dogs in Texas. Actually, that's part of what I want you to hear in the meeting; there's going to be some changes around here."

"Oh," I said. "How come you weren't interested in the football player?"

Her smile was a cold, fishy smear. Probably I shouldn't have said that; but it was a known fact—anyway, it was a fact that I knew—that even though she was married to poor Balthazar (poor only in personality, which he had none of) for years she had been conducting, in what she imagined was complete secrecy, an affair with a man named Rete Newman—Rete was a married man with three grown children, and a baby by his new wife, and he owned a two-thousand-acre thoroughbred farm in Virginia. On a monthly basis he came up to New York—once a year Amber devoted an entire issue to Rete's friends and associates. That was how these things worked, in New York. The rich people stuck to themselves, as if they might be contaminated by association with anyone from the outside. "You've been seeing quite a lot of Daniel lately," she said.

This made me nervous, even though I hadn't done anything wrong. "Just for a drink," I said. "I—uh, I was asking him for financial advice."

"Financial advice!" she said contemptuously. "His father gives him all his money. Let me tell you something, Pamela, as your friend: I'd be careful. Daniel's been with Virginia forever. Whenever he gets bored he goes out and has an affair for a little while, although I can't imagine why he would pick you. You're dealing with something way out of your league, and I would hate for you to be hurt. People with four hundred million dollars live in their own world, with different rules than normal people; believe me, because that's the background I came from, and I know you don't. It's nothing for Daniel or Virginia to have an affair for a little while, but they'll always stay together."

I didn't mean to get drawn in to what she was saying, but I couldn't help myself. "What keeps them together, then?" I said.

A cheerful glitter came into her blue eyes. "I'm telling you this in strictest confidentiality," she said. "Virginia likes men to beat her up; before he fucks her, Daniel puts a paper bag over her head and ties her down."

"Daniel?" I said. "But he's so weak."

"People can be very mysterious, Pamela," Amber said. "Actually, Virginia was going out with Hans Beinhorn, before she met Daniel." Hans Beinhorn was the vaguely familiar name of the wealthy heir to a German banking fortune. "But he wouldn't marry her, so she broke up with him after a suicide attempt. Then she had a fiancé, who she was madly in love with, who genuinely liked to beat her up. But he was poor. So she couldn't marry him."

Just then Debbie came into the room. She was dressed in a baby-blue flounced skirt—apparently the garb of a virginal flamenco dancer—and her hands were covered with so many rings if she had thrown a punch she could have broken somebody's jaw. "Where is everybody?" she said. "I came in and the lights were off and I almost tripped over some guy who's passed out. He puked right by my desk!"

"I was just telling Pamela how Virginia only likes sex when she's fucked with a paper bag over her head," Amber said.

Debbie shrugged. "I think she's sweet."

A voice called from the front. "Hello, where is everybody?"

"We're down here, Virginia," Amber yelled. "In the advertising office."

I stood in shock for several seconds while we waited for Virginia to come down the hall. Weren't Debbie and Amber ashamed to know such intimate details of another person's sex life, and to discuss it so freely moments before that person was due to arrive? Plus, I couldn't believe that Daniel, who seemed so sweet and unhappy, was in fact such a sleazy character. Since the night when I thought he was going to fire me and I went to his house for a drink, we had seen each other quite a bit. I hadn't told him about Abdhul; his wife was out of town most of the time, and though he wanted me to go out to dinner and to various fashion shows held at night to raise money for AIDS, I always made some excuse and went home after an hour. But when the twins were home he wasn't all that disappointed. He liked to be at home to watch them eat the food and have their baths.

During our meetings he managed to tell me most of his life story: raised by his father, who was mostly never home, he was left with various Swiss nannies in luxurious surroundings, such as a house in Belgrave Square, another in Montserrat, still others in Newport and Palm Beach. His father was a manly sort of wheeler-dealer. Daniel had always been a disappointment to him (or so he said) because he weighed only three pounds when he was born, and wasn't very athletic or coordinated. But later on, when the father realized Daniel was probably going to be his only son and offspring, he grew more accepting of him. This culminated in an episode when Daniel was sixteen. Father and son were staying in adjoining suites in St. Moritz, where his father arranged for two prostitutes to be sent up and instructed Daniel to take his pick. The father commandeered the second, and father and son retired to their suites, each with a woman.

Alas this led to Daniel's present malaise and unhappiness. Such were the small tragedies of great wealth. He grew allergic to small animals of every kind and yeast products. Also, he had a slight problem with heroin—a habit he had acquired during his Sumerian studies at Harvard—not that he shot it, but it was common among the students to snort the stuff, a custom he hadn't outgrown in the fifteen years since his matriculation.

Though he didn't make a pass at me, and no definite plans were made, he spoke on more than one occasion of his intention to divorce Virginia and sell his house and buy another. He said this so often, and looked at me so lovingly whenever he said it, that I couldn't help but think he had some plan that involved the two of us, although for the life of me I couldn't see why.

Still, stranger things had happened in the past, such as a man giving up the Kingdom of England, probably due to his homosexual tendencies, for an American divorcée, and also I think a governor marrying his cleaning woman, or maybe it was a man with a fortune from floor wax and baby oil.

A woman now appeared in the doorway of my office. "Hello," she said with a superior smile. "I'm Virginia Loomis." My heart sank at her perfection; surely Daniel's interest in me had to be some hateful joke. Once I had read about a psychology experiment in which a number of very handsome young men at a university were recruited to pay tribute, flatter, and ask out on dates a homely, overweight, unpleasant woman on campus. I forget the point of the experiment, but the woman, though at first baffled by the unexpected attention, soon grew so used to it she confidently rejected a number of suitors. And the men soon forgot that they had been recruited to pursue her, and—seeing that everyone else was interested in her—began to call her up and ask her out without being told to do so.

If there was one truth in life, it was that as soon as one man began paying attention to a woman, a lot of others were interested in her too, because men were like dogs, and if one dog started to follow a bitch in heat, then plenty of others decided to go along for no other reason than to follow the other men dogs.

That was why I tried not to think too much about Daniel's interest in me, because I wouldn't have been at all surprised to learn that he had taken me on as an experiment in human behavior or conditioning, possibly after witnessing me with Alby in the coffee shop—and this was corroborated after I saw Virginia in the doorway. She was tiny, with black sooty hair cut in a little bob, set off by her red suit nipped in at her tiny waist, and her dark eyes were richly fringed; it was hard for me, even though I was of the same sex, not to fall instantly in love with her, not that I would have wanted to have sexual intercourse with her, but I would have been happy just to spend many hours or days looking at her. She was the sort of person that just to look at made other people feel happy, and it was easy to see why when she looked the way she did. It was like looking at a ballerina or a doll, and it was a wonderful thing to know that a human being walked on earth who looked the way she did, even though I didn't. Nor did she look like a fashion model, tall and unreal; no, her tininess made her accessible.

"Debbie!" she said, and her face lit up with warmth that was either real or artificial, it hardly mattered. She embraced Debbie and then turned to kiss Amber. When she looked at me her face fell. Perhaps Daniel had mentioned me to her, although I doubted it; it was a look I had seen on faces all too often, when they looked at me. "I haven't seen you in ages,

Debbie!" Virginia said. It was curious that she had a sort of false, imitation English accent, something I would have considered a defect, but which perhaps was a charming attribute. "Are you going to come over for dinner soon?"

"I don't know," Debbie said. "I'm kind of busy."

"I have somebody special in town I'd like you to meet," Virginia said sweetly. Debbie shrugged. But this was . . . incredible! Not only that Debbie would be so privileged to be invited to a party in a luxurious mansion, but that she would be indifferent to such an invitation! *I* would go in a second; that was probably why I would never be invited. "You know there's a man passed out in reception," Virginia said.

"I know," Debbie said. "I called the super but the guy in the lobby said he's on vacation in Juan les Pins." Was I losing my mind? How could the super afford to take a vacation in Juan les Pins, and surely there should be some backup super or custodian on call in such an event.

"You better go get him out of there, Pamela," Amber said aggressively.

"Me?" I said.

"You better hurry up, if you want to be able to sit in on our meeting," Amber said. "We'll be in Daniel's office. Buzz me if Rete or Balthazar calls."

I went out to the receptionist's desk, followed by Debbie. The man lay on the carpet; to my surprise he was dressed quite nicely, in an expensive three-piece linen suit, although he was unshaven and there was a pool of vomit near his face that I tried not to look at and a strong smell of ketone. The smell of ketone was a sign of acute alcoholism, although it was possible he also had diabetes, because only recently I had read a story about a woman who was highly allergic to ketone, after working for many years in a Japanese factory where ketone or benzene or some other chemical was a waste by-product, and her husband had killed her due to the fact that he had not known he had diabetes. One day when he kissed her he had a lot of heavy ketone on his breath, and she died; the husband felt terrible.

I gave the man a little nudge on the shoulder. "Mister," I said. "Please, mister, wake up. You can't lie here." The man didn't move but let out a pained groan. It was awful, because it might have been me, a few weeks before, when I nearly fainted on the street and had to give Alby a hand job under the table. In a strange way, I was disappointed that Alby hadn't gotten in touch; maybe my hand job just wasn't good enough? It seemed strange, when he had acted so crazy about me. Obviously I was deluding myself in even thinking about Daniel as a possible romantic lead in my life. I grabbed a hunk of the man's hair and pulled up his face, which was facing down on the carpet. He certainly was gorgeous, although to my horror . . . he was Alby.

I looked up; standing behind me were Amber, Virginia, and Debbie, with the interested expressions of cows at the edge of the pasture. Where I grew up, during high school, I knew a boy who used to go with his buddies at night when they had nothing better to do and tip over sleeping cows that were standing up. There wasn't a lot to do in the country, but I suppose tipping over sleeping cows was better than what had happened to a lot of cows out in the Midwest, who were drained of all blood and mutilated by what were probably UFOs; I had only read about this, but the conclusion was reached that the UFOs were doing this, because there were were no footprints around the bloodless cows, and it would be difficult to go out into the middle of a pasture and drain a cow of blood and then mutilate it without leaving footprints, unless a person or an alien had a UFO, although why the aliens needed to drain cows of blood and mutilate them was never explained in any article I read about the phenomena.

"I know this guy," I blurted. Their expressions changed to dismayed disgust and I half-expected them to start mooing as they bolted, but all that happened was they simultaneously took a step backward and crashed into one another.

"You know this guy?" Amber bawled. "That's disgusting, Pamela! Clean up the mess!"

"Clean up the mess?" I said. "But I hardly know him. I didn't ask him to come here."

"Gross!" Debbie said. "He's kind of cute, though. What does he do?"

"International finance," I decided.

"Is that your boyfriend, Pamela?" Virginia said with a pitying smile. Before I could answer she had turned and walked down the hall. "I'll be in your office, Amber," she said. "That is, if you have some free time this morning." Why had Alby had to choose this moment to show up and pass out? Suddenly I was overcome with an overwhelming sense of reality, almost a déjà vu. My life was to be composed of such small moments of humiliations and pointless episodes that later I could look back on and see had added up to nothing. Then I would die.

"Clean up the puke and get that guy out of here and don't come to the meeting until you've taken care of it," Amber said before flouncing down the hall after Virginia.

Debbie went to her desk and sat down. "It really stinks in here, Pamela," Debbie said. "Boy, is Amber pissed." She took out an elaborate makeup kit from a drawer of her desk and began to separate her eyelashes with a primitive instrument. "She's expecting Bronson Newman up here for the meeting, too, about this new magazine, and you better get this guy out of here before *he* comes."

"What new magazine?" I said.

Debbie ignored my question. "Between you and me, I think Rete is going to dump Amber, but he just doesn't know how to get out of it. Last month when Rete was in town Amber said that if any calls came for her I could reach her at the Royalty, and she gave me an assumed name. I wonder how Balthazar puts up with it? She treats him like a dog."

"She must have some sexual trick up her sleeve," I suggested. Debbie stopped prying her lashes apart for long enough to glare at me coldly. It was unbelievable, that it was possible for one person—myself—to be the object of so much scorn and derision.

I gave Alby a prod with my foot but he was completely unconscious. I decided to at least roll his body away from the vomit; it was a shame he had an awfully nice linen summer suit, although maybe it would be possible to have it cleaned. Debbie could see I was struggling with the corpse, but obviously was not going to offer any assistance. Finally I rolled him away, back against the door. This must have disturbed him from his rest, because one bleary eye opened a crack. "Bubbela's dead," he said. "My Bubbie."

Who the hell was bubbela? In Russian, or perhaps Yiddish, bubbela meant little grandmother; then I remembered his dog, brain-damaged and half-paralyzed. But before I could ask him how Bubbie had died, his eye rolled shut again and a little saliva mixed with vomit came out of the corner of his mouth. "Need a hankie?" Debbie said. "I have a tissue."

"Aw, let me go to the bathroom and get some paper towels," I said. I got the key from Debbie and went down the hall. One of the stalls was shut and someone was in there, which struck me as a trifle unusual because there were no other occupied offices on the floor, so I didn't know who else would be using the women's room unless someone had had to come up from another floor if their bathroom was out of order.

I went into the next stall to pee while I thought of how to get Alby out of the reception area. A pool of water had collected around the floor, some kind of leakage was taking place, which reminded me of how I hadn't done anything about the gelatinous material on the floor of the bathroom at home. Maybe it was star-gel; this was stuff found in the fields, also in the Midwest, that a long time back people thought was material or organisms descended from the stars, big jellyfish blobs that would just mysteriously come out of nowhere and that thus far nobody had been able to tell what it was.

The reason I had so much information about this type of phenomena in my head was that my mother was now almost a full professor at a university that could practically be considered Ivy League, in the Psychic Phenomena and Studies department, a division of the sciences. It was quite remarkable how this had come about, because when my mother married it was back in the days when there were no careers for women, although she had majored in chemistry in college even though at that time it was not considered unnatural for women to want to get married and raise a family.

There were still a few women now for whom this was not unnatural, but they were located in the Midwest. Hence after my parents' divorce, like so many other women of her era, it was necessary for my mother to obtain a job in a local junior-high and high-school cafeteria in order to support her family with alimony supplement.

However, in my mother's case, after a while she obtained a job as a volunteer at the university, for a professor who was conducting psychic experiments with a grant received from a tobacco company. One thing led to the next: my mother became a paid assistant for the professor, she went back to school part-time to refresh her science background (university employees were allowed to take courses for free) and though the university protested at first the creation of the Psychic Studies division, the professor who had begun the program had full tenure and a chair; also, he had won a Nobel prize with several others years ago—albeit in another department— and his name lent prestige to the university. Lastly, the grant money was substantial, and this, followed up by a lengthy and only mildly controversial article in the Sunday *Times* magazine and the fact that my mother had had a brief affair with the professor, led to her academic career. All in all I was very proud of her.

I had been brought up never to sit on a public toilet seat without first covering it with paper, but now I was in so much despair over thinking of what to do about Alby that I sat down without troubling myself; besides, a janitor was supposed to clean the women's room every night, and generally the only other people who used the bathroom on this floor were Debbie and Amber, apart from a few years back when my predecessor at the magazine was raped and stabbed, although I don't know if her attacker had sat on the toilet seat first.

But now there was another person in the bathroom; glancing over at the ground I saw she was wearing very attractive mannish shoes, probably custom made, brown wing tips, and more than anything I would have liked to have a pair of these masculine little shoes. I almost asked her where she had gotten them and if they were very dear, but I felt somewhat disgusted that someone had come up from another floor to use the toilet to do number two, unless she had cramps; honestly, it was my belief that people should try to do number two in the bathrooms in their own homes, how weird to wait until one had arrived at work and was in a toilet situation where others were sure to enter and use the next-door stall. Even in college I had had trouble with this, particularly since I lived on a coed floor; it was scarcely removed from the lower life forms of animals, that human beings would line up in square boxes together to urinate, but to take a shit was even worse.

From time to time the woman shuffled her feet and I heard the turn of pages, but I tried to keep my thoughts to myself. This delayed me in urinating. Finally I finished and, flushing the toilet, went out and grabbed a handful of rough brown paper towels which I soaked briefly in the sink.

Alby was still slumped on the floor; I suppose I had secretly hoped he would have roused himself and staggered out by now. I mopped up his vomit while Debbie pointed out spots I had missed. It really was disgusting but I felt sorry for a man who would fall apart to this degree at the death of his dog and have so few places or friends in the world to turn to that he would have to come to me. "He really is gorgeous," Debbie said. "Where do you know him from?"

Since nobody else ever answered my questions, I decided this was my opportunity to do the same. I tried to pull him across the floor by his arms but he was too heavy. "You know, they're waiting for you," Debbie said.

"Come on, Debbie, help me," I said. "I can't move him, he's too heavy." To my surprise Debbie left her desk. "Where do you want to put him?" she said.

"I don't know," I said. "Behind your desk?"

"No, what if he pukes again?" Debbie said.

"Fine, then let's just drag him to the supply closet until he wakes up," I said. Luckily the supply closet wasn't far, because even with each of us pulling on one arm it was difficult to move him across the rug. I opened the door; a big piece of metal toppled off a shelf, narrowly missing my head. Even though nobody else was allowed to, Amber kept all kinds of personal junk in the closet—manufacturers sent her free samples, fly-fishing equipment, the latest crossbow and arrows—not that she needed it or used it, she just liked to gloat. Finally we dragged the lower half of his body in and pushed the door shut against his legs. "Should we lock it?" Debbie said.

"Lock him in?" I said.

"Bobette came home one night and passed out and when he woke up I had already left for work and he was still so dead drunk he trashed the apartment."

"Why?" I said.

"Because he didn't know where he was. Ever since then, if he seems really drunk, I tie him to the bed; he doesn't mind, because it's easier than cleaning up the next day."

Somehow I couldn't follow what she was saying, but maybe she had a point, and I agreed we should lock the door to the supply closet—making sure his legs were in first, of course. Then I went down the hall to Amber's office. Virginia and Amber were deep in conversation but stopped instantly the minute they saw me. "Did you bring the coffee?" Amber said after a pause.

"I—" I said.

"All right, all right, forget it," Amber said irritably. "Just sit down, we don't have much time." I looked for a place to sit; Amber and Virginia were in the only chairs, and the brown leather couch along one wall was absolutely covered with books and papers. Even though *Hunter's World* was a magazine only about hunting, Amber had arranged with the publicity departments of every book publisher in town to receive the latest copies of new books. Of course, a few of these were in fact hunting books, which might possibly be reviewed, but the majority were the latest tomes—art books, biographies, fiction—and what Amber did, every few months when the piles became overwhelming, was to make Debbie take them down to the Strand, a bookstore that bought review copies for a small percentage of the cover price.

Since Debbie was having to do all the work of hauling the books there, Amber generously split with her whatever money was made. More than anything I wanted to read a lot of these books that came in, but although once Amber had given me one for a Christmas present, she was very territorial about the books and got angry if I ever tried to look through them. It seemed awfully sad, that out there some poor author had struggled and labored for years, writing a book and trying to get it published, only to have it shipped directly over to Amber where it sat ignored for months before being sold, brand-new, unread, for a dollar and a quarter, and not even donated to a hospital or some charity. I looked for a spot to sit. "Go get a chair!" Amber snapped.

So I went into my office and grabbed the folding metal chair and took it back into hers. I set it up alongside the couch, sat down, and waited, hands in my lap. "All right," Amber said, lighting a cigarette. "Here's the story:

However, it's strictly confidential, no one knows this apart from me, Virginia, Bronson Newman, and Debbie, so I would expect that you'll be able to keep quiet about this too, if you get any calls from the media. Virginia and I have decided to revamp the magazine. Over the next six months, we're very gradually going to change the focus of the magazine until it becomes a women's fashion magazine."

"You're going to change a hunting magazine into a women's fashion magazine?" I said.

"Gradually, yes," Virginia said. "We're going to start by running good-looking men who hunt on the cover, and include some articles about fashion for women hunters, and hunting dogs, and the world's most beautiful locations to hunt, and I'll be writing the editorials up front. By the end of six months, although it might take a little longer, the slant will be entirely different, but without necessarily losing all of our former circulation. That's our intention."

"What does Daniel say?" I said.

"Bronson's going to be the new art director," Amber said.

"Danny hasn't been interested in running the magazine for quite some time," Virginia said coolly. "He's going to stay home for a while and be a house husband and work on his painting."

"His painting?" I said. Oh, but Virginia was so pretty, with her sooty hair and porcelain skin and her tiny red Chanel suit. The price tag was practically written all over her. On one of her impossibly perfect little doll's hands was a huge square-cut emerald ring; some poor Brazilian miner had probably lost his life over it.

"The point is, Pamela—" Amber said, and now her voice rose to a nasal whine—"the point is, we need a new ad director in here. Somebody who's going to be able to make the transition with us. And your background is entirely in manufacturers of hunting equipment, which was fine, of course, but now we need somebody else in here with a broader base."

"That's no problem for me," I said. "I can easily—"

"You're missing the point," Amber said. "Believe me, I'm not trying to be difficult. But you're not involved with the fashion industry; we need someone who can bring in the cosmetics accounts, the restaurant trade, and still be able to hold on to the original accounts, which frankly I just don't think you're up to."

I tried to look Virginia in the eye, but she ignored my gaze. Pinned up on the wall was the layout for the next month's issue: alongside was an ad, a two-page spread that was supposed to go in the beginning of the book, for Feigelman's World's Largest Gun and Tackle Dealer. On November 28, the ad stated, Feigelman's was offering a FREE hunter safety course. There were various depictions of the latest products, a Smith & Wesson Model 3906, double-action pistol, Feigelman's special @ $414.99; a cold Office MIK IV series, semi-auto pistol, $592.99; a Remington ammo sale, $2.69 per box of 100 rounds.

Virginia and Amber fell silent, watching me. "You're saying I'm fired?" I said.

"Finish up the week," Amber said. "I'll give you two weeks severance pay, which I think is generous considering there's nothing in your contract, is there?"

I had known this was coming, I had sensed it for weeks, if not months, yet I had done nothing about it. I deserved to be punished, after all, for working for a magazine advocating death and destruction. How had I been able to justify what I was doing for all these years? Oh, it was just that I told myself that everything was equally filthy, and that if I had gone to work on a magazine that told rich women to go out and buy a ten-thousand-dollar French couture gown there was something just as disgusting about it. Maybe it was just that I never thought too closely about what I was doing. Or if I did, it was only to think that at least what I was doing was honest. What if I had gone out and tried to find a position raising money for a zoo? Would that have been better, to help feed animals trapped in cages? Or if I went to work for a bank, a bank that foreclosed on mortgages of people unable to pay, while the bank owners got richer and richer on money invested in some lousy diamond mine?

The truth was, in my philosophy everything was pretty terrible, and selling ads for a magazine that wrote about guns wasn't like going out and shooting someone—no, whether I worked for the magazine or not, people would either buy guns and shoot deer or they wouldn't. I had nothing to do with it.

"Pamela, it wasn't easy for me to tell you this," Amber said. "Let's have dinner, in a week or two, and keep in touch." There seemed to be nothing further to say. I stood up to leave. "Take a book with you, if you like," Amber said.

"Oh, okay," I said. "Thanks." I picked up whatever was closest to hand and walked down the hall in shock.

"I hope she wasn't too upset," I could hear Virginia saying.

"What are you going to do?" Amber said. Perhaps they didn't know their voices were carrying. "Frankly, I should have gotten her out of here years ago, but I felt sorry for her. She'll be all right."

Leafing through the book I had grabbed I couldn't even feel angry or blame anyone. It was just how things worked; probably Amber or Virginia had someone else they wanted to bring in as ad director, it was nothing to do with me, and surely it wasn't easy for Amber to have to fire me. That was the problem with trying to put oneself in someone else's shoes; it left me with a feeling of emptiness.

The book I had taken without looking was *A Gastronomic Tour of the Scandinavian Arctic.* I flipped to a page of a recipe for smoked reindeer open sandwich. Finely sliced smoked reindeer was to be arranged on sparsely buttered slices of white bread. Mousse of snowgrouse served cold; freshly fried cods' tongues with seasonal salad. A saddle of hare in a rich sauce with juniper berries.

I went into the hall to go to the women's room. The key was still on top of Debbie's desk where I had left it. "Everything okay?" Debbie said, looking at me timidly. So even Debbie knew that I was going to be fired! It made me feel worse that Amber had invited Virginia to be in the room when she did it. If only I could have been Virginia; she had everything, looks and money and servants and a large house. How unbalanced it all was, it was awful having to be me, ponderous and lumpy and unpleasant.

Inside the women's room the manly shoes were still visible from beneath the door of the next stall. She must have been in there for hours. "Are you all right in there?" I said. "Do you need any help? Are you sick?"

A hoarse, muffled voice said, "Is that you, Pamela?"

"Daniel?" I said.

"Is anybody else in here with you?" he said.

"No," I said.

"Quick, lock the door." I went to the door and locked it. How strange that the women's room door lock had never been removed; surely someone would have thought of that since the terrible bathroom tragedy of years ago. On the other hand, maybe the lock was there for security reasons, so that women could lock themselves into the toilet. The one time I had gone to camp, as a child—it was during the breakup of my parents, at the height of their altercations—I had gotten locked in an outhouse, an event that to this day I had never really gotten over. The outhouse was miles from the campers, or so it seemed to me at that age; somehow the old metal lock, quite rusty, got stuck when I shut the door and for an hour and a half I was trapped in the john, a hundred and two degrees, along with a huge wasps' nest, although the wasps weren't trapped, they could fly in and out through a tiny window of their own accord. I kept calling and calling, but since the other campers and the counselors were off swimming, nobody heard me.

"What are you doing in here, Daniel?" I said.

"I was coming in to work when I saw Virginia getting on the elevator, and I didn't want to have to deal with her, so I came in here. Is she still there? Has she gone yet?"

"She's still inside," I said. "Amber fired me, Daniel."

"Oh," Daniel said, emerging from the stall. He looked around the room as if perhaps I had drawn him out in order to trick him; maybe Virginia was somewhere in here after all. "Gee, that's too bad."

"Can't you do something about it?" I said.

"I should have tried to tell you earlier," Daniel said. "But . . . oh, Pamela, I really love you!" He threw himself approximately at my waist.

"I was admiring your shoes before," I said. "Did you have them made for you?"

"What?" Daniel said. He disengaged himself and looked down at his feet. "Oh, yes. In Milan. Do you really like them? Or do you think they're a little . . . fey."

"No, they're nice," I said. "But Daniel, what am I supposed to do now? It's not just the job; but now I don't have any health insurance and how am I supposed to begin my psychiatric treatment?"

"Your psychiatric treatment?" Daniel said.

"You know, with Martin. *You* told me to go and see him."

"Oh, yes," Daniel said. "Well, why don't I pay for that for you?"

"I don't want you to have to do that," I said. "Can't you do anything? I feel so bad, being fired. And they said you're not going to be the publisher anymore."

He looked pensive. "I know," he said. "I'm going to stay home now, with Archie and Alice. The way I see it, children are only young once, but a person can be immature all his life."

"But you're really relinquishing the magazine?" I said.

"Martin has helped me a great deal. I've finally found the courage to go up against my father. I want to devote myself to painting, before I get any older. Or else I might become a fashion designer." His nose twitched so frantically I couldn't tell if he was serious, but finally I decided he must be and I went over to the sink and plunged my face into some cool water from the tap. It was an awkward maneuver to try to fit my head under the running water. Just then he came up behind me and his arms shot out and around my waist, and he clutched me violently in a youthful orangutan fashion, as if I were the mother primate and the two of us were about to mount some ancient kapok tree.

A wave of panic came over me and I nearly bashed my cheek into the tap. What if he were the bathroom rapist and stabber of my predecessor from years ago? I looked up into the mirror and flashed him a nervous grin. My God, my teeth certainly looked gray and stunted. Out of a dentist anxiety or phobia I had avoided going in to have my teeth cleaned for quite some time. I blamed this on the fact that the last time I had been to the dentist I had filled out a reminder postcard, after instructing the receptionist that I didn't want an appointment to be made for me in six months, but just a notice in the mail that I should arrange to come in. But when the postcard arrived, it had been carefully filled out with the time and date.

I called the office to say I would not be coming in on that date at that time—in other words, I canceled. But a few days later there was a telephoned reminder of my appointment on my answering machine. This so enraged me that in order to punish the dentist I didn't show up or reschedule an appointment at all.

A number of years had gone by since that time, and now I was bitterly sorry. My front teeth in particular were so cold they might have been chips of ice embedded in the dull pink gums. Probably they would fall out almost immediately, now that I had no medical insurance. My face dripped and I tried to move away from Daniel to grab a paper towel but he didn't release his feverish grasp.

"Pamela, Pamela," he breathed heavily behind my torso. "I've been waiting to make a pass at you, but I was too nervous." Surely a man grabbing me around my waist could not be constituted as making a pass. And why me, after all? His beautiful wife Virginia had been able to humble me with a single scornful glance. But it was better not to denigrate myself too much, not even in my thoughts; each flower in the garden has its time, and like the daylily, which opens to live for only one single day before shriveling up, my day had perhaps come.

"I'm going to move out of my house, Pamela," Daniel said. "I know a woman who'll let me use her apartment—until I find my own place. I can't go on with things the way they are any longer. Of course, I'm a little nervous about staying in her place, because she may come back to town, and this woman is a very big . . . well, drug user, and I'm trying to quit."

"Gee, I guess you could stay in my place," I said. I tried to think out loud. "Me and Abdhul can sleep in the bedroom, and you can have the couch, even though I'm not sure it's very healthy, actually."

"Abdhul?" Daniel said, letting go and crossing the room.

"I didn't tell you about him—it's a boy who's been . . . staying with me."

"How old?" Daniel said.

"That's hard to say. Maybe six, maybe eight or nine. Sometimes I wonder if he's not actually a dwarf, maybe thirty-five years of age; some things he says sound like a grown man."

"Ah," Daniel said. He scratched his face. "Listen, I believe I'm having a nervous breakdown. Would you think the less of me if I just had a little snort, right now? It's the last I've got, and as soon as I finish it up, I plan to quit."

"You want to snort some heroin?" I said. "Listen, I'm not your mother. You don't need my approval."

"Oh, okay," he said. "Thanks." He took something out of his lapel pocket and darted back into the stall. "I have to do it in private, because there's something extremely erotic about sticking something up my nose in front of other people," he called. I heard a couple of quick whuffles from behind the wall.

Certainly it wasn't very sanitary, and perhaps there was something sexual about inserting dope in the nose. After all, the nose was an orifice, and the human body had only six; seven if you counted both nostrils. That was why it seemed peculiar that eating was such a public gesture. Then it dawned on me that Daniel really intended to leave his wife for me. How sorry I felt for him, sunk in his misery, leading a life without love or values or the milk of human kindness. Without his money, after all, he would have been just another person.

Suddenly I was overcome with nausea and wanted to throw up in the sink, although I couldn't bring myself to do so while he was in the room. Perhaps I had had too many cups of coffee before I left the house, or maybe I was merely identifying psychically with him, for I knew that people who took heroin often threw up afterward, not that I had ever done so, taken heroin, I mean. But that I was able to feel compassion for him! This was a sign of some spiritual growth on my part, and, overcome with tenderness, I wanted to pat myself on the back.

When he came out of the stall his eyes were lacquered and wooden but he smiled politely at me and at least he appeared somehow calmer unto himself. "Here," I said, pointing to the row of sinks. "Sit up here, and relax for a minute." The sinks were sturdy metal basins set onto an old marble slab, and he hoisted himself up so obediently it was like commanding a zombie, but I was worried for his safety and well-being, which he himself now appeared indifferent to.

He leaned back against the dim mirror and half-closed his eyes. I parted his legs gently; how light they were, practically no bigger than eight-to-ten-year-old tree trunks in green khaki trousers. Then I unzipped his fly and reached in to fumble for the merchandise.* It was hard to reach my hand downward from this position and then into his undershorts, which were quite tight jockeys and the little slit was somehow off-center from his outer fly, but at last I located his equipment and pulled it free. It was a bit chilly and curled slightly in my hand. So this was the organ, then, with which I was to spend the end of my days!

He moaned slightly. "Nice, Pamela," he said by way of encouragement. I angled his legs a bit farther apart so that I could have free access with my mouth as I leaned over him. He loved me, that was what was important, although I hadn't made him analyze his statement when I first came into the bathroom and caught him—out of shyness, I suppose, or surprise. But his remark had not gone unnoticed.

"Tell me, Daniel," I said, lifting my head slightly. "There's something I've always wanted to ask a man. Does your appendage . . . feel like it's attached to your body? I mean, does it feel like it's part of you?" I looked up; his eyes, which had half-closed, opened wider.

"What do you mean?" he said.

"I mean, does it feel like it's firmly attached, or that it might sort of fall off? Is it *part* of you, in an integral way?"

His body tensed slightly. "It feels like it's part of me," he said after a pause. "I mean, do your fingers feel like they're attached to you?"

"Yes, yes," I said, lowering myself, "I see what you mean. I always wondered." I put the tip of what there was of his organ into my mouth. The poor man; it must have been awful for him, married to a woman who wanted to be beaten while wearing a paper bag over her head, when obviously he was a gentle little flower waiting to be defoliated. I did not mind taking the aggressive stance in sex. He whimpered as I held it firmly in one hand and ran my tongue around the rubbery rim. And I wasn't even drunk! I was proud of myself. "Each man has a sexual secret," my mother had told me. "And when you discover what that is, he's yours for life."

One of his hands pressed firmly on my head, either pushing it down or away I couldn't be certain, but I took a chance and swallowed up a bit more of his penis, although it appeared nothing much was happening, no doubt due to the effects of the heroin, which in literature at least was always described as causing impotence. "I'm very shy about this sort of thing," Daniel said. "I've never been able to have an orgasm in any woman's mouth."

---

*This is fairly typical behavior for women of Pamela's age group toward the end of the twentieth century. —Author*

"Really?" I said. "How come?"

"What?" Daniel said.

I leaned back. "How come?" I said.

"I—" Daniel said. Just as he started to tell me, there was a banging on the door.

"Is that you in there, Pamela?" Amber whined. "Are you all right?" Daniel jumped; the poor thing must have skewered itself on his fly. In my nervousness I tried to jam the thing back inside. It must be hard for a man, to have his most sensitive area surrounded by metal prongs; I got it inside all right, but then had to give it a little twist to fit it back into his underpants slot. Perhaps such things were better left to the owner, because he let out a little yelp and pushed my hands away from his groin.

"I'm all right!" I yelled. "I just . . . uh, I just needed to be alone for a little while."

"Unlock the door, would you?" Amber bawled. "Because I have to go." She was joined by another voice outside the door. "Pamela, Pamela, it's me, Debbie," Debbie said. "You better get out here, because your boyfriend's woken up in the closet and he sounds kind of mad."

"Your boyfriend?" Daniel hissed.

I put my hand over his mouth. "Ssshh," I said. "I'll explain everything later. For now, we better figure out how we're going to get you out of here." I could hear Debbie and Amber squabbling outside the bathroom door. "You locked that drunk in the supply closet?" Amber said. "What about those weapons I've been keeping in there?"

"What weapons?" Debbie said.

"The crossbow and the arrows," Amber said.

"I thought you took that out to Long Island?" Debbie said.

They were joined by another voice. "What's going on?" Virginia said. "Is she all right in there? Honestly, it's not that big a deal, to be fired from a job."

This momentarily peeved me. How the hell would Virginia know about what it meant to be fired, with two weeks severance pay and a child to support? Even if she and Daniel divorced, she was set for life; and probably she had *never* had to worry about money. I started to say something and looked over at Daniel. He was fumbling with his groin, rubbing it pathetically. Well, I had to be saddled with a tiny mustache and I had learned to live with it; so he, too, had his cross to bear, only in his case it wasn't much of a cross, only a tiny, tiny little one.

"Is that her?" he moaned stonily. "Virginia's still out there!" His eyes closed and he leaned back against the mirror. "What am I going to do?" I tried to find some avenue of escape for the poor man. Obviously it would not do at all for him to be discovered in this condition with me in the bathroom.

"Come on, Pamela, you've been in there for ages!" Amber snarled from the other side of the door. "Stop being so selfish. I have my period."

I looked around the room. There was indeed a window, long since blackened by grime and soot, but it was blocked with a heavy metal security grid, bolted into place at the bottom and locked; there was no sign of a key. Then, above his head, I saw that there was a trapdoor leading into the ceiling, no doubt it was a double ceiling with slithering pipework within; in fact, as I now saw, the ceiling above the bathroom floor was perhaps more modern than the original installation, made of thin foamy sheets of some crumbling substance. "Do you want to get out of here?" I said.

"Yes, yes, get me out of here," Daniel whined. Really, couldn't he stop playing with himself?

I pointed above his head. "Hurry," I said. "You have no time to lose."

He hauled himself up with some effort, using the top edge of the near toilet stall for assistance, but even standing atop the row of sinks he was at least a foot and a half away. I climbed on to assist, despite an ominous squeak and a wiggle from one of the legs that held up the marble slab; I kicked off my shoes and flipped them onto the floor. Then I grabbed Daniel around the waist and attempted to lift him into the air, but I could only manage to hoist him a good six inches or so, his outstretched arms wiggled inches away from the trap hatch. But certainly it was possible to enter it; after all, men must climb up there to work on the air-conditioning units.

It occurred to me to mount the top of the toilet-stall wall. "Hold my legs," I said to Daniel, although he now appeared barely steady on his feet, a fact I attributed to the fact that the entire row of sinks was shifting back and forth loopily as if an earthquake were in progress. Thank G-d (as my grandfather would say) I was just able to reach in this position the trapdoor, which with a little effort I slid to one side.

"I found the spare key," I could hear Debbie saying eagerly on the other side.

"Quick, quick," I told Daniel, and jumped down onto the marble slab just at the moment the whole thing gave way and three hundred and fifty pounds of stone, steel, and cement broke loose from the wall.

With a kamikaze chortle Daniel hoisted himself onto the toilet-stall wall and stood on the top. From my position on the smashed appurtenance I could see his head, then his torso and lastly his wriggling legs disappearing into the hole in the ceiling. He must have collapsed in exhaustion, because one of his shoes fell off and I could still see both his feet, one clad and the other in a navy sock with a hole in the bottom, protruding from the cavern; I prayed either he would slither farther in or that nobody would think to look up, for gallons of water were pouring rapidly out of the three separate sets of pipes that led to the former sinks.

It really had been quite a crash, when I went down with the sinks, but with the remnant of my strength I grabbed Daniel's shoe that had fallen almost on my head and gave it a toss upward and back into the air, hoping it would hide itself. Just then the spare key finished its rape of the lock and the door swung open; Debbie, followed by Amber and Virginia, burst into the room and then all three stood stock-still by the door.

The floor was already an inch deep in water; while more poured out, the marble slab half collapsed and cracked. I was propped up in supine position against the wall of the toilet stall, part of the sink basin beneath me. It was some moments before any of them spoke, although with the ringing in my head, which I must have cracked sharply against the wall, and the rush and gurgle of the water, it would have been hard to hear them in any event. "What the hell's going on here?" Amber said at last. I was surprised at her quickness and grace; for a plump woman with short arms she moved quite rapidly. "Where's the turn-off valve?" She slogged through the water and reached her hand under the higher end of the marble slab, searching for the faucet to shut off the water. Just then, loosened by the water, the other two legs holding up the basins gave way, crushing her arm at shoulder level and knocking her down into the water.

Why were her arms so short, anyway? This was something I had pondered in the past. Was it some sort of genetic defect, such as Crohn's disease? Could her mother have taken a mild dosage of Thalidomide or other medication while carrying her in the womb? They weren't so short as to be a truly horrendous defect, and perhaps I was the only one who had noticed. It was simply that they seemed an inch or so too short for her torso, although my thinking might have been due to the fact that my own arms were unusually long. In the past Amber had often commented about the state of my fingernails, which seemed to attract dirt. Of her own hands she was inordinately proud, and I suppose by some standards they were pretty hands, but not to my taste, being pink, plump, and dimpled. She kept them immaculately groomed, the nails lacquered in buff-brown, and they always reminded me of the hands of some spoiled little girl in a party dress, a six-year-old princess.

One thing I had to say about my father, was that however uninterested he had always been in me, he always wanted me to hammer in nails, and femininity and helplessness were traits he despised. He always told me, "Pamela, most women think they're here on earth to feed off of men, and always remember that when you grow up nobody's ever going to support you or look after you but yourself." In fact, he wasn't too pleased with the fact that he had to support me even when I was a child, but at least because of this, even though I had never actually become a plumber or car mechanic, I was proud of my self-sufficiency and that I was not a woman who felt the world owed me a living.

I should have gotten up to help Amber, but perhaps I had a mild concussion; really, the crash of the marble slab, with me atop, had been quite a blow. And now I was afraid that if I stood up the rest of the weight might fall farther on Amber. If I had asked for revenge out loud I couldn't have hoped to receive it more quickly or violently. "My arm!" Amber screamed suddenly.

"What were you trying to do, Pamela, hang yourself?" Virginia said from the doorway. Oh, please don't let her look up, I thought, but involuntarily I glanced quickly overhead; Daniel's feet were gone.

"Well . . ." I said noncommittally with a wave of one long, hairy arm. Let her think what she wanted.

Debbie now broke from her trance and ran to Amber's side. "Don't move," she said. "You may have broken something." It seemed to me this was a mistake, because if Amber didn't move, crushed as she was into the tile flooring, within minutes, as the water rose, she might surely drown. Nobody cared about me and whether my head had been split open, that much was certain. Still I could not complain. Only once had I seen justice served in such rapid fashion; that was in second grade, when Cornelia Hightman had commented cruelly on the hairiness of my arms and only moments later was violently hit over the head in the hallway when my briefcase, red canvas and black vinyl, fell out of my locker of its own accord just as she passed by. Perhaps the human psyche had all kinds of hidden powers that people did not know how to utilize.

The water must have reached Amber's face as she lay on her side, for she let out a peculiar glugging sound. "Can't you turn off the sink?" Debbie said.

"I think my arm's broken," Amber said, but she was able to reach the faucet, because the geyser sound ceased, and briefly everything was quiet except for the soft swish of water across the floor as it slapped around the wall.

"Oh, for God's sake," Virginia said, taking a step farther into the room. "My shoes are ruined. Let me just pee, quickly; don't move, and I'll go and try to find somebody to help." She slushed through the water and into one of the stalls. "You know, you can be arrested for trying to commit suicide," she said, shutting the door. "What the hell's this?"

"What's what?" I asked.

"It's a man's shoe," she said. "Somebody's put a man's shoe in the toilet."

"Better use the other toilet," I said. "That could be what's caused the backup."

"The backup?" Virginia said. "The entire bathroom's destroyed." In England, where the culture was different, no one referred to a bathroom unless it was a room with a bath in it. Over here, people rarely said *toilet* even when that was what they meant. Surely if Virginia wanted to present mock-English airs she shouldn't use the word *bathroom* when she meant *toilet*.

It was awful for me, that I had to be the kind of person who would simply look at other people and then think about them. I knew that Virginia considered herself to be a superior person; she believed herself to have breeding, and intelligence, and good looks, and while this was true, it didn't make her useful in any way. But at the same time, the fact that she thought all these things about herself made me feel worthless.

My mother would have said that I did not have to go along with the game, and that probably Virginia was basically insecure and therefore had to concentrate on this type of thought every second in order to force me to believe it was true.

She came out of the stall and saw my shoes where I had tossed them. "Oh, whose shoes are those?" she said. "Those are nice."

"Mine," I said, pleased.

"I had a pair like that I just threw out," she said. "I can't use this bathroom. It's absolutely filthy. Debbie, you stay here with Amber. I'll go see if I can't find some man to help us."

After Virginia left, I crawled off the collapsed slaughter table and stood barefoot on the floor. The cool water on my stockinged feet was quite refreshing. Debbie, crouched over Amber, was murmuring gently. "Hang in there, Amber," she said. "I remember when my roommate, Bobette, OD'd and he fell and hit his head on the toilet. Blood everywhere, and the whole toilet was shattered."

"What did you do?" I said.

"We told the landlord the toilet just broke," she said.

It was obvious that while the marble slab was serving as a mausoleum for at least a portion of Amber's anatomy, it was not actually crushing her, the full weight was still precariously propped up above her arm by a fragment of a millimeter or some other mathematical measurement. Her expensive scent wafted toward me; of what rare alpine flowers were the perfumes of the rich composed, the ambergris of the world's remaining whales and the musk of civet cats, delicate beetle shells and petals plucked from obscure grasses de France? "Hey, what kind of perfume are you wearing?" I said with some envy. My own perfume was of the discount drugstore variety, at least when I remembered to wear it, and though I tried to justify my odor by believing that there was no difference between it and the two-hundred-dollar-an-ounce scent, there were obviously qualities in hers not found in my own.

I didn't want to cause her any undue anxiety, so without speaking I grabbed her arm firmly at its root and gave it a yank. Amber let out a shriek, but she should have been grateful that even if her arm was broken it was no longer in danger of being crushed. However, she must have been crippled or stunted in some way, because she didn't move but merely lay on her side. With her enormous rear end in full view.

And suddenly, I don't know what happened—I saw myself grabbing this woman, who was absolutely undesirable, at least from my point of view, with great chunky big legs, big animal legs, like an elephant, with a huge ass, and I just saw myself grabbing her and fucking the hell out of her, right there on the floor, yes, I could see myself, ramming a penis into her, a big fat dick into her huge pussy.

She was an unattractive female and a giant sex object. But I was no lesbian; therefore, how could I have thought this? For a second it was as if some male mind had occupied mine, and when I looked up, puzzled, I saw Alby standing by the doorway, holding the crossbow. With his drunk, slitty eyes he resembled a little runion or grunion, in his creased and vomit-streaked expensive linen suit.

He was looking down at Amber quite calmly and plainly, and I thought, He's the guilty party! And he didn't even look embarrassed, or sheepish— this was probably a normal thought for him! Grabbing a big plain woman with piano legs, simply because she had been knocked over onto the floor and practically crushed to death and therefore was in a helpless position. Here was this lunatic: drunk, probably jobless, having made a fool out of himself, and he had the nerve, the audacity, to feel superior to a woman, to want to come up behind her, right there on the filthy wet bathroom floor, hold her down, pull out his dick and shove it up into her from behind.

And yet, during the time that I had been forced to have Alby's fantasy, I could honestly say that it was truly enjoyable, and I had genuinely wanted to grab Amber and rip off her pantyhose and fuck the hell out of her.

Well.

I mean, what could I say? Even though to me men didn't somehow quite exist, even though from what I could see the men I came across weren't exactly like real people, they still ruled the world, out of some episode from a television science-fiction program, giant gray dicks from another planet, bossing and controlling and deciding who was in favor this week and who was not.

But where had I ever gotten the idea that I might at least be allowed to be master of the events inside my own head? Now I could see that even this was not going to be the case, and that I was always going to be at the mercy of male thought forms, although perhaps I was temporarily denying the fact that only moments before I had believed myself to be under the force field of Virginia's thoughts, and she was female.

Finally Amber flipped like a fish in a too-shallow puddle, and wiggled over onto her back; she caught sight of Alby standing in the doorway holding the crossbow and arrow and let out another scream. Honestly, for a verbal person she had been rather quickly reduced to a nonverbal level. Where had Debbie disappeared to? She was nowhere in sight, and it seemed clever of her to manage to escape immediately before a mass execution. My best bet was to try and speak to Alby as if he were a person.

"How'd you get out of the closet, Alby?" I said. "You were locked in." He waved the crossbow in the air and looked blank. Many hunters advocated the use of the crossbow rather than guns to shoot deer, claiming it was a more honorable pursuit. But as far as I was concerned, to shoot some poor deer with any instrument was foul play. It might have been more fair if the deer themselves were outfitted with some type of explosive, but for the most part they were not, and no danger to the hunter was posed in killing wild animals, apart from other hunters. The thing was, a cow or a sheep could not survive without being looked after by human beings, and therefore it was their own fault that they were summarily executed for meat at a certain age. But a deer, who looked after him- or herself; it was horrible to think of an animal running for its life. Nor did I care for venison, although once I had had a date with a man who no longer wished to be homosexual, and he took me to an expensive restaurant and ordered a saddle of venison with lingonberry gravy, which I sampled. But it was not his record of homosexuality nor his desire to eat deer that troubled me; rather, it was the fact that by selecting me as the one woman who could transform him into a happily married man made me feel somehow masculine, and it was obvious he was just waiting to be seduced, and since I was, too, I just didn't see how it was going to work.

I tried to lift Amber into an upright position but I must have grabbed the wrong arm, because she let out a scream. Perhaps her shoulder was dislocated; helpfully I tried to shove her arm back in its socket. A slew of garbled blather began to pour from her mouth. "You sah et ah much cawl . . ."

"Amber, I can't understand what you're saying," I said. Her bovine body shuddered and she appeared to be gathering herself together.

"Get me out of here now!" she said. I looked over at Alby, standing in the doorway; I was not about to force my way past him. The steely crossbow, highly painted in red enamel, glinted in one chunky hand. Just then Virginia's voice could be heard down the hall. "This stupid, silly woman was trying to hang herself in the loo," she was saying to some unknown companion. "*She* was unhurt, naturally—I'm sure it was just a ploy for attention—but the ladies' room is completely destroyed." I noticed when she said the word *stupid* that she pronounced it as if it were spelled "stewpid." Perhaps I would acquire that delightful pronunciation as a mannerism of my own. Stewpid—it sounded like an elegant yet peasanty dish composed of rabbit and legumes, seasoned with rosemary over an open-pit fire. "I've had some experience with my brother," the male voice said just at the moment they entered the room and came upon Alby and his spurious weapon. Did he plan to use it? And if so, how much pain would it cause? But I was not to find out; just as Virginia was announcing, "Here's Bronc, the only one around here with—" her voice dwindled, then faded into uneasy silence. Whatever it was she was referring to was permanently lost.

Apparently Bronc was Bronson Newman, the new art director and the same man I had had the disappointing interlude with in the sex booth. He glanced around the room, and, barely hesitating a moment, let out a sort of wrestler's grunt; then he leapt forward with surprising deftness and gave my poor Alby a semblance of a karate chop just below the hand holding the crossbow, which (I had not picked up on this before) was set with a needle-nose arrow. Alby's hand jerked; the arrow was released with a shrill whanging sound and flew up and across the room, piercing the soft skin of the ceiling. Only the tail end was left protruding. My God, what about Daniel? I wasn't going to be the one to give away his secret; on the other hand if he was wounded, or possibly even killed outright, it would only be a matter of days before his body began to decay in the heat, and that would be one hell of a mess, although it was true by then I would surely be long gone from the premises.

With another grunt Bronc knocked Alby down on the floor (naturally, though I didn't say anything while Virginia and Amber were busy applauding politely, it was not all that difficult to knock over a drunken man, particularly when his attacker must have weighed more than fifty pounds more) and with one cowboy-booted foot Bronc crushed Alby's hand, still clutching the crossbow, into the muddied floor. "Why doesn't one of you go get me some rope to tie him up with?" Bronc said.

"Rope?" I said. "I don't remember seeing any rope around here."

"Use an electric cord!" Virginia snarled at me. "The stupid cunt!" she announced to no one in particular. "That's her boyfriend. My God, these people and their sordid, dreary lives."

I had to admit, she had hit the nail on her head. Debbie emerged from one of the toilet stalls where she had been hiding. She was holding Daniel's shoe daintily between two fingers. "I fished it out," she said. "What kind of sick person would do that?" She looked at me accusingly.

*"I* didn't do it," I said.

Meanwhile on the floor Alby had burst into girlish sobs. I went back to my office to find a cord to tie him up with. There was a rather nice lamp near my desk; it would be a shame to yank the cord out of it, as it would probably cost quite a bit for the rewiring; but perhaps there was a way they could tie his hands behind his back still attached to the light fixture itself. Then I remembered nothing in the office was mine any longer. Oh, what did I care; but still I couldn't bring myself to disembowel the light fixture. It was a free-standing old brass floor lamp, dating back to the early days of electricity and quite heavy, but I unplugged it from the wall and lugged it back into the bathroom.

In my absence Bronc was now comforting Alby. "I had a dog too, once," he was saying. "It was the middle of the summer, and they were tarring the streets, and the dog went out into the road and got tar all over his feet. My mother tried to clean him, with kerosene, and he died. I was just a little kid, but Jesus, I didn't fall apart over it! Get ahold of yourself!" The two of them were practically embracing.

Virginia was busy annointing herself at the remains of the sink; oh, she was lovely, patting powder over what could scarcely be considered a nose, just two tiny flanges capped with a confectionary of freckles, like expensive Dutch cocoa dusting the top of a thirty-five-dollar cake from some Madison Avenue bakery. She caught sight of me admiring her and managed to convey a glance that simultaneously accepted my worship while dismissing me. I was determined to force her into understanding that I existed. "Here's the lamp," I said, thursting it toward her. "We can tie him up with the cord."

"Oh, God, why don't you women leave the poor guy alone," Bronc said.

"I had nothing to do with this," Amber said—imitating me. She gestured in my direction. "It was Pamela who drove him out of his mind. I never knew, Pamela, what a walking disaster you are."

All I could think to say was, "You sound rather hostile." She narrowed her eyes and flounced out of the room, cradling her arm. Let her try and fire me; it was too late. I had already been fired. But Amber didn't go far; she stood in the hallway. "Bronc, I want him tied up immediately or I'm going to call the police."

Bronc took a couple of sloshing steps through the water. "Aw, Amber, I think it's going to be all right. He's drunk but he's harmless."

"Tie him up, Bronc! I don't care what you say. Frankly, I'm ready to call the police. He could have killed somebody." She came back into the room and glared at me. "I think my arm is broken. You're lucky I don't have you arrested too, Pamela. I'd like to see you get some psychiatric help. Do you want me to send Debbie to sign you into Bellevue?"

"I'm planning to see a psychiatrist later this evening," I muttered. "Bellevue won't be necessary yet."

Bronc seemed somehow aroused at being ordered around thus. He picked up the lamp from where I had deposited it on the wet floor. "Will one of you help? I'll hold his arms if someone can tie a good knot."

Both Virginia and Debbie began to sashay toward Bronc, but Amber stopped them aggressively. "I'll tie him, Bronc," she said. I was going to point out that if she were capable of tying a knot I doubted her arm was actually broken, but my manners stopped me. Oh, it was awful: these were people without any real values, without any sense of morals—no wonder I had so few friends, when everybody in New York was competitive, ambitious, and busy sucking up to anybody with money or power. Amber stood defensively in front of Bronc as if she were guarding him on a basketball team. Believe me, Amber, I wanted to say, I have no interest in stealing Bronc from you, even if he is an Important Art Director. He had the face of a depraved TV weatherman, clownish and somehow corrupt; one could easily imagine him being caught in the act of raping a twelve-year-old Thai girl. I wondered if Amber was having an affair with him, despite his previous denials. What about poor Balthazar, Amber's long-suffering husband? Didn't he mind being cuckolded thus? On the few occasions I had met him he seemed very sweet and obsequious; as a public act of charity Amber raised seeing-eye monkeys for the quadriplegics, and they kept eight of them—capuchins, I believe—in their home, an old brownstone that had been in Balthazar's family for a number of generations.

Bronc had hoisted the semiconscious Alby to his feet while Amber knotted the electric cord, still attached to the lamp, around his wrists behind his back. "As soon as I'm finished, I want you to go get us some coffee and danish," Amber told Bronc.

Bronc grinned helplessly. Really, he was looking less and less handsome; his jowls sagged with the strain of holding Alby, and I hoped he didn't have a sudden heart attack, which had once happened to a boy I knew who was only eighteen at the time with no previous warning and in appearance at least wasn't half so soft and mushy. If Bronc were in my care I would put him on a diet and send him to the gym, but maybe Amber liked her men to be giant babies.

A big chunk of spongy material suddenly crashed into the water near my feet. Then I saw that more bits of the particle-board ceiling were falling down all over the room. Nuggets of ancient extruded foam wafted into Virginia's hair, but nobody seemed to notice; they were all too busy watching Amber strap Alby upright to the standing lamp. "This'll keep him on his feet," Amber said firmly. Bronc watched her admiringly. The end of the cord dangled on the floor. Bronc kept Alby up in a standing position, his hands under Alby's armpits; I didn't know what would happen once Alby was completely bound, despite Amber's assurances—in the tone of a cardinal of the Spanish Inquisition—that once she was finished Alby would have no choice but to remain upright on his stake.

Suddenly the lights blinked off briefly and then flickered on. Perhaps this was a sign that Daniel—if he was still above our heads—was not dead after all, but intent on ruining the antiquated electric wiring. It occurred to me that there was probably nothing else here I could do. I went to find my shoes in the slime. They were floating along like little alligators. The top part was some species of reptile, but the soles were made out of rubber, so perhaps they weren't completely ruined. Didn't Virginia realize she was paying all this money for shoes that didn't even have real leather soles? If I were a rich person and could buy celadon-colored shoes from the fanciest French designer salon, I would want to make sure they were of the finest construction.

However, now perhaps was not the time to complain. I slipped them on my wet feet and began to head quietly for the door. A bit of the electric cord attached to the lamp had been yanked free and several wires protruded;

I thought of maybe telling Amber that if Alby struggled long enough he could probably loosen it the rest of the way. But before I could say anything the lights flicked off again and this time didn't come back on.

There was a moment of silence and in the dark was audible the sound of bits of ceiling flaking down and a slithering humping noise above our heads; then the lights in the hall went off, and everything was plunged into complete black.

Before my parents' breakup, there had been a giant snowstorm and a number of trees were knocked down. My dad went out after the snow stopped to cut them down, and when he chopped the first crumbling birch tree, speckled with pancake-shaped fungus, it toppled over and hit the power line. All the lights in the house went out. He came back in and called the operator to say what happened. "Listen, mister," the operator told him. "The lights in your house are out? All the lights on the Eastern seaboard just went out." It gave my father a certain feeling of power, that he was responsible, and we did nothing to discourage this, for my mother wanted to bolster my father whenever she could.

"Oh, fuck," Bronc finally said in the dark. "I want to find some kind of crowbar or weapon." Perhaps he had a fear of the dark, which I found rather touching. But I would not let him suffer for long. Even though I had never been able to see very well in the dark, I knew where I could find a light; the plug was right at Amber's feet, and I had long ago noticed an outlet along the wall.

I stumbled in the dark and rummaged by her ankles until I located the end of the plug and picked it up. With my free hand I felt blindly along the wall; my eyeless fingers caressed the bump that indicated an outlet was to hand, and without thinking of the first rules of electricity I inserted the metal prongs into the wall.

Wow! It must have been God, Buddha, Krishna, or some other deity's will, even I felt a tiny sparkle, but the three of them—Amber, Bronc, and Alby—were suddenly illuminated by an unearthly, neon-blue silhouette, a sound resembling frying grackles crackled across the airwaves, metallic smoke began to pour out of the wall, along with another discharge, the scent of burning hair, although maybe this wasn't from the wall but from the three of them.

Dear me, I was electrocuting them, that was four deaths or maimings I was responsible for, at least in part, during the course of one morning. Quickly I yanked the plug out of the wall. "Good thing my shoe-soles were made out of rubber," I announced to no one in particular.

Even though the room was still pitch dark I picked my way along the wall and fumbled down the hall until I reached the elevator banks; the lights were on in this section and the elevators apparently in order, so the blackout must have just been along our—I mean, their—office section of the floor. I had done my best, but rather than wait around to assist any further, when the elevator stopped I got in and went down to the lobby and into the street.

I set off as quickly as I could so I could go home and call my mother before it was time to pick up Abdhul from camp. What was I going to do without a job, how would I be able to pay my psychiatrist bills when I hadn't even begun to meet with him yet? "I'll pretend you've moved home with me, and I'll arrange for my university health insurance to be extended, to cover you and Abdhul," my mother said.

This lessened my anxiety somewhat. "And I have a credit card," I said. "All over the United States there are people with no money whatsoever, but they're able to buy huge television sets, and cars, and expensive, thick, woolly sweaters, for no other reason than that they have credit cards. I don't know how I could have gotten into such a panic."

"No, no!" my mother practically shouted. Now she was the one who sounded panicky. "How many times do I have to tell you, that's not our philosophy?"

It was only in the past few years, since her teaching job was fairly secure, that she had even acquired a credit card. And when we were kids, she never purchased anything unless she had the money to pay for it. If we needed new clothes, we went to the Salvation Army. I had always wondered why the poorest person always seemed to be able to afford more things than we had, but I'd never suspected it was due to my mother's abnormal, un-American behavior, until she began to teach in the Psychics Department and there, during her first year, befriended a student—a woman with four small sons—who had been able to go back to school after her divorce by taking out student loans.

My mother's friend's name was Melanie, and Melanie lived in a far nicer apartment than my mother. My mother's, when she first moved to upstate New York, was the shabby upstairs half of a two-family house, and when I visited it was so cold during the winter that once I took out my contact lenses and cleaned them before going to sleep; I left the little saline solution-filled contact-lens case on the windowsill, and when I woke up in the morning the contact lenses were embedded in two chunks of ice.

But Melanie's apartment was toasty warm and furnished with all sorts of possessions acquired from the local shopping mall as well as a huge color TV and VCR and a number of pay channels. Melanie had acquired everything by charging it. What would happen to her when she couldn't pay? They could come and take the things away, that was about it. And it dawned on me, that was why people had things, whether or not they could pay for them. Because it was highly unlikely they would be thrown in jail. Of course, Melanie's sons, over the years, got into all sorts of problems—my mother would tell me the latest episode every week. One became a father when he was only thirteen. Another stole Melanie's credit cards until she had him sent to reform school. One found a boyfriend, a fifty-year-old man, and moved to New York to live with him until the man was arrested for acts of necrophilia (he was a coroner for the city, and this story made all the papers, but luckily Melanie's son, who was only seventeen at the time, wasn't prosecuted but made a lot of money selling his story and photographs to various magazines and even appeared on national TV shows). One—but the point was, these boys might have turned out that way whether or not Melanie put everything on charge cards.

"This sort of thing happens to families all the time," I said. "Even to families who're able to pay the bills, so why shouldn't I go out now and get a TV, like Melanie?"

"Because," my mother said, "we're not like that. You have to live within your means."

"But I don't have any means," I said.

After this I went to pick up my surly child from camp. I say surly because when he saw me, across the room in the basement, where he was at work constructing what was apparently a life-size naked torso of a woman in plasticine, he finished fondling her nipples and ran over and bit me on the arm. I was so startled I gave him a shove backward. "What the hell was that all about?" I said, rubbing my arm. Luckily he hadn't broken the skin, but there was a neat round circle of teeth marks. Perhaps the honeymoon stage was over. A spoiled-looking little girl watched gleefully. She had a flat face, a bunny nose, and straight, long blond hair with bangs. From my lofty position of maturity I could see how stupid she really was, but she brought back memories of how often I had tried to befriend this sort of kid when I was a child, and how I had always been snubbed. She was the epitome of American wholesomeness, with her retarded blue eyes, directly out of a Norman Rockwell painting. And though once I would have envied and coveted any friendship with her, and begged to be one of those privileged to comb her hair, I now knew that in a few years she would be sent to prep school where she would take drugs and be highly promiscuous; eventually she would attend one of the colleges for stupider yet monied American youth and spend the ten years after graduation "partying" and trying to find a status-symbol boyfriend while working as an aerobics instructor or something similar, before losing her looks.

Times had changed since old Normal Rockwell was painting his American paintings, was all I could say. They did not have "partying" back when he captured his race of Aryans on canvas. Probably some whiny Jewish guy trying to write screenplays would marry her in the end and she would have to walk up six flights to a crummy sublet with a baby in a stroller. "Partying" had to be one of the ugliest, most criminal words to come into modern usage. Attend a party, Miss Fish, I wanted to tell the little girl, okay, but if you want to "party" then why not simply say that you plan to take cocaine, drink beer with a bunch of morons until you throw up and pass out, and then allow yourself to be gang-raped with a baseball bat. The self-hatred and lack of spiritual grace that accompanied modern times! Why not stay home and read a good book? But no, Jennifer or Emily or Elizabeth, whatever the au courant names were for eight-year-olds, would never grow up to read a book; she would watch TV and go to the movies and one day, if she were lucky, Arnold Schwarzenegger or some other movie star would pick her up in a restaurant and take her home for a one-night stand, after first requiring her signature on a piece of paper swearing she would not discuss it on TV, which she would anyway.

Abdhul was now leaping about the room, darting back and forth to his nude torso from time to time to slap more gray plasticine atop the primitive breasts, which had taken on monstrous proportion. "Calm down, calm down," I said, grabbing him by one of his scrawny arms. "Try to get a grip on yourself. What's gotten into you, anyway?" Just then Ralph, the limping counselor, came over to my side. "You're here early today," he said.

"I'm sorry," I said, struggling to subdue Abdhul, who wriggled frantically. "Has he been a lot of trouble? Is that what you wanted to see me about?" It seemed sad, that there were so few men involved with childcare in camp programs such as this or at the elementary-school level. And despite the fact that one was not supposed to feel this way, the men who did choose to devote their careers to working with children always seemed somewhat pitiful and unmanly. Of course, if such jobs paid any money, they would, no doubt, be run entirely by men. But Ralph, with his one short leg, his wispy black pubic goatee, had to have selected this job for *some* reason. It was possible he was a child molester. Or that he thought of himself as the last of the hippies. Perhaps in order to remain a man in his thoughts he convinced himself that he was at work on a novel, a gentle and touching tome about a man whose wife had died unexpectedly, leaving him destitute and causing him to quit his high-paying position to go and work with the children, where he would meet a) a single mother and they would fall in love or b) a tiny nymphlike Jennifer or Tiffany and they would fall in love or c) a single father and they would fall in love or d) all of the above. ". . . Oh no, Abdhul's wonderful. It's a real treat to have him around," Ralph was saying. "Just this morning he took his shower with me—we shower before we swim—and then he invited me to come and join you for dinner, so I don't know how you feel about that, hee-hee-hee! His artwork is marvelous, really he's very talented. Have you seen his nude figure he's been working on? It's very Henry Moore and yet somehow different. I think I might be able to get ahold of'—and here he named a prominent art dealer—"to come by and look at it—wouldn't it be fabulous, cast in bronze? It's too good to simply keep in plasticine. No, I think he's very, very talented, and starting this young . . . well, artists these days make a great deal of money. What I really wanted to ask you though, is . . ." Ralph glanced around the room. "Abdhul, why don't you and Amanda go to my office and get the Tofu Treats and the rice cakes for the afternoon snack and carry them to the courtyard in back?"

"Okay!" Abdhul said, and with a whoop he grabbed the snub-nosed bimbo by the hand and they ran up the staircase together. It really was rather sweet, that an offspring of mine would be popular in a way I never was. "Oh, by the way, I don't know if you're aware of this," Ralph said. "But he's very good at sports; I know he'd love it if he could join a Little League softball team, we don't offer that sort of thing here, or golf? I would have loved to be athletic, but with this leg . . ." He looked down wistfully. "I was in a plane crash, when I was eight; I had been in an Albanian orphanage, and my adoptive parents had me flown over. I was in a cast for a year from the waist down, but this leg never grew after that. Anyway, of course now they can do all sorts of things—graft in new sections of bone, or artificial material, but at that time . . ." Oh, I felt just terrible! Here I had been thinking all sorts of mean thoughts, when in actual fact Ralph was one of the true saints who roamed around devoting their lives to worthy activities. Why did I have to be the sort of person always to think the nastiest things? Thank God I wasn't a Catholic; in which case it would have been a sin, to think bad thoughts (anyway, this was what Catholic people I knew had told me). Luckily I could just think bad thoughts and then feel guilty, instead of having to go to hell or say a Hail Mary, which would have taken up a lot of time. "Pamela, let me be frank: is Abdhul really your child?"

It was like a bucket of icy water had been dumped over me. My legs broke out in goose bumps. "Mmm," I mumbled. Should I say I was looking after him for the summer? Or should I just simply lie outright? I had always been a terrible liar, and this had kept me on an honest path. Before I could answer further, however, Ralph nodded sympathetically. "I don't want to frighten you; but a woman's been hanging around, the past few days, claiming Abdhul is her child, that he was lost and she wants him back. I didn't want to call the police; the woman seemed so obviously mentally ill, I thought I would speak to you first."

"Who is she?" I said. "What did she look like?"

"She was . . ." There was a long moment of silence. "She was . . . no, I don't really know."

"But how old was she?" I said. "Was she young? Did she have blond hair or brunette? What was she wearing? Was she well dressed?"

"I can't say," Ralph said finally. "I'm not really a very good observer. She might have had on a dark dress. Listen, I really wouldn't worry if I were you; why don't you just come and pick up Abdhul from now on? I'll keep him here until you've come."

"But where did she see him?" I said. "Did she give you her name?"

"Go look outside now," Ralph said. "Maybe she's still there."

I ran up the steps and out the front door, but there was no one on the street. The long narrow lobby in front of the auditorium was empty as well. I went back to the basement. "If she comes back . . ." I said.

"Oh, I'll make sure nobody gives out your home address or phone number," Ralph said. "We're very careful here; this is New York, after all. We were on a field trip one day: she came out of nowhere and tried to drag him off."

"He never said anything," I said. "If you see her again, will you take her name? Her phone number? I'd like to . . . talk to her."

"That's probably not a good idea," Ralph said. "But if you want, I'll see, if she's willing to tell me." I followed Ralph out to the courtyard. Amanda had pinned Abdhul onto the ground and was stuffing Tofu Treats up his nose. I went up alongside. Amanda turned and gave me a superior smile. "I've never eaten sugar in my entire life," she said. "Your hair's all gray in the front. Abdhul eats sugar all the time. That's why he's so weak."

"Come on, Abdhul," I said, ignoring Amanda. "We've got to go now."

"Okay," Abdhul said cheerfully, scrambling up. "See ya!" He kissed Amanda on both cheeks and then ran to Ralph, who bent down in order that Abdhul could again perform the same. "Hurry up, Pamela!" Abdhul said, running out the door.

I decided not to send Abdhul back.

★   ★   ★

"It's not that I have no good memories of my father," I tried to tell Martin Feurey that evening in between his trips to the bar to get drinks. "Once a week, on Saturday mornings—perhaps in lieu of synagogue—my father took me with him to the country dump. Sometimes my brothers were included, but often—"

"Oh my God," Martin said.

"What?" I said.

"That's my patient over there," he said.

"Where?" I said.

"Right there! Oh my God, what if he sees me? I'm going to go hide. I'll be back in a few minutes. Better still, why don't you come knock on the ladies' room door when he leaves."

"The ladies' room?" I said.

"The women's room," he said. "Whatever. Sorry. I'm not trying to be sexist."

"No, I mean, why are you hiding in the women's room and not the men's?" I said.

Martin grinned gleefully. "I'm going to think about that one," he said as he exited.

I was left alone with my thoughts and a bottle of beer, glassless. The man Martin claimed to be his patient took out a Scrabble board and began to play with himself near the jukebox. Ah, well, so it was to be left to me to begin treatment; frankly, I wasn't sure if anything was really wrong with me, apart from having been born. . . .

Together my father and I loaded the week's worth of garbage (all dry goods, plastic, etc.—the scrapings and foodstuffs were all sentenced to the compost heap, along with chicken droppings, pig manure, horse and cow shit, to rot for a year and then spread out over the garden) into the back of the old pickup. And then my dad would drive the twenty miles or so out to the dump, the town dump on a dirt road off the road leading out of town. The ground was sand; as it was always a Saturday the bulldozer was at rest, like some behemoth or stunned, evil dinosaur with a shovel-shaped mouth at the end of a pencil neck, near the far end where the burned garbage was buried.

From time to time the dumping section was moved, so that gradually over the years acres of land had been uprooted, dumped on, burned, and buried, and the trees at the far ends of the landfill had had their leaves burned off, dark lacquered skeletons, as if here—though it often seemed to be this way everywhere, during my childhood—it was always winter.

The smell of garbage and old smoke was immensely pleasurable. And the look of the place—the carcasses of refrigerators, the heaps of crushed metals, old cars the color of soft solder and tellurium. The chunks of boulders, crates, plastic bags whipping in the wind, the slag heaps and baby strollers, coils of barbed wire and broken crockery . . . I got out of the truck and studied the old sand studded with bottlecaps, broken glass fused and etched, labels from wine bottles, a stack of cracked 78s . . . the air was sour with ammonia.

My father unloaded the bags of garbage from the truck. Often I climbed up onto the back of the flatbed and handed the bags down to him, which he carried over to the edge of the pit and threw down on top of the other piles, coffee grounds, heaps of slate, pools of slimy earth scented with the decay of vegetables that we call mold. Empty cans—Campbell's cream of mushroom soup, Libby's peaches, Dole pineapple, the labels smeared but still legible. A wrecked television set, its iris crushed.

After the bags were tossed I wiped up any spilled juice, oils, or gunk. "You wait in the car," he said. "I think I see something over there I want to check out." He went off through the dangerous pit in search of valuable treasures. Sometimes he spent an hour or longer browsing through the rubble, as dainty a shopper as if Harrod's or Saks Fifth Avenue had been caught in an avalanche and he was the first shopper allowed in after the disaster, to pick and choose from the wreckage at his leisure.

At last he returned. "Take a look at what I found!"

Eight unopened good cans of Spam, perfect for the pigs (at that period he kept four sows, monstrous pink women who on hot days lay on their sides in a muddy pen, and one boar, Grumpus, who all us kids were warned against going near. But how we loved those little pink piglets! One summer I was allowed to keep one as a pet . . . it ran after me like a dog until fall came and it was sent off with the others to the man up the hill who did the butchering; a coil of tangled mylar fishing line, to be unraveled on a winter night; a partly broken jar of nails, grommets, and washers; an ancient typewriter, later found to be missing the letters *T* and *D;* a can with a handle and long spout used to squirt oil or grease into small crevices; a child's battery-operated record player. "I think I can probably fix it," he said shyly. "I'll clean it up; then it can be yours."

"Neat, Daddy," I said as he loaded his finds into the back. We climbed into the cab. His own smell—that of the animals, whose stalls he mucked out with me and my brothers on weekends, of sweat, of male musk—was now masked by the powerful smell of garbage. His big shoes, which he had acquired back in the army, black, heavy, crushing boots, were now caked with sand, wet tea leaves and sometimes globs of more offensive gunk.

He was never much of a talker, was Dad, but sometimes when just the two of us were together he would speak. "I don't know why I ever became a women's doctor," he said. "Some of these women who come in to see me—my God, they have no more brains than animals! Eight or ten kids, no idea about birth control, overweight—I don't know how their husbands can bring themselves to touch them, but they keep getting pregnant. One girl came to see me, seventeen years old, six months along with her second child and this is the first time in her pregnancy she's come in to see me. Believe me, I get no joy out of discovering half the human race is subhuman. Sometimes I think the only reason I went into gynecology was because of my mother."

"Grandma?" I said.

"Mmm," he said. "She trained me to believe she was so weak and helpless that it was my duty to take care of all women. I would be in big trouble if you ever repeated this, Pamela—"

"I won't, Dad."

"But some of these girls who come in to see me want abortions, they don't have the money to go to England where it's legal, and occasionally— only once or twice, mind you—I do a D and C and write it up as endometriosis. They have no idea of their own anatomy, can't insert a diaphragm and can't remember whether or not they've taken their pills. One thing I would hope for you, Pamela, is that when you're ready to have sexual intercourse you'll be able to enjoy it. To take pleasure in your own body."

"Okay."

"When you're ready I'll personally provide you with birth control."

Oh, Daddy, how at one with each other we were then, the old truck rattling on the back roads, reeking of garbage—just you and me. But alas, the moment I reached puberty all this was to change, and, like my mother, I was abandoned. After that you had no more use for me, except the occasional casually flung words of contempt. You never liked my shoes, for example. And how often you warned me that for a person such as myself it would be a mistake ever to have kids. It was too bad my psychiatrist wasn't around to listen to any of this; what an epiphany I was having, although exactly what the epiphany was I couldn't be certain.

I must have been sitting there thinking my juvenile thoughts for quite some time. Martin's patient was well into his solitary Scrabble game. I got up and went to the women's room. Martin was standing at the sink, washing his hands. He looked up at my entrance and seemed disappointed that it was me. "Has he gone?" Martin said. "Has my patient gone yet?"

"No," I said. "Tell me, Martin, did you hear from Daniel today?"

"Daniel?" Martin said, turning off the faucet and delicately removing a piece of paper towel from the dispenser. It was apparent that he didn't want to touch the object itself. "No, I didn't. I'll give him a call later. We usually speak every day. Why? Is there something you wanted me to tell him?"

"Oh, no," I said. "I just wondered whether he was all right. Don't you usually see him at lunch?"

"I can't reveal that," Martin said, feverishly wiping his forehead with the towel. "Doctor-patient confidentiality. But you know, he's not very happy. Every day he comes to me and whines about one thing after the next. Sometimes I feel like slapping him; I mean, it's hard for me, when he's so rich, to listen to him complain. So his wife likes him to tie a paper bag over her head before he fucks her—what's the big deal? All he has to do is turn the lights out."

"I thought . . . they didn't have sex anymore," I said.

"Let me tell you something—I used to go out with Virginia, right after I met them. She called me up one day and invited me over to dinner. Naturally I assumed it was going to be a dinner party; I didn't know Daniel was out of town. It turned out I was the only guest! That's right, I was the dessert course. Well, it certainly brought out a side to my character that I hadn't known existed. And I found it wasn't entirely unpleasant. Say, Daniel tells me that the two of you are romantically involved? Or is that something I read in the paper?"

What low life the human race was composed of! I felt like taking Martin's head and plunging it into the toilet, but the way things were going he probably would have begged for more, and I wasn't certain that this was something I wanted. It was true he was single, but he was so self-absorbed. "No, there's no involvement between me and Daniel," I said. "We're just good friends."

"I don't know what to do about my patient," Martin said, beginning to wash his hands. "He's still out there?" It was remarkable how Martin always turned the conversation back to himself.

"Why does this bother you so much, Martin?" I said.

"Oh God, I don't know," he said. He snatched another piece of paper towel from the dispenser and wrapped it around the door handle before pulling open the door and peering out down the hall. "Yes! Yes! Damn! He's still there! Help me, Pamela!"

"It's no big deal if your patient sees you," I said. "Is it that you're afraid of embarrassing him by acknowledging in public that he's in therapy?"

"No!" Martin said. "It's because he's a nut case!"

"What's wrong with him?" This question was said perhaps a bit slyly on my part; if I had had more dignity as a human being I wouldn't have asked, because it was apparent that Martin was completely unable to prevent himself from telling everyone everything.

"His name's Moe; he was the heir to a lot of money, but his father remarried before his death and left everything to his new wife. Moe used to be very smart, but then a long time ago his wife was hit by a tractor-trailer on their honeymoon, and he was permanently brain damaged."

"But surely brain damage isn't a psychiatric problem?" I said.

Martin shrugged. "At first the stepfather and his mother sent him to all kinds of expensive clinics and institutionalized him. But then his family got tired of spending the money and they sent him to me. He's close to being cured, though." He looked hopefully at the door. "Can you believe it, not a single woman came in here all that time?"

"It's pretty empty out there," I said.

"Should we go back out there?" Martin said. "I'm afraid."

"The thing is, Martin, I should probably get going," I said. "My little boy is waiting for me at home."

"Oh, okay," he said with some relief.

"But I wonder, if you just have maybe five minutes, because I don't really have anybody to talk to, apart from my mother, and there's some problems I'm having in my life right now that there's probably specific things I could do to solve."

"Your mother?" Martin said. "Are you very close with your mother? How often do you speak to her?"

"I speak to her," I said.

"Excuse me for saying this," he said as we walked back to our table. He was hunched over with one arm up over his face. "But Jewish women are so wrapped up in their mothers. I'd never want to get involved with a Jewish woman. I can say that, because I'm Jewish, and as you know Jews are the most anti-Semitic."

"Just a question or two . . ." I said.

"Well, all right, but let's hurry and finish this up. I have a date, with a blonde I met at the clinic where I work one day a week. We meet secretly, it's a secret, because I don't want anybody at work to find out!"

"Does the fact that she's blond have some significance for you?" I said.

"Frankly speaking, yes. I'd pick a blonde over a brunette any day. She's English, and a nurse." He grinned creamily and licked his lips. It was odd, because even though everything about Martin offended me deeply, I was also fond of him. He reminded me of one of my own lowly relatives, perhaps a distant cousin whom I was meeting only now. Something about him made me feel genetically connected. This was all I had to hang on to in my life at present. My feelings of connection with the human race were so tenuous that to communicate with another person was impossible; but at least a feeling of familiarity was something.

"You know, in the old days people were close with their parents," I said. "They all lived near each other, there was a sense of family. Now women who speak to their mothers are considered sick."

Martin hunched over the table. "Ah, what do I know?" he said. "I'd like to order some onion rings, but I'm afraid of the kitchen. God knows what's back there: rat hairs, the cook jerking off into the fat fryer. My stomach is sensitive."

It pained me to meet a walking cliché. But perhaps I was a cliché in my own way. I suppose everyone is, really. "The thing is, Martin, let me just be brief."

He tapped the empty beer bottles impatiently. "Should I go get us some more beer?" he said. "It's three-fifty each." He stood at the moment his patient Moe also rose from his seat. Moe had wiry, thick red hair, a firm, bushy blond beard, and was dressed in the manner of a lumberjack or Yukon goldminer in 1890. "Hi there!" Martin said and, knocking his chair over on its side, scampered off to the bar.

Moe looked at Martin quizzically. He appeared to have something caught in his teeth. His tongue pushed out the side of his cheek. Then he reached back there with a finger. He kept staring at Martin over at the bar, but it was apparent, at least to me, that he had no idea who Martin was; he had merely been getting up to leave when a complete stranger waved and said hi. By the time Martin came back from the bar Moe had folded up his Scrabble set and silently stolen away. "Did he leave?" Martin said. "Did he say anything to you?"

It was remarkable how much my life had changed in the course of only a few weeks. Before, I knew so few people. Now, I knew so many. And wherever I went, it seemed, I met new ones. I remembered the woman I had met in the post office, the one who had given me a little package. What had become of that present? I had never gotten around to opening it. And what had become of the woman? It was sad that I hadn't seen her again; she was part of my life now, and I longed to know where she had gone. "Okay," Martin said, sliding a bottle of beer over to me. "Shoot."

"A few weeks ago a child followed me home," I said.

"Wait one second," he said. "Excuse me, but that's three-fifty each."

I fumbled in my pocket for the correct change. I knew Martin wasn't cheap, he was just broke. I had once had a girlfriend who accused me of being cheap, and it was a cruel statement I had never forgotten. Even now I occasionally thought of writing her a note (I hadn't seen her in years), to explain to her how poor I had been. It wasn't fair, for a person with a trust fund that was quickly spent on cocaine, to accuse someone who had no money of being tight with it. *I* would have liked a trust fund to spend on cocaine. My head felt hot and swollen, as if it had been put in a 350-degree oven. If I could just prick a little hole in the tender scalp and let some of the thoughts ooze out, thick and white as the innards of a roasted clove of garlic! . . . I supposed if a human head were actually to be roasted in an oven someone would have to trim the hairs from it first. The baked brains might then be scooped out and served on—toast? Or perhaps a bed of broad noodles. Oh, I had to stop this internal deranged muttering.

Martin was watching me with bright-eyed studiousness. "That's it," he said at last. "I'm afraid our time for today is up; I don't want my date to bump into you."

"For God's sake, Martin," I said. "I need some help with a concrete problem."

He took a folded piece of paper and a pen from his lapel pocket. "There'll be plenty of time for us to talk," he said. "But I think you should ask yourself why you waited so long into our session to bring up what's bothering you. Maybe you don't really want advice?"

I spluttered into the neck of my beer. "You—you're impossible!" I said.

He smiled wanly. "I've been working on this crossword puzzle," he said. "Is there a type of pudding known as pease?"

I thought for a moment. "Well, there's pease porridge," I said. "There's pease porridge, hot. There's pease porridge, cold. And there's *pease porridge in the pot, nine days old.*"

Martin scribbled frantically for several seconds. "It fits!" he said triumphantly. "It fits! Now, if you'll excuse me, I'm afraid I have my next appointment."

"Oh, sure," I said and waited for him to leave.

He tapped on the side of the bottle. "I'm afraid you'll have to go now."

"Oh!" I said, embarrassed. "I thought—when you said, 'if you'll excuse me'—that meant you were leaving."

"Move along," he said carefully. "I think perhaps you should come back tomorrow. It might be best if we were to see each other every day, at least while you're so obviously falling apart."

Oh, did I want to smack him! Move along, he said! It was a public bar, wasn't it? What was to stop me from simply sliding over to another table and waiting until his next patient, or his date, came in, and then eavesdropping and commenting aloud on the entire farcical procedure? But he would probably enjoy the attention and feel important if I insisted on pulling a scene. I got up to leave. "Another appointment with you won't be necessary," I said. "I can get the sort of help you offer just as well from my friends."

"Whatever you want," he said. "I don't need your sort of patient, you stupid woman. All day long I see alcoholic morons. I don't need to see them at night as well."

Surely his words were rather harsh, I thought, standing up with a bit of a stagger. But perhaps Martin felt close enough and comfortable enough with me that he was able to forego the customary distance between doctor and client. Still, the thing that really irked me, in addition to his insinuation that I was an alcoholic, was his statement earlier about how he preferred blondes to brunettes. It was the person who counted to me, not the hair color, or some other trivial attribute. Frankly speaking, I would take what I could get. Benjamin Franklin was not a shallow person, and it was he who first remarked that all cats were black in the dark, which enabled him to marry a wealthy widow twice his age, of a plain appearance.

I was about to point this out to him, as my parting words, when Amber came in, her arm in a cast and a sling, followed by a policeman. I guessed she had done something wrong; it was a bit unusual to be accompanied by a policeman, but she had him apparently so cowed he had agreed to come along with her to a bar before taking her off to jail or wherever. "Amber!" I said. "What are you doing here?"

"You have the keys to the offices," she said. "I've asked Officer Berlino to come with me to make sure you give them back."

"How did you know I was here?" I said.

"We went to your apartment," Amber said. "There was some little kid there." She looked at me accusingly. "I didn't know you had an illegitimate child, Pamela."

"Hey, there's no stigma attached to illegitimacy today," I said. Oh, what was I saying? Quickly I rummaged through my bag; it was true, I had inadvertently taken a set of the office-and-bathroom keys.

"It's some little kid she found on the street," Martin said with a helpful note of concern.

"You *found* him on the street?" Amber shrieked.

"Oh no, no, nonsense," I said, looking Officer Berlino in the eyes as I forcefully pushed the keys at her. "It's just—the child of my aunt, I mean, my younger brother, you know, the one who donates to sperm banks, that I'm baby-sitting for a while. I was telling Martin, earlier today I found him *playing ball on the street*—but I guess he wasn't really listening."

"He's such a cute little kid," Amber said in a more subdued tone. "A person like you shouldn't even be allowed to baby-sit, leaving him all alone in the house."

"You're right, you're right," I said, stepping past her and doing my best to avoid her crippled arm. "If you'll excuse me, I'll go and check on him now."

As I left the bar I could hear Amber's high-pitched voice, carrying clearly across the room, "Isn't there some sort of *law?*"

3

WHEN I GOT HOME ABDHUL HAD
fallen asleep on my bed. I didn't want to disturb him; shortly thereafter I
fell asleep, too, and woke a few hours later with the ringing of the phone.
It was only midnight, but too late for anyone to be calling; the answering
machine in the living room picked up, and with the volume turned down
I could barely hear the voice. "Pick up the phone! If you're there, pick up
the phone!"

If you expect me to answer you should at least identify yourself, I
thought, before falling asleep again. I didn't like being woken at midnight
to be commanded to do something, but a short time later someone began
to bang on the window, over and over, until it sounded momentarily as if
the glass were going to break. It was true there was a metal grille over the
window but it wasn't very sturdily fixed, in fact if someone wanted to break
in they could easily tear the grille from the wall, smash through the screen
(I had left it half-open), and climb in. Being a basement-size window, up
at ceiling level, it would be a tight squeeze for a burglar or murderer, but
entirely possible. Abdhul woke and began whimpering. "What's happening?" he said. "Who's out there? I'm scared."

"Don't worry," I said. "I'm going to call the police." I fumbled in the
dark for the phone and dialed 911. "Somebody's trying to break in," I said,
and gave the address. In fact, I had been burglarized one previous time,
which was how I acquired a number of my possessions. I was away at the
time; my upstairs neighbor called me at my mother's—I had left my number
with him in the event of an emergency—to tell me that the previous
evening both of our apartments had been broken into, and that my place
was such a shambles he couldn't tell the police what, if anything, had been

taken. He said that when he returned home that night the burglars had already been through his place, and he called the police, who surprised them in my apartment—they then ran out the back. To my great relief when I returned home everything was just as I had left it, apart from the fact that there was now a tape-cassette player and a variety of ethnic music tapes that had not previously been there—German marching music, Italian accordion tunes, and a Japanese boys' choir, to name but a few. My upstairs neighbor, Randy, denied ownership of these items, and though the next day I rang the police station to say that I had been burglarized and some things were left, the officer who had handled the case the night before said I might as well go ahead and keep the cassette player and the tapes, since nobody had reported any such items stolen. "You might as well have something, after what you went through," Officer Berlino said. "I've never seen such a disaster as when your neighbor let me into your place that night. They completely trashed the place! Looked like a tornado hit, the fucking bastards, excuse my language." I hung up without bothering to explain that, from what I could judge, not a single item had been touched or moved out of place.

I heard the wail of police sirens. A commotion was taking place outside. "Freeze!" and "Put your hands behind your back and lie down on the ground" shouted as if some aerobics class were being conducted. At last I got up and peeped out the front door and then shut it in alarm: The metal security door was open, pushed inward. Perhaps the burglar had picked the lock. There was a knock on the window. "Hello? Hello?" a voice said. "Anybody home?"

"Who's there?" I said.

"Police. You called us?"

"That's right," I said.

"I was trying to ring your doorbell but there was no answer."

"The doorbell's out of order," I said. "I put a sign up in the window to knock." There was a momentary silence. "Oh yeah, I see it," the voice said. "You want to come outside for a minute?"

"Is it safe?" I said.

"Yeah," the voice said. "Bailey's got the perpetrator over by the car."

"Just let me get a bathrobe," I said. I was wearing a pair of old sweatpants and a filthy T-shirt, acquired at the discount remainders store, that had come from Japan and was printed with the words LAYING MASH on one line and on the next FULL-O-PEP. I had enjoyed wearing this T-shirt very much for a time, since many people always stopped to ask me what it meant, but at last I had permanently ruined it while lying on the bed as I ate dinner and watched TV with only my head propped up, so that a quantity of indelible food had saturated the area on my chest surrounding the chin.

"What's happening?" Abdhul said sleepily from the bed.

"Nothing," I said. "They've caught the perpetrator, and I'm going to go out to meet him. You go back to sleep." I had a momentary anxiety attack—what if the burglar was Brenda, trying to recover Abdhul? Then the police might take him away until some King Solomon made a judgment, but with the modern legal system this could take years. I put on my bathrobe and slapped a little red lipstick on my mouth. I dreaded seeing the faces of the police officers and the assailant when they looked at me without makeup. If only I could have been one of those women who, bald-faced, looked luscious; but I had seen the shrunken face of shock all too many times when by chance the mailman caught sight of my tiny, unenhanced eyes, blotchy skin, dark circles, and fluffy mustache. A few layers of foundation and eyeliner did wonders, but in this case it seemed regrettable there was no time for lengthier preparations. I opened the front door. One of the policemen had Alby pinned up against the car. "He says he knows you," the cop said.

What would it take for this guy to learn his lesson, whatever that was? "I, uh—" I said. I didn't want to come out and lie outright and say that I didn't know him; on the other hand . . .

"Do you know this guy?" the cop asked.

"I'm her boyfriend!" Alby said. "Get rid of that lipstick; you know I hate that fucking shit!"

"I look better with makeup," I said. The policeman seemed baffled and released his grasp. "He's not my boyfriend."

"Yes, I am!" Alby said. He pointed beyond my shoulder. "Who's that?" he said. I looked down. Abdhul had gotten out of bed and now peeped around my waist. "That's, uh—" I said.

"I can't believe you would do this to me, Pamela!" Alby said.

"I hardly know this man," I told the police.

"I know everything about you!" Alby shouted. "Ask her where she got that kid!"

"It's, uh—he's staying with me, for the summer."

"He appeared out of nowhere!" Alby said. "I've been watching you, Pamela, and that's not your kid!"

The other policeman had been in the squad car, filing his report or whatever it was they did in there, and now he came over to the top of the staircase. "Whose kid is it?" he said with some interest, looking down.

"He's—" I said.

"I'm her sister's," Abdhul said helpfully.

"She doesn't have a sister!" Alby said. I wondered how he knew this. It was true that some time ago we had spent an evening together on what vaguely resembled a date; but it seemed impossible to believe that even if I had mentioned at that time that I had two brothers he might have been listening. "He's my brother's child," I said at last. "Abdhul is confused with kinship names." I looked down at him. "You see, Abdhul, my brother would be your father. His wife would not be my sister, but my sister-in-law. I would be your aunt. However, were I to marry, my husband would be your uncle. If we had children, they would be your first cousins. If your cousins had children, they would be your first cousins once-removed, or possibly your second cousins. If I had a daughter, and you wanted to marry your first cousin, I believe in most states this would be legal. But you might want to undergo genetic testing. Now—"

"So what do you want us to do with this guy?" the policeman said.

"Aw, gee, I don't know," I said. "What are my options?"

"He hasn't really done anything," the other cop said.

"Disturbed the peace?" I suggested.

"What peace?" the policeman said. Alby looked at me disgustedly.

"Take him away," I said. "Work him over!" I was tired of being victimized. Probably if it were not for Alby crashing my office I could have hung on to my job. What did he want from me, anyway? Once I had seen this woman on television complaining about an obscene phone call she had received, and due to the fact that she had been abused as a child she immediately ran out and bought recording devices and one of those machines that prints out the number where the obscene caller is dialing you from, and then she just waited for the obscene caller to phone her again, and when he did she encouraged him to keep calling her until she had enough evidence to go to the police and humiliate him. When I first saw this I thought the woman was a nut case, because if I ever got an obscene phone call I would just hang up, rather than encourage the guy to call again and use expensive equipment on him. But now I understood how a person could be pushed too far, and eventually she would just snap and get tired of being a victim. Let somebody else feel like a jerk for a change, was my feeling.

The two cops stood looking uncomfortable. "Hey, I think my softball team played you guys a couple of weeks ago," Alby said.

"Yeah," the short one said. "I thought I recognized you. Third base? Two weeks ago, in the park, right? You play with the Turds?"

"The Turks," Alby muttered.

"We beat those guys, eight to two," the cop said proudly. "All right, all right, what do you want us to do with him?" he asked me uneasily.

"Injure him," I said.

"Just cool out," the other policeman said. "We'll take him away and get him a cup of coffee. You go back to sleep." It was obvious I was not appeased. "You going to come back here and bother her again, Al?" the other policeman asked him, grinning smirkily.

"I'm not coming back here!" Alby said in a hurt tone of voice. The three of them got into the squad car and drove off with happy expressions, the policeman in the passenger seat waving good-bye. "Come on," I said to Abdhul, who was still looking worried. "Let's go back to bed."

It took me hours to fall asleep. Of course I was in the wrong. I had done nothing to try to find out who Abdhul belonged to. Now I was going to be punished, probably publicly. It was awful, not being able to sleep. To have to simply lie in bed, trying to get someplace, like waiting for a train that had been derailed en route. Normally I had no trouble falling asleep. Indeed, falling asleep was one of the things I did best. I had only to lie down when my eyes would close and a blissful pea-green wave would wash over me, the pleasant in-between state, and that was generally the last thing I knew until I woke up, when I always felt worse than before. Yet something wonderful must have been happening while I slept, else why would I be so eager to re-create the experience? Dim memories occasionally floated back to me—my dreams—of waiting on line to use a filthy women's room, usually in a gas station, where there was no toilet paper and the plumbing was out of order, or sometimes where the doors were broken or the stalls so tiny one could barely squeeze inside. And other dreams—shopping for groceries, buying antiques at a very cheap price and finding after leaving the store that they were all broken. Sometimes I took tedious trips in a car, in my dreams, through dismal landscapes of stunted vegetation. My dream-life had the same remarkable qualities as reality. But now there was no trick I could play on myself to drift off. Perhaps, first thing in the morning, I should drag Abdhul down to the police station and deposit him there, without so much as a final good-bye.

I had barely dozed off when the phone rang and it was morning. "Hi," my mother said, "I'm sorry to bother you at home."

"That's all right," I said. "It's the only time I'm here. What's wrong? You sound weird."

"Why are you still at home?" my mother said. "Did you take the day off from work?"

"I was fired," I said. I looked over at the clock. It was already ten thirty. Abdhul wasn't in the bed; usually he got up before me and made himself a bowl of Frosty Flakes or one of the other hideous breakfast cereals he was partial to. "Listen," my mother said, "this is an emergency. I think I finally killed your father, and possibly Angela as well."

"What did you do?" I said.

"I've been conducting a series of psychic experiments to ensure their demise," my mother said.

"But what was the specific reason for wanting them dead, apart from the fact that Dad stopped sending you the hundred dollars a month alimony, although he agreed to do so for the rest of your life?"

"He kept the house; he hardly paid any money or child support, but at the time of the divorce that was part of the agreement, that he would keep giving me the money. Then he abruptly announced he wouldn't do so any longer, because he was retired. Naturally this irked me, because I, too, would like to retire—we're the same age, after all—and he has plenty of money, yes, plenty. Over the years he's managed to amass a small fortune. I suggested, in a letter, that if he wished to stop paying me this sum I would like some assurance that when he dies his money will be left to you and Ralph and Mitchell. I didn't want to tell you this before—you know I don't like to say anything against him—but he wrote back and said naturally his estate will go to his children, in the event of Angela's death. In other words, he's leaving everything to Angela."

"But Angela's only five years older than me," I pointed out. "It seems unlikely she'll die before me, and even if she does, once Dad dies there's nothing to stop her from remarrying and writing out her own will leaving the money to whoever she wants."

"Exactly," my mother said. "What kind of father wouldn't want his own kids to inherit his money?"

"Of course, a lot of his money is Angela's," I said.

"Plenty of it is his own," she said. In the end my father's license to practice medicine had only been temporarily revoked, and after it was reinstated, due to the publicity, his practice grew larger than ever. Even though he and Angela lived out in the back woods of Maine, and he had sold the heavily mortgaged clinic, he had still been able to open a small office in the moldy basement of their home, and many women drove for hours from Boston and even flew up from New York in order for my father to treat them for infertility, using local herbs and those imported from Indonesia or some Asian locale—he had a system worked out with a witchdoctor or homeopathic doctor over there, and the women would be photographed and a copy sent to this person. Six weeks later a variety of weeds would arrive which he would make into pills or stuff in teabags, and give to the patient. She was supposed to drink the tea and use the suppositories, and quite often, amazingly enough, the end result was a pregnancy, although I had my suspicions as to how this was accomplished.

Reports came via my brothers that Dad had found an old stone quarry on the property (it consisted of nearly five hundred acres of swampland, in addition to the pastures for the horses that Angela raised) and spent all of his days on his tractor, dragging slabs of stone over to a meadow where he was constructing a pyramid in the center of a Stonehenge-like arrangement of rock to celebrate the vernal equinox. Perhaps my mother, using her psychic concentration, had contrived to have these stones topple over and crush him? Dad had had his near-death experiences before now. Attempting to dismantle a beaver dam (beavers swarmed the property, fabricating dams and gnawing down trees, so that each year the swamp area grew by many acres) using scuba-diving gear, only a couple of years back, he had become stuck under a massive log just at the moment the dam burst and he ran out of air. Luckily the force of the water was so great he was pushed free and washed downstream nearly a mile, ending up in the state park reservoir below. The state sued him for fifty thousand dollars (it was illegal to interfere with waterways in Maine), but luckily his insurance company settled out of court. Most of the swamp on Dad's property was only five or ten feet deep, but there was an area where—on what was once a little valley—the water was as deep as seventy feet. Here, many years ago, a small town had been flooded, and the old ruins of four or five houses still remained. It was while exploring these shambles in search of buried gold or other valuables under the floorboards that my father came down with a bad case of giardia, acquired from swallowing water contaminated by the feces of beavers, although how he knew that it was on this site that he got sick I never really understood. "Tell me," I asked my mother, "what makes you think anybody's dead?"

"Because nobody's heard from him in weeks," she said. "Usually he calls Ralph and Mitchell every weekend. Finally Mitchell got worried and called him; but there was no answer. And both boys say your father and Angela had no plans to take any trips. As long as you don't have a job anymore, I think you better go out there and find out what's happened. Rent a car. Or else you and Abdhul fly up there and rent a car at that end. My only hope is, that if he's dead, she is too, or else there's no point to the entire business."

The last time my dad had been in the hospital—he fell off a ferryboat and broke his leg, although at the time he thought he had had a heart attack—Angela had not even bothered to call any of us. It was entirely possible that if he had keeled over now, she had simply buried him and taken off on a worldwide tour without notifying his immediate family. Still, I wouldn't have been concerned, except for the fact that my mother did have a tiny bit of psychic ability, and if she felt something was wrong, there was a slight probability she was correct. "Even if you wished and experimented for his death, Ma, I really don't think you should feel responsible," I said.

"Well, I do feel bad," she said. "After all, Mitchell and Ralph do love him. I feel like I can't go on living with myself. All my life, I thought that when I got older, I would stop making embarrassing mistakes. Now I'm fifty years old, and I'm still stuck with my idiotic behavior. How much longer do I have to go on living with this person? What can I do to get rid of her?"

I laughed merrily. "How wise you are," I said.

"It seems you can either shut yourself up and never see anybody or speak to anybody, which is what I've done," she said. "Or else you can go out and play the game in society's terms, which is basically trying to accumulate more and more material objects, in order that other people can admire you and wish they had the things. But all these people who are out there accumulating—what's the point? Whether they have a lot of things or nothing, they're all going to die. It's like when you and Ralph and Mitchell went to help Grandma Vi move to Florida, and she said you could have the things that she wasn't going to take with her, but every time you said you liked something, she said she was going to bring that with her and that she wanted to keep it. So by the end, when she was ready to move, she was stuck with all the stuff—crowded into one room, with a lot of things she didn't want, and nobody else wanted either! Things are only good as long as somebody wants them. But the only reason somebody wants them, is if somebody else wants them. By the way, why were you fired?"

"I was politically shanghaied," I said. The day before, when I told her I needed health insurance, I hadn't bothered to explain that this was due to the fact I had been fired; I simply said I no longer had any coverage. Normally I blurted out the most intimate details of my daily existence, but as I had been running out the door to see my psychiatrist, I didn't have time. "The thing is, I don't feel that bad about being fired, although I did feel bad that Daniel Loomis refused to do anything to defend or assist me. It changed my feelings toward him, that and the fact that I thought his feelings toward me were sincere, when in fact it transpired that he and his wife like to have affairs as a sort of competition. But now I'm worried about how I'm going to support myself and Abdhul."

"You can both come up here and live in the spare bedroom," my mother said.

"That wouldn't be my first choice, as a mature woman," I said.

"But I'm not sure, in any event, that's the best move for you right now. Have people been coming around questioning you about where you got him?"

"Yes!" I said. "Two times, yesterday."

"Then I think, if you want to keep him, you better get out of there. I have a feeling somebody's going to come and take him away. First go and find out if your father's dead, and if so, dispose of the body. Then contact me, from a pay phone, and I'll give you your next instructions."

"And my apartment?" I said.

"Abandon it. I believe it to be a harbinger of evil."

Ah, modern lunacy! But I always did what my mother said. I never believed there was any other choice. I went down the street, took my savings out of the bank, and then, using a credit card (although I knew that through its use it was possible I might be traced, but they insisted on a credit card I guess in case I decided to steal the car) I went to a Rent-A-Wreck rental agency and rented a subcompact car.

It didn't seem fair that I had to drive twelve or fourteen hours up to Maine with a screaming, bored, and whining child. Why couldn't Mitchell or Ralph go? But Mitchell was in medical school in California and Ralph was managing a chain of restaurants in Arizona and couldn't leave work. I suppose if I had been thinking more clearly I might have managed to track down the nearest neighbor—or called the local police up there—but I was not thinking clearly. Abandon ship! For I saw now all too clearly that my mother was right. They were closing in on me: Abdhul would be taken from me, I would be jailed on a variety of counts, and something was so terribly wrong with this apartment that it seemed incredible that I had inhabited it for all this time. There was no time to lose. Already in my absence—I had instructed Abdhul not to answer the phone—the messages were piling up, from Daniel, from Bronc, from Martin, from Amber and even Debbie. Something was clearly wrong, that all these people would bother to call me. Quickly I dialed the telephone company and arranged for a disconnection; the final bill, I said, should be sent to my mother, and I gave her address. Con Edison, the same. I did not know whether to call the landlord, or simply let him keep the deposit after it became apparent that he would receive no more rent and I was gone for good. And then, what possessions to take? There was no time to pack and ship things—in any event, my mother's apartment was too small to sustain any more possessions. Well, what did I have of any value? A tiny TV set—I could unplug it at the last minute and fling it in the car trunk—a few books, old tax returns, piles of shabby clothing, some cooking utensils . . . oh, there were plenty of objects in the place, that much was certain, but scarcely a thing I might have wanted to own. It was true that I would only have to run out and buy the same flimsy items again, were I ever to settle down; but I would face that later. Irrefutable refuse! In my panic I hastily tossed stuff into one of the many empty cardboard boxes I seemed to have acquired and kept in the closet. Then I found an outfit I had long since forgotten. It was a dress resembling a ballerina's tutu, for a grown woman, but quite minute in size, with a stretchy tube top and layers of pink tulle studded with sparkles. I was beginning to hatch a plan; but just then some foreign body—an eyelash, a flake of skin long ago deposited on some dusty shelf—fell into my eye, and midway between tossing objects around (for now I found several old and queer-smelling suitcases, which would no doubt be useful) I ran into the bathroom, still carrying the tutu, and tore at my eye. "What's going on?" Abdhul said, following me. He looked at me quizzically, with a certain mature air, as if I had taken leave of my senses, which it appeared I had. "We're leaving," I said, and thrust the tutu at him. "Put this on."

"I'm not going to wear that," he said. "That's for girls."

"You need a disguise," I said. "People are after us. Whoever is looking for you is looking for a boy. They'll never suspect a ballerina."

"You never tell me what's going on," he whined. "Why don't you ever tell me?"

"You never listen to me," I said. "You're too busy watching TV. Get into the dress and grab a suitcase and pack your things." A sudden attack of bilharzia or some other liverish ailment swept over me, and I bent over the toilet, but no upchuck was forthcoming, although I wouldn't have been surprised under such circumstances to have been infested with some weirdly tropical ailment. The gelatinous pâté that inhabited the bathroom floor came and went with changes in the weather; after the initial sighting it had disappeared, only to rejuvenate some days later, and this despite my attempts to render the floor uninhabitable by pouring quantities of rubbing alcohol and bleach over the tiled surface. But apparently after a rainstorm the base of the toilet had a tendency to leak, and on whatever microbes were in the sewage the gelatin rebirthed itself and fed upon. Schistosomiasis? For I never remembered to wear slippers in the house, and thus Abdhul and I puddled through E. coli and virulent bacteria strains deposited in the toilets of others, that regurgitated onto our floor. It was a miracle that more cases of cholera, typhus, and bubonic plague were not hatched in New York every day; hepatitis too. Perhaps the Board of Health was aware of this but conspired to keep it a secret?

The foreign body was out of my eye and I turned. Abdhul had positioned himself by the bathroom door; thank God he had slipped into the tutu. He gave a little pirouette. "How do I look?" he said.

"You look gorgeous," I said. "But you still look like a boy. Isn't there something we could use for a wig? Go look and I'll tell you what's going on." He disappeared into the closet and I went to the kitchen. It seemed a shame to waste the cans of foodstuff and products in the refrigerator. Six ice cream bars, enrobed in chocolate @ $1.95 apiece—these would have to be left behind, to dwindle in the shortly-to-be-disconnected freezer. A can of glossy lychee nuts—I slung them into a box. Stale pretzels, a jar of Spanish capers, a packet of Melba toast, a bag of red lentils, a small, elderly canned ham—I would like to say that only a woman would include such items when attempting to flee in haste for reasons that would later become clear, but this would be wrong of me. Perhaps a few men would run to the cupboards, perhaps not all women— or perhaps anyone who had been brought up poor. In the back of one cabinet I found a small jar of Vegemite, a yeast extract. Where had it appeared from? I had never purchased spreadable yeast extract in my life. Had it materialized from the spirit plane? Oh, there were wonders in the world to behold.

Abdhul came into the room wearing an elderly straw hat topped with cherries and ivy. "Where did you find that?" I said. In all likelihood it was a present from Grandma Vi; from time to time she sent me a box of thrift-store finds. Some of these would have been very nice, except for her ministrations: she had the habit of discovering antique clothes, such as a beaded cashmere sweater, and then washing them in the washing machine so that they shrank. "You look lovely," I said.

"Oh, come on," Abdhul said, snorting.

"You remind me of my brothers. They always snorted in just the same way." If only he had been a little girl; then he might have been somebody I could be friends with. Still, he was awfully good at packing, and the stuff I had already thrown into the suitcases and cartons he took out and reorganized, rolling his eyes at my inability to be compact.

"You're right," I said. "The hat's a bit silly. I wonder if Randy upstairs has a wig we could borrow?" I ran out the door. Luckily Randy was home. "Listen, Randy, do you have a wig I could borrow?"

"What?" Randy said. "A wig? Oh yeah, yeah sure." He disappeared and returned a moment later with a long almost platinum-blond fall.

"Thanks a lot!" I said and dashed out with it under my arms. What a shame it was so blond; it wasn't my first choice of hair color for Abdhul. But I ran back in, took off his hat, and put the wig on his head.

"My Dad lives sixteen miles down dirt roads in the middle of the country. You'll like the country, Abdhul. Hiking, swimming, canoeing, hauling brush, weeding the garden, plucking vegetables, chopping and cleaning, sponging the kitchen sink—"

"Are you taking *this?*" he said, holding up an open bag of scabrous prunes.

"Dried fruit," I said. "Quick energy, nutritious and natural."

"Yuck," he said. I found a small canister of bug repellent. "This, we'll definitely need," I said. "You know, they took this stuff off the market just recently. This can is the last of its kind. I couldn't believe it, when I read they weren't making it anymore! I used this my entire childhood."

"Maybe that's what's wrong with you," Abdhul said. A healthy, organized home life had certainly gone to his head quite quickly. I might not point out just yet that what we were likely to find in Maine was a couple of ripe cadavers, but I would certainly keep that information up my sleeve for somewhere en route when he grew cranky. That morbid piece of news would probably buy me a couple hours peace while he mulled it over in his male mind. My experience might be limited, but I knew what boys liked. By now bags and boxes were stacked by the front door and I got ready to carry them out to the car. "This is your last chance," I said. "Do you want me to take you to the police station, in the hopes that they can track down your real family or send you into foster care? Or do you want to stick with me, with very little chance of a real future?"

"Oh, for Christ's sake," he snarled. "Let's go already if we're going."

That was as much reassurance as I was likely to get. This was it, then; I picked up a suitcase and was just heading out to the double-parked rented wreck (actually it didn't seem so bad, although there was a distinct doggy perfume to the interior) when the telephone rang. I had already unplugged the answering machine, but the phone would not be officially turned off until late today or the next. Should I bother to answer it? It was probably some lunatic—maybe the one out to get Abdhul. The phone rang and rang while I stood transfixed. Eggshell blue, lemon-curd yellow—a bit of fabric from some mangy dress I had yanked out of the closet was draped over the chair. I picked up the phone. "You haven't left yet?" Thank God, it was my mother.

"Abdhul's in disguise," I said, my eyes following him as he grabbed the car keys and carried one of the suitcases out the door. "He really looks adorable."

"What sort of disguise?" my mother said.

"Ballerina tutu," I said. Abdhul came back in. "Hold on a second," I said.

"There's a woman out there," he said.

"So?" I said.

"She said she was looking for you."

"Who was she?" I hissed. "Was it Amber?"

"I don't know," he said. "Why are you acting so weird?"

"What did you tell her?" I said.

"I told her you were going out of town, and that she should come back another time."

"Geez, Ma, there's a woman out there, looking for me," I said.

"Who was she?" my mother said.

*"I don't know!"* I said. "Abdhul, what should we do? What should we do?"

Abdhul shrugged. "Maybe she's from the social services department," he said.

"Oh my God," I said. In my study of the subject I had read that the city social workers went to the houses of people who had foster children and looked in their refrigerators, in order to decide if children should be returned to their real homes. There was nothing I wanted to see less than a social worker, not the way my refrigerator looked. There was no form of life on earth lower than a social worker, accepting low pay in order to go out into the world in order to do good deeds.

"Is she still out there?" I said to Abdhul.

"How should I know?" he said. "Could I have some lipstick?" He tossed his blond hair over his shoulder. "You're wearing a disguise, you're not supposed to be in drag," I said.

"Turn off the lights and talk quietly," my mother suggested on the other end. "Why haven't you left yet?"

"Because I had to go and rent a car and we were just carrying the stuff out when you called!" I snapped. "What's up? Did anybody get ahold of Dad and Angela?"

"I dialed their number, thinking if they did answer I could just hang up—at around six this morning—but there was no answer."

"Are we going to get a dog?" Abdhul suddenly shrieked. "You said we could get a dog."

"Not right this second," I said, trying to listen to my mother at the same time.

"I'm just going to tell you one thing, quickly," my mother said.

"You said we could get a dog!" Abdhul yelled.

"Carry the stuff out to the car!" I snapped. "If that woman comes near you, start screaming."

"What should I scream?" he said.

"Child abuse," I said.

"You always make me do everything," he said. "I'm not your slave. I'm not the servant."

"Yes, you are," I said.

"Women have always been willing to trade their souls for one night's good sex and the hope of being supported," my mother said.

"Why are you telling me this now?" I said.

"Because it's going to be up to you to change the way things are," she said.

"I'm trying to flee!" I said.

"But men aren't going to support women," she went on. "Men are not evolved. I haven't mentioned this to you before, but there's only three things men are good at. Some of them are good in bed, some are brave . . . and I forget the third. Men are not intelligent, Pamela. Women are going to be number one. We're not going to be victims anymore. Men are given one-hundred-point starts, just simply because they're men." Something was tapping on the window.

"Ma, it's too late!" I said. "The women's movement failed miserably! There's no status for women; they're back to writing moronic articles for the Sunday *Times* about being carried off on a white horse."

"It's not too late!" she said. "You can be in the vanguard, and you can teach others!"

The tapping continued. In a panic I hung up the phone. Luckily it was only Abdhul, who had locked himself out. "She's not there anymore, if you're worried," he said with a flounce as he threw himself onto the sofa. I took one last look around. It seemed a shame to abandon so many material possessions and leave the place in such a mess; but that was how things worked in Manhattan. Almost once a week on the block somebody died and then the landlord—or the relatives—came and threw out an entire lifetime of accumulation. If only they had been able to work out a way so you could take it with you! Before I shut the door for the last time I quickly called back my mother. "I'm sorry I had to hang up," I said. "I thought there was somebody at the door."

"Remember when I got you a scholarship to that school for mentally disturbed children but you refused to go?" she said.

"No, I don't!" I said. Without my mother there was no one I would be connected with in the entire world, yet why did she irritate me so?

"You don't remember that?" she said.

"Maybe vaguely," I admitted. "A bunch of spoiled rich kids. I never would have fit in."

"Remember when the neighbors came over and they were drunk and wearing Halloween costumes and trick-or-treating and you got so angry?" she said.

"Who?" I said. "Where?"

"You don't remember? Troy and Vicki Bridges?"

"Troy and Vicki Bridges came over drunk and wearing Halloween costumes?" I said. "Why would this make me angry?"

"Because you said they were too old to go trick-or-treating," my mother said.

"Vaguely," I said, although in fact I had no memory of this. When I was around fifteen and Ralph and Mitchell went to live with my dad for six months, my mother took a position house-sitting for a couple who joined the Peace Corps, in return for free rent for the two of us. This episode had ended in disaster; the two sons of the couple (they were in their fifties and it had always been their dream to join the Peace Corps, so they waited until the boys were in college) had returned home abruptly, having dropped out of school in their parents' absence, with a collection of pistols and rifles, and my mother and I were forced to leave. Troy and Vicki Bridges—it dimly came back to me—were the next-door neighbors, and the master of the house had been having an affair with Vicki for some twenty years. . . . How much I had blocked from my mind! It was incredible, the whole huge chunks of my history that were missing from my brain. Was it something in the water that caused me to forget? "You know, I'd like to give a dinner party," my mother said. "But I can't think of what to make; every time I try to think of what I should prepare, I feel so overwhelmed it just makes me want to forget the whole idea."

"I've lost my job and I'm kidnapping a child to go and find out if my father and his wife are dead or alive, and you're wondering what to serve at a dinner party?" I said.

"Speaking of the Bridges, I remember when we were living next door to them and I made the moussaka, and when we came back half of it was gone and you accused Vicki Bridges of sneaking in and eating it," she said.

"Who ate the moussaka?" I said.

"Don't you remember? It was the dog."

"Mmm," I said. "I do remember. It was so neatly divided in half, it looked like it had been sliced. I couldn't believe a dog could make such a neat edge."

"But what kind of thing is that, to accuse the neighbor?" she said. "You see, Pamela, you've always had a mind of your own; and I've always encouraged you. Somewhere along the line you lost it, though, that courage—and now it's up to you to regain it."

"Either you're insane and I'm normal, or I'm insane," I said.

"Ah, what difference does it make?" my mother said. "It's all up to you. Good-bye, and good luck."

Once entirely farmland, and before that forest, New England is now made up of nothing but endless highways. Where there are not highways there are houses, and shopping malls, and fast-food restaurants, but little else remains. The area outside of Manhattan is surrounded by gray skies, industrial developments, a few miserable representative trees; perhaps because I was not looking at a map, it took us nearly three hours to reach the city outskirts known as White Plains. Something had gone terribly wrong in the civilization of this country. The cars were bumper to bumper, going nowhere.

Maybe my father had the right idea when he moved to the middle of nowhere and resolved never to see or speak to another human being. But even though I was fed up with humanity, I couldn't really see myself living in complete isolation. Anyway, according to my mother, my father had chosen to remove himself from civilization only because he was a genetic throwback. This had dawned on her after watching a TV show about a group of primitive Russian peasants living in Georgia. They liked to crush grapes, make cheese, and eat potatoes. Each had a job, such as hammering or sawing. It was from such stock my father's ancestors derived.

Take this genetic measure of hearty peasant broth alone, and I would not be the person I was no doubt destined to become. But luckily, on the other side, my mother came from a far more refined and rafinée pool, the great-great-granddaughter of Austrian meat-grinders and butchers; along with this was some blood of a Chinese Jewish person, for indeed some time ago a number of Jewish people got lost and settled down in an area where plenty of Chinese take-out such as Peking duck was available. Of course, as my mother pointed out, originally everybody on the planet came from Africa, but I was pleased with my magical ancestral blend, melding as it did the hearty with the delicate. As I believe I have mentioned previously, my grandfather on my mother's side worked for the Bureau of Motor Vehicles and on the other my grandfather, now long since deceased, was a Communist who had owned and operated his own business, that of selling postage stamps at a substantial markup in various machines located in the remote wilds of Clifton, Passaic, and Rutherford, New Jersey. I tried to amuse Abdhul with some of my interesting history as we drove; this would be helpful if ever he were forced to prove he had come from my blood. "It's sad that you never got to meet Grandpa Irving," I said. "But it's probably for the best that he's no longer with us. The downfall of communism would have killed him."

"Where are we going?" Abdhul whined. "How much longer till we get there?"

"Have you been listening to what I've been saying?" I said, glancing away from the road to look at him. One of his fingers was probing the interior region of his nose. "Straighten your wig. And don't pick your nose, at least not in public."

"How come?" he said.

"It's just one of those things," I said. "It's disgusting."

"But lots of people do it," he said.

"But we don't do it," I said. "We're not that sort of people. Now, repeat what I've just told you."

"We don't pick our nose, at least not in public," he said.

"No, not that," I said. "Repeat my ancestral past and make it sound like yours."

"My mother was probably some kind of crack addick," he said in a monotone.

We were in the right lane of the highway and I almost swerved into a particularly nasty metal guardrail, fabricated at the taxpayer's expense, I was so startled to hear him say anything about his past. Out of the corner of my eye I saw what appeared to be a big human head, protruding halfway out of a garbage bag, deposited on the shoulder but there was no way I could stop without causing an accident, and I wasn't sure I wanted to.

Maybe it was just an old cantaloupe; but a half-mile farther on I saw what seemed to be a dismembered human hand. The grim highways of America were repositories for all sorts of foul discards; even though there were signs up saying it was illegal to dump refuse from the car windows, or leave things in trash receptacles at the few hideous rest stops, nobody paid any attention to this. After all, stuff had to be dumped somewhere, and in this country it made no difference where anything was dropped, it all ended up in the highways, or in the oceans, or buried halfheartedly in leaky landfills. Only recently some jerk had attempted to cross an eight-lane highway, been hit by a car, and spent four days semiconscious in the center divide, feebly trying to wave down a motorist; it took four days before anybody did anything. "What makes you say that?" I said.

He opened the glove compartment and was apparently inserting or storing the toys he had taken along at the last minute: a switchblade (he had cajoled this from me after seeing it in some store and asking for it every day for two weeks) that with the press of a button flicked open into a natty comb; a small cubelike device that had several switches which when pressed made various bomblike sounds; and an LCD wristwatch too large for his wrist, that in addition to telling the time supplied the temperature, could be used underwater, and had three different electronic games. "What makes me say what?" Abdhul said.

"Why did you say your mother was a crack addict?" I said. "Ad*dict*. Ad*dict*."

He fiddled with the radio and at last found a particularly unpleasant screaming deejay, who was screeching in a neo-Nazi voice about action-packed stock-car racing taking place that night in New Hampshire. "Did you ever hear of fetal alcohol syndrome?" he said quietly.

"Yes," I said.

"The six of us used to live in one room at the Martinique Hotel," he said. "And Brenda used to drink a lot."

"But that doesn't mean she was drinking while she was pregnant with you, or whoever your mother was," I pointed out. He shrugged and switched stations. "Is your seatbelt fastened?" I said. He certainly was unfathomable. "What about your brothers?" I said. "Do you ever miss them?" There was no use my trying to question him. He reminded me of *my* brothers, who lapsed into silence whenever my mother tried to quiz them about any thoughts they might have. I used to think it was malicious stubbornness on their part, until I learned it was simply due to the fact that they were male. "What about my puppy?" Abdhul said. "You said we were going to get one."

"I'm trying to drive now," I said. "Are you happier being with me? Or would you rather go back to your old life?" I wasn't trying to threaten him, but it was a pitiful thing that I needed reassurance from a nine-year-old, or whatever his age was. "What about that woman who was looking for me?" I said, when it was obvious once again he wasn't going to respond. "Who was she? Was she still outside when you went back out to the car?"

"She said you had her package," Abdhul said.

"What?" I said. "What package? Where was she from?"

"She said she was from the city."

"From what part of the city?" I said.

"I don't know," he said, as if I was the stupidest person he had ever met. "I didn't ask her where she lived."

"But was she from social services? Or the tax office? Why would she think I had a package of hers?"

"I don't know," he said. "All I know is, you wanted to leave, so I got rid of her."

"But she thought you were a girl, right?" I said. A pop singer was now crooning lyrics I could barely determine, either, "I don't know what it is to choose," or, "I don't know what titties to choose,"—probably the latter. "Listen," I said. "Why is it that half the time you don't answer me? I'm waiting and waiting for your answer, and you just ignore me like I'm beneath contempt."

He seemed surprised. "I don't know," he said at last. "Maybe I'm not listening. I'm hungry, Esmerelda." Where this Esmerelda business came from all of a sudden I didn't know, but somehow I was touched. That he had a pet name for me—even a temporary one—must have been a sign of love. Perhaps it was best, if some social worker was in fact looking for me and him, that we didn't call each other by our correct names. "You think of a new name for yourself, too," I said. "And keep your eyes out for some place we can stop and get lunch. I could use a cup of coffee."

"Okay," he said. "Did you see the head back there on the road?"

Now it was my turn not to answer. "What do you mean?" I said after a pause.

"What's that on the road? Ahead?" he said and laughed uproariously.

"I saw it," I said. "The old cantaloupe, you mean."

"No, it was a head," he said. "And there was a hand, too. Hey, get off at the next exit. There's Wendy's, McDonald's, Roy Rogers, and Burger King—ahead." What a morbid child he truly was. I pulled off the exit ramp and we drove nearly five miles back in the direction we had come from before finding the little group of fast-food outlets; the highway, a four-lane affair here, destined for local travel and containing stoplights every few hundred yards, climbed sharply up a hill, and there in the decline, a half mile away, was the collection of restaurants, nestled together like lice behind an ear. "Something in this car sure stinks," was Abdhul's only remark in the way of thanks. Maybe the jar of Vegemite had broken in the trunk.

Everyone on the planet is by now familiar with the prestigious interior of Roy Rogers—formerly a star of stage and screen, now best loved for his dollhouse-like restaurant chain decorated with plastic chairs and tables, replete with "free fixin's" bar and specializing in limbs of fried chicken. I ordered a chef salad and Abdhul went for the cheeseburger. A curl of roasted beef lay feebly atop a mound of lettuce shreddies; over this I doused a gluey white liquid from a packet marked BLUE CHEESE DRESSING. Abdhul pumped vast quantities of sugary red ketchup over his cheeseburger before taking the seat across from me. "Maybe Abdhul isn't even your real name," I said. "Maybe if you think hard, your original name will come back to you." He swiveled back and forth in his seat while he ate. "I wanted to go to Burger King," he said. "You can win a million dollars instantly, and a part in a Hollywood movie."

"You should have said something earlier," I said. "I happen to like Roy Rogers because they serve a roast beef sandwich here, and so they put a real slice of roast beef in the chef's salad, whereas at McDonald's you just get packaged strips of roast beef."

"What about Burger King?" he said.

"I don't know," I said. "Actually, I haven't tried their chef salad."

"See?" he said triumphantly. Ketchup was smeared around his mouth His eyes were wild and yellowish. His wig was standing on end and strands were stuck together where they had dangled in hamburger juice. Little snot-face! I was overcome with a sudden blister of love, watching him put his legs up on the seat and swivel like some deranged water bird. He was going to be handsome when he grew up, that much was certain. And I didn't think he had fetal alcohol syndrome, or that his mother had smoked crack—maybe he was a trifle hyperactive, although I had nothing to compare his behavior with, it seemed likely that all small boys had his energy. If anything it was a good sign. What if he were suddenly to choke on a bit of bread or meat, bouncing back and forth like that while eating? I would do anything to save him, although it would be awful if I had to perform an emergency tracheotomy. "Sit still while you eat," I said. "You could choke."

This remark seemed to appeal to him. "Heimlich maneuver!" he shouted suddenly. Luckily the restaurant was practically empty, but the biscuit-faced Roy Rogers food-service gal looked over in our direction with torporous interest. What a miserable and futile profession! Even if it was only her job during summer vacation from school, I could think of nothing more grim. Why not simply sign up for a term in prison? Yet, even dressed in her drab brown chickenish uniform, a masterpiece of humiliating design, she was attractive in that way so coveted and desired in the United States. The expressionless face, nearly featureless, that blank, stupidly milky look in her blue eyes, her blond, frazzled hair, carefully coiffed in the flip fashion of television commercials—no foreigner would have given her a second look, but here in Connecticut I bet she was the most desirable of female commodities. No doubt she prayed nightly that some important male customer would come into Roy Rogers and take her • away—perhaps a rock star, or a photographer for *Penthouse* magazine—or that the crew of a movie shooting locally would stumble in and sweep her in front of the cameras. And perhaps something of the sort would happen, so pleased with herself did she look. Those were the women who got ahead, the ones who seemed immensely self-satisfied and in love with themselves. I wanted to go over to her and shake her out of her platitude—she must be made to understand that she was nothing more than a Roy Rogers server, after all—but meanwhile Abdhul had jumped up and was demonstrating how he would practice the Heimlich maneuver on himself in the event that he were to choke and no one were there to help him. "I'll practice the Heimlich manuever on you, don't worry," I muttered. I got up and went to the bathroom while he was leap-frogging around. Nasty little cupboard! For the lighting had been specifically designed, perhaps by Roy Rogers himself, to humiliate and age the viewer who looked in the mirror. Big circles under my eyes, greasy pores the size of moon craters—what a sad thing it was, that all it took for me to be depressed was a glance at my own face. I had seriously debated the idea of plastic surgery. If a small fraction of my nose were to be removed, my entire appearance would be improved; but what would be the point, when all that would happen is then people would comment on the fact that I had had my nose fixed? Always to be haunted by the ghostly remnants of my nose . . . this made me think of the head on the road, and what should be done about it. It wasn't really my responsibility after all, although it seemed a shame to just leave it there, even if the person to whom it belonged was dead. A piece of paper had fallen to the floor by the sink, and I bent to pick it up. A Xeroxed flyer, announcing the sale, locally, of a litter of six-week-old affenpinscher puppies. But this was remarkable! In fact, I couldn't believe the workings of Fate or Kismet, because affenpinscher was the type of dog I had been in love with in first grade, when the mother of a classmate (his name was Kelvin, and I believe his mother's name was Muffy Worthington Ramirez) raised and showed the tiny dogs that looked exactly like monkeys. Many was the night I had lain awake trying to remember the name of this particular breed. Oh, but they were wonderful dogs, never have I seen a dog that looked less like a dog and more like a monkey than those affenpinschers. And they weren't common, either; I had never seen one since those days when Kelvin's brothers took me out to the meadow in the middle of playing Army and made me take off my underpants. Maybe I'd never have another chance to get one of those dogs; and if Abdhul had a puppy to play with, he would certainly be happy on the remaining eight or ten hours of the trip to Maine.

I rummaged in my handbag for a quarter. No name was listed, but there was a badly reprinted photograph of one of the pups and its parents, pedigreed, all shots and wormed. I memorized the number and, folding the paper, put it into my bag; I would surprise Abdhul, if going to buy one of the pups was not too much of a detour. I left the women's room and went out to find a phone. Abdhul was taking slices of raw onion from the free-fixin's bar and apparently eating them; two rings were hanging over his ears. The pre-*Penthouse* Pet had left her position from the fried-chicken rack behind the counter and had come out to join him. "You're eating onion raw?" she said with some amazement.

"Mmm, that's right," Abdhul said. "I'm traveling to Maine, with Esmerelda." He hadn't noticed my return and chatted animatedly. "She lost her job, and we're going to find her father, who just died. She's not my mother, though; I bumped into her on the street and she took me in."

I didn't want to be an alarmist, but I grabbed him by the arm. "Oh, Tiffany, what are you doing?" I said with a sickly smile that I directed at the server. "You're not supposed to eat things directly out of the fixin's bar." I glanced over at the dirty blond. She was wearing a little nameplate that indicated she was to be called "Bonnie." "Sorry about that, Bonnie," I said. "What were you telling the lady, Tiffany? You really have some imagination." Luckily Bonnie didn't seem to register what he was saying; it was possible she was drugged, most of these young high-school students were, or perhaps she was involved in some satanic cult, as shown so often on TV, and was busy worrying about her upcoming sacrifice. "We've just come from Tiffany's ballet-school recital, isn't that right, Tiffany?"

Abdhul looked blank. "And what did you play, Tiffany?" Bonnie said. Oy gevalt, I had no idea what he would say now, but he emitted a belch and said, "Sugarplum Fairy."

"She's so cute!" Bonnie said blandly. "How old is she?"

"Tell Bonnie how old you are, Tiffany," I said.

"Search me," he said.

"Well, bye-bye now!" I said, dragging him after me by the arm. "Isn't it silly, I couldn't get her to change after the show. Come on now, Tiffany, we have a long way to go before we get to Grandpa's." Boy, would my father die if somebody were to call him Grandpa. Even I had to call him Dick, once the divorce was finalized; at that time he wrote me a postcard, saying he hoped I would understand but he considered himself more of a

friend than a father. "What the hell's wrong with you?" I said once we were
safely outside. "You don't want to go telling complete strangers everything,
Abdhul."

"How was I supposed to know?" he said furiously. *"You* tell everybody
everything."

"I do?" I said. "No I don't."

"Tiffany! What kind of skunky name is that?"

I was momentarily humbled. "Sorry," I said at last.

"You're always on the phone, telling your mother everything. I don't
have anybody to talk to." Now I felt even worse; the poor kid was probably
right. "Tell me," I said, "have you told other people about our little secret."

"I don't know," he mumbled.

"What?" I said. "Who did you tell?"

"Nobody," he said sullenly.

"Who?" I said.

"Nobody!" he said. "I didn't tell anybody. And don't call me Tiffany."

"What would you like to be called, then?" I said.

"Beryl." I had to let it go at that. There was a pay phone near the car,
and while he rummaged sulkily in the shriveled grass, I dialed the number.

"Things are kind of hectic at the moment," said the woman who
answered the phone. "We're just heading out the door to go to the quarter
final round of the Hughes Cup in Pittsburgh. My sister is married to Max
Eng, the famous Chinese tennis star. Anyway, they haven't been getting
along very well for a month or two, but I make a habit of going to all the
big matches—naturally, since my sister is married to one of the top-seeded
players I'm able to go into the VIP areas."

"Uh, we were just passing through," I said. "But I thought, if we could
see the puppies, then we'd buy one and take it to the country with us.
We're just over at the Roy Rogers."

"That's not far," the woman said. "My name's Joy Wilson, by the way.
If you could get over to us in the next fifteen minutes I guess we could
wait." She gave me an elaborate set of directions which I did my best to
scribble down. "The thing is, we really have to leave pretty soon because
I promised that my daughter would baby-sit my sister's two-year-old during
the match. My sister and Max tried for eight years to have kids, and they
couldn't; a couple of years back they adopted a Samoan child—she's four
now—and then naturally my sister got pregnant on her own immediately.
She went to some specialist . . ."

"Up in Maine?" I said.

"Yes!" Joy said. "I think so!"

Joy certainly wasn't very discreet. It was entirely possible that she had a part-time job giving phone sex, as so many women did these days, since it was a job they were able to do out of their own homes.

Abdhul had already gotten into the passenger seat and was staring out the window pretending to ignore me. "Listen, I'm sorry if I hurt your feelings," I said. "I didn't meant to embarrass you: I just got nervous that if you told Bambi or Bonnie or whatever her name was that we weren't related she might call the police as soon as we left. I could be reported for child abuse, you know." His little jaw was set but although he didn't say anything I could see my apology was accepted. I handed him the piece of paper on which I had scribbled Joy's directions. "You'll have to be the guide," I said. "We're making a slight detour, to get you a surprise. You tell me how to go."

"I don't want to wear this disguise anymore," he said. "It itches."

"Fine, fine," I said. "After we get your surprise you can change."

We had to keep driving back toward the city before finding the entrance ramp onto the highway. That meant we were going to pass the alleged head again. "Be on the lookout for that cantaloupe," I said. "Let's see if it's still there, or if somebody ran over it."

"The head, you mean?" Abdhul said. "Slow down—I can see it, right up there." Whatever it was was sticking out of a black flapping garbage bag, and though this was a dangerous and possibly even criminal maneuver, I slowed the car and pulled over onto the shoulder. If I didn't find out now what the hell the cantaloupe-head actually was, I would be up all night brooding over the matter; or even worse, feel obligated to turn around in twenty or fifty miles and come back for a look. I knew myself fairly intimately, and this was the sort of person I was.

The wind was whipping by from the cars so fast that the garbage bag blew this way and that, rendering it impossible to view the melon. Abdhul started to open his door. "Don't do that!" I said. "You stay in the car! Never get out of a car on the highway."

"I can't see what it is, though," he said.

"I'll get out," I said. "You climb over me, so I can get out on your side." He squeezed over me and wedged himself under the steering wheel. I got out the side door. What a stupid thing, but it would only take a second. Then I could come back and tell him it was just an old piece of fruit. Without the air conditioning of the car, on the open road, the air shimmered metallically, parched of oxygen; my lungs felt instantly seared, as if they had been ripped from my chest and placed on a heated barbecue grill.

Tentatively I walked in front of the car and toward the degradable garbage bag. I assumed it was a degradable bag; nowadays almost all the trash bags on sale at the supermarket were marked degradable, although I had never been able to figure out whether that meant they were subject to humiliation or would fall apart after they were full of garbage. The cars, racing past on the lanes, seemed to be deliberately swerving toward me, and I flattened myself out along the guardrail. There was a sharp drop on the far side, filled with refuse, and beyond this a row of houses with near-human expressions.

When I got closer I saw—as the bag blew back and forth—that it appeared to be a cleverly fabricated mannequin head, complete with bloody neck-stump, that must have been used in some horror movie or purchased at an elaborate specialty shop. To my left a car horn blared, startling me; I darted forward and snatched the hefty bag, and then turning around held it up to Abdhul in the car and with my free hand gave him a wave. What a find! I knew he would love the head, which if purchased new might have cost hundreds of dollars, and could show it to his friends, if he ever had any. The damn thing weighed close to twenty pounds. But to my horror he must have slipped the car out of neutral; though he was too short to see over the steering wheel, the car was moving—slowly, thank God—coming straight toward me. The bag still in hand I ran back to the rolling car and grabbing the passenger door yanked it open and jumped in. "What are you trying to do?" I said. "Are you trying to kill me?" I tossed the bag over the back seat. "Put your foot on the brake!" I screamed at him. The car was accelerating and now directed straight into the lanes of traffic. I was not at my best in emergency situations. "Stop, stop!" I screamed, and tried to put the shift into park; but pulled too hard and flung it into reverse. Luckily this confused the car to the degree that momentarily it went nowhere and I had the time to yank the emergency brake.

Badly shaken, and with Abdhul now crying in fear, I pushed him over the seat and into the back, turned off the engine (we were almost in the lane of oncoming traffic), put it into park, started the car again, turned the wheel and then in drive pulled farther off the shoulder so I could collect myself. "My God, what were you doing?" I said.

"I didn't do anything!" Abdhul sobbed from the backseat. "I didn't touch anything."

"The car just started moving, by itself?" I said bitterly. "Do you know how easily you could have been killed?"

"You scared me!" he said, "when you started screaming at me like that."

"Yeah, well, you scared me," I said.

"And my arm hurts, you pulled my arm and shoved me over the seat. I didn't do anything. And this wig itches." I panted heavily while he complained. If the car had gone forward two feet farther to the left it would have been sideswiped almost immediately. A few feet forward, I would have been run over. The steering wheel was slobbery with the sweat from my own hands. Now it seemed even stupider that I had pulled off the highway in the first place; if a patrol car came by, I probably would get into all sorts of trouble for pulling off the road.

I waited until there was a gap in the traffic and stepped on the accelerator, pulling into the lane while trying to get up to speed. Neither of us spoke for some miles. What a crushing near-disaster. I was driving on automatic. If there had been any alcohol in the car, I would have drunk it. At least there was a stop coming up, if I could ever find Joy whatever-her-name-was's house. I fumbled on the seat for the piece of paper on which I had printed the directions. "Read them," I said, tossing the paper over my shoulder.

"Where are we going now?" Abdhul said.

"Some woman's house," I said.

"Are you going to get rid of me?" he said.

"No," I said. "Who the hell would want you?"

"Are we still friends?" he said.

"Not right this minute," I said. "But perhaps we will be in the future."

"I want to go home," he said.

"We don't have a home at present," I said. This certainly was a cruel statement on my part, but since it was similar to the way I always spoke I knew he was used to it by now. "We're going to get your surprise, remember, not that you deserve one." I remembered when I had gotten my own first puppy, after begging for a dog for years; the timing was perfect, since we went to collect it immediately after a slight tragedy had taken place. My folks took me to get my hair trimmed; at age eight it came down to my waist and was always getting tangled, so it was decided a trim at the local beauty salon was in order. Unfortunately the hairdresser had his wires crossed, and without unbraiding my two long braids he took a scissors and chopped off each one at my scalp. That was traumatic, to find such a large portion of my anatomy lying on the floor. Luckily after that we went to fetch the pup, so I forgot my misery.

Abdhul was silent in the backseat, but it still seemed best to wait until we arrived at the House of Joy before telling him what was up. "Look in the bag," I suggested as a temporary stopgap amusement. There was a pause and then he screamed; his two little paws grabbed me around the neck and tried to strangle me. "My God, get your fucking hands off me!" I said. "Do you have a death wish? What are you doing?" He was apparently trying to crawl into the front like a deranged cat. I had to drive with one hand and pry his hands free with my other, which only caused him to cover up my eyes. "There's a head in the bag! There's a head!" he said.

Out of the corner of my view I saw the exit ramp and slowed the car, turning off. Somehow I got his hands away and after turning right at the bottom managed to come to a halt at the red traffic light. I turned in my seat and gave him a shove that sent him flying across the backseat. "It's not a head, it's not a head," I said. "It's one of those things from a joke shop or a horror movie, dummy. You can use it to fool your friends. Those things cost hundreds of dollars."

"It's not," he said. "It's real."

"How do you know, Abhdul?" I said patronizingly.

"There are bugs in it that are moving," he said.

"What kind of bugs," I said.

"White bugs," he said. "With eyes. And it's dripping blood onto the floor."

This did seem to corroborate his opinion. "Oh," I said. There was a pause while the light turned green. "Which way do I go now, Abdhul?" I said.

"Make your next right," he said.

"You have a good sense of direction," I said in what I hoped was a complimentary tone. "Tell me, is the bag itself leaking, or just from where it's open at the top?"

"At the top," he said.

"Here's what I'd like you to do," I said. "Tie up the bag as firmly as possible, and then climb back over the seat and sit next to me." Why did I think such things couldn't happen? Of course such things happened; things like this happened every day. We were driving down a long suburban passage where big houselike objects, quite hideous, were set on plots of land, surrounded by apparently artificial trees. My God, the sort of people who must live in this place! They had lawn mowers, and dishwashers, and all sorts of cooking utensils; day in and day out the television signals poured into their homes, telling them what to buy and what to laugh at—in other words, how they might best fit in to society. And yet it was probably somebody in one of these homes who had murdered his wife or her husband, placed the body in a full-size food freezer until it was chilled enough to dismember, and then tossed the parts out alongside the motor highway. "Keep your eyes out for a dumpster or a garbage pail," I said. "By the way, was it a man's head or a woman's?"

"This is the house, Pamela," Abdhul said. "It says Wilson on the mailbox."

There were no cars behind me and I turned up on the drive. A couple of metal trash cans had been placed by the road, and I hesitated briefly, but this seemed to me to be a poor choice to deposit the head. Even if I paid for the pup with cash, surely some neighbor would remark on the car—in this sort of place there were always spying neighbors—and when or if the head were discovered it would no doubt be traced to me; blood from the head would be found on the floor (even if I washed and vacuumed the backseat carpet, modern forensic science was capable of finding even the tiniest drops of blood, there were all too many accounts of this in newspapers and books) and it seemed impossible I would be able to explain my way out of it. Oh, why hadn't I simply ignored the head on the road in the first place? Or at least simply called the state police and given them an anonymous tip? For it now dawned on me that—wherever I chose to deposit the head, even in the most remote roadside park dumpster—there was a strong chance it would be blamed on me. People were lurking everywhere, behind shrubs and from windows with binoculars, pretending to sleep in parked cars but actually gazing out the bottom of the window; if I had been a real criminal I might have gotten away with tossing a head out the window, but as I was not, I would surely be caught. It seemed as if all my life I had had a sense of impending doom; no doubt this sensation was what was known as foreshadowing and this event was what psychically I had always unconsciously anticipated. It was like being locked in a kitchen cabinet. I should never have drunk that last cup of coffee at Roy Rogers. My heart was trying to escape from my chest, I couldn't get any oxygen into my lungs, black dots flickered into my vision. I had had anxiety attacks before, and while they were never pleasant, they were based on having imbibed too much alcohol the night before and saying stupid things; usually my mother could talk me down with a few well-placed words, but in this case the only thing I could think of doing was to get myself to a post office, purchase a box, and mail the head. Get rid of the head, get rid of the head I chanted over and over, parking at the top of the driveway and getting out of the car. Originally I thought, for security reasons, that Abdhul had best wait in the car while I got out and acquired a pup, but now it seemed too cruel to leave him in the hot car with the head, and so I said nothing when he got out the passenger side and followed me to the front door.

I rang the doorbell and a woman—I supposed it was Joy—opened the front door. She looked slightly apprehensive; I guess we were an unusual sight, I covered in sweat, hot, hair scattered and standing on end, while

Abdhul, shrunken, wig askew, gibbered quietly to himself. I gave him a little shake on his shoulder to shut him up. "Pamela?" the woman said.

"You—how did you know my name?" I said.

"You said, on the phone," the woman said. "I'm Joy. Come on in. I was just on the phone with my sister. I really better get going, right away. She's hysterical because she thinks her husband is having an affair with a trapeze artist from that show 'Circus of the Stars.' The rest of the time she's an actress." She gave Abdhul a peculiar look. "Straighten your wig!" I told him, and gave him a little nudge. "Oops. She—uh—she's had some chemotherapy."

"Oh, golly," Joy said. "And what's her name?"

"Her name?" I said, panicking. "This is—uh—" Abdhul smiled. "Tell Joy your name, honey."

"*You* tell her," Abdhul said.

"She's very shy," I explained. "Isn't that right, uh . . . Belva?"

"Beryl!" Abdhul spat out with a certain vicious satisfaction. "And I'm itchy. And I'm not going to wear this for much longer."

"We were just at Beryl's dance recital," I said. Luckily Joy wasn't the kind of woman who paid very much attention. She was a woman around my age, maybe a little older, brown hair cut in a silly cap with sort of spaniel ears of hair that hung down to her shoulders. Her blue eyes were thickly fringed with a heavy coat of mascara, giving her the appearance of a startled spider, but apart from that she was one of those people who have no qualifying characteristics; with so many people like her around, it was easy to understand why the Chinese complained of being unable to tell us apart. Once, seemingly only a few months ago, I, too, had tried to follow this role model of normalcy. Now, gazing past her shoulder into the gold-spotted mirror on the wall, I could see more readily why she looked apprehensive. It was not just that I was covered with sweat and that my hair was a mess. Everything about me was all wrong. Parts of my hair had recently—very recently—gone quite gray, my nose was as white as a mushroom, and there was an alarmed look about me as if I had recently escaped from a halfway house for manic-depressives.

We followed the chattering Joy through the tiled entryway and into the living room. Her home was a masterpiece of inconsequentiality. Yes, the pale yellow plaid-chintz couch, the overstuffed armchair covered in peach-and-yellow striped fabric, the pecan coffee table topped with an oversize book called *American Masterpieces of the Old West,* the large floral hooked rug beneath our feet . . . bookshelves with a few Book-of-the-Month Club selections, the oversize television set, and thick yellow balloon drapes over the two windows that faced the yard. . . . Somewhere along the line it had been decided that this was what a living room was supposed to look like; Joy had followed all the rules, every item was probably expensive—in fact, she may have used the services of a decorator—and yet, were she to try to sell the various objects, no one would want them, she would be lucky to get a tenth of what she had originally paid. Yet all over the country people were aspiring to achieve this exact mundanity and live on an estate with other homes all exactly alike or nearly.

In the kitchen she stopped and opened two cages, neatly lined with newspaper; two fully grown dogs and four puppies all ran out and disappeared into the other room. "Damn," she said. "Michelle! Michelle! Would you please get those dogs and bring them in here?" Just then a plain girl, her head down, with close-set eyes and a surly expression, came into the kitchen. She must have been around sixteen. This is my daughter, Michelle," Joy said. "Michelle, this is Pamela and Beryl." Michelle looked at Abdhul and let out a sort of squawk.

"Can I use the bathroom?" Abdhul muttered.

"Michelle, show Beryl," Joy said. Michelle gave an evil flash of silver braces and left the room followed by Beryl. "Michelle's father, one of my ex-husbands, is Peruvian. We were married for ten years; he's a famous Grand Prix driver. Now he raises budgerigars. Michelle's my only child, though. I had six miscarriages." In a way it was strangely soothing to have her chatter on telling me things that I would have considered personal. She was like somebody selling gum in an advertisement, one of those healthy American types. "Then I remarried twice," Joy said earnestly, as if it were imperative for me to know. "Of course, Michelle's father, the Grand Prix driver, was the most famous." That she had three husbands, one of whom was a famous Grand Prix driver! How odd it seemed, for apart from her innocuousness and her supreme self-confidence, I didn't see what she had going for her that would make her so desirable. "But I know you're dying to see the dogs," she said, as they returned to the kitchen. "This is Happiness," she said, pointing to the male, a sort of steel-wool miniature gorilla, "And this is Charisma." Charisma was apparently the mother, a small orange orangutan-type dog. "And these are her pups—Fame, Fortune, Goodness, and Mercy. My ex-husband, the Grand Prix driver, gave me Happiness. We used to live in a mansion, outside Lima, and I had lots of animals then: two ponies, a donkey, and dogs and cats. We had a fourteen-acre enclosed garden!"

In many ways it was like listening to a Barbie doll gone to seed: how dumb could her Grand Prix Peruvian have been? I was longing to ask his name, but I thought—rather pettily—I wouldn't give her the satisfaction. Probably if it was somebody really famous she would have told me his name by now. But the puppies were so cute, with their wrinkled, squashed, worried expressions, I didn't want to antagonize Joy and so I tried to look admiring. "Oh, they're all so cute!" I said. "I don't know which one to pick—I should let . . . Beryl . . . decide. It's really going to be Beryl's dog. Where is she, anyway?"

Abdhul came into the kitchen in his underpants. He was obviously a boy. "Beryl!" I said. "Where's your tutu?"

"It itched," he said.

"Why don't you pick your dog and run out to the car and put on your jeans," I said. I smiled wanly at Joy. "It's the radiation treatment she's been undergoing."

"Oh, how awful," Joy said. Abdhul looked at the puppies suspiciously. "What are they?" he said.

"Don't you want one of the puppies?" I said.

"These are dogs?" he said.

I laughed merrily. "Aren't they cute?"

"It's so ugly!" he said at last.

"Just pick one!" I snarled. He pointed at Mercy. "Mercy, good," I said. "Now go out to the car and put your fucking clothes on!"

He left. "Tell me, what's wrong with your little girl?" Joy said after a pause.

"Tumor," I said. "You know"—I indicated my crotch.

"Oh, how awful," Joy said. Nobody could be that stupid, I thought, feeling ashamed. Yet something was so wrong with this typical American household. Maybe she had a reason for seeming so naïve. It dawned on me that perhaps Joy had recently murdered one of her boyfriends or husbands, and I had inadvertently picked up his discarded head on the roadside and carried it back to the scene of the crime.

"It took me ages to breed them," Joy said. "Happiness would rather fuck my leg." She held up one long, neatly shaved leg protruding from cut-off jean shorts, as if to demonstrate its desirability. "You know, with little dogs—and they're very rare—it can be difficult. The second time around when Charisma came into heat I had to get Happiness drunk with a few tablespoons of brandy to relax him. However, he's very well hung—his prick must take up his entire body—which explains why he has so few brains, because when it's out he can't even walk. It goes down to the ground. None of my husbands have ever been that well hung."

Abdhul came back into the room in jeans and a T-shirt. Thank God during this time he had not removed his wig; even so, could Joy have been so unobservant not to notice some form of child abuse was in progress. I must remember to explain to Abdhul the difference between the birds and the bees, that much was clear. "You know, Beryl, Mercy is my favorite," she said. Abdhul grunted, but he picked up the dog.

"Let me give you the money," I said, rummaging in my bag.

"I'll walk you to your car," Joy said.

"No, no, that's all right," I said.

"Oh, I insist," Joy said. "I have to go out anyway. Michelle, let's get going!" Joy and Michelle followed me and Abdhul out onto the drive. Michelle had a little smirk on her face; God knows what was going on in her mind. "Bye, now," I said, opening the driver's door. "Thanks so much!" I should have left the windows open; already the most putrefying whiff had arisen from the back. Abdhul got in the front passenger side. "Say bye-bye, Beryl!" I said.

"Oh, just a minute!" Michelle said with a little cackle and she ran into the house. Damn, I thought; I hoped she hadn't gone to get a camera, pretending she wanted to have a photograph of the dog but really in order to take our picture and hand it over to the FBI, as so many children were fond of doing nowadays. "I wonder what she's gone to get?" Joy said, leaning in the window on my side. I pretended to accidentally remove my foot from the brake so that the car began to roll back slightly. Anything rather than have her see or smell what was in the back of the car, even if it was her own husband. "We should really let you get going," I muttered.

"Oh, she'll just be a minute."

Michelle ran out the front door, holding a teensy-weensy dress, apparently designed for Confirmation in some Latin American country and covered with masses of lace, and a doll with long purple hair. "These are for you," she said, passing them through the window to Abdhul. "I used to wear the dress when I was little, but I outgrew it. And I thought you'd like the doll." Surely that wasn't a knowing smile on her face; I was being paranoid. "Neat!" Abdhul shrieked suddenly, surprising me. "It's very pretty! And I always wanted Dolly Wet One!" Rudely, unable to wait any longer, I backed up as fast as I could. "Wave bye-bye!" I snapped at Abdhul, "before they follow us down the driveway." How had he even known about Dolly Wet One, anyway? And I only hoped he was being sarcastic, or a good actor, when he made his remark about the lacy dress. Not that a mother was responsible for her son's homosexuality; everybody knew this was determined at birth. On the other hand . . . "It stinks in here," Abdhul said, waving listlessly at Joy and Michelle. He threw the dress in the back.

I was ashamed at thinking such mean thoughts about Joy and Michelle, when they had really been very nice to us. The puppy was cute, and immediately curled into a ball and lay down as if he had been traveling with us all his life. It was hard to be so paranoid and judgmental, but there was nothing I could do about it, unless I changed my personality completely—and then who would I be? I would be a completely different person, *a stranger to myself,* and apart from Abdhul and my mother, I was the only person I could trust and be comfortable with. If I were a stranger, it would take years to get to know myself. And right now, I just didn't have the time.

At last we were out the drive and I turned the car around. "Read me the directions in reverse so we can get back onto the highway," I said. Mercy stood up and urinated on the seat; I could only look down briefly, but I felt my thigh grow damp. "Do me a favor and put Mercy in the back," I said.

"Why?" Abdhul said.

"If we have an accident, Mercy could be thrown through the window," I said. "We have seatbelts. If you want to play with the dog later, you can get in the back."

"Mercy's so ugly," Abdhul said. "He looks like a goldfish. Why couldn't I have a golden retriever?"

"Because we're not that sort of people," I said shortly.

"Can I change its name?"

"Sure," I said. "What do you want to call him?"

"Murder," Abdhul said.

"I don't think that's going to work," I said.

"Why?" Abdhul said.

"Because," I said. "Just think about it. I mean, you can't go around yelling 'Murder! Murder!' if he gets lost."

"Then my second choice is Dalgleish," he said finally. Poor little Abdhul, with the kind of puppy he didn't even want.

"Okay," I said. "Dalgleish it is."

Abdhul slumped into silence and it was nearly an hour before he spoke. "I'm tired," he said.

"Shut your eyes and go to sleep," I said.

"I can't sleep unless I'm lying down," he said.

"Climb over to the back and put the stuff on the floor and go to sleep," I said.

"I'm not getting in the back with that head," he said. I had nearly forgotten all about it. There was enough wooded area at my father's that it occurred to me I could go out when my dad wasn't looking and bury it someplace. This perhaps would not be the most satisfactory of solutions, but it was the only one I could think of at present. As I have said, so many people in trying to dispose of a body in a public place have been traced and caught at a later date; inevitably a bit of evidence is left behind, a laundry ticket or checkbook stub; a couple having illicit sex in a parked car jump out and out of curiosity decide to examine the contents of the sealed cardboard box. Recently there had been an item on the news about the new system set up by the state police to record speeders—a camera set up behind shrubs, connected with a radar detector, snapped photographs of travelers driving too fast and speeding tickets were then sent by mail. With my luck, the camera would accidentally take a picture of me, whether or not I was going too fast.

"I think you're being awfully fussy," I told Abdhul. "But keep your eyes out for a rest stop, and if nobody's around I'll get out and put the bag in the trunk. I don't see that anybody would report me for doing that. Then the back will be clear for you to sleep." Glancing over at Abdhul's sulky, pinched face I was overcome with love. *He* accepted me for who I was; *he* had chosen me, and liked me for myself. He was mine, and maybe would always mean more to me than any child I might ever have, because a congenital child could always blame me for having given birth to him or her. But Abdhul could not. He inhaled wildly. "Don't snuffle," I said. "Use a tissue." He snorted again, breathing in a noseful of snot.

"What's wrong with you?" I said. "Are you getting a cold?"

"No," he said.

"Are you allergic to the dog?" I said. He didn't answer. "Are you mad at me?"

"No," he said. "But I will be, if you keep asking me."

"What do you mean, if I keep asking you? I just asked you once," I said. My God, did I feel like giving him a smack! This seemed to me to be wrong—probably he had been smacked around enough already—but I was sorely tempted. "I don't like the way you talk to me," I said. "What a typical male."

"There's a rest stop up ahead," he said. "You're going to miss it if you don't slow down."

"Turn around and see if there's anybody behind us in the right lane," I said.

"Oh no," he said, looking over his shoulder.

"What?" I said. "What's wrong?"

"You'll find out," he said. "You can pull over now." I signaled and pulled into the right lane. The rest stop was a soiled bit of dried grass, two picnic tables, and a metal dumpster. There was a truck in the parking lot, one of those eighteen-wheelers, but there was no sense in waiting for a rest stop that was completely empty, if all I was going to do was tie a knot around the top of the garbage bag and shove it into the trunk. I suppose I should have simply driven to the nearest police station and handed over my find. How could I do this, though, when there was at least a possibility that I had been reported as a kidnapper; by now Ralph the camp counselor might be suspicious that Abdhul had not returned to camp so soon after he had informed me that a woman claiming to be Abdhul's real mother had been around. And then there was that woman from this morning, looking for me; maybe she had been sent by Alby. I would die if I were to lose him. Oh, I was old enough to know I wouldn't die; nobody died from grief, not anymore. But to live the rest of my life not seeing him, or speaking to him—the thought was unbearable. And even if they took him away and I obtained lawyers and fought and fought to get him back, years would go by, he would be in his teens, a grown man, things would never be the same.

The crumpled grass was littered with detritus: beer cans; foam containers spongy and white, more permanent than the Sphinx; used condoms; broken green and brown glass bottles. It was filthy, filthy. Above the green dumpster was a sign, black on white enamel, announcing NO DUMPING, $500 FINE. Candy-bar wrappers, chunks of nougat, chicken bones—earliest man, sitting around a campfire, had been a neater and cleaner animal than this! A pair of panties, a tampon tube—I got out of the door and walked around the back on the passenger side. The baked air reeked of car exhaust, the few trees planted around the rim of the asphalt had seared, crumpled leaves, crispy, resembling a person who has had her hair dyed one too many times. I started to open the door when I let out a gasp and backed away in horror. "Oh, no!" I yelped. The pup, who I thought was asleep, had gotten into the bag containing the head and indulged himself in an afternoon snack. His punched-in face was covered with blood, there were stringy bits of gristle and skin strewn this way and that, over the plastic seat and chunks on the floor; half the bag was open, and several of the maggots—anyway, I assumed they were maggots, what other insect larvae, white and juicy, came along to feed on deceased corpses I didn't know, although probably at my dad's house there were a number of nature books in which I might look up such information—were lying helplessly on the back of the seat. The pup appeared to give me a guilty grin. He had a distinct underbite, his little underslung jaw gave him a vague resemblance to Sammy Davis, Jr.

Then I realized that was a terrible thing to think: by comparing him to Sammy Davis, Jr., was I being anti-black? Or anti-Semitic? Or, anti-one-eyed people?

I opened the back door of the car. The dog sneezed, gave a wriggle, jumped down off the seat, then from the floor squeezed past me and ran out the door. He seemed to know exactly where he was going; he made a big circle across the tarry parking lot, dashed for the grass, and squatted briefly to urinate (he hadn't learned to lift his leg yet) and then took off for the shrubs at the edge of the grass and disappeared out of sight. "Help! Help!" I yelled. "Dalgleish, you come back here! Come, Dalgleish, come!" Uh-huh. "Abdhul, get out! The dog ran away." He opened the door slowly and then jumped out quickly. I could see that one half of him would have liked to spite me by either not responding or behaving sluggishly, but the other half of him didn't want to lose his new dog. He was just like every man I had ever gone out with, nice at first and then deliberately malevolent. Anyway, maybe I was just being paranoid. "Please, find him before he runs out onto the highway and gets run over," I said. "But don't you run out, if there're cars."

Abdhul took off for the bushes. "Dalgleish, Dalgleish!" he screamed. "Bad dog. Come, Dalgleish!" I wanted to go after him, but I had to clean the backseat first; anybody who pulled up in a car next to mine and glanced in would certainly be taken aback. It was all smeared with blood and with the door open a number of eager flies abandoned their chicken wings and made a beeline for fresher meat. I gave a tug on the ripped-open bag. The head had a vaguely familiar look to it—its mustache and hooked nose reminded me of . . . Hassim, the man who worked in the pizza parlor. Of course it wasn't, there were certain differences, and thank God somebody had closed the eyes, but that it was familiar in appearance I found somehow soothing. The poor man, although possibly he had deserved decapitation. I picked it up in my arms and attempted to rewrap the now-torn bag around it. There had to be something I could swaddle him in, before more leakage occurred. If only I had thought to take a few extra garbage bags along. But how was I supposed to know at the time? There was a soft-sided suitcase on the floor and I put the head back down on the seat and unzipped the bag, quickly tipping out the contents onto the pavement. What a stench. Now that the air conditioning was off and the head exposed to fresh air I could barely breathe. I snatched a knee-high sock from the ground and tied it around my nose. The smell was something a person once having smelled it could never forget; it was unlike anything else specific, vague overtones of rotting meat and fruit, so shrill and decayed it made me want to vomit.

In the event that the weather ever turned cold, I had bought for Abdhul a flannel one-piece pajama set, one of those cute numbers with the dump-flap in back. Maybe he was too old for this type of thing, but the pajamas were so cute, complete with bunny feet, that I couldn't resist, and for whatever reason these were one of the items in the duffel bag. I unsnapped the front, and, removing the head from the bag—there was no point in keeping the bag, it was all torn to bits and dripping—I shoved the head into the pajamas, which I then bound using the arms and the legs, and then placed the whole enterprise into the suitcase. Probably it was eventually going to leak, but at present what else could be done. I opened the trunk and moved some of the boxes and suitcases over to make room for the head.

I really felt very sorry for myself. I had never expected life to be so difficult. I was getting older and things weren't getting any easier. I slammed shut the trunk but now I didn't know whether to go and look for Abdhul and Dalgleish or to clean off the backseat of blood and tissue. Plus I had to pee and this was not a rest stop with toilet facilities. I hated the idea of going over and squatting behind some bushes, which was not only embarrassing but ecologically unsound. The thought came to me from nowhere that if I were ever to live in the country and have a little home, there I would like to keep a chicken. I would only want to have one chicken, two at the most, the fancy sort with big white legs and a red wattle plume on its head.

Then something awful happened: the nail of my thumb must have had a tiny split along one side, because it snagged on my NY METS T-shirt and I felt it sort of rip. This hurt a lot, and when I looked at my thumbnail I saw it had split or torn well below the tip of my thumb, almost halfway down. It was incredibly painful, and I didn't have a little scissors or an emery board or anything to file it. There was no choice but to try and bite it off, but since the break had occurred so low down—this was possibly due to a vitamin deficiency, although I had always had very soft fingernails that tore easily—I couldn't really get a sufficient grip on it with my front teeth. Sighing, I closed the back door, grabbed a box of Kleenex tissue from the glove compartment and set off for the scruffy bushes behind the picnic tables. "Abdhul, Abdhul!" I called. "Dalgleish! Dalgleish!" Neither of them were anywhere in sight. I prayed the pup had not headed off toward the highway where the cars came racing past.

It was unimaginable, the kind of filth that had been deposited or blown back here in the prickly bushes. Old brambles, blackberry and wild black-cap raspberries, with dried-out berries, crisp as fried eyes, limbs covered with needle prickers, tore at my legs. Even though I grew up in the country, having to squat among the creepers, pants and panties down at my ankles, was something I hated to do. It was hard to position oneself so that the urine didn't run down one's legs. There was a woman in New York—she had died not long ago, AIDS—who was perhaps best known for her ability to urinate standing up, like a man. Because of this she would often wait until the men she was with were urinating on the street or off some dark pier, and then shockingly she would join them. Still, this wasn't something I really approved of. Even if she could pee like a man, there was no reason for her to stoop to their level. It was one thing for a dog to piss on the street, but human beings should wait until they found a restroom. If there was any advantage to being a woman, it was that women, even when they were desperate to go, could hold it in, whereas once a man announced it was his time, he was weak and helpless to control himself.

Now the urine was trickling down toward my tennis shoes, I could hear it splattering over the dry, dusty leaf mold, and I wiped myself with one of the Kleenex and quickly tucked it under a bit of vegetation. Anyway, a tissue would disintegrate pretty quickly, I guessed, and I didn't want to carry it around with me all day or even take it out to the dumpster, since anybody watching would then know what I had been doing out here. At least the dog and Abdhul hadn't suddenly appeared right in front of me at the minute when I was doing my business. Glancing around nervously I yanked my panties and trousers back up. "Dalgleish, Dalgleish, Abdhul!" I called. I went back out, picking my way carefully through the prickers, onto the lawn. A hunched-up Abdhul appeared across the grass, a mournful expression on his face. "I can't find him," he said. "What are we going to do?"

"I have an idea," I said. "Now, watch this." I got into the car and opened and shut the door loudly several times.

"We're not leaving, are we?" Abdhul said. "We can't just leave him here!"

"You'll see," I said. "Dalgleish, hurry up!" I yelled. "Get in the car! We're leaving! Time to go!" With that, from down the road Dalgleish came running, tongue lolling, a fiendish grin on his face, which was still covered in blood. His little fangs were protruding; he saw the open car door and ran toward me, jumped in across my feet, clambered around and then up onto the seat, where he sat looking quite pleased with himself.

"Wow," Abdhul said. "How'd you know that?" He got in on the passenger side. "Dalgleish, you bad boy," he said. "Where were you?"

I nibbled at my ripped thumbnail to no avail. "Oldest trick in the book," I said. When I got my first puppy, after my braids were chopped off, even though he had never seen me before, the woman we bought him from told my dad as we were leaving to get into the car and call, and sure enough the dog came running and hopped in.

"Let's get out of here," I said. "We'll never get to Maine at this rate." I tried to turn on the ignition but the keys were gone. "Where'd I put the keys?" I said. I looked down on the seat. The bug-eyed Dalgleish beamed up at me guiltily. "We've got to give that dog a bath," I said. "Maybe we'll pass a lake, and we can throw him in." I rummaged around my pockets. "Abdhul, get down on the floor and look to see if the keys are there," I said. I got out of the car and felt in my pockets once more. No keys. I opened my little handbag, but I hadn't put them in there. I walked around the car looking on the ground. Maybe they fell out of my pocket when I went to urinate. When was the last time I had seen them? I tried to think carefully. Thinking carefully was like operating one of the early, slow-working IBM computers. *We pulled into the parking lot; the keys must have been in the car then. I stopped the car, turned off the ignition, got out, took out the head . . . then I had put it in the trunk. I must have last had the keys when I opened the trunk.* I went to the back of the car, but they were not in the lock. They were not under the exhaust pipe. Oh no, this just could not be. I had locked the car keys in the trunk. I clutched my temple in my hands. No, no, no no. No, no, no no. No, no. No, no, no. "Abdhul, I think I dropped the keys in the bushes," I said. "I'm just going to go look. If you get out, don't let the dog out of the car." I trudged back across the grass, head down, looking for a bit of shiny metal. Beer-can tops, a bright quarter, which I picked up. A piece of crumpled aluminum foil. Back through the bushes in search of the spot where I had my squat. It was hopeless, ridiculous even. They were not to be seen. I had locked them in the trunk.

Trampling the crispy grass I returned to the car, gnawing feverishly on my defective nail. "Okay, Abdhul, out of the car," I said. "We have to remain calm. Here's what we have to do: I've locked the keys in the trunk of the car."

Abdhul hopped out, making sure the dog was safe behind him. "What do you mean, here's what we have to do?" he said. "What?"

"We have to remain calm," I said. "Let's not get excited! Try and think!"

Abdhul shrugged. "Why don't you go see if the guy in the truck can open it?" he said.

I looked at him gratefully. "Good idea," I said. "Do you want to go and ask him?"

"I don't want to go ask him," he said. "*You* go ask him."

"I'm shy," I said.

"So am I," he said.

"You're not shy!" I said. "You're just saying that because I said it."

"I am too shy," he said stubbornly. "I'm afraid he'll try and take me away from you."

I made a sound of disgust but I went over to the cab of the truck. It was one of those big eighteen-wheeler things; maybe the driver was asleep in a berth above the front, but the way things were going at present, by disturbing him I would probably trigger some sort of murderous rampage. In all likelihood he was a serial truck-driving killer. I climbed up the steps on the driver's side and looked in the window. He was lying on the seat reading a paperback book by Somerset Maugham. "Excuse me," I said. I leaned in and tapped on the sole of one of his shoes. He let out a yelp and shot up. "Hullo," he said in an English accent. "You startled me."

"Sorry," I said. "We locked the keys in the trunk and I was wondering if you had any tools to break in." I had to think it, this guy was really gorgeous. He had a pencil-thin mustache and a sort of dissipated Errol Flynn appearance; what he was doing driving a truck I couldn't fathom.

"Blimy," he said. All my life I had waited for somebody to work that expression into a conversation and I was thrilled it had finally happened. "I'm not very good mechanically, but I could take a look if you want."

"That would be so kind of you," I said. I climbed down the steps and quickly opening my handbag applied a little powder to my nose as he got out behind me. I wheeled around as he came down the steps and stuck out my hand. "My name's Pamela," I said. "Pamela Trowel. The car's just right over here." I walked across the lot. Damn, why hadn't I thought to cake some mud over the license plate, rendering it unreadable? That was what people were always doing in true-crime novels. "I'm Rodney Arthur," the English person muttered behind me. "Nice to meet you."

"This is my son, Angelo," I said, pointing at Abdhul. "And this is the trunk of the car, that I locked the keys in." He blinked uncomfortably in the bright light. He gave the trunk a little tug, but obviously that was not going to open it. Abdhul got out, holding the bloody-faced Dalgleish in his arms. "What are you going to do?" he said. The dog wriggled uncontrollably, trying to get free.

"I don't know," Rodney said. "Nice pup. What's he called?"

"Dalgleish," Abdhul said proudly. "I don't have a leash yet, though."

"I'll see if I have a bit of twine," Rodney said. "But I don't know what to do about opening the boot. The, uh, trunk. If you locked the keys in the car, then I could probably get in with a coat hanger. The trunk, though, I don't know." His sleepy eyes, I noted, were an attractive green hue. "Where are you headed?" he said.

"We were on our way to Maine," I said. If only I could learn to lie more consistently! Already I couldn't remember what I had said Abdhul's name was. Rodney went around to the back door of the car and opened it. "What are you doing?" I suddenly shrieked, for all at once I realized that the backseat was covered with patchy blood and other bits of stuff from the head. If only I had at least wiped off the seat. Luckily he didn't seem to notice, not even the two juicy maggots that were curled up with helpless expressions. Rodney jumped at the sound of my voice and froze momentarily; that was a nice thing about those English people, who were brought up always to think they were doing something wrong. "I just thought," he said apologetically, "that I would take a look to see—sometimes there's a way to get into the boot from behind the backseat."

"Good thinking," I said. "Tell me, Rodney, where are you from?"

He was pulling at the cushions of the backseat. "Outside London," he said. "Sorry."

"Why are you sorry?" I said. I wanted to add that he should be proud to come from another country than the U.S.

"Excuse me?" he said. "Whyahya?"

"What?" I said. "Oh. I asked you, why are you sorry."

"Oh," he said. "I'm from Surrey."

"Ah," I said. "And what . . . brings you here?"

"Well, I'm driving a truck," he said. "Across country."

That was life in modern times for you; everybody had seen too many movies, and felt obligated to reenact them. Probably Rodney was ashamed for being an effete Englishman when he had really wanted to be born a truck-driving man from Oklahoma. "It looks like there is a little space down here at the bottom of the seats that is open to the boot," he said finally. "I think if I could find a long probe, I could work it in and maybe undo the lock from inside."

"Ooo, baby," I said in a jokey tone. Really he was jumpy as a rabbit; he leapt back a bit, knocking into me, and gave me an injured look. It wasn't my fault; normally I didn't make suggestive remarks, but he was so attractive with his James Bond—or maybe it was Ronald Colman—good looks, dressed in tight black jeans and a black T-shirt, although given time I hoped he could be persuaded to rid himself of the pencil mustache, even if it meant having to wait until he was sleeping and then shaving it off myself. The poor man, all alone, driving across country with his mustache, no doubt mocked and jeered at every truck stop. Finally I moved out of his way and he went back to his truck. Quickly I tried to mop up some of the more gruesome bits with a paper towel, wiping the larvae off the seat onto the ground. Luckily from everything I had read I knew that English people were for the most part fairly discreet, and just as he had obviously been uncomfortable being asked questions, so in return I suspected he would not attempt to question me. If he were unable to retrieve our keys, perhaps he would let us hitch a ride with him. The long days and nights we would drive, across the dusty plains, country-western music in our ears. At night pulling in to some honky-tonk motel, the truck parked outside, passionate lovemaking in the blue mineral light of the moon. We would take turns driving; each of us in turn would tutor Abdhul, and from Rodney he would learn Latin, the rise and fall of the English Empire, and the terrible conditions of life under Margaret Thatcher or whoever was in charge.

Based on his accent I assumed Rodney was what might have been called well-bred—anyway, he didn't drop his haitches—and perhaps he was even some sort of English lord, or the younger brother of one, on the lam from the Old World and its decay, possibly collecting material for a novel or a book of humorous travel monologues. I particularly liked his manly jaw and aquiline features, coming at a time when most Americans to me seemed weak-jawed and fairly homely, at least the men. What a difference between him and Daniel Loomis, who I could barely remember. That mealy-mouthed monster! Leading me on simply in order to satisfy his depraved lust for excitement, and to torment his wife. Still I would have liked to have found out what happened to him; last I had seen him had been just before he crawled up into the hole in the ceiling.

Meanwhile Rodney returned from his truck, carrying a crowbar; a long thin metal pole; and a piece of cord, which he gave to Abdhul. "Here you go, mate," he said. "Should do for a lead temporarily."

"Hey, thanks!" Abdhul said. Already he seemed more cheerful at being in the presence of a man. It was a shame that almost an entire generation of little boys were being brought up without any active male role models whatsoever. Their parents were divorced; they saw the fathers only rarely, if at all; the daycare and elementary school teachers were all women. I thought Rodney showed a nice fatherly touch, never a consideration with me before now. "I found this piece of metal," he said, pointing to the thin pole with a sort of S-shaped hook on one end. "I don't know what it's meant for, but I thought I would try to use it to open the boot from the inside. And if that doesn't work, if you really want, I could smash the lock with the crowbar, if you're desperate to get out of here and don't want to call a garage."

"Great!" I said. "You're really terrific, Rodney. I'm sorry we had to bother you like this, but really I didn't know what else to do."

"Not at all," he said gallantly. He got into the back of the car and removed the seats once more. Then he inserted the metal pole. Obviously with all the junk we had put into the back it wasn't so easy for him to search out the lock; he kept shoving it in with grunts. Abdhul and I crowded behind him to watch. "I hope you don't mind if anything gets broken," he said. "I don't see how I can find the lock without just forcing it through whatever's in there."

"Don't worry about it," I said. "I don't care—nothing's valuable, it's just clothes and food and stuff, if something's broken I could care less if we get the trunk open and the keys." But the pole had apparently come up against an immovable object; however hard he grunted it didn't budge. "I might give it a tap with the crowbar," he said. He looked over his shoulder into my face. "If you two will just move back a few feet, I can maneuver and give it a quick blow."

"Sorry," I said. "Abdhul, get out of the way. We'll never get to Shrewsbury at this rate." Shrewsbury was the nearest town to where my father lived.

Rodney gave the thin pole a sharp tap with the broader end of the crowbar. It didn't move, so he hit it again. Maybe the other end had come up against the side of a suitcase, or the food-cooler. He whapped it several times again, and at last the pole was hammered in. "Anyway, now the pathway's clear, I think I'll pull out the pole and then slide it into the latch," he said. "Angelo, if you could run around to the back, and wave to me at the position of the lock, it might give me a better sense of where it's located." Neither of us moved, and then it dawned on me he was talking to Abdhul. I gave him a poke in the side. "Run around to the back, honey," I said. Meanwhile Rodney began to pull out the pole. The end was covered with clots of gore and what I could only assume was clumps of brain matter. Oh no, I thought, the immovable object he couldn't push the pole through must have been the head. "Good Lord," Rodney said. He turned to me. His face was white and covered with a film of sweat. I felt so sorry for him I would have liked to kiss it away. "Good Lord," he said again.

"Oh, gee," I said. "I, uh—there was a bottle of ketchup and mayonnaise back there, that you must have probed." He was backing up rapidly now, nearly knocking me over in the process, and to make matters worse I now saw that attached to the S-shaped hook was a large chunk of pink gum to which was still attached by the roots a tooth. That was going to be a little harder to explain. Honestly, he really was overreacting; without even paying attention to the fact that he had almost knocked me over he had climbed out of the backseat of the car, stumbled across the parking lot, dropping the metal pole in the process, and run up the steps to the cab of his truck. Abdhul came to my side and we stood in silence as Rodney started up his engine—he didn't actually start it up, it had been running all this time, somewhere I had read that if a truck driver was stopping for only a short period they never turned off their engine because it cost more to stop it and then start up than to leave it running—but anyway, he threw it into a higher gear and began to pull out of the parking lot. I caught one last glimpse of his face—high cheekbones, white skin, staring eyes—as the truck turned in a semicircle and with a frightened roar pulled out of the lot.

"Well," Abdhul said, "That's that. Nice guy, though."

Thank God in his haste he had left the crowbar behind. I hoped he didn't get into trouble, if the crowbar wasn't his. It was probably an expensive piece of equipment, although I couldn't remember ever having priced crowbars. The pole he had dropped with a clatter in the middle of the space between his truck and my car. I told Abdhul to go and clean it off; then I took it around to the back of the car, gave the lock a couple of good hard whacks, and with the cloven tip pried open the lock. The hood of the trunk popped open at once; naturally the keys were right inside, on top of the hard-sided blue suitcase. I grabbed them and slammed shut the lid. Just as an experiment I tried to see if the trunk would now open with the keys, but it was broken. It was just as well, anyway, if nobody could open it; if I had to break in again with the crowbar it would have to wait until we got to my father's, when I had a chance to dispose of what was within. In the event that we were pulled over by the police, it would be simpler to say that the trunk was broken if they decided to search the car than to have to open it and get into a lengthy discussion as to what was inside and why.

Around ten hours later I broke out in an uncontrollable itching in an unmentionable area and it was then that I learned I had squatted in poison ivy.

Perhaps unconsciously I had given Abdhul the temporary alias of Angelo because I was thinking of my father's wife Angela. She was a big woman, nearly six feet tall, who had inherited quantities of money from her first husband, despite the protests of her former stepchildren. She used the money to start a horse farm, until one day while horseback riding her stallion ran into a tree and she was paralyzed from the waist down.

When it was left up to my father to look after the horses he mysteriously became allergic to them, and after her accident they were gradually sold. I always felt sorry for the children of James Junior, Angela's first husband—after all, he had only been married to her for four years, surely she could have arranged to see to it they were left *something*. But now Angela and my father led what they considered a simple life: her days were spent in welding garbage my father still collected at the dump into huge pieces of outdoor furniture and making vast quantities of zucchini pickle, relish, and jelly. Together she and my father considered themselves experts in the field of human psychology and many was the time by letter (which they composed and signed together) or in person, they had informed me of my contemptibility and the fact that I had an Oedipus complex.

I did not see how I could have an Oedipus complex, since I was not a man who wished to murder my father and marry my mother—maybe what they meant to say was an Electra complex—but the truth was, like so many others, my father still had a great deal of control over me. Probably this would go on my whole life, his ability to make me feel guilty; my mother pointed out that in one of her Introduction to Psychic Development courses she had an eighty-two-year-old woman as a student who said she was taking the course because she wanted to make her father proud of her, and that she had spent her whole life trying to please her father, even though as my mother said the woman's father was by now almost certainly dead. Many women, however, suffered from the same condition, that of trying to please a daddy who really didn't have much use for them; and that was one reason why now I was rushing up to check on his condition, even though ever since Angela's accident two years ago I had been asked not to come to visit until she got back on her feet.

Fine—so nobody's parents were normal (though it was my belief that my parents were the first on the block to become abnormal, by taking drugs and divorcing, which later became the norm) but at least there might have been some rules or regulations so that modern behavior was at least comprehensible! In the old days everybody made sense; there were certain things people did not do, and the things they did were to marry, get jobs, the women stayed home with the children until the children left home, the men retired, and then they died. But now, the whole system had fallen apart.

At least my father would have the grandson he might have hoped for. The last time I had spoken to him he said sadly that he was afraid it was his fault that my brothers and I had turned out so badly. This was his way of apologizing, I guessed. Although as we drove the endless industrial miles I did not know what I would find up at the house. Perhaps they had gone off on one of their hiking and camping trips (when they took a vacation they always tried to find a spot more remote than where they lived) and had together fallen off some rocky mountaintop not intended to be climbed by a man pushing a wheelchair with a woman in it. Or perhaps they had both OD'd on bad LSD (they had both had birthdays recently, and they usually liked to celebrate with various kinds of meat, lobsters, and drugs) and because of this they were wandering around in a trance, unable to take out the garbage or answer the phone. It might be up to me to nurse them back to health, even if they were never able to speak again.

Through the torporous twilight we drove, past the discount cowboy boot supply houses, the House of Wicker Furniture, the Olde New England Antiques and Basket outlet, the Super Flea Market Arcade (50 Flea Markets under One Roof). Kowalski's Fruit and Vegetable, Local Corn and Fresh Koconut Kandy. Pave the American Landscape! Cover it with Taco Take-Out, Drive-in National Banks, and Toyota dealerships! The Australian Opal and Magick Crystal Arcade, the Discount Liquor Shoppe with billboard advertising cherry wine cooler and Budweiser beer by the case. Caldor's, K mart, Zayres, Bradleys, Stop and Shop—there was no reason why, in a few years, the entire country might not be covered over in asphalt with places to buy, buy, buy. Oh, sure, there would always be a few people who strapped on expensive backpacks and hiking boots and went off to the Appalachian Trail or to climb the Himalayas, but there was every reason to hope that, given time, these places might be neatly paved, the trees marked and labeled, with plenty of snack shops and 7-Elevens and Piggly-Wigglys en route. Hah-ha! I chuckled merrily to myself, for it would serve them right; the only people rich enough to leave their jobs and take time to go off on a hiking expedition were those rich enough not to have to go to work, or who at least had a TV crew following them around to record the experience for public television.

Abdhul had fallen asleep; I drove for a time with a general sense of unease—perhaps someone was following us, though I didn't see how. My attack of paranoia I attributed to a false sense of importance. Honestly, there were so many kids all over the place these days: stuffed unwanted into Romanian orphanages, in inner-city foster care homes, every night on the news there were interviews with overworked social workers complaining they had a hundred pregnant drug-addicted thirteen-year-olds in their case load already and saw no end in sight. The highway had emptied considerably; now it was past rush hour, and though people commuted vast distances to work, from the sprawling suburbs that extended from Greenfield, Massa-

chusetts, to Hartford, Connecticut, from Boston and Providence all the way
to Manhattan, we had reached a stretch of nothing but trees. Abdhul woke,
muttered some cranky obscenity, and flicked on the radio. "I'm hungry,"
he said. "When do we get there?"

"A couple more hours," I said. "I could do with something to eat,
too." Oh, I would do anything to please him, to placate him; I glanced over
and in the yellow light of the dashboard the lids of his eyes looked swollen,
his face hot and feverish. I felt his forehead with my right hand; he pushed
it away, but not before I realized he was abnormally warm. "Do you feel
hot?" I said.

"No," he said. I was worried, though. Across the road was a brightly
lit House of Pancakes and Waffles; I got off at the next exit and circled back.
The vast parking lot was practically empty of cars; the place was illuminated
by huge high-powered lights, searing the night with a yellow glaze. I
stopped the engine and got out. The air smelled better out here; the
blackness fell in a sheet around the edge of the parking lot and above my
head thousands of insects swarmed up to the shimmering light bulbs, moths
and mosquitoes and billions of frantic gnats, all trying to immolate themselves on the false sun. Only one lone truck at the far edge of the asphalt.
Abdhul got out behind me. "Now there's every reason to hope we don't
speak to anyone in here," I said. "All we have to do is go in, order our food,
eat, and leave. Okay?" He didn't answer. "What I'm trying to say is, there's
no need for us to make ourselves memorable. We leave the dog in the car,
we go in, we eat, and we leave."

The interior of the pancake house was brightly lit; large glass windows
provided a splendid view of the parking lot. A sign in front said "PLEASE
WAIT TO BE SEATED BY HOSTESS" but since the restaurant was empty and
there was no hostess in sight I sat down in the nearest booth. A man, his
back to us, was sitting at the far end talking to a waitress, and after a while
she came and brought us two oversize plastic menus. Anybody living in
Russia would be envious: it was unbelievable, the amount of food this place
had to offer. Pancakes with chocolate chips, with nuts and raspberries;
meatloaf, Greek salad with feta cheese, omelets with mushrooms and green
peppers, fried chicken, bacon and eggs, tuna delight platter, grilled bacon
cheese lettuce and tomato—if for some reason some sort of poison gas
suddenly flooded the environment and we had to hole up in here for an
indefinite period at least there would be plenty to eat. "I'm going to have
the Silver Dollar pancakes with blueberry sauce," Abdhul said.

"What about something healthy?" I said. "For a change?"

He looked at me with hatred. Surely this was an opportunity for me to lay down the law, but frankly I didn't have the strength. Let him eat pancakes! "You'll have a glass of milk," I said feebly.

"I'm allergic," he said.

"Since when?" I said.

"Upsets my stomach," he said.

"You like milk!" I said. "Plenty of calcium. Chocolate milk?"

"Oh, all right," he said.

I ordered an egg salad sandwich and while we were waiting for the food to come I got up and went to the pay phone in back. I dialed a collect call to my mother. "Where are you?" she said.

"Some house of pancakes and waffles on the highway," I said.

"You're not there yet?" she said.

"We had a few delays along the way," I said. "Did I wake you up?"

"Not yet," she said. "A few people have been calling here looking for you."

"Calling you?" I said. "How did they get your number?"

"I don't know," she said. "Maybe you gave it as an emergency number at work."

"Yes, yes," I said, "nearest relative to notify in case of an emergency. Oh, God, who's been calling? What did you say?"

"Daniel Loomis," she said. "He wanted me to tell you there's a warrant out for your arrest in New York State." She laughed inappropriately.

"Oh, you're kidding," I said. "What are you laughing inappropriately for? Are you making this up?"

"No," she said. "Apparently Virginia and Amber have decided to prosecute you for some reason. . . . He said you didn't take well to being fired and . . . went off the deep end?"

"I didn't do anything, Mom," I said. "It was Alby who wrecked the place."

"Daniel said you're not to worry," she said. "He said that the office has insurance, and it will just be a question of suing the insurance company and settling for damages—if you're lucky."

"But I was fired before the damages took place!" I said. "That means the office insurance company was no longer representing me."

"Daniel said he would have told them to drop the whole thing, but he's anxious to leave some money to Archie and Alice when he dies that didn't come from his father, and he can put this in a special account for them."

"Archie and Alice don't need any money!" I said. "That family has something like four hundred million dollars!"

"He said, even if the insurance company doesn't pay, you don't have to worry, because there are ways they can arrange to garnish any salary you might earn in the future. You can pay it off a few hundred dollars a month for the rest of your life."

"What are you saying?" I said. "Whose side are you on? Oh, God, I'm so depressed."

"I'm just repeating what he told me," she said. "Believe me, I'm on your side. However, I do have one idea."

"What's that?" I said.

"I think you should write him a letter that says, 'Dear Daniel, In bed you were the best, I will never forget you.' "

"But he wasn't any good in bed!"

"That's why you should do it. Stick it in the mail now."

I sighed. "Yes, Mother," I said. I didn't exactly follow her reasoning, but I knew my mother was smarter than me. Probably by writing such a letter I would be the first to admire his nonexistent prowess, and he would always think of me fondly and decide not to sue. To sue! Things were worse than that if there was a warrant for my arrest! I would never fit into jail. I didn't even fit in to the mainstream population. "You'll do that for me, then?" my mother said.

"Yes, Ma," I said.

"Good. Now just try to enjoy your life!" she said. "You're having a good time—driving around, with Abdhul, you don't have to go to a job—what more could you want?"

Somewhat reassured, I hung up and went to the cash register. There was a bunch of postcards on a rack. I grabbed one without looking and took out a felt-tip pen. "You sell stamps?" I said to the cashier, and when she nodded I handed her the change and plastered one on. "I'll leave it here," I said. I was about to go back to the booth when I saw that Abdhul was no longer there. He was at the far end, talking to the only man in the place, the other customer. The minute I told him not to do something like speak to strangers he went and did it! God knows what he was chattering about so enthusiastically. Just what we needed, another stranger to become involved in our little saga. I gestured to the waitress and handed her a ten-dollar bill. "I'm going back out to the car," I said. "I don't feel so good. I wonder if you'd tell my little boy that I'm in the car?" Everything seemed slow and tedious, as if I were swimming in liquid. The light hurt my eyes and there was a strong smell of bathroom disinfectant mixed with maple syrup, as if that was what they used to wash the floor. *Just have fun!* my mother had said. But that wasn't so simple, was it? I couldn't even remember what was actually fun; maybe it was something I had never come across. Or maybe it was impossible to remember, like a trip to the dentist, where later on one couldn't really imagine what had happened while strapped into the chair.

"Don't you want your food?" the waitress said, looking at me strangely.

"I'll just grab my sandwich," I said. "I don't need it wrapped."

"All right, but the bill was twelve fifty-four," she said.

"Twelve fifty-four!" I said. That jolted me out of my trance state. "For some pancakes and an egg salad sandwich?" She looked at me ferociously. "Okay, okay," I said, handing her another five dollars. "Keep the change." She pocketed the excessive tip without even a grateful look. I went out to the car, my egg salad sandwich soggy in my grasping paw, dripping shreds of blubbery egg white and mayonnaise on the parking lot floor; let Dalgleish lap up most of it (obviously he should have been on some sort of puppy chow, but where to acquire it at this time of night) and sat waiting for Abdhul's return. What was he doing in there for so long? Through the glass front of the restaurant I could see a cheerful scene in the brightly lit interior: the waitress carrying Abdhul's pancakes down to the table where he sat with the man; the man apparently gesturing for the waitress to join them; and the three of them gathered like some happy American family around the banquet, out for an evening of fun and pancakes, Abdhul's mouth opening and closing in fishy delight, now talking with animated expression, now devouring huge gobs of pancake, while from time to time the waitress—facing my direction—broke out in smiles.

He was saying more to strangers than he had ever said to me! I was jealous, jealous; I thought of leaving the car, going in, and leading Abdhul out by the hand, putting an end to the fun and games. But how mean could a person get? I let him talk; eventually, I supposed, he would come back to me.

It was after 1 A.M. when we arrived at my father's mansion. From the highway it was twelve miles down a lesser road that dwindled to a gravelly dirt trail. Abdhul was asleep and I didn't wake him. The road veered sharply; the house was off to the right, at the end of the peninsula that jutted out onto the hundred-acre swamp. None of the outside lights were on, though this was to be expected, since if nothing was wrong they would have obviously long since gone to sleep. I pulled up into the dirt parking area between the front door and the overgrown rock garden, stopped the car, and got out. I was slightly apprehensive, for I knew they kept a number of guard dogs that ran freely outside at night—three half-breed chow chows, rescued from an inner-city ASPCA when they were a year or two old, who I hoped would remember me at least vaguely enough that they wouldn't attack. But to my surprise no dogs came running. They were kept outdoors winter and summer; to get out of the snow or rain there was a large doghouse to my left, built to resemble the main house, which my dad had designed himself and styled after what he imagined was a Zen Buddhist monastery, with a central atrium of rocks and gravel indoors open to the sky. By now they surely would have been disturbed from their sleep and come out to see who had arrived; when nobody came after a few minutes I called "Hello? Hello? Anybody home?" and tried the front door. It wasn't locked. I left Abdhul and Dalgleish sleeping in the car and went in.

On the stereo the last few bars of some Grateful Dead song played over and over. Obviously something here was wrong. It was beyond me how a grown woman could listen to the Grateful Dead, but that was Angela's taste in music for you. I walked up the stairs and into the living room; turned on the lights, and shut off the music. "Hello?" I said again nervously. Now I was frightened. The house had a peculiar stale smell, a sort of rotten hay or alfalfa, as if they had been smoking marijuana and not bothered to open the windows. Why hadn't I simply called the local police or sheriff's office to come out and check on the place when I had had the chance? I supposed it was because I hadn't ever really thought anything was wrong, and I needed to get out of the city. My family had always been good at calling the police on each other. Once years before when my mother had first moved to upstate New York, she had been living in a rented trailer; she came down to visit me in the city for a few days, and on New Year's Eve we drove the seven hours back to her trailer. There had been a storm, and the phone wasn't working, and the water had frozen in the pipes; there was nothing to do but go to sleep. The next morning—New Year's Day—at 8 A.M. a knock came on the door. It was two state troopers, called in by my grandmother, my mother's mother. "Miz Trowel?" the trooper said to my mother, who answered the door in curlers and bathrobe. "Your mother's very upset that you didn't call her."

I went into the kitchen, stumbling over stacks of newspapers and boxes before I found the light. For a Zen-monastery setting the place was certainly filled to the roof with stuff. There were at least twenty chairs around the table and lining the walls; Angela and my father were frequent flea market attendees, and each of them was unable to prevent themselves from buying all sorts of things. Fiesta ware and American pottery lined the open shelves, along with jars of zucchini pickle, raspberry jam, hundreds of bottles of spices. A filthy frying pan full of cooked mushrooms covered with mold was still on the stove, and on the table, two huge, partially eaten plates of what was apparently the same unfinished fungi. A half-eaten loaf of green bread, an open tub of spoiled margarine, the table piled high with books and papers—my God, it was like the Collier Brothers' home, or the house of the demented twin drug-addicted sadistic gynecologists (during a stint in the Army my father had worked with these two brothers briefly). I didn't even know where to begin, it seemed a little late at night to start cleaning up the mess, not that I had a particularly fastidious nature. I was in a cold sweat. Hey, I didn't do anything wrong! It wasn't like I had broken into the home of strangers, no, I was related to my father and had every right to be here. Still, something was terribly wrong, and it wouldn't have come as too much of a surprise to suddenly see my father looming behind me carrying an ax, with bloodshot eyes.

Dearie-me. I went upstairs to the bedroom in the turret; the bed was neatly made, unslept in, covered with its customary bedspread. My father had made the bedspread himself, from bullfrogs he had shot with a BB gun, and then painstakingly skinned, tanned, and stitched together. From here I could look out across the lake. The moon was setting now, but in the reflected light I saw the stumpy hummocks of cranberry bush and dead trees. The racket of croaking frogs, hooting owls, chiming insects echoed off the water, a screaming cacophony of night much louder than that in the city. Really, how could they stand it? My father, who was so attuned to noise that he had removed the motor from the refrigerator and attached it via wires in the walls that led to the root-cellar, simply in order that he not be interrupted from his meditations by the sound of the refrigerator switching on and off. My father, who had once stormed out of my apartment complaining bitterly of being kept awake at night by sirens, so sensitive to noise was he. Well, this was no time to brood over old injuries. I went out to the car and carried Abdhul inside, followed by Dalgleish. I put Abdhul in the bed; Dalgleish was waiting at the bottom of the stairs, apparently he had not yet mastered stair-climbing skills, and looked at me timidly. "It's all right, boy," I said, and carrying him up the stairs gave him a drink of water from a bowl I found in the sink that I rinsed clean of old muesli. Then I took him upstairs and put him on the bed next to Abdhul. The bedroom door had a lock on the inside, and after lying down next to the dog and Abdhul I got up, thinking I would bolt us in. Then I remembered the head in the trunk of the car. It would be a mistake to leave it there all night, dripping and oozing.

Probably I should have waited until morning, when I could think straight. But I noticed, in the last miles of the trip, that the trunk no longer stayed shut; what if it had blown open in the drive, and toward dawn someone came up the drive and noticed the contents? Plus, spiritually speaking, it was some sort of desecration, to leave a head lying around like it was an old suitcase. I went back down the stairs. The wind was blowing harder now; outside the wind chimes tinkled all at once. I went out to the car, grabbed the leaky bag, and came back in.

At the end of the living room was a short staircase leading down to the hot-tub room, a glass greenhouse connected to a solar heating system. I lugged the bag past dry foliage of dead houseplants. Nobody had watered these in some time. How peculiar that they had no friends to drop by unexpectedly, to check on them when they didn't answer the phone. Some years back Angela had been friends with the divorcée from down the road; I remembered this because once at ten in the morning she dragged me down to watch her make her stallion have sex with the woman's own palomino. The two women studied me with great interest as the stallion mounted the mare, but for me it was a little early in the morning, which caused them to tell me with no little delight that I was "uptight" as well as "surly" and for some reason "spoiled." Since then the divorcée had had a child—father unknown. Perhaps the two women had stopped speaking since then, as so often happened in friendships between women, and that was why the divorcée hadn't stopped by to check on them.

The hot tub was full of stale water, algae. I went down to the laundry room and got a bottle of bleach, which I poured in the tub. Then I tipped the head out of the bag and dumped it in, replacing the cover . . . All at once it became clear to me, what had happened to them. Never, never eat wild mushrooms, even when you think you've identified them absolutely. I thought they had given up the practice. They had eaten the mushrooms, and, violently ill, had stumbled out of the house and drowned. It might have been that just before becoming sick my dad had put Angela in one of the canoes, and in the center of the lake, at its deepest point, they had capsized. Her red enamel wheelchair twinkled by the door. Only a few years before my father had told me of an episode in which they gathered some morels and Angela had gotten severely poisoned. He told this story with a great deal of contempt, because he hadn't been ill, and he obviously believed that Angela hadn't really gotten sick from the mushrooms but something else. But I had read only recently in the *Reader's Digest* (a back issue I found on the street on the night that people put out their papers and magazines for recycling) about a man who was married to a Korean woman and when her friends came over she served everybody some mushrooms she had found in the woods that looked exactly like the ones she used to pick in Korea, and within five hours one person had died in great agony and everybody else had to have liver transplants, and they only lived because somebody had found them in time.

It was at this moment that I was overcome with an itching and throbbing in the genital and upper-thigh region so hateful I did not even have a chance to evaluate my grief. Probably later it would hit me with full force, but at the moment all I wanted to do was scratch. Due to repeated exposure I had become highly sensitized to poison ivy, although at this moment it did not dawn on me what was wrong. I was having some sort of nervous reaction, I thought, or maybe just premenstrual tension, although apparently due to stress I hadn't gotten my period in several months. I let out an involuntary moan. For a second I thought of climbing in the hot tub, but when I lifted off the lid the sight of the head, mouth agape, teeth in not very good condition, put me off the whole thing. I didn't even have the strength to cover the tub up again. With a sigh I went upstairs, located the calomine lotion in the bathroom cabinet, annointed myself, and crawled into bed alongside Abdhul and Dalgleish.

4

I AM NOTHING IF NOT A PRODUCT OF THE twentieth century and well aware that in Freudian terms all this means something. To find a head in the road might be a quirk of fate, but to find a head in the road and then to stumble upon the scene of one's father and stepmother's demise—obviously some larger psychosis or neurosis is involved. But hey, so what? I mean, who the hell actually cares? Life is short and psychoanalysis is long. In the end the only cure is death. In the meantime, as my mother always told me, the main point of existence was to have fun and grow as a human being.

Ten to fourteen days is the recovery period from a bout of poison ivy, according to one of my father's out-of-date medical textbooks, and quite frankly calamine lotion applied to this particular area did little good. Perhaps because of this I was more irritable than usual; this may have helped contribute to Abdhul's gradual drawing away from me, though Lord knows I tried.

The first day, while I took stock of the situation, and made an attempt to straighten the kitchen, Abdhul carried all our possessions and the additional food in from the car. Poor little boy! He really was so sweet in so many ways, and it occurred to me he might enjoy having a funeral service for the head, although when I was a child I never thought of having a funeral for any of my pets that died. I still remembered when a rabbit I owned gave birth to ten young and had eaten four of them when I discovered her in the process of eating the fifth. It was alive, but badly cannibalized; I flushed it down the toilet.

Abdhul was in the living room. He had unzipped his suitcase full of toys and was playing with Matchbox cars in a minuscule clear space on the floor.

"Oh my God, I almost forgot," I said. "You didn't touch any of the old food on the stove or the plates, did you? The mushrooms?"

"No," he said, looking up briefly.

"Well good," I said. "They're some kind of deadly amanita, I think. Or it may be that the herbs in which they were cooked were deadly nightshade, which is also poisonous. In fact, I'm just going to clean the frying pan and the plates right now." Really I was shocked that my father and Angela had made such a juvenile mistake. Why, right next to the stove were six volumes of Euell Gibbons's cookbooks, in which he forced people to go out and collect weeds and herbs and then come home and cook them. How many of my childhood visits to my dad had been spent having to pick milkweed buds and daylilies and then eat the inedible mess for dinner in butter I couldn't say. I wondered as I dumped the slop into the garbage bin and washed the plates if my mother hadn't somehow been behind the whole thing. I wouldn't have put it past her to find some mail-order shaman or Indian priest-doctor in the mountains of Mexico who for a fee would mail anonymous magic mushrooms—no return address—that my father and Angela would happily sample as some new hybrid peyote. "By the way, don't go down into the hot-tub room just now."

"Why not?" Abdhul said.

"Because I say so."

He stood up immediately. "Why? What's there?"

"You don't want to know," I said.

"What is it?" he said. "I want to see."

"If you must know, I put the head in the hot tub."

"Wow," Abdhul said. "I want to see!"

"Leave it alone," I said.

"Say, where is Gramps and Grandma, anyway? How come this place is such a mess?"

"Abdhul," I said, "Dick and Angela are dead. I think they ate the poison mushrooms."

"Where are they? I want to see!" He ran from the room. "Are they in the hot tub, too?" As soon as he was out the door I reached down for a good scratch. "Abdhul, did you take Dalgleish out yet?" I called. "Take him outside! Go for a nice walk in the fresh air! But don't go too far, Abdhul— just up the drive and back!" I put the plates in the dish rack. "Later we'll go for a long hike," I said in a quieter voice.

Where to begin? It seemed that until I had an idea of what to do it would be better if nobody knew we were here; how long that would be I didn't know, so I made some attempt to clear off the table and then I got everything resembling food out from the shelves. I had always secretly loved a challenge; if I were resourceful enough we might be able to remain here undiscovered for quite some time. An unopened box of ground almond flour—recipes listed on the back said milkshakes could be made with two tablespoons of the flour and ten ounces water. This would do as a milk substitute. A jar of cashew nuts, stale and chewy. Four small cans of Mexican hot peppers. A bottle of Korean pickled cabbage kimchee. Two pounds buckwheat flour. Half an opened box of linguini. A ten-and-a-half-ounce can of salmon. Hellman's real mayonnaise, large bottle. A can of sauerkraut. I opened the liquor cabinet. Christ, what a paltry assortment. A gallon of Gallo, opened but only a little gone. One inch of Jack Daniel's and a bottle of gin. Not much selection.

There had to be something else. I opened the refrigerator—the full force of my grief had apparently not yet hit, for I found myself sobbing as the smell of sour milk greeted my nostrils. The half-gallon container, only half full, had spoiled and I poured it down the sink crying and grabbing a piece of paper towel on which to blow my nose. My poor daddy, usually he liked his coffee with milk in the morning but he never ate breakfast because his father had died of a heart attack in his early fifties, shortly after I was born, so I never knew my grandfather. And my father had been determined not to gain any weight, but he had still only managed to live to age fifty. It was so sad. And the orange juice was spoiled too, although thank God there were two cans of concentrate in the freezer, four pints of expensive ice cream in various flavors and, miracle of miracles, eight separate containers of what appeared to be spaghetti sauce probably made from last year's garden vegetables. Also in the doorway of the freezer was a Band-Aid box where the drugs were kept. How could I forget my father's words to me on my last visit here before his death? "Hello, hello," he said. "Help yourself to the liquor cabinet; Angela's made hashish brownies; and in the freezer there's psilocybin, LSD, and I think a little bit of cocaine."

"I didn't know you liked cocaine, Dad," I said.

"I don't!" he said jovially. "That's why there's still some left in the freezer. Somebody gave us a packet—I tried a bit, but I didn't care for it. But if you like it, it's yours for the asking."

Oh, Daddy, why hadn't I smoked marijuana with you when you wanted me to join you? Was it simply stubbornness on my part, a refusal to become one with you? But the truth was, I didn't care for marijuana or any drugs, except alcohol, and even that didn't really agree with me. As I explained to Dick, marijuana made me anxious, and other women I had spoken to felt the same. But Dick claimed that marijuana only brought out the emotions within; therefore, it meant that I was an anxious person. But I wasn't particularly anxious, unless I smoked marijuana. Now I was sorry I hadn't experienced a little anxiety if it would have pleased him. And I had never had a chance to tell my dad how proud of him I was. Nobody could say he was ordinary. And he had an animal magnetism and verbal skills I had never come across in any other man. When I had finished inside I would take Abdhul and go out to find the Stonehenge he had said he was building. Now that he was dead he would probably be discovered by the art critics as an artistic genius; his heart had never really been in gynecology, even though he had worked wonders for so many women. But whenever he had a free moment he was happiest in his workshop, chiseling stone into unsold sculpture. His dream, forever unfulfilled, was to have a show in a Manhattan gallery—but of course the New York art world wanted no part of the chefs d'ouevres of a country gynecologist specializing in fertilization techniques.

A jar of Mrs. Betterby's Sweet Gherkins. Four and a half slightly hard English muffins—thus far, this was the only bread to be seen. In the vegetable bin, potatoes and onions, four carrots, and a soggy cucumber. A plastic bag on the first shelf contained half a green, cooked lambchop. Tupperware tubs of varying sizes held old peas, a dab of ratatouille, cole-slaw, and some smarmy basil-pesto sauce. I longed to pick up the phone and call my mother, so I could describe to her the contents of my dad's refrigerator. One of the big reasons for their divorce was, according to my father, that my mother insisted on keeping all the leftovers in the refrigerator until they turned rotten, although my mother denied this. Here was proof that it was his doing—however, she had warned me against calling her or contacting her from the house, and until I decided what to do I wanted my presence here unknown.

Returning to the kitchen some half hour later Abdhul pronounced the ripened head "neat" and expressed a desire to confiscate Angela's wheel-chair for his own usage. I didn't see the harm in this; it was a modern lightweight racing number. As a child I, too, had always had the desire to push myself around in a wheelchair and would gaze longingly at the sight of a handicapped person. Well into my adult years I had shared with my mother a taste for the morbid in literature: among my favorite books, passed on to me from her collection, was a story of a boy who had become blind due to a mishandled firecracker; the first-person account of a woman who, at the age of twenty-two, had breast cancer, badly managed by her doctor; and my favorite of favorites, *Awake, Monique (Awaken to the Meaning of Love)* in which a newly orphaned Dutch girl was adopted by her handsome uncle who ultimately seduced her.

Uprooted so frequently in his young life, why shouldn't Abdhul be indulged in this whim, although as there were no paved roads in the area nor sidewalks, it didn't seem to me that it would be much fun for him to wheel himself around in the chair—obviously he wouldn't be able to get up to high speed. Squeezing my thighs tightly together under the table where I sat, I said the wheelchair could be his if he could help me figure out what to do with the head. "Bury it," he said.

"Good idea," I said. "Go look in the workshop." One end of the house was a sort of barnlike structure with huge doors, where my father chiseled his slabs of marble and local granite, while to the side was where Angela welded garbage. Beyond this was the guest bed, although few guests who slept in the middle of the vast chilly room, air nearly unbreathable with the fragments of metal and stone-dust chips, ever felt much like returning. Abdhul scampered off and came back with a shovel and a pitchfork.

Oh, it was hard not to stereotype men when he was so mechanically minded and he hadn't learned it from me. It was sad my dad wasn't able to see Abdhul; he would have been proud. My dad had always been so dreadfully ashamed of my inability to hammer and saw. According to him I was extremely manipulative, which was a female trait. Because when I was a child he had had to build me a treehouse, and a cage for my rabbits, both of which were my idea. I was so manipulative that when he found me, age eight, feebly sawing a board into a crooked strip, he took the saw from my hand and did it himself. I was sorry I still harbored some bitterness, when the flower of life could be crushed at any minute. Nobody liked to be around an angry or sour female. Each day was a chance for a new beginning, or so it was said on the Dinah Shore program, one of those TV talk shows.

It took us several hours to dig a hole along the marshy edge of the swamp. It was amazing how firmly the roots and tubers of the nearby trees and the sharp-edged sawgrass clutched the soil; they fought desperately to avoid being torn from the ground, but in the end Abdhul and I won, even though the hole wasn't very deep. "Now what are we going to do?" I said. "I don't want to touch the head again."

"Impale it," Abdhul said. "On the pitchfork."

"Yuck," I said; but I went into the house, down to the hot-tub room, opened the lid, impaled the head, and carried it back out—followed by Abdhul and Dalgleish—where I shook it off into the pit. We then covered it as best we could with rotting pine needles and several scoops of muck from the water. There were a couple of big rocks scattered around—my father had hauled them over on chains behind the tractor, to form a Japanese garden—but these were too heavy for us to move. So we gathered pebbles and stones from the driveway and placed them in a cairn-shaped memorial mound atop the burial site.

"Now," I said, wiping my hands together, "let's go out exploring. We'll have a nice long hike around the premises."

Abdhul was like an animal released from a zoo after many years; every muscle in him was tensed, and when he glanced over at me his eyes were bright and fierce. The pine trees, maybe seventy or a hundred years old, grew up along either side of the gravel path, and the ground was covered with a thick bedding of pine needles. Low mountain laurel bushes, fragrant with bay scent, blueberry bushes, wintergreen creeper. Dalgleish followed behind, barking with excitement. "Oh, Abdhul," I said. "If only I had been a tree, how much differently things would have turned out for me. Of course the life of a tree could be hard."

"How come?" he said.

"First a seedling, competing with the others for light and space. If I get to the sapling stage, there are more obstacles to overcome: drought; bark being nibbled by insects or animals; larger trees all around anxious to smother. But let's say I made it to maturity, in the protection of a woods such as this, or in a nature preserve. Now that would be heaven. The days passing in peaceful, eyeless glory. My roots in the ground, my leaves basking in the sky. Surrounded by the other trees, some communication would take place, but it will be a blind, sexual communion, without language."

Abdhul snorted disgustedly and rolled his eyes. "I think you're crazy," he said and pushed on ahead of me. Dalgleish scrambled to keep up. Meanwhile I swatted at a variety of stinging fly that had taken a personal liking to me. We circled the edge of the swamp and then cut through on a path leading up a hill to a cliff of rock. Here I clawed my way up behind Abdhul, over the outcrop. The swamp, the pine trees, the little house perched on the tip of the jutting peninsula, the balding hardwood trees blighted by gypsy moth; all spread out like a vista before us, minute and on the same scale now as the broccoli-like lichens, the pixie cups and redcaps that studded the surface of rocks and boulders when examined from close up. We sat for a time in amiable silence. Even Dalgleish lay peacefully in a fragment of sun. From a distance came the drone of a chain saw. "Tell me, Abdhul," I said at last. "What do you think you want to be when you grow up?"

"Cocktail waitress," he said with a scowl, before rising and charging back down the rocky crest.

★ ★ ★

It was an idyllic time, apart from my depression over the deaths of my father and Angela and the difficulty of not speaking to my mother for so long. To speak with her was like talking to myself, only a version of me who was intelligent and not quite so vicious.

I wondered what people did who didn't have my mother to talk to. How lonesome and isolated most people must be. Of course Abdhul was my friend. But over the next weeks he became more and more of a wild animal. He was up before dawn with the dog—luckily I'd found a big bag of dog kibble in the barn, so at least Dalgleish had a balanced diet—and then disappeared until dark, though what he was up to out there I never knew. I was afraid to use the car (gas was costly, and what if we were recognized) so I stayed around the house. At night I prepared various meals, progressively more inedible: night after night we ate spaghetti sauce, there was no more pasta so I served it as a sort of soup. One night we had beans and sauerkraut, hot-dog-less; there was the time I tried to prepare a pseudo-Thai saté, serving peanut butter atop toasted cashew nuts. Stunted potatoes from the garden, boiled, butterless. A salad of dandelion leaves, sheep's sorrel, and daylily buds, doused with plenty of oil and vinegar. I mixed up a thick slush of almond-flour milk, flavored it with vanilla and cinnamon and froze it, thinking we could pretend it was ice cream, but that was the day the electricity went off. Naturally the electric bills must have been unpaid. My dad and Angela had a post-office box someplace, I should have gone in and collected the mail before somebody grew suspicious. But at least the solar panels heated the hot water.

I sent Abdhul out at night with the BB gun to shoot frogs; he came back after midnight with five, very proud of himself. After all, he really was just a very little boy. I don't think it was all that easy to shoot them, even though the place was hopping. But that was on a night when the moon was full. Without electricity I was afraid to use up the kerosene in the hurricane lamp, and there were only two extra batteries for the emergency flashlight. When the weather turned cold I knew there were only four or five cords of wood split, stacked, and seasoned, not enough to get us through a whole winter, even if we did go to bed as soon as it got dark.

Yet it was pleasant during these few weeks. The occasional woman appeared in the drive, someone who had made an appointment to see my dad six months or a year before, but I always managed to make up an excuse and turn her away without much difficulty. It was perhaps lucky my dad had gone into semiretirement a year or so back; his office, in the basement, was unused and dusty, he only made appointments to see a few patients a year.

From the kitchen table I watched the leaves beginning to change around the edge of the lake; there were cold spots in patches, and here unexpectedly overnight a harsh swatch of red or gold would appear, as if somebody had gone out and thrown buckets of paint over a select tree in the night. I was nervous that Abdhul's childhood was going by and he wasn't receiving an education of any sort. For a few days I tried to make him stay in during the afternoons while I read aloud parts of the encyclopedia; but it was one of those things my dad or Angela must have picked up at a flea market, and dated 1890. Anyway, he was so bored and restless I again let him go back out all day, though I made him promise he would take a book along and read for at least an hour. There was quite an extensive library in the bedroom, though of course I'm not sure they were books he would have read had he been enrolled in school—*Candy,* by Terry Southern (I had read this book myself, when I was around ten, and remembered being baffled by the hunchback who urinated on a piece of bread and then ate it). Which reminded me of a hunchback man who followed me for four blocks around 96th Street a year or two ago. He was around forty-seven years old, a bald hunchback who drooled and wasn't very tall. He didn't have any teeth either, but he liked me, the poor man. But it didn't really give me an ego boost, not that I was anti-hunchback.

Anyway, the books. No book was more recent than 1967, apart from every single copy of the *National Geographic.* Had my dad and Angela simply stopped reading on that date? I supposed if we stayed here for the next ten years until Abdhul was eighteen or twenty, he would have a unique education. By that time we would be well into the twenty-first century, and he would be the only person of his generation unable to operate a computer or any electronic equipment. He would be a good fifty years behind any of his peers, yet the only one to have read Anatole France. In a way it would be an interesting experiment. It was only a shame that the available material was not even older. Just think if everything had been published no later than 1900. What a unique person I would have raised in that case! He would never use the words *fuck* or *shit,* at least not in everyday conversation. Modern art would have no existence. The future would be his to reinvent as he chose, and perhaps because of this he might create something wildly original.

Still I knew it was important that I try to teach him different subjects, even though I had a slight problem with math, such as adding and subtracting numbers, which I had to do on my fingers, and with the multiplication table I could only multiply numbers times two or three, and then after that I had to add on the rest by hand.

After dinner one night—four small musty fish we had caught together, a sunny, two perch, and a catfish tasting faintly of algae, along with a small amount of wild rice I found in a bag and boiled with some Mexican hot peppers—I sat Abdhul next to me at the table and attempted to teach him about fractions. "Let's say a man had four hundred pages, and he wanted to take away one-fourth of these pages," I said.

"Then he would have three hundred," Abdhul said.

"Not exactly," I said. "Because let's say the man had to subtract a fourth from every hundred pages. From the first one hundred pages he would deduct twenty-five. That would leave him with three hundred seventy-five. Then from the next one hundred pages—one hundred to one ninety-nine—he would deduct twenty-five. That would leave him with three hundred fifty. Then from the next one hundred pages he would deduct twenty-five. But one-fourth of the remaining twenty-five is not twenty-five, but rather a little more than six. Do you see what I'm getting at?"

"No," Abdhul said. "You're not making any sense."

"All right, let me try to demonstrate physically," I said. I went to the drawer by the defunct telephone and removed four pieces of paper from a pad. "A man has four pieces of paper and three friends. Now, he wants to remove one-fourth of each page. But he doesn't want to spoil all four sheets of paper."

"Then he should just throw out the fourth piece," said Abdhul.

"No, no, you don't understand. He doesn't want to cut a fourth off of each page; so from the fourth sheet he cuts one-fourth, for his first friend's sheet. For number two, he cuts a fourth from the fourth sheet. For number three, a fourth. That leaves him with one-fourth of the fourth page. But now, he doesn't need to throw away the entire last fourth, because he only needs to remove one-fourth of it. That leaves him with three whole pages, and a little piece of the last one."

"Pamela, you're not making any sense whatsoever!" Abdhul said. "What's your problem? One fourth from four is three! You're just confusing everything!"

"Temper, temper, my little Heathcliff," I said. His face was quite flushed. Really I should never have given him *Wuthering Heights* to read. What a book! I even made him read sections of it aloud to me by candlelight. We were both saddened by the end, when almost everybody was dead. I tried to explain to him that that was how life operated in those days. But as he pointed out, things weren't all that different now. Because now, even if people didn't die, chances were good that you were never going to see them again, so what was the difference? Ever since then he had worked himself into babyish fits with regularity. "I know you think I'm stupid, and you can talk down to me as much as you like," I said by way of reassurance. "But you'll still have me and I won't leave you."

"Easy come, easy go," he said and shrugged. But he left his seat and, pulling up his T-shirt, came and sat on my lap, an indication he wanted me to scratch his back, which both of us found comforting.

Several things troubled me as I occupied my days going through the papers in the filing cabinets, straightening and organizing and looking for a will that would tell me what to do in the event of both my dad's and Angela's deaths. Come spring, I figured, their submerged bodies in the lake might float to the surface.

And not among the least of my worries was that I hadn't gotten my period. Probably I had some sort of cyst condition, but it made me uncomfortable that I had missed it—twice—and felt progressively more bloated. But it was impossible that I could be pregnant. I leafed through an old photo album of pictures taken in my childhood that somehow my dad and not my mother had kept after the divorce. There was a picture of me holding hands with my brothers, in the middle of a field of pumpkins. What a pretty child I had been, snub-nosed, with red-blond braids; who would have thought, looking at that picture, that my condition would deteriorate so much over the next twenty-five years and that I would not turn out to be a beauty. If only I could have been flash-frozen at that age, physically, while my mind was allowed to grow—I could have conquered the world if I had an eight-year-old's body with the mind of a grown, manipulative woman, even though I would have been somewhat short.

Frankly, I couldn't think of when the last time any sexual intimacy had actually been consummated. Of course there was the Alby hand job under the table, and a brief interlude with Daniel Loomis in the bathroom. Abdhul was right: Life today was like life in the books of yore. (*Yore* was a word he was very fond of). Characters appeared briefly and exited, never to be seen nor heard from again. Or if they were—the way Alby materialized and tried to break in one night—it wasn't for reasons that made any sense, or furthered any sort of plot. It was all arbitrary; there was no glue holding people together. Because of this in many ways I considered myself practically virginal.

Then, too, the head buried outside bothered me. But to drag the police in at this stage would only lead to further difficulties. Perhaps the peat-bog soil around the edge of the pond would preserve its condition until I knew what to do. In many ways I was still in shock, for as I say, to find a head in the road was a terrible tragedy, but to find a head in the road and then realize that one's father and stepmother have eaten poisoned mushrooms and staggered out into the wilderness to die, having already stated that one would inherit nothing, withered the spirit. It was not that I felt myself to be alone or unique in the way I was being treated by the Fates. No, I had read too many trashy newspapers to believe that, and watched too much TV. Many people arrived home to find their entire family had been slaughtered during their absence; a lot of people got married and then forty years later had to perform a mercy killing of their husband due to senility. My upstairs neighbor, Randy, was talking on the phone to his friend who was calling from a pay phone on the street when a guy came over and shot him in the head after asking for money, and his hearing was permanently damaged. Airplane Crash, Disgruntled Serial Killer marching into the office at work with a machine gun, ready for mass execution—hey, my situation was just one of a long list. Probably it would only make page two of the *New York Post* or *Weekly World News*. Of course, it was different when you were the person living through it; then it was more than just light reading.

I decided at last to take the chance and hike through the woods down to the little general store in Wain, just beyond Mosquito Gulch. I wouldn't drive—I had rented the car for just a few days, it was supposed to be delivered back to the city—and God knows by now any charges must have been well over the limit on my credit card. It was possible the Wreck people had even reported it as stolen. One afternoon I lassoed Abdhul into helping me camouflage it with pine needles and branches. At the general store I figured I could use the pay phone and also pick up some supplies, although I didn't see how much I could carry in a shopping bag through the overgrown paths. "All right, Abdhul," I said. "I've decided today's the day I'm going to have to risk it and go to the store."

"I want to come," he said.

"Look, I don't want anybody to know you're here," I said. "What if that social worker has been around, or if your picture is on the back of the milk cartons as a Missing Child?" But if I went at the end of the day, just before the store was closing, the clerk or whoever ran the place might not pay too much attention to me in his eagerness to close up shop. Then I could hide myself in the bushes until it got dark before heading back up the road and cutting into the woods. It would be hard to see where I was going, however, in pitch blackness. "Abdhul, is this the time when the moon is up?"

He gave me a long, patient look. "No, Pamela, it's morning. The sun is up."

"But is this the time when the moon is full?"

"No, it's the time when the sun is up!" he said.

"But sometimes the moon is full, and other times there's no moon in the sky. What I want to know is, is this the time when the moon is full?"

"The sun is out during the day, Pamela!" he yelled.

"Was the moon out yesterday?" I said.

"The sun was out yesterday," he said. I could see he felt sorry for himself having to speak to somebody who was so demented. I found a backpack—this would help to carry stuff—and got some of Angela's clothes out from the closet, in order to make myself as local and innocuous as possible. The way people dressed around here was truly something. They tried to look nice and fashionable, and that was where they made their mistake. Wrap-around blouses with motifs of blue clouds on a red background. Puffed sleeves. Aqua-blue pants suits. Yellow plaid ruffled skirts for evening wear. Meanwhile in the city they were buying and wearing expensive flannel-lined overalls. Apparently in the country they felt obligated to dress in city fashions dating from 1973, while in town they were dressed in tweed country clothes circa 1957. Couldn't Angela keep up with the times? Finally I had to settle on wearing one of my dad's shirts—a pumpkin-colored velour (1969) and a baggy pair of jeans that Angela wore horseback riding. I took the last of my cash from my pocketbook and set off for Wain.

You can never get all the parts of your life to match up at one time. If you have extra toilet paper, that's the moment you run out of paper towels. If you remember to purchase coffee, it turns out there's no milk. Here I was in the country, but without an adult male to share the pleasure with, and I was in peril, even though I couldn't exactly remember why, only that I had done something wrong. Trudging down the drive trying to find the path that would lead through the woods and worrying about all my various conditions, I was reminded of a guy I had gone out with many years back, one of my first boyfriends. I was maybe eighteen at the time, and in college. The only way he was able to have sex was to pretend I was a man. He was a lot older than me, maybe thirty-five, and since I hadn't really gone out with anybody before, I assumed his behavior was normal. He liked to discuss what sort of penis I would have had. "It would be short, but thick," he said. I don't know how he came to the determination, but I guess he thought I'd be placated by the thickness, despite the fact that according to him it wasn't going to be a big one. Somehow he must have envisioned me as one of those mustached leather-clad men so familiar on the streets of Greenwich Village or Fire Island, wearing chaps, and with a lot of hair growing on my back. Thanks a lot for nothing, I wanted to say, but I just assumed that this was probably necessary in order for men to have sex, though quite frankly even after I went so far as to paint my existing facial hair with black mascara he still fell limply into disappointment when it became obvious that I only had a pitiful clitoris. Probably Martin, my ex-psychiatrist, would have said I had penis envy or else I wouldn't have found myself in such a position. But what about womb-envy, huh, Martin? I mean, which would you really rather have, a short-yet-thick penis or the ability to have a baby?

I was already sweating profusely in my father's mock turtleneck. Finally I found the turn-off point, some sort of old logging trail that I thought would lead down to Mosquito Gulch. The dirt road was hot and dusty, a gash carved between boulders and rocks, maidenhair ferns, wild trillium, daylilies, stunted birch, and white pine. Beyond the road a small stream trickled around and over rocks, then followed a little passageway where it crossed under the street. I paused to splash some water on my face, then moved a big rock over to one side. What a scurrying of bizarre insect life! Things with large eyes limped and hobbled away at the destruction of their home, horribly wormy creatures beginning to form wet wings—things that were probably thinking, if everything went well they would be the ones ruling the earth in a couple million or billion years.

When everybody had a chance to escape and the murk washed away and the water had collected sluggishly in a foot-deep pool, I scooped up some of the sweet water in my palms and drank. Just at this moment a gnat, or perhaps a green fly, decided to take a little stroll around the outer shell of my right ear, and before I could swat it away it had plunged itself into the honeyed inner depths. Oh, no! I bashed myself rapidly several times along the side of my head, but the thing wouldn't leave. It was lost in there. To have an alien living creature inside my head; I stuck the tip of my little finger in there, hoping to silence its angry, airplane-like buzz, but to no avail. Surely the damned bug would take it upon itself to get out of there; it must have the intelligence to find its way out; but I could sense it staggering this way and that along my eustachian tube, if that was the name of the passage.

Now I was sorry I hadn't allowed Abdhul to come along. He was so clever manually; the awful thing was, that whenever I argued with him about something he was almost always right. I didn't know where he got his information, but once when I had pointed out a leather chair for sale he said it wasn't leather but plastic, and sure enough, he was correct. And another time, when I brought home an antique tiny merry-go-round horse on a music box, he said it was new and made to look old. Probably he would know some technique for insect-removal from the inner ear, even if he had to use his tongue or manufacture some suctioning device. The whole thing gave me a colossal headache; it was as if in addition to the insect some large, hot, carnivorous bird had come along and landed on my head.

I left the stream and walked along in a state of misery. Hiking in the heat made my itching worse, too, and I stopped to scratch, my hands down my pants, just at the moment a pickup truck came crashing along down the road, though I'm sure too much dust was raised for them to be able to see what I was doing. Fuck the country! Why did I have to be punished in this fashion, when I wasn't trying to do anything wrong? If only I had been a nun, then I could have enjoyed my torment and used it to my advancement.

Finally I arrived at Zabruder's. It was an old chicken coop of a building, with a creaky screened front door, big rips in the screen that were repaired with plastic tape or not at all. I opened the door; inside it was dark. "Close the door!" a voice creaked in the dark.

As I turned to close it I saw that on a shelf next to the doorway, alongside a red plastic fly swatter, was a large collection of deceased flies neatly arranged on their backs. The last was still in its death throes. So this was my reentrance to civilization! I was so excited I didn't even know where to begin. Oh, the things I would buy to take back to Abdhul— canned peaches, and Hershey bars, and dried beans for bean soup! There was even a cooler/freezer off to one side, I didn't know if I could carry back ice-cream toffee bars before they melted, but certainly I could lug along a couple of cans of Coca-Cola, which he had scarcely gotten over his addiction to. I treasured the moments before making my selection. It would be so wonderful to surprise him, to watch his face as he unpacked the contents of my knapsack. To my right was a pay phone on the wall; perhaps I would call my mother first, although I didn't know what was more thrilling, to speak to another adult human being or to shop for Abdhul. If I made my selections and then carried them to the cash register, I would have to load up everything in the knapsack, so perhaps I'd better make my call first. The fly buzzing my ear made me feel I was deep under water. My eyes were beginning to adjust to the gloom. "Do you mind if I make a phone call?" I asked the man behind the cash register.

"Pay phone," he said. "Free country."

I picked up the phone and dialed collect; but I could sense the clerk's hulking presence, and I realized I would not be able to tell my mother everything that was in my heart. Then the phone rang five or six times and I grew nervous. What if she had gone out of the house? She almost never went out of the house, except when school was in session and she had to teach. But on the seventh ring she answered the phone and the operator asked her to accept a collect call from Pamela. "Will you accept?" she said.

"Yes, I will," my mother said.

Why it was just as if I had been wandering some Yorkshire moors for many days, through gorse and snow and sleet, even though it was practically ninety degrees outside! "Ma!" I said.

"Where are you?" she said.

"I'm at a pay phone," I said, "in the middle of a store."

"So you can't talk?" she said.

"Not really," I hissed, blinking over at the man. Now that my eyes had adjusted, I saw what a mockery of humanity this guy was. Gaunt, dressed in overalls with a soiled bib, swollen nose, and greasy red-blond hair and beard—he was playing some type of board game, alone, and there was something vaguely familiar about him. "Are you at your father's?" she said.

"Near," I said.

"And how is he?" she said.

"Uh-huh," I said.

"Deceased?" she said.

"Uh-huh," I said.

There was a pause. "But otherwise, are you having a good time?"

"I can't hear you very well," I said. "There's a fly in my ear."

"Do you want me to drive there?" she said. "If I can find a substitute to teach my classes?"

"No!" I said. "That would only make things worse." Much as I loved my mother, I knew that very quickly after I saw her I would revert to adolescent behavior, due to the fact that during my adolescence I had never rebelled, and some part of me was making up for that now.

"Are you depressed?" she said.

"A little," I said.

"Maybe you're getting your period," she said.

There was something strangely unsatisfying about the conversation. Maybe too much time had gone by since we had last spoken and she had changed. "Well, this isn't much of a conversation," she said. "I guess you can't talk."

"That's right," I said.

"Something remarkable has happened here," she said.

"What?" I said.

"One of my students put her blue jeans in the washing machine and when she opened it she discovered a British Revolutionary War uniform. It's in excellent condition, practically new, and we're going to take it to the costume and clothing department of the Metropolitan Museum."

"Aw, Ma," I said. "She probably had one lying around or made it."

"I don't think so," she said. "It would be impossible to fake it; they can do tests to determine its age through the fabric."

"So what do you think happened?" I said.

"I believe the washing machine was temporarily attached to some conduit opening onto the past. Now somebody in the Revolutionary War has a pair of new Levi's."

"If only something like that would happen to me!" I said.

"I know," my mother said.

"I would give anything for just one experience like that. Or if aliens landed and took me in their spacecraft, and injected me with some painful substance and then deposited me on the highway!"

"Have you seen any spacecraft out there?" my mother said.

"No," I said.

"Why don't you and Abdhul go out at night and look?" she said.

"Mm," I said, keeping one eye on Silas Marner. He really was rank, too, just my luck. Didn't it offend him to live with his own odor, or did he enjoy it? It reminded me of a man I had once found through an ad in the local paper to type some of my essays and my thesis in college. He had smelled, too. Human beings were very odd, I had forgotten this after being away from them in the woods.

"You really should keep your eyes out," my mother said. "I was just reading, how recently the CIA captured an alien, and apparently he's escaped. I'd send you the clipping, if you had a mailing address."

"Does the alien—have a strong scent?" I said in a hiss.

"What are you saying?" my mother said. "Does somebody there smell?"

"Yes!" I said triumphantly. That was all the proof I needed just now that my mother and I were still attuned to one another.

"Hold your nose," my mother said. "You know, I really feel very sorry for Abdhul."

"What do you mean?"

"How is Abdhul ever going to learn any morals, with you for a mother?"

"I don't follow you," I said.

"Forget it," my mother said. "But is everything all right? What are you going to do now?"

"Yes," I said.

"You know, it's hard talking to someone who doesn't say anything. Do you have enough money?"

"I found twenty-eight dollars in a drawer."

"Do you want me to send you some money?"

"Not just yet," I said. "Maybe later." Maybe later I would find a way to unobtrusively get to the post office and have her send a money order to me, but for now I was certain if I went and collected the back mail there would be questions asked. I didn't even know how long the post office would continue to hold old mail, without payment made on the P.O. box.

"You know, you and Abdhul can always come here," my mother said. "I have a job, and there'll be enough money for the three of us. You can be the housekeeper, and Abdhul can go to school while I work."

"A housekeeper?" I said. "Do you want me to wear a uniform?"

"Just when company comes," my mother said before we hung up.

She was a very powerful woman but I couldn't help but feel she was in some way responsible for the predicament I now found myself in. For years whenever I told her I had met a new man she suggested I get pregnant and ship the baby up to her to raise, although she hadn't stated this quite so bluntly. It was only natural for a woman to want to have grandchildren, I guessed; there must be something so wonderful about a baby that people never got over it. Maybe there was always hope that next time around they would do a better job. Of course with Mitchell out there so busy selling his sperm she probably had plenty of grandchildren already, even if she hadn't seen any of them that she knew of.

But both my brothers had sworn they never wanted children of their own. Ralph's hobby was raising ferrets, and Mitchell said that as soon as he finished medical school he was going to go off to some Third World country; he was fond of the tropically diseased. Now I was sorry I hadn't told my mother to call up Ralph or Mitchell and send one of them to me—but maybe she had already done so. I got along better with Ralph than with Mitchell, but it would have been nice to have either one with me. I needed help, I now saw. I would give the situation a couple more days and if neither of them arrived I might come back to use the pay phone again. I stood for a minute by the pay phone collecting myself and then set off down the dank aisles. What should have been a pleasurable experience filled me with dismay. The wretch who ran the store had apparently eaten half the produce and put the empty and half-empty cans back on the shelves. Four antiquated tubes of toothpaste, two of which had obviously been opened, lying squeezed and depleted on the shelf. Several opened cans of

Libby's pear halves. Everything was sticky with syrup. An ancient bag of oyster crackers. Twenty or thirty jars of orange marmalade, the last thing Abdhul and I needed in a house where in the basement larder were already fifty or sixty jars of raspberry preserve dating back innumerable years. A tiny can of Vegetable Medley—peas, carrots, and potatoes—the photograph on the label resembled food served to children in a cafeteria. A partially consumed can of black-eyed peas. A can of pork pâté, some sardines, cocktail olives, Spam, several relatively fresh boxes of Rice-A-Roni. I took whatever hadn't been opened. I gave a sour glance over at the gaunt figure behind the cash desk. He was avidly rubbing his left breast and gleaming at me. What kind of filthy pig would litter his own sty? Perhaps my analogy wasn't apt, but pigs were generally neat animals, and if a pig were a man he wouldn't have behaved this badly.

If only I had joined TWA's frequent flyer program when I had the opportunity! Over the years by now I might have accumulated enough mileage points for a free flight somewhere for Abdhul and myself. But it always seemed too complicated and I was never really certain of how to join up. Now I was sorry I hadn't taken the trouble. He picked up a fly swatter—not the one by the door, I noted—and, still massaging his chest with his right hand, flicked a bug on the counter with his left. I half expected him to pick up the fly with his fingers and pop it into his mouth, but luckily things weren't so bleak. I was so fascinated by him that I didn't notice a long piece of flypaper dangling from the ceiling fan and walked straight into it. I put my hand up to my hair; a nattering tangle of sticky brown glue studded with ripe raisins of insects. The presence of its companions seemed to set off a sort of stirring in the mite inside my head; either the bug or a broken string of some sort inside my ear tube suddenly let out a shrill, high-pitched whirring sound, causing me so much pain I wheeled rapidly and crashed into one of the racks of half-eaten food, still trying to detangle the long gooey piece of flypaper in my hair. A can of Durkee's French Fried onion rings I hadn't noticed before (what a special treat for Abdhul this would be: take one can cream-of-mushroom soup, mix with canned or frozen green beans, and then sprinkle the onion rings on top) hit me on the shoulder and began to roll along the floor, so I dove down to get it before it disappeared out of sight for good, but this unfortunately caused the aluminum bars holding the knapsack to my back to hit several opened cans of fruit cocktail and peas, which poured down on me.

There was still some life in him after all; he came running out from behind the counter yelling, "Hey, you! Quit it!" and grabbed my arms behind my back. What did he think I was trying to do, distract him while

I shoplifted? This was the last place I would think of shoplifting, a bunch of old mangy half-eaten food, and he was probably the sort of guy who kept skinned and flayed heads or private parts in empty boiled-egg-and-beet jars around the filthy mattress where he slept. Believe me, I had read enough books about what went on out here in the country. Lying on the floor trembling in a pool of sticky substance, all I could think was that I wanted to go home, even though I didn't really have one. Now I felt bad for telling the same thing to Abdhul when on several occasions he had said he was homesick. The geezer was coming toward me. I couldn't move, the ridiculous backpack made it hard to twist around. Did anybody else ever come in this loathsome shop? Oh, please, let some car stop, let somebody shout out for gas, let Alby or the crazed social worker in search of Abdhul appear at just this moment. My arm felt as if it had been pulled from its socket, but I managed to reach my hand up to my mouth; my fingers smelled curiously of pizza. Probably this guy had eaten a pizza at one time and then with his filthy, greasy, unwashed hands smeared the juices from pepperoni or sausage all over the merchandise, touching the unopened cans, and then I had gone along and picked them up, and clutched them to my body—though they had in my spill rolled this way and that—and now I had his creamy juices contaminating my skin. This was no nostril hallucination. Garlic, tomato sauce, onions, and some sort of meat. I should never have permitted myself those masturbatory fantasies in which I was being raped. But after all, there was nothing wrong with a rape-fantasy, it still didn't mean the person actually *wanted* to be raped. All it meant was that one portion of my brain wanted to lie around passively while some man came along and held my arms down, overcome with animal desire for me that he was unable to control. I wasn't alone in this fantasy either; plenty of women, who had to live in this day and age when no men wanted very much to have sex, dreamt the same thing. Whereas, if we had been living in the cave-man era, when men still had an abundance of testosterone, then no doubt the prevalent fantasy would have involved a very gentle, weak, and helpless man with a face like a girlish angel, who lay on the grassy lawn and was overcome with gratitude at a woman floating out of the bushes to place her wet vagina atop his excited dick.

Involuntarily I let out a scream as the big stinker came closer and began to bend over me on the dirty linoleum. Oh, how clearly I saw what was to come. A filthy snot-filled rag shoved into my mouth, to prevent me from further utterance. Carried off to some disgusting mattress, possibly in a spider-filled cellar smelling of mold. There I would be stripped and bound—perhaps he would shave me of all body hair—and then press his soiled and reptilian organ against me, as many as eight to ten times a day. Who knew what depraved positions it would take to please him? My mind raced in its hole, no exit up *there*, though possibly given time I would learn astral projection, similar to that practiced by the Tibetan lama Lobsang Rampa, who was captured by the Chinese and tortured in a cell where he perfected his ability to leave his body and travel into the sky, which prevented him from crying out in pain, in a fashion similar to that promoted by the screen actress Shirley MacLaine. The reason I knew about Lobsang Rampa was that my mother had read all of his books and told me about them, even though I hadn't actually gotten around to reading them myself, and even sneered at his sad story a little bit, though now I was deeply sorry for this.

Unfortunately, as I am willing to concede, I was not always the best judge of human nature. "Hello, I'm Moe Newman," he said, "I own Zabruder's." He reached out a hand at the exact moment I reached a can of burrito dinner and threw it with all my might at his head. "Let me help you uuuuhhh," he said. I felt so mad at myself for my misdirected rage that I leapt up, slipping across the sticky puddle and grabbing his head between my hands—the can had hit him just about his right eye on the temple—and pulled it down toward my bosom, rubbing the sore spot as if it were my own.

I was amazed at the quickness of my upwelling maternity, though perhaps this ran in the family. One time on a bus my mother knocked off a man's hat but didn't notice while my brothers and I walking behind her up the aisle roared with laughter. "What's so funny?" she said. "You knocked off that man's hat," we told her. Without thinking she turned around and walked down the aisle, picked up the man's hat, and replaced it on his head; however, she must have been in something of a trance, because she looked at him quizzically and began to adjust it on his head, pushing it down this way and that until finally some dim fury entered his brain and he pushed her away. It was as if she were arranging a fedora atop a mannequin, muttering apologies all the while, and now I heard myself (in only one ear, however) doing the same. "Goodness, Moe, I'm so sorry, so sorry," I said, rubbing his domed brow as if it were Aladdin's lamp. "Apparently I've retained something of my softball pitching skills, all these years." What a little champ I had been, and it was a shame I hadn't continued with it and fought my way through the Supreme Court to be permitted to be one of the only women in the minor leagues to play ball. How sad it was to reach mature years and find certain pathways permanently closed.

Moe fluttered this way and that, trying to escape my grasp. "An aspirin might do the trick," I said, looking around, and wanted to add, "if you've got any in this slop hole," but stopped myself in time. It would take me no time to make the shop clean and tidy; I might make fresh-baked breads, and fruit pies from local fruits in season, and sell them for an exorbitant sum, along with herbal teas and spices. With a little work, my insistence on daily baths or showers, Moe might turn out to be quite presentable, and in front I could grow flowers, while in the old mill out back Moe could teach Abdhul woodwork and carpentry, and each day a yellow bus would take him off to school. Given time we might be blessed with little offspring of our own; how gratefully Moe would look at me, tears in his eyes, at how lonely he had been and how happy he was now. Poor, poor Moe! And poor me, although I did not like to feel sorry for myself, for after all, self-pity was a disgusting thing, was it not, for some reason that I momentarily couldn't remember.

I started to straighten up, gathering my cans and jars into a heap on the floor, so Moe could be sure I wasn't planning to steal any of his wretched merchandise. My actions were rewarded; there under the bottom shelf, in a pile of fluff balls, was a small two-pound bag of unbleached flour—now I could teach Abdhul how to bake bread, provided that the flour was not full of mealworms. According to Ralph, my father and Angela had often spoken about the fact that I was a "dysfunctional" personality. Ralph was too delicate to tell me this himself, but he had told my mother, who repeated this to me. Apparently once some years back, Angela and I had gone to the supermarket together (though as I couldn't remember this I didn't know whether it was in Manhattan or some other location) and there I had purchased a two-pound bag of flour. Only a completely incompetent person would buy a two-pound bag of flour, because as everyone with any sense knew, it was more economical to buy a bigger quantity. Of course, there were all sorts of reasons I might have bought only a two-pound bag at the time, though as I say I had no memory of any shopping expedition with Angela, so I couldn't accurately justify my actions just this minute. It might have been that a) I didn't have enough money to buy a bigger bag, or b) There was so little room in my kitchen cabinets in New York that there was no room to store a larger bag, or c) I probably didn't use that much flour, living on my own, and if I had bought a bigger bag it might have gone bad before I had a chance to use it all up. But that was my father and Angela for you. Women fell into three categories—those with low self-esteem; those with dysfunctioning personalities; and those who were overcompensating. Now I would never have a chance to explain to my father why I had only bought two pounds of flour those many years ago.

What a shame I hadn't bought a bigger bag of flour when I had the chance, so that my father could have died with a better opinion of me.

I saw now that my major fault had always been in not living each day of my life to the fullest. I should have been enjoying every nuance, not being so nervous or anxious—appreciating it like a child, like Abdhul—and buying economy-size boxes of detergent, flour, and other products. What if I had been the one to die, and not my father? Well, there was no time for such philosophizing now. I chattered happily to Moe, picking up the cans from the floor and thrusting them into his begrimed arms. "I'm buying all these things, you see," I said. "I wasn't just grabbing cans to create disorder. If you carry them up to the front, I can pay you." Clutching the cans he shuffled back to the register. He didn't have what I would categorize as a brilliant personality, but far be it for me to judge. "You know the Trowel place?" I said, putting a can of beans and the flour down on the counter. "That's my dad. I'm house-sitting, while he's away." On a short pole with hooks different kinds of squat smoked sausages were hanging in plastic—"Beef Jerky" and "Spicy Mini-Sausage"—and after checking to make sure I had enough money I grabbed a bunch of these and put them on my pile of stuff. Sure, they were loaded with nitrites and carcinogens, but both my brothers when they were little had loved these meat treats, and probably Abdhul would enjoy them too. If they had been homemade, I would have thought twice, but they were in sealed wrapping with the name of the manufacturer. Otherwise I might have wondered if Moe wasn't grinding pieces of customers out in the shed in back, which believe me had happened in the past. Murderers were into all sorts of kooky techniques for getting rid of their victims, it boggled the imagination, the kind of things in the paper. I took all the jerky strips he had, at the low price of forty-nine cents each, and the one lone plait of "Camper's Pemmican." The label said this was an old Indian Treat of preserved meat and raisins, and even if Abdhul didn't like it, it could be a teaching device about the ways of the Indians. There was a lone package of Ballpark wieners, and I snatched these up eagerly. It might not have been the healthiest diet, but I knew plenty of people who were on macrobiotic diets, and they were often scrawny and gray; and I had once had a girlfriend (not exactly a close friend, but I had hopes that we might become close) who had worked briefly at *Hunter's World* as an art director but who left after she got pregnant. And during her pregnancy she was determined to be the perfect mother, and so she never drank, nor smoked, nor took aspirin, and she ate only healthful things. And when that baby was born (she nursed it and said she would never, ever give it a bottle) it was the scrawniest, most homely baby I had ever seen. Around every two minutes she would whip out a breast to feed it, while it made horrendous slurping sounds, and its little face was all pinched and gray from trying to get enough to eat. Probably if she could help it her child would never taste dried Indian pemmican, nor Ballpark wieners—and she would be right. And here I was, secretly contemptuous of this woman's noble aspirations for health and clean living, carrying my hotdogs over to the cash register and being a lousy mother. A crippled fly chose that moment to dive-bomb onto the package; it must have been crippled or at least genetically deficient, because when I swatted it with my free hand it didn't fly off in time and I killed it. I felt bad, too, not just that I had killed a living thing that I could have just as easily brushed away, but because it made a huge greasy smear on my hotdogs. Probably its bad diet had slowed it down; it really was overweight and too fat to fly fast. I didn't know what a balanced diet for a fly should be, but whatever it had been feeding on here was not nutritiously sound.

"You staying at the Trowel place?" Moe said, sluggishly and methodically ringing up my products.

"That's right," I said, putting down my hotdogs smeared with fly topping.

"How is old Doc Trowel?" he said.

"He's away," I said.

"Is that right?" Moe said. "You have any idea when he might be back? I was supposed to get over there last year to talk to him about cutting down some trees in the orchard up there. Haven't gotten around to it yet. Been kind of busy with this place."

"He's out of town," I said, "for an indefinite period."

"Might stop by in a day or so," he said, "see if he's back."

"I'll let you know when he comes back," I said. "I'll tell him to get in touch."

"He wants that lot cleared," Moe said. "Told him I'd give him a hundred dollars, too. I'll stop by the house first, if I get up there with the chain saw."

Why had I been so foolish as to tell him I was staying at my father's? I could have just as easily said I was a traveling hiker, on route to the Appalachian Trail. "I used to get over there quite a bit," Moe said. "We had a Scrabble game going pretty much once a week. Your dad, Doc, was quite a help to me some time back; we had sort of a falling out a year or so ago, though, and I haven't seen him since. Then I moved to New York, briefly."

"Oh yes?" I said. "Why was that?"

"Well, your father kind of inspired me. I decided I wanted to go back to school and become a doctor."

"A gynecologist?"

"No; well, I thought more along the lines of a psychologist. I didn't think I wanted to spend four years in medical school and four more in residence. Plus I would have had to take some undergraduate science classes first. But I have my B.A.; right now I'm going back to school at night for my psychology degree." What sort of people would want to go and see a psychologist who smelled so bad? It seemed farfetched—but I myself knew of a nutrition specialist in New York who was a coke addict, and I had gone to a doctor—he had been highly recommended—who weighed close to three hundred pounds. "Sorry about my present demeanor," Moe said, almost as if he could read my thoughts. "My ex-boyfriend is supposed to be stopping by in a little while, and I'm hoping to discourage him."

"Listen, would you mind if I gave you a check?" I said frantically. "I seem to have bought more things than I have cash for." Maybe this was a terrible thing to do, because I knew I didn't have any money left in my account, but I didn't see what else I could do. We needed food. Anyway, later I could write him a note saying he could have the wood he was planning to buy from my dad, for free. Under other circumstances I might have been tempted to linger longer; but Abdhul was alone, and probably hungry. I wrote out a check, slung the merchandise in my knapsack, and headed out the door.

In the twilight Dalgleish was gnawing on something on the front steps. He looked up at my approach; his face was covered with blood. What the hell had he found, anyway? "Oh, no," I said aloud. "Bad dog! Bad dog!" I clapped my hands together and ran at him to frighten him off. Oh, yuck. He had managed to dig up the head and had dragged it over to the house. If only Barbara Woodhouse or some other dog trainer were here to offer assistance. What was I supposed to do under such circumstances? "Abdhul!" I called. "Abdhul, get out here and look at what your dog's done." The assorted remains were really too grotesque to examine closely. Abdhul opened the front door. "Hiieeee!" he said.

"Look what he did," I said, pointing.

"Oh, no!" Abdhul said. "Bad dog! After all the work it took, digging that hole."

"I don't know what to do," I said. Dalgleish licked his lips. "Just a sec," Abdhul said, going back into the house. Great, I thought, suspecting him of returning to whatever game he was playing and leaving me to clean up the mess. But he came back out holding a gray metal wastebasket. "Put it in the wastebasket," he said.

"Good idea," I said. "Put it in the wastebasket."

"I don't want to touch it," he said. *"You* touch it."

"I'm not going to touch it," I said. "Put the wastebasket on its side and kick it in." Abdhul sighed but he did as he was told. "Yuck," he said, tilting the wastebasket upright again. "Now what are we supposed to do with it?"

"I don't know," I said, "Just leave it there for now. At least it's a cool night out. Come on, I bought us lots of groceries." We left the wastebasket near the front steps and went inside. Then I got to work.

"If you could eat only one thing now and forever and ever, what would it be?" Abdhul said, over dinner.

"You mean you'd have to eat the same thing three times a day?" I said. The meal was practically the first decent thing we'd had in weeks; the rank hotdogs, bloated and pink, on a bed of canned baked beans, sauerkraut and potato chips. Surely there was some old Shakespearean expression that was appropriate, about living for today, but at the moment I couldn't think of it.

I fed Dalgleish a half a hotdog under the table while I thought. It occurred to me that the fly in my head had stopped buzzing; years from now, if I ever had an autopsy, some coroner would no doubt find it embedded in ear wax like a fly in amber. "Gee, I don't know," I said. "That's sort of a hard question. I like lobster, though I can't really imagine eating it for breakfast, but I guess I could skip breakfast and then have it boiled with butter for lunch, and maybe broiled at dinner. Remember, though, lobster's not kosher."

"I'd have hamburger," Abdhul said. "With french fries. No, maybe onion rings."

"I guess my choice would be pizza," I said. "Onion, sausage, and mushroom. If I got tired I could just pick off certain ingredients for a change."

"But you like salad, don't you?" Abdhul said. "Why don't you pick chef's salad, and that way if you got tired of it sometimes you could just eat the cheese."

"That's not a bad idea," I said. "Although salad, day in and day out, could get pretty boring." Dalgleish was having a hard time eating the hotdog; he was in the process of losing some of his baby teeth. His guppy eyes bulged but he chomped industriously, holding the meat between his two front paws. Then he got up, stretched his legs luxuriously, and urinated on the floor. "Bad dog!" I said. "Abdhul, you've got to teach him! There's

no reason he shouldn't know by now to go outside." Dalgleish lifted his
eyebrows at me and walked briskly from the room, his red orangutan fur
sticking up in matted patches on his head. "The moon's going to be up
tonight, Pamela," Abdhul said, finishing his vittles. "It was almost full last
night. What do you want to do? Do you want to come out with me in the
canoe to shoot frogs with the BB gun?"

"Why not?" I said. "You know, when fall comes, all the frogs will
disappear under the mud and there won't be any more frog legs to eat."

"What was it like today," Abdhul said, "at the store?"

"Oh, it was unbelievable," I said. "It was really run-down—half the
cans on the shelf were open—flies everywhere, tubes of squished toothpaste—and the guy who ran it apparently knew Grandpa. He smelled really
bad, because he was trying to discourage his ex-boyfriend, who apparently
was still in love with him. I guess he was gay, or he had been ambivalent
about his sexuality, but Dad—Grandpa—cured him, and then they had
some sort of falling out. Grandpa was a very talented person, even though
he always felt depressed because he hadn't become a famous sculptor.
Actually, you haven't painted in a long time. We should look in the
workshop for his paints and stuff, and then you could paint a picture. You
have a lot of talent in that direction."

"No, I don't!" Abdhul said modestly.

"Anyway, Dad—Grandpa—probably could have gotten very rich, cur-
ing guys, because he always had some young guy hanging around him, who
would always start out being very passive and effeminate, but after Dad put
him to work chopping trees, day in and day out, and lecturing him, the guy
invariably went out and found himself a girlfriend to boss around. But Dad
preferred to make his money fertilizing women. That reminds me, if only
I could find that goddamn will. I've looked everywhere and I just can't find
it. We have to make a move pretty soon. I don't know what's happened
to their bodies or when they'll turn up, but I'm not sure I want to know.
But without the will . . ." Abdhul had taken our plates, nearly licked clean,
over to the sink, where he was languorously pouring the contents of a bottle
of dishwashing detergent on them.

"Dad would have liked you, Abdhul," I said. "It really made him mad
if people didn't jump up as soon as they had eaten and clear the table. One
of his favorite pastimes was to invite a bunch of people over, telling them
it was for a party and a barbecue cookout. Then when they got here he
would make them carry logs over to the swamp—you know that pathway
made of sticks that goes over the water? It's the same type of log path that
the early settlers used to build, backbreaking work, believe me. And imag-

ine the surprise of my dad's guests, thinking they were attending a party and then being put to work! Sometimes he had them help him construct a dam, too."

Abdhul turned from the sink dreamily, wiping his hands on a dish towel. "Let's go find the paints and paper," he said.

"Mmm," I said, going over to the window. It hadn't taken me as long to walk back as I thought: This was a good thing; the moon wasn't yet up, I could hear the leaves of the birch trees chattering uneasily just beyond. My own face reflected back in the glass, though I was barely able to see it, and I grabbed the cigarette lighter from the general store to light the hurricane kerosene lantern. Thank God for the wood-burning kitchen range. It even had a little side compartment to bake things, although I hadn't yet tried. I carried the hurricane lantern down to the workshop studio, Abdhul following me. Shelves crammed with jars of nails, screws, bits of string, a jackhammer still on the floor next to a chunk of local stone of some sort, possibly marble. The two of us began opening drawers and boxes; I knew that somewhere were various paints, acrylic and oil, turps and sketchbooks—in the past I had seen my father drawing or sketching, I doubted he had thrown the stuff out, since nothing here ever was—except for a TV set, which they had once sold at a yard sale, at a time when I didn't have a television set nor could afford one, and so I requested this old set, but my request was denied and it was sold for five dollars. It was terrible to harbor a grudge; really I hoped I wasn't that sort of person, but unfortunately I probably was. "Actually, the truth is that everybody harbors grudges, but they have the decency to pretend they're mature individuals who have put the past behind them and forgiven," I said to no one in particular, since obviously Abdhul wasn't listening but pouring a lot of pennies out of a coffee can into a heap on the floor. "Hey, look at these," he said. "These are all different weird kinds of pennies and nickels." He carried a few over to me: zinc and wheat stalk, buffalo head and silver dimes. "These might be worth something," he said. "Maybe I'll collect them." I murmured admiringly and opened a cabinet: there was all the junk, the crayons and pastels and Cray-pas, slabs of spongy paper and brownish rolls of newsprint. "Here you go!" I said, getting the stuff out.

Then, behind where the art supplies had been, I saw a metal security firebox. "There it is!" I said. "This must be where he keeps the will." I took the box down. Just as I was about to open it, Dalgleish pranced in, with the end of the roll of toilet paper in his mouth. "Oh, no!" I said.

He had apparently grabbed the dangling end and carried it from the bathroom, unwinding the rest of the roll as he went, meandering around chairs and workbenches. "Look what he's done!" I said. The entire roll, hundreds of feet, was raveled in a path behind him. Abdhul left the coins on the floor and darted after the dog; Dalgleish decided to run, toilet paper still in mouth, and within seconds the whole workshop area was bedecked with pink-tissue streamer. "Toilet paper is in short supply!" I said. "Stop him, and reroll it." I put the box down on the table and looked at it. The moment of truth was at hand; what a terrible person I was! All I did was think mean and bad and hostile thoughts, and now I felt guilty. I was guilty, I knew my father believed I didn't care for him, otherwise I would have called and visited more frequently. I hadn't touched the telephone since my arrival—probably it had been disconnected—but there was a lumpy gray phone here in the workshop, and I picked it up. The dial tone whined in my ear. Ah, what did I have to lose? I rang my mother's number; she picked it up on the second ring. "I found the box that I think has the will in it," I said. "And I'm afraid to open it. I feel so terrible. Terrible and guilty."

Abdhul was still chasing Dalgleish in circles; the dog dropped the toilet paper and was grinning like a fiend, while Abdhul shrieked. Bits of torn paper were flying everywhere. "I don't want to hear about it," my mother said.

"How could I have been such a rotten person?" I said. "I should have been visiting Dad while he was alive; I should have gone to Florida to visit Grandma Vi; I should have come up to spend time with you. Life is short, I never meant to be a bad person, but everything slipped past and now I feel guilty."

"Why would you feel guilty?" my mother said. "My last words to you are—if you feel guilty I'm going to come to you from beyond the grave and kick you in the rear end."

"What do you mean, your last words to me?" I said. There was a banging on the front door. "Oh my God, somebody's here," I said. "I have to go." I hung up. Abdhul stopped chasing the dog. Dalgleish suddenly looked frightened; he ran over to a pile of boxes covered with an old Hudson Bay blanket and squeezed underneath. Some watchdog—the little monster was hiding from the burglars! Still, I couldn't feel too ashamed that the dog was a coward; it showed a certain humanness that was rather adorable. Well, there was no sense in making Abdhul open the front door; I went and opened it myself. This was probably an indication the ghost of my father was lurking someplace about, because to me one of the great joys of having a child was being able to say, "Abdhul, go answer the door," or, "Do me a favor and bring me a glass of Diet Pepsi with one ice cube"— commands similar to those given to me by my parents. However, if my father had been here, he would have said, "Pamela, don't make Abdhul answer the door! Get up off your tush and answer it yourself," or some statement to the effect that managed to make me feel like a lazy slob.

It was Moe, rubbing his left breast and looking gray and nervous. Really, it would have been a nice touch if he had shaved off his musty beard on my account, but it was still there, long and red. Maybe he had to keep it, to hide some facial neuralgia. Even so, he was quite froggy in appearance; still, I had always liked the way frogs looked, especially the frog butler in *Alice in Wonderland*. Somehow the fact that he wore specs hadn't registered on me earlier, but they contributed to his goggle-eyed demeanor, although no frog had such full, ruby lips. Perhaps I had gotten him all wrong: he was now dressed neatly, in a white shirt with high, button-neck collar, and no longer seemed quite so country-bumpkin, though he let out a ribbety gulp. "You, uh, left some of these groceries back at the store and since I was passing by I thought I'd drop them off," he said.

"Thank you," I said and started to take them from his arm.

"I'll bring them in for you," he said. I really didn't want him to come in; but then it occurred to me that if he stayed outside, there was a strong chance in a minute he was going to stumble or trip to see the wastebasket right next to his feet. Luckily he was peering over my shoulder, apparently trying to see what was in the house. But at any moment . . . "Come on in!" I said suddenly, grabbing him by the arm. "Don't stand there outside in the cold!"

"It's not cold out," Moe said, puzzled.

"Then it's too hot!" I said. "Come in where it's cool!" Moe followed me around to the workshop. "This is Moe," I said to Abdhul, who had picked up the metal firebox and was leafing through the contents. Dalgleish, on realizing Moe was no burglar or thief, came running out from his hidey-hole, tail wagging, and dragged himself humbly along the ground and over to Moe's feet. "I brought you a few other things I thought you could use," Moe said, putting the paper bag down on the workbench next to the vice.

"What is all that stuff, Abdhul?" I said, going over to his side and taking a sealed letter from his hands. Maybe I had jumped the gun and there was a revised will or addendum in the box. I looked at the fat envelope in his hand. This was it! As soon as I opened it, I knew I would have the evidence that the ancestral pad was never to be mine, my brothers' and Abdhul's; now we would have to leave. It really wasn't very nice; though my father was notoriously absentminded, due to his daily marijuana intake, or so I believed, surely he could have remembered he had children to leave his property to. Still, I had resolved to let go my anger, and I tried not to feel mad at the injustice. I was longing to rip open the will and read it right now, but somewhere I had read, maybe in a newspaper advice column, that it was rude to open one's mail and read it in front of others, although maybe I had gotten my facts wrong. If only Moe would leave—but how to get him out of here without his bumping into the head in the wastebasket?

Moe seemed a bit abashed at Abdhul's presence and the fact that the dog, though youthful, had abruptly entered into a premature sexuality, for overcome in a paroxysm of lust Dalgleish was attempting to mount Moe's shin. The poor man must have really wanted to make a good impression; perhaps he was trying to win back my father's affections through me, because I looked in the bag of groceries and saw a fresh carton of milk and a little jar of caviar, among other stuff, and none of it were things I remembered having picked up in his store. Maybe it came from some other private stock, or maybe he had stopped at some gourmet shop miles away in town. "Oh, look at all this!" I said.

"It's, uh, just my way of apologizing," he said. "I guess I'll be going now."

"Going?" I said. "Oh, no—not yet. Stay for a drink."

"Gee," he said. "I really can't."

"Abdhul, why don't you run upstairs and make us a couple of drinks," I said. "Gin and tonic all right with you? You know where the liquor is, don't you, Abdhul? And, uh, while you're up there—*move the garbage.*"

"Yeah, yeah sure," Abdhul said, giving Moe a thoughtful stare.

"And look, Moe brought us some fresh milk, wasn't that nice of him?" I said. "After you *move the garbage* you can mix some Nestlé's Quik into it, I saw a jar of strawberry flavor in the cabinet over the refrigerator."

"I can take out your garbage, when I go," Moe said.

"Oh, no, he can do it," I said, handing Abdhul the bag of groceries to carry upstairs. I certainly didn't want Moe snooping around the rest of the house; it really was a complete disaster, and he might begin to wonder— what had happened here? Moe was shaking his leg, trying to detach Dalgleish; the glossy pink lipstick tip of his wobby baby penis flashed before my gaze and I sighed. He was so young, but I supposed I could find him an old blanket or a towel and tie it to a doorknob for him to have sex with. My childhood dog, the one I had received after my braids were removed, had a lifelong affair with a towel tied to a doorknob, although to be perfectly honest I never understood that his humping activity was sexual in nature. What I thought he was doing with the towel I don't know, but it was tied there by my parents to save the legs of my brothers and me from sexual abuse. "Well, I guess I better get going," Moe said.

"Tell me—what's Moe short for?" I said suddenly.

"Maurice," Moe said. "I don't know if you know the family history, but your father's wife, Angela, was my stepmother for a brief time. After my father's death, my brothers and sister took the whole case to court, because, quite naturally, it didn't seem right that our father had left us nothing, and he was quite senile at the end—none of us could believe that Angela hadn't somehow manipulated him into rewriting the will at the last minute."

"Abdhul, did you *move the garbage!*" I yelled. I turned to Moe. "Ah, yes, I see. And you weren't involved in the court case with your brothers and sister?"

"Well, you see," Moe said. "I've had quite a few years of problems. My wife was hit by a tractor-trailer on our honeymoon and killed. And this caused me to become homosexual. I'm very open about my past, but I'm sure your father has mentioned me. Anyway, after years of therapy I finally made my peace; living here so close by, running my little general store, I got to be quite intimate with your father."

"Yes, yes," I said distractedly, listening for what I hoped would be the sound of Abdhul opening the front door and moving the wastebasket into the woods.

"But then, I got very angry when your father sued me for thirty thousand dollars over a land dispute. See, the state said that the dam on his property that I helped him build was illegal, and that he had to take it down, but I own the adjacent property, and he claimed that it was my land that was interfering with the flow of water down to Hatcher Lake. I was so annoyed I left for New York and came back only quite recently."

Abdhul came into the room. "There's no garbage in the kitchen," he said. He had three drinks on an aluminum tray. He was so clever; really he was talented in all sorts of different ways. He must have left the wastebasket where it was and instead nipped out to pluck a few mint leaves from the mint that had gone wild and taken over a plot of ground underneath the kitchen windows—because Moe's drink, which he carefully pointed out to him, had a sprig of mint leaves protruding from the top, and it was only a shame there was no ice in the house.

"How pretty," I said.

"Actually, I better get going," Moe said. "I really only stopped by to tell you something, but . . . this really isn't a good time, and I'll come back a different time."

"Oh, no," I said. "Let's talk. Abdhul, why don't you take the paints and brushes and go and *move the garbage* while I talk to Moe?"

"What about going out in the canoe to shoot frogs?" he said. "You promised."

"Yes, I can see you're busy," Moe said. "Thanks for the drink."

"That's your drink," Abdhul said to Moe intently. "Aren't you going to drink it?" Moe picked up the drink, looked at it, and put it down. "Abdhul, alcoholic drinks aren't meant to be drunk like soda or juice," I said. "You're just supposed to sip them." I took a swallow of the stale tonic and gin in my glass. "Have your drink, Moe," I said.

"Actually, I'm allergic," he said, but he took a tiny sip and began to walk away.

"Wait!" I said. "Don't go out the front door. We're not using the front door. The front door is broken."

"It wasn't broken when I came in," Moe said.

"Yes," I said. "But it might break. That's why we're trying not to use it."

"I can take a look at it," he said.

"No!" I said. "Not right now. Go out this window. I'll climb out first, and escort you to your car." He looked puzzled but I slid open the window and climbed out. "Let's go right to your car," I said. "No need to take a look at the door now." I stuck by his side, chattering, while he got in. "Thank you so much for coming," I said. "It was lovely to see you again. And now, Abdhul and I are off frog hunting—we're going to use a BB gun."

"I'll come back in a day or so, to fix the door," he said, driving off.

I ran back to the house and grabbed the wastebasket with the head, lugging it inside. How wrong I had been about Moe! That just shows you, I thought, carrying the head up the stairs and into the greenhouse, I might have thought I was a judge of human nature, and I was, but maybe not a very good judge. One thing I had always hated, was when a person was unfriendly (and therefore I decided that I disliked the person in return) and then if the person suddenly acted friendly. It was like getting a rug pulled out from under you; people had no business changing their behavior in such fashion. I put the head back in the hot tub for the time being. It would be safer there, until I figured out what to do. It wasn't my fault that my father had been suing Moe for thirty thousand dollars; maybe Moe now suspected that my father hadn't gone on a trip but was deceased?

I went back into the workshop and gulped down the rest of my drink. Too bad Moe hadn't thought to bring some liquor, though perhaps if we became good friends I could ask him to come back with a case of beer, because otherwise I would be forced to begin opening my father's private stock of homemade wine in recycled bottles—elderberry, cherry, and dandelion were but a few of the labels. "What did you think I was trying to tell you, when I told you to *move the garbage?*" I said to Abdhul, who was happily engrossed with sorting a box of crayons.

"I took the garbage out yesterday," he said.

"I was talking about the head!" I said. "I was trying to make you understand you should move the head, so that Moe didn't trip over it on his way out."

"Oh," Abdhul said.

Dalgleish was engaged in an act of sexual intercourse with an invisible partner. I picked him up under his forelegs and held him outstretched before me in the air. Luckily his penis temporarily vanished into its sheath. Not even old enough to lift his leg and already a sex maniac. Across his pink belly a juicy flea fled into the safety of fur. I picked up the drink abandoned by Moe. "Don't touch that!" Abdhul said.

"Why not?" I said.

"That's the guest's drink!" he said. Really, I didn't want to chastise him, I knew he would be embarrassed, but maybe we had been isolated for too long. Looking at him through the eyes of a stranger he was quite rude, even belligerent, bossing grown-ups the way he did. Also I wondered if he was growing as fast as he was meant to. He appeared quite shrumpy, neither shrimp nor hump but something in between; whereas I had imagined at this age—whatever it was—he would grow in great chunks, changing almost overnight from chunky near-toddler physique to lanky, lithe boy. But before I could enter into any discussion of his behavior there was a sharp, rapid, nattering knock on the front door. "Oh, God, that must be Moe again," I said, putting down the glass and going out to the entryway. Maybe he had left something behind. Anyway, I had moved the head just in time.

"Did you forget something?" I said, opening the door a crack.

"I forgot," Moe said. "There were actually a few things I came to tell you. I was going to . . . ask you about your dog." Dalgleish poked his head into the doorway between my feet and growled. "He's an unusual little fellow. I'm something of an expert on ancient Greek vases, and it's interesting to note the three varieties of dogs that appear on them, which I've managed to identify. There's the Maltese, that fluffy little white dog still in existence, which appears almost exactly the same now as it did then. The other two varieties were the Malthusean hound, a large dog possibly slightly related to the greyhound, and the Laconian dog. I always said that if I were to get a dog, I would want one that looks like the Laconian. My ex-boyfriend, Eric, was a professional dog handler, specializing in schnauzers; but I'm sorry I mentioned him to you now, because it really doesn't give me a chance with you, does it?"

"I don't know what to say," I muttered. What a nut case! I was determined to block his reentrance into the house.

"No, I should have kept quiet about it—that's what your father would have said," Moe said. "I've always liked women more than men. The only reason I was gay, however, was that after my wife's death I was afraid of killing more women." On the one hand everybody was some peculiar cliché or variety of stereotype, but on the other hand nobody's character seemed gelled. They were all a mishmash of various attributes loosely thrown together in the same kettle but uncongealed; the different elements refused to blend. So that while the stereotype appropriate to Moe was that of the neglected son of a wealthy family who rebelled by moving to the country to run a general store—a type that I had read about frequently in various self-help books written by psychologists under headings such as "Moe—a Case of Escape from Responsibility." But in actual fact, were this case history laid out under a magnifying glass, what would be visible were the diverse lumps, unblended, that had been used to form this entity like so many others. I bared my teeth in a pathetic attempt at a smile. "Well, good night," I said, starting to shut the door.

"No, wait," Moe said. "I've come to warn you. They've found your package—with the letter. They know your plans to blow up the building on Christmas Eve to protest the Palestinian situation." He gave me an admiring look. "I didn't know you were an Arab terrorist."

"I'm not!" I said. "I'm Jewish."

"Oh," he said coyly. "The Jews are always the worst."

"I'm not pro-Palestinian," I said. "The Israelis bought the land from them—following a mandate from the British! Why don't we just give Texas back to the Mexicans! Let the other Arab countries find room for the Palestinians—the Israelis have nowhere else to go! No other country in the world would take in the Jews during World War Two . . ." Then I stopped. "What package?" I said.

"The one in your desk drawer," Moe said. "At work. With the plans. I spoke to my brother. He told me all about it. That's what I meant to tell you. Listen, I'd better come in." He forcefully pushed his way past me and went back down to the workshop. "There's something else I should tell you, too. Ah, to hell with it!" He picked up his drink and guzzled it down.

"How do you like the drink?" Abdhul said from the doorway. Some help this kid was.

"What's that?" Moe said. "Yes, yes."

"I made it myself," Abdhul said. "How many times a day does a dog go to the bathroom?"

"Gee, I don't know," Moe said thoughtfully, putting down the glass. "Probably as many times as a person."

"Oh, really?" Abdhul said. "How many times a day do *you* go to the bathroom?"

Moe thought for a minute. "Maybe five?" he said.

"Because Dalgleish is peeing on your foot," Abdhul said. We all looked down. The dog finished squatting and trotted off, leaving Moe's right shoe in a steamy yellow pool. "Oh, sorry about that," I said, rummaging for a piece of paper towel. How offended could he have been, though, living in the center of a fly-infested general store with open cans of stewed prunes? Maybe he was one of those cases with multiple personalities; he sure seemed different than he had that afternoon. Perhaps he suspected I was shortly due to come into my inheritance and had thoughts of marrying me in order to make a fortune. "Well, are we going out in the canoe or what?" Abdhul said. "The moon's up by now."

"We're going frog hunting," I explained to Moe. "I hope you'll excuse us."

"Oh, gee, that sounds like fun," Moe said. "Could I come? I could show you how to spear frogs with a stick." I blanched—anyway, I felt myself blanching. "You know, it was my brother that I was speaking to earlier who told me everything about you," Moe said.

"Your brother?" I said.

"Bronson," Moe said. "Bronc. You know him."

In the past there were two canoes. Perhaps we would find the other, partially capsized, out on the lake. The canoe that was left was an old red battered fiberglass construct lying upside down at the shallow end of the swamp. Moe flipped it over and pushed it out into the water, the back end still on land; Abdhul perhaps in front, an oar in one hand, while I took the middle and Moe the back. The BB gun Abdhul stored for the time being on the bottom of the boat. From a branch of a nearby willow Moe chopped a long branch; one end he carved into a point, and he kept this on his lap, shoving us off the land with the tip of the paddle. We left Dalgleish on shore, barking frantically; but the idiot animal decided to swim out after us.

"Stop, stop!" I said to Moe and Abdhul, both of whom were paddling furiously out into the moonlit water. "Dalgleish is following and he can't swim. Back up so we can pick him up." They backstroked briefly while I leaned over the right side and grabbed the dripping dog, pulling him over the edge. He sneezed and snorted profusely. He had such a little snout, all the water ran straight into his nose and he couldn't seem to figure how to cough it out. Then he shook himself, scattering droplets of water over all three of us. But the night air was so milky, and the water so murky and warm it was not unpleasant. My ear still hurt, but at least the buzzing had ceased. The moon overhead was shining and huge. The branches of the trees rustled around the edges of the lake, and lumpy hummocks rose in the steely light around the side. I had often inspected these hummocks in daylight; astonishing citadels, on which grew a scruffy cranberry bush, curious lichen, and pulpy plants designed by some evolutionary quirk to catch and consume insects. The slap of a beaver's tail gave a warning on the water. The beaver lived in a massive lodge at the far end. This was where Moe suggested we now go. The more leaves and muck at the edge the more likely frogs would be lying in wait, although for some reason this evening they were curiously quiet. Perhaps frog season was over; usually the bullish bellows and croaks broke the night more loudly than any city siren or ambulance.

The pungent smell of wet dog and Moe's rotten scent wafted up into my nose. The only place one could swim was in the immediate vicinity of where the canoe had been parked, by the dam—and in the very middle, where the water suddenly dropped off and a few old houses were buried deep in the muck. But the rest was three or five feet deep, a thick soup of decay. Thank God Dalgleish hadn't jumped in elsewhere and come up strewn with fetid clumps of algae. According to my brother Ralph, when my father had once toppled out of the canoe in search of a dropped fishing pole, the stench of a person submerged in this pea water was so great it was like an exhumed body—though how Ralph would know what an exhumed body smelled like, unless there was something he wasn't telling me, such as he had murdered his girlfriend and kept her corpse in the bathtub, I didn't know.

We paddled—anyway, the men paddled—silently for some minutes, the oars darting into the shiny water, nearly phosphorescent in the moon. When we were about ten feet from what passed for shoreline (though so dense was the land with scrubby trees, and the water so thick with lumps and bulges it was impossible to get any closer) Abdhul slipped the BB gun out from under the wooden seat and took careful aim at an object I couldn't even see. Some forty-five minutes or half hour had passed since we left the house, the moon not yet at its zenith but swollen and heavy midway in the sky.

Sitting in silence gave me a chance to think: *package . . . plans to blow up the building on Christmas Eve . . . Moe had come to warn me—but why?* Then dimly it came back to me . . . *the woman . . . in the post office . . . who had handed me a package while she went to use the fax . . . the police came in . . . she vanished . . . I went with Alby to a restaurant . . . hand job . . . under the table.* Suddenly from behind me Moe let out a tremendous bellow and I bucked. "Wait!" he said. "Wait! Oh my God, will you look at the size of that fucking thing?"

Carefully I turned around. "Don't move!" I said. "You'll tip us!"

Moe's eyes were huge and terrified; he began to stand, weaving curiously from side to side, holding his spear up over his head. "What the fuck is it?" he shouted. "Is it a frog?"

"What are you talking about?" I said. I couldn't see any poor old frog, not even a pair of red eyes, though obviously I didn't have the best vision at night, since Abdhul was deliberately aiming and seemed to know what he was doing.

"The frog!" Moe shouted. "The frog! Is it a mutant? I've never seen a frog like that!" Maybe he had a low alcohol tolerance? The canoe was violently rocking. "Sit down," I said. "Will you please quit it!"

"We can't stay here," Moe said. "This is crazy!"

*You're* crazy, I wanted to say. "Where is it?" I said patronizingly.

"There, there," Moe said. "Don't you see?" He pointed at what looked like a cranberry hummock. Abdhul swung the BB gun toward where Moe pointed. "Don't shoot, don't shoot," Moe said. "You'll never kill it with a BB. You don't want to make it angry." Abdhul half turned in his seat. He gave me a curious, sickly grin, turned in the other direction, and fired. Even though it was just a BB gun, the sound was loud. "Got it!" he said. He started to paddle the boat toward shore, though there was too much growth here for the canoe to push through.

At this moment Moe let out a bellow of rage. "It's coming toward us!" he screamed, his tone turning to one of terror. He threw his spear out at the hummock—anyway, as far as I could tell it was a hummock, though as I say I have lousy night vision, so if it really was a giant frog it was possible I just didn't see—and pitching forward toppled out the back of the canoe, splashing into the thick murk of algae and muck. The canoe rocked violently from side to side, the back end, now lightened, shot up into the air, and clutching the edges I peered over; momentarily his feet clad in brown workboots and his backside were visible. With a gurgle he disappeared into the mud.

"My God, what a lunatic," I said to no one in particular. "What the hell is wrong with him?" Thick, congested bubbles of mucous consistency rose to the water's surface. Abdhul continued to paddle forward. "Stop, stop," I said, rummaging around on the bottom of the boat with my hands in search of the other oar, so I could put a stop to our forward motion. Moe must have been holding on to it when he flung himself out of the ship. I was worried that if we moved too many feet away I wouldn't be able to find the spot where he had gone down. All swamp looks the same in the moonlight. There was a brief blubbery disturbance off to one side, as if some prehistoric monster were rousing itself from the depths; Moe's slimy head emerged, the sound of a fishy burble, a gasp for air. Then he went down again and everything was momentarily quiet apart from the dip of Abdhul's paddle into the slippery primordial soup. "Did you do something to that man, Abdhul?" I said. He flashed me a stunning smile; his teeth were white and feral, and momentarily I felt better about not having found the time to take him to the dentist, because with my encouraging him to brush two and even three times a day with fluoride toothpaste, they were looking much better.

"You said people were out to get us," Abdhul said. "You said they were going to try to take me away from you."

"What did you do?" I said sternly.

"I put the stuff from the Band-Aid box in the freezer into his drink," Abdhul said.

"You put everything in the Band-Aid box in his drink?" I said.

"Just the pills and the powder," Abdhul said. "But not the mushrooms. Anyway, I think they were mushrooms—hard, dried brown pieces?"

"But what did you do that for?" I said.

"To get rid of him," Abdhul said simply. Oh, poor, poor Moe—I wasn't even certain what had been in that box, LSD and mescaline and a packet of cocaine maybe, I hadn't bothered to examine it and certainly the contents weren't labeled. "And also some pills I found by the drawer under the telephone." This could have been anything—my father continued to receive free samples from various drug companies despite his retirement, whether it was tranquilizers or estrogen supplements there was no way of telling until we got back to the house and I could examine the empty packet. But in a strange way at least it was nice to know that Abdhul was worried about being taken away from me, when half the time he acted as if having to live together were some sort of punishment.

The canoe was two or three feet away from the allegedly deceased corpse of the frog that Abdhul had shot, and he now leaned forward over the prow of the canoe as far as he could in order to be able to reach the frog; I could see a white belly floating alongside a platter-size lily pad. From behind the canoe Moe rose up out of the water, grabbed the side of the canoe, and pulled. A tremendous stench of rotten waterplants filled the air, and before the boat went over I caught a glimpse of his wild, yolky eyes, his slathery, spumy lips and face plastered with brown-green bile.

Then I fell in. The water, warm, was only three feet or so deep, but beneath that was apparently another six feet of rotten organic material, warm and lascivious, that seemed to suck me down. My feet were waving frantically, struggling to touch bottom, but there was no bottom and it was like being tossed into a vat of warm pea or lentil soup; I couldn't tell which way was up, the stuff came down my throat and tasted so putrid I involuntarily gulped in several huge mouthfuls more.

My hands were waving, brushing against sticks and branches that scratched; something was crushing me—the side of the canoe, or some floating branches—I tried to calm myself by thinking that whatever I had ingested probably had great nutritional value, like tofu, although the last time I had purchased tofu in the supermarket when I got it home and opened the sealed packet in which the white cube floated in milky liquid it had turned and the stench was so fierce I had to bring it back to the store for a refund.

Anyway, these were but a few of my thoughts as I flung myself spasti- cally around in the ooze; finally I got my head out of the water, but something was grabbing at my ankles and I went down again. All I wanted to do was find Abdhul and get him onto shore, it was possible he hadn't been flipped from the canoe when Moe deliberately tried to topple it, but if he had I was worried, Abdhul was so little and the mud really had a sucking effect, maybe it was quicksand, but were there any cases of quick- sand in the Northeast region and was it possible for quicksand to be covered or hidden by a few feet of water? I came up again and this time managed to drag myself over to one of the prickly hummocks; the tree or whatever it was was still clawing at my feet, but holding on to the hummock with one hand—there was a prickly shrub, firmly rooted—I was able to reach down and pry the branches loose. The canoe had righted itself, I guess it had only half tipped, but with the disturbance of the waves had blown out into deeper water where it drifted high on the surface. Abdhul was up to his knees in muck by the shore, bobbing back and forth anxiously. "Pamela, Pamela!" he said. "Don't try to get to shore this way, there's at least eight feet of mud even though it looks shallow."

"How am I supposed to get over to you?" I said. "Where's Moe?"

"He's over here," Abdhul said. "By my feet." And looking closer I could see a tremendous reptilian object churning and struggling in the mud. "You better help him up," I said. "He's going to drown."

"In two inches of water?" Abdhul said contemptuously.

"A person can easily drown in two inches of water," I said. "Anyway, a baby can, so he might." Abdhul pulled up his right foot, making a huge sucking sound. "Listen to this," he said, putting his foot back down and extracting the other.

"Stop playing around," I said. The thrashing of the reptile was weakening. It would have been exciting if there really were giant prehistoric reptiles in the swamp.

Abdhul picked his way through the mud, muttering, "If I had a pair of boots like the ones I wanted, this would be easier," until at last he arrived at the reptile's side. "I'll find a stick to poke him," he said. "He's not too far out."

"Just go out there and pull his head out of the water, Abdhul," I said. "Hurry up before he suffocates. By now he's probably sufficiently anesthetized, I doubt he'll lash out at you."

"What does anesthetized mean?" Abdhul said.

"Put to sleep," I said.

"Oh, very well," Abdhul said.

"You're lighter, so you don't sink so deep," I said, gingerly releasing my grasp from the prickly sticker bush and attempting to float on my back on the few inches of water above the mud. With this technique I was able to float a couple of feet farther in toward shore, when I stood and began to make my way through the effluvial waste. What I wouldn't have given for a good wallop of Listerine right at this moment. Standing in the muck I watched Abdhul pull Moe's head up; Moe's mouth hung open, he choked wretchedly and though his head must have been heavy Abdhul bravely held it up by the hairs with one hand and with his free fingers (the BB gun apparently had fallen into the water) he reached his hand inside Moe's mouth and pulled out a quantity of goop. Moe moaned, shut his eyes and opened them, shook his head, and with a yodel rose up out of the water, knocking Abdhul down in the process, and pulled himself pathetically through the mud and onto the shore, where he crashed between the bushes and disappeared into the woods. "Not very nice," Abdhul commented, picking himself up and falling down again, though at last he made it back onto shore. "Well, that's that," he said. I was up to my knees in mud, it was another ten minutes before I picked my way onto dry land.

It took Abdhul, me, and Dalgleish nearly two and a half hours to find our way back to the house, slashed and cut by branches, stumbling forward and backtracking; under the canopy of overgrown trees it was dark, no moon to light our way.

Dripping with mud, stinking like fish, we stripped off our filthy clothes at the door and had barely finished taking showers and drying ourselves with the last of the plush, clean towels when Moe barged into the house. He was now apparently in midstream of his mixed trip, and it was my belief he should have been locked up. Moaning and cursing, he entered the kitchen and plucked a long strand of green water growth from what was formerly his lapel. Then he sucked it into his mouth. "My God," he said. "Thank God, your door was open. Do you know what's happening out there?"

"You're on drugs, Moe," I said. "You're having a bad trip."

"Nonsense," Moe said. "I don't take drugs." He picked another snatch of green goo from his chin and chewed on it thoughtfully. Then he reached into the tattered shreds of his shirt and removed a massive glob of what might have been frog's eggs. It was far too late in the season for a frog to lay eggs, I thought, however I supposed there might have been a female frog out there who was biologically screwed up—recently I had read about a sixty-seven-year-old woman who became pregnant for the first time, so anything was possible—and he held the translucent mass in one hand, looking at it as if he were gauging the weight of a woman's breasts. Then he handed the goopy mound to Abdhul. "Fry it," he said. "I must take a mikvah bath. I believe your father has a hot tub and Jacuzzi bath, does he not?" With great dignity he unzipped his fly, urinated a small amount under the table, shook it off, and exited the room. "Oh my God, wait!" I said. "Moe, wait! Come back!" I jumped up and followed him out the door to the sounds of Abdhul laughing hysterically. "You're some help, you are," I said. "Who the fuck's going to clean up this mess?" A long trail of slime like the trail of a slug extended from the front door up to the kitchen and down the hall in the direction where Moe had gone. How could the guy see where he was going, anyway? He must have spent some time in this house, to be able to find his way around in the dark; holding my candle in one hand I went to the hot-tub room just as Moe, who had already removed the top cover, was climbing in.

Without going into further detail I will say it was a mistake to put the head in the water; the results were not flattering. I had hoped that Moe would simply dismiss the head as part of his ongoing hallucinations, but he let out a low, sissy whimper, turned, knocked into me—extinguishing my candle—all the while murmuring, "Dr. Trowel, Dr. Trowel," and bolted from the room.

I heard a crash and I went into the hall. Moe was lying unconscious on the floor next to a chair. Abdhul stood alongside, an empty wine bottle in his hand and a foolish expression on his face, though I couldn't be certain whether he had bludgeoned Moe on the head or if Moe had knocked himself out. "What's this chair doing here?" I said.

"I was going to change a light bulb," Abdhul said.

I didn't want to discourage him from being helpful by pointing out we had not had electricity in quite some time, so I simply said, "I don't know what we should do now. When he wakes up I'm sure he's going to remember seeing the head in the tub."

"What a mess this has turned out to be," Abdhul commented. "He stinks, too."

"Poor guy," I said. "He took a bath before coming over here and brought us all that food, too. Some people might think he was homely, but you know, Abdhul, I think when you get to know a person you can't see what he looks like anymore. Even if you marry a model, after a few weeks when you wake up in the morning you don't think, gee, he or she really is good looking. You just think, there's Molly or Jim or whatever their name is. It's just a person to you."

"What's going to happen now?" Abdhul said. "Are they going to put me in a foster-care situation or something?" For a while we had watched a news series on TV about the terrible state of foster care for children in Manhattan.

"Maybe you'll get lucky and go to a nice family," I said. "In the country. By the time I get out of jail you'll be grown up, and we can get married." Perhaps it was all for the best since Abdhul was turning into a real juvenile delinquent and I was obviously mismanaging his upbringing. I felt furious at the way things had turned out for us. If only I had gotten married, perhaps straight out of college, to a man who was good at doing the income tax returns and had a health insurance plan through work that covered the entire family. By now I would have had a child or two of my own that were Abdhul's age that nobody could take away from me unless there was some kind of computer screwup or a neighbor called the welfare department accusing me of child abuse. How had things gone so terribly wrong? Other women had houses in Scarsdale with vacuum cleaners and Brazilian maids who came in to clean at least once a week, possibly more frequently. During the winters their husbands took them on vacation to St. Barts.

"Well, don't just stand there, Pamela," Abdhul said plaintively. "Can't you do something?" We had never troubled ourselves to give the head a name. Poor Abdhul, suffer the little children. Really, he had a point. There were two types of people in this world, those who were passive—the ones to whom life happened, and these people either lived lives of complete blandness, waiting for something to occur or going from one disaster to the next with a sort of Hindu acceptance—or those who went out and did things to solve the problem. The best examples of the latter were probably people like Donald Trump, J. Pierpont Morgan, and Henry Ford, although Henry wrote a terrible anti-Jewish pamphlet about how the Jews were responsible for a conspiracy to take over the world, which certainly wasn't true in my case. "All right," I said to Abdhul, who was staring at me in my trance with a worried expression. "You're right. We don't have to stand around and take this crap. Go get me the will and we'll have a reading."

He ran off to the workroom and I went into the kitchen and lit a candle. When he returned I unfolded the document. Abdhul sat and watched a mouse masturbating—maybe it was just cleansing its genitals—in the corner while I read aloud. Naturally I couldn't follow the legal jargon all that readily, but it seemed to indicate that everything was to be left to Angela, in the event of my father's death. And in the event of Angela's death, everything was to go to: Angela's parents; her brothers and sisters; her cleaning woman; and her stepchildren from her first marriage.

"Well," Abdhul said. "That's that. Now what are we going to do?"

"What do you think of this idea," I said slowly. "What if the house were to accidentally burn down? It's a wooden house, highly flammable, and when my dad and Angela built it they didn't let the wood age long enough, so it's full of oozing pitch. In addition, everyone knows that wood-burning stoves, improperly cleaned, have a tendency to catch on fire from the buildup of creosote in the chimney pipes. Without a will the property will go to Dad's kids."

"What if there's another copy of the will than the one we found in the workshop?" Abdhul said.

"Clever boy," I said. "If there's another copy of the will, my brothers and I can argue in court that Dad had recently mentioned he had updated his will and left it in the house. At the very least we'll get half."

"And will we burn up Moe?" Abdhul said.

"What's that?" I said. I looked over at the semiconscious figure on the ground. "No, no, of course not. We'll drag him outside before we go. If the police come, and he says something about the head in the tub, nobody will believe him, because he's obviously stoned. And if they find the head . . . oh, let them think what they like. Let them think that Moe's the one responsible, although I want to make it clear—that's not a very nice thing for us to do." So much for my spiritual development.

"What about the fire department?" Abdhul said.

"I thought you might say something about that," I said. "There is no fire department out here. My dad always said he was unable to get fire insurance because there are no fire hydrants. I don't think there's even a volunteer fire department. But if there is, by the time they come it'll be too late. By the way—how come Moe passed out? Did you hit him over the head?"

"Who, me?" Abdhul said.

It took us half an hour to drag Moe's body down the hall, each of us pulling on an arm, and I'm afraid that we were none too careful with his body going down the stairs headfirst. He was going to have one hell of a hangover when he woke up, that much was certain. Dalgleish ran alongside, biting his feet and ankles. I had to keep reminding myself that up until this time I hadn't committed any actual crime. Finally we got him to what I thought was a safe distance away from the house. There wasn't much more to do.

I could have spread some kerosene around to assist in the accidental fire, but these things had a way of backfiring on the arsonist; although I doubted there would be any sort of follow-up inspection; in the unlikely event that there was, many fire marshals were apparently able to determine that gasoline or other flammable solutions had been utilized. However, I left the kerosene lamp directly next to the wood-burning stove, and moved a pile of old newspapers nearby. There was so much junk scattered around the place that anybody who had ever been here and was questioned in a later investigation would swear they had always wondered why the place hadn't gone up sooner. I also turned on the gas stove. God Almighty, what a sick cookie I had become. Probably I would figure out some way to punish myself later on. "Can I light the fire? Huh? Can I light it?" Abdhul said.

"No," I said. "Go find the matches."

"Why can't I light it, huh? Please?" Abdhul said.

"No," I said. "How am I going to feel, twenty years from now, when you realize the magnitude of your actions?"

"I don't care," he said.

"Well, I do," I said. While he went to find the matches I collected a pile of old *Country Pleasure* magazines where they were stacked by the toilet. One of them fell open, revealing a whole slew of ads in the back. "World's Most Advanced Home Greenhouse," "Walnut Acres—Healthful, Delicious Organic Foods, Delivered to Your Door," "Birkenstock Sandals," and "Mehu-Maija Juice-Extractor-Steamer-Cooker"—why hadn't I gone to work selling ads for such a magazine, instead of *Hunter's World?* Obviously that was where I had gone wrong, building up bad karma at such a frantic pace it had led me to my present predicament. Probably I was guilty of primitive thinking; probably this type of thinking belonged to the same people who watched those allegedly religious shows on TV, where in order to get good luck and health they were told to send money to God, in care of Robert Tilton or some other evangelist's address. If only I had belonged to some primitive tribe where animism and voodoo was the accepted explanation for why things were the way they were.

I crumpled up the magazines and spread them around, then collected my bag of makeup to take out to the car. Abdhul had found the pack of matches and was hopping up and down with excitement in front of the wood-burning stove in the living room. I went into the workshop and carried the papers from the firebox upstairs. "There's only three matches left, you know," Abdhul said. "You light two and I'll light one."

"All right, all right," I said. "You take Dalgleish out to the car first, though. I'm not coming back into any burning house to get a dog." I was pleased with how carefully I had thought things through.

"Goody, goody!" Abdhul said, picking up the squirming Dalgleish and dashing down the stairs.

I gave the place what I thought was one last look. What a shame, that the beautiful, delicate house had to be destroyed. Of course it was far too full of stuff, if it were mine I would have gotten rid of the junk and redecorated, maybe with simple Korean antiques, since Japanese antiques were very expensive, but from what I had read there were plenty of old Korean furnishings, rustic and attractive, at very low prices. What if the place only caught on fire a little bit and then went out? Things wouldn't look good then; unless the county coroner was a complete alcoholic there was no way he wouldn't be able to tell that the head wasn't newly deceased. But the nice thing, I thought, looking at a life-size sculpture of my mother, nude and pregnant, that my father had carved out of pink marble shortly before I was born and that now stood behind the couch, was that with any luck the stone sculptures would survive the fire, and some day when I was more mature and settled I could try to arrange for a show of my father's work in Manhattan. Maybe then he would forgive me.

Abdhul came back into the room, his face flushed with excitement. "Can I go first?" he said.

"Let's just try and think," I said. "Can you think of anything we didn't do, to cover our tracks? Is there anything that's going to incriminate us later?"

"Not that I can think of," Abdhul said.

"All right, this might be dangerous," I said. "You can light the first match, but I want you to run out immediately, okay?"

"Okay, okay," Abdhul said, hopping. I tell you, a little kid like that during the course of a day uses up so much energy in things like hopping up and down, deciding for no reason to try and touch a branch over his head, tapping his foot under the table—if I had been able to hook him up to some sort of squirrel or hamster wheel connected to operating a dishwasher or electric generator, I could have kept the whole system going. People were worried about the energy crisis; why didn't they hook the little kids up to treadmills and also all the people who were out jogging and doing aerobics. Then they could have gotten their exercise in and done something useful as well.

He set the match to the paper and we both stood mesmerized while a little fire sprang up on the wooden floor. It was strange to see a fire in the middle of the living room like that, not enclosed. It was just a paper fire, throwing up a lot of smoke and somehow reluctant. "Okay, what did I tell you—get out of here," I said.

"Aw," he said, but he trudged out. There were only two matches left and the first ignited and then sputtered out, the back of the pack was a little damp. I lit the second and held it up to the edge of *Country Pleasure.* Maybe it helped that it was made out of recycled paper; anyway, I used the flaming corner to light a number of other papers scattered around the room, especially the ones around the hurricane lamp. There was the stump of a white candle and I lit this, too; too bad Angela and Dad didn't believe in curtains or draperies, these were usually flammable objects that went up quickly. I went down to the hot-tub room and tried to ignite the dead plants with the candle stub, but the leaves burned only halfheartedly and extinguished themselves. But at the top of the stairs the room was filling up with smoke, black and curly, and I slipped open the glass side door and went out.

The nightlife had apparently gone to sleep, everything was quiet and still. I walked around to where we had hidden the car and opened the driver's door. Abdhul was sitting in the passenger seat, strapped in. "But Abdhul, it's still covered with the leaves and vines," I said. He hadn't cleaned it of the camouflage; I brushed the front windshield free of pine needles. I should have reported the rented car stolen, at least then I wouldn't be responsible for not having returned it in time, particularly when my credit card had a maximum limit of one thousand dollars that I didn't know how I was going to pay. I went around and brushed off the sides and the top. The thing was, in the garage drive-through beside the house was a perfectly good Subaru, only a year or two old, but if I took it then it would be proof we had been here at the house. Still, my situation with the Rent-A-Wreck company was something I would have to deal with later.

I waited a few minutes standing outside the car until I saw smoke squeezing its way out of the house. Then I burst into tears, I didn't want Abdhul to see but I was frightened. So much for my spiritual growth and salvation, maybe it would do me good to be in jail for ten or twenty years. I wiped my eyes and tried to find a tissue in my pocket but stupidly there wasn't even a scrap of paper towel and I had to blow my nose on my fingers and then wipe them on a handful of old oak leaves. I got into the car. Abdhul peered over at me in the dark. "Where's the keys?" I said, fondling the ignition. "Do you have them?"

"I don't have them," he said.

"You don't have the keys?" I said. "Well, where are they?"

He opened the glove compartment. "Not in here," he said. "When did you last see them?"

"I don't know," I said. "I thought you had them."

"Want me to go inside and look?"

"No!" I said. "I don't want you to move. Are you sure they're not on the floor?"

"They were by the telephone in the kitchen the last time I saw them," he said.

"All right," I said. "I'll be back in a minute. Don't move. We've got to get out of here." If somebody did see the fire even though there was no fire department it was possible they might drive over to try and help. I doubted the fire had progressed very far, but there was a smoky smell in the air. I walked behind the car and over to the tree where we had planted Moe. He was lying facedown in the half-fetal position. At least he seemed to be sound asleep. I doubted he would remember a hell of a lot when he woke up. If I had time I would grab one of the nearly empty bottles of liquor from the cabinet and lean it up against the base of the tree. In his present condition he certainly didn't look like a reputable witness. Idiot! How could I have forgotten the car keys?

The moon was still high in the sky, like a giant bowl of Frosty Flakes. I trudged down the drive, expecting to see flames shooting into the air, but no, there was nothing, perhaps the fire had gone out and I would have to reset it. Suddenly the contents of a dream I had had the night before came back to me, in which I had been stopped by a policeman who complained about the condition of my clothes, which he said were torn and dirty. Luckily he was a Spanish policeman, and I explained that I had been to Spain only a short time before, so he let me go.

Cautiously I opened the front door. It was weird, there was a strange atmosphere inside now, as if some living alien being had moved in, intangible, invisible, yet wrong. The air had a certain wavering electric quality, though I could see no flames. The smoke perhaps had risen to the ceiling; yet as I stepped in and went up the hall it dawned on me that there must be flames somewhere, the house was brightly lit. In the distance I heard a thin whistling sound, ominous as a snoring giant with congested nasal membranes. I tried to move quickly, I went up the stairs and into the kitchen; the keys to the car were in a basket, already they felt slightly warm to the touch and I grabbed them and then took a quick peek into the living room. The room was filled with honey-colored flickers. Just at that moment there was a curious—not an explosion, it was soundless, but a physical sort of whumpf, the entirely room shuddered, all at once there were flames everywhere, jackknifing and pirouetting on the plum-colored couch, shooting up the walls, steel blue and topaz, running like a burst bottle of syrup. I didn't even notice the heat, I was so entranced. The books and burning papers, the wooden fan hanging on the ceiling that now began to spin around and around, fueled by the fire on top, the large timbers that traversed the room pinpointed by sugary licks of flame that darted over and around. The leather ottoman, the melting bowl of wax fruit from Mexico, apple and pear, the Turkish kilim rug embraced by its new pattern of liquid light—everything had gone up at once. My eyes felt like those marbles my mother had taught us to fry as a form of childhood entertainment and the next time I inhaled I took in a lungful of searing intensity, as if I were breathing in a vacuum or the Sahara desert, and then I noticed that the ends of my hair were on fire, surely I should move, I should get out of there, and yet this was so soothing, so pleasant, the fire seemed to be my friend. My legs had become two sponges, without muscles. Little hairs inside my nose were being neatly seared, I could feel the heat of the floor through my sandals. Something creaked over my head. Perhaps soon the ceiling would begin to collapse? The little flames beckoned me to join them.

The fire began to roar, it had gathered force, within seconds it was transformed from dancing flicks of light to a hot, huge animal, it did not need to bother to disguise itself any longer. Tarry smoke filled the air; imagining I was trapped, the fire did not pretend to be delicate, amusing, or tiny dancing fairies, but showed its real self, a bottomless mouth. Quickly

I turned and ran down the hall, I couldn't see and could barely breathe, the doorknob was scorching to the touch and as I opened it there was another gasping sound and the whole place exploded behind me.

I ran down the drive. There was Abdhul, hitting me over the head, extinguishing what I guess were the flames. I breathed heavily in the night air, but my lungs felt dessicated, friable. No oxygen seemed to reach my bloodstream. "Are you okay?" Abdhul said. "Say something, Pamela, I thought you got burned up." He let out a whimper and wrapped himself around my waist. I wanted to say something to reassure him but I couldn't speak. My hair smelled smoky and burnt. I had to get into some water, and with Abdhul still clutching me I shuffled down to the water's edge, walked in a foot or so and stuck my head down into the water. It was cool and murky; I ran my fingers through my crunchy hair without even noticing that I was still clutching the car keys. Then I felt better.

"See, I'm fine," I said, standing up. Abdhul was hopping around on the shore; I splonked through the mud and gave him a hug. "I told you not to get out of the car," I said. The house was crackling behind us, now there were flames shooting up out of the ceiling, a groaning sound as part of the roof gave way and the shrill pop and hiss of melting pitch. Flames ran down the pagoda-shaped roof and lapped around the overhang like erect icicles. "Come on, we better get out of here," I said. "You can probably see this by now from on top of the mountain, although it's doubtful anyone who lives up there is awake. Where's the dog?"

"In the car," Abdhul said.

We got in the car and I started to back up, then stopped. "Look, you better get out and make sure I'm not backing over Moe," I said. "There's no point in crushing his legs." Abdhul jumped out and ran behind the car; in a few seconds he came back. "He's not there," he said.

"Not there?" I said. "Well where is he?"

"He must have gone home," Abdhul said.

"But he wasn't behind the car?" I said. "You're positive?"

"Nope," Abdhul said.

I backed up and then drove carefully down the drive; it was possible Moe had woken briefly, staggered off, and then collapsed again. I really didn't want to feel the smack as the car hit some lump on the road. But there was no sign of him and at last I pulled onto the dirt road and we drove in silence for several minutes. "I still have my frog," Abdhul said. "Want to see?"

I glanced over briefly. "I can't look now, Abdhul, I'm driving," I said. "It looks like a big frog, though." All I had actually seen out of the corner of my eye was a couple of dangling legs poking out of his fist. "Where did your bullet go?"

"I can't see any mark," Abdhul said. "It's possible his mouth was open and the BB went down his throat." This seemed unlikely to me but I let it go.

"And you kept it all this time?" I said. "You carried it for two hours through the woods, and remembered to bring it out to the car and everything?"

"Yup," Abdhul said. "But the BB gun's gone. Can I get a new one?"

"Where did you lose the BB gun?"

"When that jerk tipped over the canoe," Abdhul said. "I'd say this frog weighs two pounds. Will you cook it for me?"

"Well, sure," I said. "But we might stop at a hotel now, for a couple of days, so I don't know when we'll be at a place with a stove."

"I mean, what a jerk that guy was," Abdhul said. *"He* fell out of the canoe, so then he had to push it over so we fell out, too. I hated that guy, Pamela. How could you have ever been girlfriend and boyfriend with him?"

"Search me," I said, too tired to explain that we had never gone out. Abdhul reached over with his frogless hand and made little pinches up my side—he was searching me. "Not right now, Abdhul, I don't want to get into an accident. Is your seatbelt fastened?"

"Yes."

"Is your door locked?"

"Why do you always have to ask me that?" he said. There was a pause. "That was really some fire, huh?" he said. "The whole house was burning up!"

"Yup," I said.

"All that stuff, too."

"Yeah," I said. There was a pause.

"And that guy's head."

"Yeah," I said.

"Well," Abdhul said, and made a thoughtful popping sound with his mouth. "I guess that's that."

Something shuffled in the backseat. "Where's Dalgleish, Abdhul?" I said.

"By my feet."

"By your feet!" I said. There was a phlegmy, coughing sound. "What'd you put in the backseat, Abdhul?"

"A blanket for the dog and some other stuff I wanted to keep," he said. "Are you sure your frog is dead?" I said.

"Hello, hello," he said, waving his fist around. "Are you dead, froggy?"

"Do me a favor and look in the backseat."

"I can't," he said. "My seatbelt is fastened."

"Unfasten it!" I said.

He took off his seatbelt and squirmed around until he was facing the back. "He's under the blanket!" Abdhul said.

"Who?" I said stupidly.

"That creepy monron jerk!" Abdhul said, a certain note of triumph in his voice.

"Moron, Abdhul, moron," I said. "The word's *moron*, not *monron*. And don't call him that, he might hear you. Is he sleeping?" There was a terrified whinny, I couldn't see what Abdhul was doing but he had flung himself halfway over into the backseat. "What are you doing?" I said.

"Testing to see if he's still alive by touching him with my frog's legs," he said.

"Well stop it," I said. "How did he get in here, anyway?"

"I don't know," Abdhul said. "He must have climbed back here when I was putting your hair out."

"Oh, God," I sighed. "What are we supposed to do with this guy now?" Suddenly Moe shot bolt upright in the back and gave Abdhul a shove that sent him toppling onto the floor in front. Dalgleish, crushed, let out a squeal. Moe was breathing rapidly and heavily, a strangely sexual sound, although it might also have been similar to the sounds of a torture victim in an Arab prison, or a woman getting her legs waxed. "Oh my," Moe said. "Oh boy. Oh. Oh." He leaned forward and bellowed into my ear. "What's happening to me? Where are we? UFO? Don't hurt me."

"Push him onto the floor before he causes an accident," I said to Abdhul. In the rearview mirror Moe's face was slobbery and mundane. Why was it that the faces of Americans seemed so featureless? The Americans were not a handsome people, I concluded. If you thought about the different countries—Norway, or India—well, those people had a distinctive look. You might not have said the French were a handsome people, but for the most part they were attractive, and even if they didn't all look exactly alike, they looked French. The Russians and the Latvians, they might have had potato faces, but there was a definite tribal unity. Italians, one thought of black hair, topaz skin, and Sophia Loren's nose, or else blond northern Italy. But with the Americans, all that intermingling with different nationalities had created nothing but a bland, watered down look: weak chins, toneless dirty brown hair, neither blond nor black, and the runty, stupid eyes of suspicion. Oh, not that I wasn't proud to be an American!

Abdhul struggled to pull Moe back down onto the backseat. Maybe my instructions were a mistake, because Moe bellowed and flailed. I was a little worried that Abdhul was going to get hurt. "No injections!" Moe shouted. "Let me stay awake."

"Ow!" Abdhul said as Moe pushed at his face. "Quit it!" Suddenly something big and green shot straight at my head, scaring the hell out of me. "Aaaggghh!" I screamed, swerving the car. "What's happening?" Moe leaned across me and gave a yank to the steering wheel; we skidded across the gravel shoulder and even though I was pumping on the brakes the car kept moving and crashed into an old-fashioned telephone pole. There was a tremendous bang; instinctively I reached across the seat and put my arm across Abdhul, even while I was being whipped forward. My head snapped back and cracked into Moe's skull with a resounding clunk. The car engine coughed and stopped. After a pause I looked over at Abdhul. His eyes were shut. My God, had he hit his head against the windshield? I gave him a gentle shake. His eyes fluttered open and he looked at me happily. "Wow," he said. "The frog was still alive!"

"Are you all right?" I said.

"Where'd the frog go?" he said. "Can we keep him, Pamela?"

I turned around on the seat. Moe was lying, arms outstretched, in a semiupright position. Apparently the same laws of physics had applied to my cracking his head with my own as those English guys who head-butt one another in various pubs after rugby or soccer matches. I always wondered how come one guy would be knocked completely unconscious, while the one who used his head as a brick to hit the other was always able to walk away unharmed. Not that I had ever actually seen this in person, but it was an English custom I had read about.

"I hate to do this, but I can't drive with this guy in the car," I said. "Let's drag him out." I turned off the ignition in the car, I didn't want the engine to flood, and we got out and dragged Moe from the backseat. "This is just an awful, terrible thing that we're doing, and I want you to know that," I told Abdhul. We pulled his body over to some shrubs well away from the road, though at this time of night on this back road there was no traffic. "But what else can we do?" I said. "He's a big boy; when he wakes up I'm sure he can find his own way home, and I didn't invite him to come along with us. I don't even know how he got in the car." Moe let out a little moan as we slid him down the gully over some sharp stones. "I hope when you grow up you'll manage your life better than I'm managing it at the moment," I said.

"I want to be like you!" Abdhul said. "This is fun."

"Be like what I say, not as I do," I said. "Take your vitamins, save your money and put it in a retirement plan, make sure you have adequate health insurance. Verbally my advice is sound; I'm just not that good at the actual behavior part."

"I can't believe the frog was still alive," Abdhul said. "Boy, I must have knocked him completely unconscious. Can I have another BB gun after we get settled?"

"Listen, I have other problems to think about right now," I said.

"But later on? When things calm down?"

"Maybe," I said.

"Goody," Abdhul said. "This is far enough, Pamela."

He might have had a point because I couldn't seem to drag Moe any farther anyway. I just didn't want him to wake up and go haring up onto the road in front of an oncoming car. I thrashed back to the car praying that the engine wasn't dead. It turned over once, spluttered out, and I tried it again. This time it started and kept running, although it sounded slightly distraught. "Come on, Abdhul," I called.

"I have to make pee-pee," he said from down the hill.

"Then hurry up and go," I said. "But do me a favor and don't piss on or near Moe. That poor man has suffered enough." I put the car in reverse; there was a sort of metallic scream as the fender unpeeled itself from the telephone pole and after I backed up I got out to look. There was a big dent in the hood and half the chrome on the left was bent in such a way to appear that some sort of primitive weaponry had been affixed to the car muzzle—it pointed out in the front, stiletto fashion. I gave it a kick but it didn't bend. "Hurry up, Abdhul," I said, getting back in the car. He ran up the hill and hopped in. "Where did Mr. Froggy go?" he said fondly. That was a kid for you; one minute with murder in his heart for Mr. Froggy, but when it survived its near-death experience he was ready to nurture and succor it.

Oh well. I peered out the window on the passenger's side. "Can you see Moe, Abdhul?" I said. "What's he doing?"

"I think he's waking up," Abdhul said. "His arms are moving, anyway."

"At least he's alive," I said. I was about to drive off, but then I felt remorse. What if his mouth and nose were filled with pine needles and gravel, and later he suffocated? I got back out and went down the hill. It wasn't very pleasant, but I held his nose and pried open his jaw.

"I wanted to tell you before," Moe moaned. "I really did. I made the mess in Dr. Trowel's house. I was going to clean up, but I didn't think anybody would show up until tomorrow." His eyes fluttered shut but I pinched off his oxygen until he moaned again. "You made the mess?" I said.

"Before they went on vacation they asked me to look after the place. I was . . . I was angry, at Dr. Trowel. And one day I went over, and I cooked a lot of food and made a mess and . . . I didn't clean up. But I was planning to, really, before they got back. Only . . . then his daughter showed up."

"Before they got back?" I said. It was hard not to keep repeating what he said.

"They called today to say they're coming back early . . . had a nice time, although Mrs. Trowel was bitten by a tsetse fly."

"A tsetse fly?" I said. "A tsetse fly?" He moaned and was quiet until I bounced his head up and down on the ground. "Where were they?" I said. "Where were these tsetse flies?"

"All over her body," Moe said.

"And the—the plates of mushrooms?" I said.

"I ate them," Moe said.

"Did you tell them on the phone I was there?" I said.

"No," he said. "I figured they knew."

"Unfortunately," I said, "we had to leave. But I tell you what: I won't say what you did, as long as you don't mention that I was there." I put his head back down to let the poor guy get some rest. Then I got back in the car. "Listen," I said to Abdhul. "Why don't you let Mr. Froggy go? Don't you think he's suffered enough? If you let him go here, I'm sure he'll find his way back to his pond."

"Naw," Abdhul said. "I want to keep him."

"Abdhul, he's a big frog who's lived a long life, and if you keep him in the car like this he might dry up."

"When we get settled I'll make him a nice pond," Abdhul said. "We can get a fish tank."

"I can't drive if there's a goddamn frog in the car!" I said.

"I'll hold him," Abdhul said. "He likes me."

I pulled out, although the car really sounded terrible and wouldn't move very fast. "Say, where is Mr. Froggy?" Abdhul said.

"Abdhul, where's the frog?" I repeated.

"Oops, he's by your feet," Abdhul said. I glanced down; the frog was incarcerated in the space between the brakes and the gas pedal, a handsome animal with tawny green and brown mottling. "The poor frog," I said.

"Abdhul, pick him up and let him go." Abdhul flung himself down by my feet. He held the frog up in the air triumphantly. "There you are! Got you!" he said. The frog let out a lowly, anguished croak. Giving me a stealthy look out of the corner of his eye, Abdhul thrust the wretched creature into the glove compartment. I said nothing. From time to time the sound of a pained, sorry belch dimly flooded the air. In something less than forty-five minutes, driving at a speed between twenty-five and thirty miles per hour, we had reached one of a chain of Night-and-Days Inns, and here I pulled into the parking lot just at the moment the car sputtered, chortled, came to a stop, and turned itself off. It was eight thirty in the morning. Reeking of smoke, covered in soot and pine needles, I got out of the car. "Put the dog in the duffel bag and zip it up," I said. "We'll smuggle him into the hotel."

In the lobby I found a pay phone and called my mother collect. "Did I wake you up?" I said.

"That's all right," my mother said. "Where are you?"

"We're at a Night-and-Days Inn, located off I-91," I said. "I'd rather not go into any great detail at just this minute. Here's what I'd like you to do—" I looked over at the reception desk, where a spotty, banal youth with a little shoal of fur above his upper lip was thoughtfully grooming the rim of his ear with the eraser end of a pencil. Abdhul had placed the duffel bag containing Dalgleish on the floor and was happily watching the bag— apparently staggering drunkenly this way and that of its own accord on the dull pink "Mediterranean"-style tiled floor. "Excuse me," I said to the receptionist, "what's the phone number here?" I grimaced furiously at Abdhul, hoping he would read my signals and pick up the goddamn bag before the receptionist caught sight of it.

"What?" the receptionist said in a high-pitched voice.

"What's the phone number here?"

"Oh," he said and rattled off a string of numbers.

"Okay, here's what I want you to do," I said into the phone. "Call the hotel and book me a room and put it on your credit card. I think it's better if I don't use mine just now." I looked over at the receptionist. "Is that okay?" I said to him. "I—lost my credit cards, and my mom is going to call you and put the room on hers."

The receptionist smiled weakly. "Sure thing," he said. "And when will y'all be needing this room?" Had they shipped this menial up from the South?

"Now," I said, and hung up the phone.

I waited in the lobby for several minutes for my mother to call the desk.

"Abdhul, pick up that duffel bag and wait outside," I hissed. Abdhul gave a peaky smile and, picking up the bag so that the dog must have been forced to slither to one end, trudged outside. Poor little boy, really he had been through quite a lot. It wasn't fair, to put him through all this insanity, but I hadn't done anything deliberately. People all over the world led very difficult lives; maybe by going through the tough part now, he would have an easier time of things later. "Walk around and stretch your legs," I called after him as he stumbled through the revolving door, smashing the suitcase into the wall. "I'll come out for you when we get our room."

The receptionist was training the fur below his nostrils, as if a caterpillar had embedded itself there and he was coaxing it to grow. The lobby, with its cocoa-colored area rugs and glassed-in atrium containing drab, mangy philodendron and dieffenbachia, was a masterpiece of hideous design. A few couches, foul plaid, had been arranged in groupings with Formica imitation wood lamp-and-table units alongside. I went and got some sticky candy bar out of a vending machine and sat down. Couldn't the architect, or designer—whoever—have been slightly more imaginative in his or her use of color, textile, materials? The stuff wasn't cheap, it just looked that way. If only we could have stopped at some charming, pine-paneled inn, but it seemed to me that in a more intimate place we would have received too much attention. Besides, those places were expensive, although this place wasn't likely to be cheap. "Do you smell fire?" the receptionist said suddenly.

"Nope," I said and peeled the wrapper from the candy bar. It was a horrible stale mess—the label said it was a "Persnickety," fresh peanuts, nougat, and caramel bathed in rich milk chocolate—that had apparently been made out of various waste and by-products, as if glue and cardboard had been dipped in fireplace ashes or brown creosote from the chimney flume. It reminded me of how back in the Victorian age cheap candy had been made out of sugar-coated clay and other inedible substances. What was taking my mother so long to make the goddamn call? It wasn't that much to ask of her, was it? The phone began to ring; perhaps it was her; the receptionist, however, was asking questions such as "When would you like the room?" and "How many people is it for?" Then he occupied himself for quite some time punching information into a computer, leaving the person on hold. At last he told whoever was on the other end of the phone that their reservation for two was confirmed for today and, thanking them for thinking of Night-and-Days Inn, he hung up. I waited for several minutes while he continued to operate the computer. I figured momentarily he would glance over at me, say that was my mother who had just called, and give me our room key. But when some time passed and he didn't acknowledge my existence I stood, deposited the uneaten candy bar in the ashtray, and approached the desk. "I think that was my mother calling, putting the room for me on her credit card," I said.

"What name is your reservation in?" he said.

"Trowel," I said.

"A room for two people, for today?" he said.

"That's right," I said.

Eagerly he began to punch various numbers into the computer terminal. "That's right," he said after an interminable pause. "And how long will you be staying?"

"Ah, I'm not really definite just yet," I said.

"I'll need to know," he said. Oh, come now, I wanted to say, this hotel is huge, obviously there are hundreds of rooms, the parking lot is empty. "Could I let you know later today?" I said, controlling myself.

He frowned. "If you could let us know later today," he said. "Now, I'll need your credit card."

"What do you mean?" I said. "The room is prepaid. You just spoke to my mother on the phone."

"I took your reservation," he said. "But now I need an actual imprint."

"People pay for things with credit cards over the phone all the time!" I said. "Don't be ridiculous—where's the manager?"

"Just a minute," he said and began typing into the computer. After a pause he looked up. "Our computer is down," he said. "I'll need your credit card imprint in the event that you were to charge things to room service or make any phone calls."

"Do me a favor," I said. "Can't you put a lock on the telephone or tell the hotel operator I can't make any calls? I won't use room service; or I'll pay cash."

"Since the computer is down I'll take your driver license information," he decided. "I'll give the bell captain instructions to unplug and remove the phone from your room when he takes your things up. And when the computer is back on line, I'll make sure there are instructions that any room service is cash only. In the meantime, please don't order anything to the room unless you pay cash."

It seemed to be taking things to extremes, to physically unplug the phone and take it from the room, but at least he gave me a plastic key card—unmarked, in the event it was lost—and told me our room was number 617. Then he rang for a bellman, but the guy was so long in coming I went out, found Abdhul, and we carried our things to the elevator down the hall and went upstairs.

Two double beds shrouded with heavy pale blue slippery casings; beige wall-to-wall carpeting; a boxy TV set/radio on a post embedded in the ground. All this for $120 a night! I let Dalgleish out of the suitcase while Abdhul ran around the room turning the lights off and on and calling excitedly from the bathroom that there was a small basket containing shampoo, a shoehorn and polish, bath gel, and two new bars of soap. "God, I'm exhausted," I said, flopping on the bed. "I'm going to take a nap. What do you want to do?"

"I'm hungry," Abdhul said.

"I tell you what," I said. "How much money do you have? Let's try and find all the money we have, including the change, and then we can put it together and order room service. We have to pay cash. We can get breakfast, and then I can take a nap and you can go and play. They might have an indoor swimming pool here; see if there's a brochure in the drawer." I took off my shoes and socks. Dalgleish scratched to come up on the bed and began tenderly to lick my feet. He was not an affectionate animal nor a particularly cuddly one. Now I was touched that from time to time he looked up from my feet and at my eyes with love. But I misread the signals; the taste of my feet had apparently roused him, he mounted my outstretched leg and rhythmically began to attempt intercourse with my calf. "What's he doing?" Abdhul said, laughing.

"I've told you before, he's trying to have sex," I said.

"Like this?" Abdhul said, throwing himself across my other leg and simulating a wild humping.

"Off me!" I said. "Get off me, both of you! We're going to have to get Dalgleish fixed, as soon as we figure out what we're doing for the rest of our lives. In the meantime, go find the room-service menu." He jumped up and, rummaging in the drawer by the bed, pulled out a folder containing various papers. "Now, I'll read you the menu while you see how much is in the bottom of my pocketbook and how much you have." It wasn't even eleven o'clock yet. Breakfast was still being served: eggs, waffles, hash-browns, omelets, a Nova salmon platter, and so on.

Abdhul tallied up the last of the cash: there was fifteen dollars and twenty-seven cents, more than I had thought. Perhaps it was foolish to spend it all, but I was hungry, he was hungry, and something had to be done. My mother could perhaps wire me some money. Maybe she could send one of my brothers to rescue us. Or she might even come herself; the highway exit where I had finally stopped was only a few hours from her house. After food, and a rest, I would know what should be done.

It was forty-five minutes before our food arrived. I made Abdhul go and hide in the bathroom with Dalgleish when the knock came on the door. Probably animals weren't allowed in the hotel. The waiter carried a large platter into the room and, placing it on the table, handed me the receipt and a pen. So I signed. It wasn't my problem, and I was sure the cash saved would come in handy.

When he left I told Abhdul to emerge. Two hateful plates of cold eggs. Dalgleish sat on the ground, looking up while we ate. How human his face looked, as if a small boy had a premature growth of facial hair. Actually, somewhere in Mexico was a whole family of kids that were covered with hair—I had seen their pictures in the paper. "Two brothers and a little girl," I said, "for whom electrolysis would have been a hideous, lengthy, and unendurable procedure, even if they could have afforded it."

"You're kidding," Abdhul said.

This reminded me that many, many weeks had passed since I had attempted to bleach my own facial hair, although I hadn't paid much attention to myself in the mirror. Dalgleish's little black lips trembled as I ate the pink sausage and a bit of the reheated frozen hashbrowns. When we were done eating I put both plates on the floor for him to lick clean. He nibbled delicately—he was a fastidious eater—and, finally finished, he cleaned his face, what he could reach with his pink tongue, and gave me an appreciative look. "You're welcome," I said. He let out a little belch, trotted across the room, and lay down. "That's it," I told Abdhul. "Go and play. I'm going to sleep. Take the room key and remember we're in room six seventeen. Don't go far. Your bathing suit's in the bottom of my bag, if they have a pool there'll be a locker room where you can change. Don't let any men approach you if you use the men's room. Take some change if you want a soda later on. If you go outside, make sure you look both ways before you cross the street. Take the book of matches from the ashtray—it has the hotel name and phone number on it, in case you get lost, but there's no reason you should. You won't go far, will you? Come back in two hours. Do you want my wristwatch?"

"All right, all right, leave me alone," Abdhul said. "Take your nap. See you later on!" Grabbing the plastic key card from the desk he ran chortling from the room, slamming the door loudly as he left. "Wait," I said. "You forgot your—" But he had already gone. I sighed. Maybe they would have boys' bathing suits at the pool, if there even was one. I changed into a sweatshirt and sweatpants, too tired to take a shower first, and got into bed, tucking Dalgleish in alongside me. He let out a feeble grunt of protest and fell asleep.

I dozed. Moments later there was a knock on the door; I threw the sheet over Dalgleish and got up. "Who is it?" I said. "Bellman," the voice on the other side said. I opened the door. "I've come to take the telephone," a lanky youth said, looking at me with a toothy grin. Maybe my appearance was a bit shocking, but I saw no need for such harassment. "It's over there," I said, pointing. He unplugged the phone and exited from the room, saying, "Sorry if I disturbed you, ma'am." Ma'am! Really, how old did he think I was? I got back into bed and slept again, this time to be woken by a maid who entered without knocking. She let out a shriek—perhaps at the sight of the small reddish orangutan face next to mine in the bed in the darkened room—and left abruptly. Then I slept again, an uneasy sleep interrupted by the sound of slamming doors up and down the hall; three men who seemed to find it necessary to carry on a loud conversation right outside my room; and the elevator, only two doors down, that was in some way defective, for every time it started up and stopped I could hear, transmitted through the floor and legs of the bed, a sort of whistling, crushing groan, as if someone were trapped beneath and the rise and fall of the elevator in the shaft was acting as a device of torture. In between I had a dream I had been forced to go back to high school; I was much older than everyone else, and the classes were too difficult for me.

When I woke it was early evening; my watch said four forty-nine; something was whimpering softly in my ear. Briefly I had no idea where I was. I got up and carried Dalgleish into the bathroom, where I placed him in the tub and he urinated. I went to the window and pulled the curtain to one side. In the distance—I hadn't paid much attention to the view before—Interstate 91 was visible, daubs of flickering cars in shades of red, blue, gray, camel, camel, camel, silver, flashing by like industrial migrating birds. How could I have slept for so long? I felt sick, heavy and eggy, and the pungent reek of fire, sweet and acrid, clung to my nose and clothes. I went back to the bathroom and splashed some cold water on my face. Dalgleish was scratching on the side of the tub, unable to climb out, and I picked him up and hoisted him onto the floor. What a hangover, and I hadn't even drunk anything. Maybe I had been more contaminated by smoke inhalation than I had realized. To my surprise I suddenly leaned over and threw up a little bit in the sink. Then I lay back down on the bed.

Dalgleish scratched to come up, and I reached over the side of the bed and pulled him next to me. He sat jabbing with his clawed paw at my arm and muttering softly under his breath. "Okay, okay, I'm getting up," I said. "You want to go out. Where's Abdhul?" Still feeling sickly I sat and reached for my blue jeans where I had flung them on the floor, but they reeked so much of smoke I didn't want to put them on. So I pulled another pair out of the suitcase, and grabbed a T-shirt, but it must have been one of Abdhul's, because it was so tiny a fold of my stomach hung out in a rather unpleasant band. Those women on TV and in magazines who wore tiny bandeaux and little shrunken-up mini-tops were completely unnatural; maybe they were really men in disguise, because it wasn't normal for a woman to have no stomach whatsoever. The point of being a woman was to have a stomach. And that was why Rubens was one of my favorite painters, because to me there was nothing more pleasurable than the sight of an eight- or ten-foot-tall woman with tiny breasts and a huge girth and thighs, in passionate embrace with a man with equal amounts of flab and cellulite.

I grabbed Dalgleish's leash and stuffed it and him into the duffel bag so we could go outside. Where the hell was Abdhul? Now I didn't have the key to the room; at least if he had come back during the afternoon and found me asleep he should have left a note saying where he was going. If they hadn't removed the goddamn phone from the room I could have called the swimming pool or the coffee shop and asked if he was there.

I rode the groaning elevator down to the lobby. The mustached receptionist had gone, perhaps off-duty; in his place was a thin woman, in her thirties, with strands of hair carefully dyed an artificial color to resemble an abnormal attack of sunshine. "Excuse me, have you seen a little boy running around?" I said. Dalgleish chose that moment to throw a fit, I picked up the bag and held it firmly under my arm as if it were a usual phenomenon, for a suitcase to attempt to unpack itself. "No," she said.

"Well, if you see him—a little boy, eight or nine years old, somewhat hyperactive—could you tell him I'm looking for him?" I said.

"If I see him," the woman said.

"How do I get to the swimming pool?" I said.

"The pool is closed," she said.

"But where is it?" I said.

"Take the elevator to the eighth floor; it's at the end of the right wing."

I wandered down the corridor to the gift shop, still holding the wriggling suitcase. It was stocked with a variety of marked-up cosmetics—tampons, Pepto-Bismol, eye shadow—priced at three to five times what they would have cost in a normal pharmacy. There was a display of New England ashtrays and dashboard dice, several stuffed bears and pigs, a few

T-shirts and sweatshirts, and a variety of magazines and newspapers. I asked the woman at the cash register if she had seen a little boy come in. "Oh, gee, I don't know," she said.

"But at any time—earlier in the day?"

She struggled to recollect her past. "I don't know," she said at last. "I really couldn't say. Was he a little boy, by himself?"

"Yes," I said hopefully.

She paused to think again. "I just don't know," she said.

"Well, if he comes in, could you tell him I'm looking for him?" I said.

"Oh, gee, I'm just about to close here," she said. "But if he comes in, I will tell him."

"Thanks," I said. There was a door marked EXIT at the end of the corridor; it wasn't locked, I pushed it open and went out. Across the parking lot was a grassy strip, maybe a quarter or half mile wide, separating the interstate highway from the hotel; in the center a few scrubby pine trees had been planted, as yet only four or five feet high. I walked across the grass, waiting until I was safely out of sight to put the suitcase on the ground and unzip Dalgleish. The dog urinated on the grass and then tore off in loopy, widening circles, yelping feverishly. My God, what if Abdhul had headed for the highway and been hit by a car? I waited until Dalgleish made a kamikaze dive at my ankles and then grabbed him and snapped on his leash. He plunged like a hooked marlin. "We have to find Abdhul," I said. It was rapidly growing darker; I walked to the center trees, hoping Abdhul would be playing quietly underneath, but he wasn't there. Surely he had more brains than to go to the highway; maybe he had befriended whoever was in charge at the swimming pool and was still up there. A wooded area lay just beyond the grass, but I didn't see the point in going there until I had searched the more logical places first. "All right, buddy, I'm going to put you back in the room so I can look for Abdhul," I told the dog.

I stopped at the front desk. "My little boy has gone off someplace, and he's got the key," I said. "Can I get a duplicate? I'm in room six seventeen." The woman at the desk looked miffed, but she must have sensed my growing agitation; from a drawer she produced another plastic card and placed it on the counter.

*Oh, please let him be upstairs,* I thought, waiting for the elevator. I opened the door to the room and called out "Hi!" in a forceful voice; he wasn't there. I filled the ashtray with some water and put it on the floor for Dalgleish, instructing him not to bark or I would have to tie his mouth shut, although actually I didn't see how that would be possible since with his pug face he was basically snoutless. On a piece of hotel stationary I scribbled,

ABDHUL, I WENT OUT TO LOOK FOR YOU. IF YOU COME BACK, DO NOT LEAVE.
The eighth floor reeked of chlorine, but the glass doors at the end of
the hall were locked. What if he had hidden somewhere inside, and come
out when everyone had gone home, and was now floating facedown in the
water? "Hello, hello!" I called. "Abdhul, are you in there?" There was no
answer.

There was no point in panicking, I told myself. The bar was one flight
up, a dark room with schlumpy black leatherette overstuffed chairs and a
view of the highway with its endless stream of cars. Everyone in the world
was going home except for me, I thought. A TV mounted up by the ceiling
was blaring in the corner; the news was on, out of the corner of my eye I
saw a woman in an orange blouse, with busy black hair and a forced smile.
"Now back to you, Kerry," she said prettily.

The bartender was occupied with transferring nuts into troughs. "Have
you seen a little boy?" I said. "A little boy—was he in here before?"

He gestured with his head in a direction behind me. "Take a look," he
said. "Nobody in here." I turned around; it was true, the room was empty.
"But was he in here before?" I said.

"Nope," the bartender said. "No little boys in here today."

"If he comes in, would you tell him to please go back to the room and
wait for me?" I said. "I'm looking for him. Is there a coffee shop here?"

"Ground floor," the bartender said. "Opposite side from the gift shop."

I should have checked there first.

The coffee shop was fairly busy; older couples, perhaps local residents
and not guests of the hotel, were busy dining on Senior Citizen/Early Bird
Specials, $4.95 Fish and Chips, 4:30–6:00, Salisbury Steak/Mashed Potato/
Veg. "Excuse me," I asked the hostess. "Has a little boy been in here? Eight,
nine years old, kind of dirty, curly hair, by himself, space between his front
teeth."

"Oh," the hostess said. "I just came on duty, and I haven't seen him.
Mary's been here since this morning—why don't you ask her?" She pointed
to two waitresses who were standing behind the counter.

I flung myself across the room.

They had little signs above their breasts, HI MY NAME IS MARY and HI MY
NAME IS KATHLEEN, and I addressed HI MY NAME IS MARY. "You've been here
all day? Have you seen a little boy, by himself, around eight or nine years
old?"

Mary had a pot of coffee in her hand.

"Oh, yes," she said. "There was a little boy in here today, by himself.
He had a Coca-Cola."

"You saw him?" I said. "What time was that?"

"Oh, I guess it was around twelve thirty or one," she said.

"And he hasn't been back since then?" I said. "Did he say where he was going?"

"No, he hasn't been back here since then," Mary said. "Did you see a little boy, Kathleen?"

"There were two little boys with their parents," Kathleen said. "I remember because I had to get the highchair for the littlest, and when they left the whole floor was covered with peas."

"No, that wouldn't have been him," I said. "Listen, if he comes back here, would you tell him I'm looking for him and I want him up in the room right now?"

"Oh, sure," Mary said. "I'm not going to be here for much longer, but I'll tell Betty. Is Betty coming on duty tonight, Kathleen?"

"I think Betty has the flu," Kathleen said. "But I'll keep my eyes open. You're staying here at the hotel?"

"Room six seventeen," I said.

Maybe he had gone back up to the room. I went back up, he hadn't returned, I went back down to look outside. "Abdhul!" I yelled across the parking lot. "Abdhul! Where are you?" I tried to keep calm, but something inside me was panicking. I ran across the grass to the wooded lot. It was almost too dark to see, but I thrashed around through the trees. "Abdhul!" I bawled. "Come on, it's getting dark." It was insane to get this worked up, I thought, as I walked toward the highway. The grass seemed to be getting wet, the bottoms of my jeans were damp. Obviously he was someplace around and had just forgotten the time. My thoughts were logical, but my ears were ringing and something inside was pounding like a toilet plunger. Heat rose off the highway and the cars whipped by, pummeling the air and discharging furious chemicals. I looked up and down the shoulder; of course Abdhul had more sense, there was no sign of a little hump of collapsed red sweatshirt and blue pants lying in a tossed and ruined heap.

At least if I could have called the room from the lobby I wouldn't have had to go up and down in the elevator so many times. I used the pay phone to call my mother collect; she would calm me, perhaps. Some message might come to her, like those psychics who were able to tell complete strangers that the missing keys could be located behind the third bookshelf on the left. But though the operator let the phone ring ten times, there was no answer. "Thank you for using AT&T," she said. "Please try your party again later." He must be in the coffee shop, I thought suddenly, and I went down the hall and burst into the room, pushing past the hostess to peer intently at tables where he might perhaps be talking to some strangers, too small for me to be able to see his back from the door. As if my voice belonged to someone else, I suddenly heard myself announce to the room loudly, "Has anybody seen a little boy around? I'm looking for my son." The noise in the room ceased; a few faces turned to smile at me sympathetically yet frightened—I was breaking some unwritten rule of society by addressing a room full of strangers in a loud voice. "Help me, somebody!" I said. There was no response. I felt like a drunk at a cocktail party. I turned and went upstairs. But he was gone.

5

ALL NIGHT, EVERY HOUR, I DIALED MY mother's phone number collect from the lobby, but there was no answer. Where could she have gone? She'd never stayed out all night with any boyfriend, as far as I knew. In the past at times her telephone had been out of order; twice she had been hospitalized, an attack of kidney stones, and it had been several days before I tracked her down. But the operator said it would be impossible to test the phone line until working hours. I called the local hospital; she wasn't registered as a patient, but there were other hospitals in the area and if she was in the emergency room it might be they had no record of her yet.

I called the police. Now I would have to explain that Abdhul was not really my child, I had found him, or he had found me, on the street; they would sure accuse me of burning down my father's house, perhaps they had found remnants, bone and teeth, of the head. The rented car, broken in the parking lot, would certainly be traced to the rental agency; then they would learn that it was due back weeks ago, had probably been reported as stolen. I had overrun charges on my credit cards. And there was more. Somewhere back in New York there were people looking for me who claimed I was a terrorist planning to bomb a building on Christmas Eve to further the Palestinian cause; that I had destroyed the office bathroom and electrocuted Amber. Perhaps there was a warrant out for my arrest.

Yet I didn't care about any of these things. Abdhul was gone. My little boy. Somebody had taken him away; he had gotten into a car with a stranger. Somebody had run him over and driven away; he had crawled under some bushes, injured and whimpering, and fallen unconscious.

While we waited for the police a security guard escorted me through the hotel and around the grounds; he had the key to the swimming pool, and at last we went upstairs.

At the pool, now closed, he flicked on the lights. I ran from the women's to the men's lockerrooms, peering under benches, yelling "Abdhul!" and tapping on locker doors—perhaps he had locked himself in. But each door gave an empty, hollow rattle, there was no indication that a small boy had suffocated inside.

Under fluorescent lights the pool was an unearthly grayish-blue; at least he was not floating in the water. The air was shrill with the scent of chlorine and disinfectant, I could taste it in my mouth. My eyes began to burn as if I had already gone for a dip. "Abdhul!" I yelled. My voice echoed back and forth over the white-tiled walls. I sat down on one of the padded lounge chairs and crushed my temple between my fingers, pressing hard. "I don't know what to do," I told the security guard. "It's not like him, he doesn't wander off."

"That's right," the security guard said kindly. "I tell you what: why don't I put in a call to Larry, he's the other security guard, he was here during the day. I just came on at five o'clock. Maybe Larry saw something."

"That would be wonderful of you," I said. How I hated to ask anybody for anything; some people would have by now befriended everyone in the hotel, strangers would be searching, covering the grounds, but due to my aloofness or some basic chemical flaw in my makeup I was alone in this mess. An indecipherable crackling came over his walkie-talkie, and the security guard turned and told me the police were downstairs. I felt so angry at Abdhul—if he were here I would have smacked him. Probably he was already downstairs, now I would have to face the police and apologize. It would turn out Abdhul had wandered down the road to the nearest shopping mall or some pizza parlor. *Please let him be downstairs,* I thought as we rode down, *I'll never say anything mean to him ever again.*

Two policemen were waiting in the lobby alongside a man who introduced himself as the manager. I had to explain the situation several times: that I had arrived this morning with my little boy, we had both gone up and had breakfast, I said I was taking a nap and sent him out to play, I had slept longer than I intended and when I woke up he was gone. The last person to have seen him was Mary, one of the waitresses in the coffee shop, around twelve thirty or one.

The policemen had already conducted a search of the grounds. "What we can do, Pamela, in a situation like this, is to get the volunteer fire department to organize a search and if nothing turns up we can call in the National Guard," one of them said.

"You know the last time something like this happened was last winter," the other said. "A two-year-old girl, mother claimed she went to the toilet and the child walked out the back door. Three days we were looking in the snow. Third day, the mother claimed the child's mittens had been sent to her in the mail—they had just come back from shopping when the kid wandered out, and the mother hadn't taken her snowsuit off yet—and then the mother abruptly confessed she had accidentally strangled the kid and showed us where she dumped the body."

"Well that's not what happened here," I said sharply. "He doesn't know the area, he never would wander off by himself, and he's too strong for me to easily strangle."

The manager looked nervous. "Nothing like this has ever happened before at this Night-and-Day, and I've been here for seven years," he said, as if I were somehow to blame.

"You were going to try and call the daytime security guard," I said to the security guard who had walked around with me.

"That's right," the security guard said. "Anybody got a quarter?"

"Use the phone at the front desk, Fred," the manager said irritably. He spoke across the room to the receptionist at check-in. "Polly, Fred's using the phone."

The taller of the two policemen began to explain to me the chain of events that would take place. He and his partner were going to drive around the area and I would ride with them to the various video arcades and pizza parlors in the area. "You know, maybe he just wandered off and lost track of the time," he said.

"He didn't have very much money with him," I said.

If that failed to locate him—in the meantime the precinct would be notified and any policemen out on duty would also be looking—then they would begin to organize community members to go out on foot. In the background I could overhear the security guard on the phone. "Uh-huh," he was saying, "a little boy, eight years old . . . Uh-huh . . . That's right." The receptionist with the frosty hair, Polly, had come out from behind the registration desk and stood near the edge of our group with an eager smile. "She lost her little boy?" she said to the manager. "How could she lose her child? That's just awful. There're so many lunatics out there. Last night, on TV, you know that program 'America's Murderers on the Loose'? They had a man who got a little boy out in the woods and cut off his penis. Now the boy is going to live, but he'll never have a penis."

"You're lucky in a way he was only eight," the policeman now said.

"I mean, if he was fifteen, we'd just have to be upfront and tell you we don't have the time or the manpower. You'd just have to wait and hope."

The security guard had hung up the phone and came back over. "That was Larry I was speaking to," he said. "Lucky I got him at home; they were just heading out to see *Bambi* at the Five Cinemas. He said he did see your little boy this afternoon and he remembers it because he was walking around the grounds when he saw him playing with a book of matches down by the front entrance road. So he warned him about the dangers of playing with matches, and took them away from him, because when he was six years old his brother had to have skin grafts when a kerosene heater blew up in the house and to this day his brother never regained complete use of his right hand. It sort of curls up, like this." The security guard held up his hand to demonstrate. "I've seen it myself. The thumb is kind of melted onto the other fingers. He can't even bend it around to hold a spoon very well."

"He saw him at two o'clock?" I said, my voice coming out a squeak.

"So then a car came by and the woman in the front got out and chatted with the boy for a little while and they drove off together. Larry figured they knew each other, that she had come to pick him up, because he got right in and then she turned around and they drove off. He wouldn't have noticed it except that he remembered the little boy was playing with matches. He said he taught his kids from the minute they could walk not to play with fire."

The policeman scratched his head. "What time does *Bambi* get out?" he said. "We can drive on over to Larry's house after the film gets out and see if he remembers what sort of car they drove off in. In the meantime, it's kind of hard to put out an APB, unless the State Highway Patrol just happens to pull her over."

"But Steve, kidnapping is—" the other policeman began.

I interrupted. "I forgot," I said. "I told a friend to pick him up." There was a moment of stunned silence. "I'm very, very sorry," I said. "I haven't been feeling very well, and so I asked a friend to come and get him for a couple of days. My apologies for the inconvenience."

I mean, what was I supposed to say? It was apparent to me that someone had been following me from the social services department—or perhaps it was his real mother—and had waited for an opportunity to reclaim him. If I were to pursue the matter any further it would obviously soon come out that the child was not mine, that I had stolen him—how ridiculous it would sound if I claimed he had followed me home—and perhaps, knowing I had done a good job in looking after him, the woman wanted to spare me arrest and possible prosecution. Or maybe she simply wanted to avoid a scene.

Abdhul must have known who she was, to get into the car with her. It was better to come off sounding like an idiot than to now suddenly explain that the child was not mine, that in fact I was the guilty party, but his real mother had tracked him down and taken him away. The manager, the security guard, Polly, the two policemen—all five of them stood looking at me with varying expressions of blankness and then contempt. "My apologies again," I said, as they dispersed.

I lay awake sweating, frantic, restless, in between trips down to the lobby to use the pay phone and try and call my mother. Finally toward dawn it came to me that the reason I was being punished was because I had no morals. Somewhere out there somebody had lain awake night after night wondering what had happened to her little boy. Maybe she still was. It might have been Brenda, or someone else. But I *had* made an attempt to find out who he belonged to, hadn't I? I had called the social services department and they had been uninterested. It didn't seem like anybody had cared that he was gone. How much of it was my fault, anyway? I didn't have the slightest idea of what morality was or ethics, and maybe nobody else did either, at the end of the twentieth century. Ethics and morality were from movies I had never seen, from another time. Was it ethical to work for a magazine that promulgated killing and death? How much less ethical could it be than, say, selling ads for a magazine that contained photographs of twenty-thousand-dollar dresses when there were people starving in the world? I mean, I knew it wasn't ethical for us to do a cover story about a new gun that just happened to be a product of a company owned by Daniel Loomis's father. There was something wrong with that—I guess. There was a pretense taking place all the time that ethics and morality were in existence. Fur coats, for example, had become unpopular—but not leather shoes or jackets. People sent money to an earthquake site on the other side of the planet, while arguing in the Xerox shop, waiting on line, that it wasn't right to give money to people begging on the street, who would only use it to buy drugs and alcohol. Believe me, if I were out on the street the first thing I would do is go get a drink.

But none of the issues at hand had any real bearing on how to make the correct choices on a daily, hourly basis in order to be able to live life like a decent human being. The choices were too fragmented, the issues unclear, the rules of behavior, etiquette, changed too fast for anyone to keep up. How could you stop to help a fallen man on the street when chances were good he had a partner waiting nearby to hit you over the head as you stooped? It was immoral, a few years ago, to have a baby out of wedlock.

They threw Ingrid Bergman out of the country. *Morals could change.* And ethics? They could be justified in practically any situation. Every dictator, every real-estate tycoon, had a fine rationale for why he was torturing citizens or burning rain forests. And the average person—reporting on a colleague at work to the boss—had his explanation too. I had tried to be considerate and kind, even when my interior thoughts were otherwise. Just the same, I had been very, very wicked. I had done something really wrong. I hadn't found the time or energy to search for Abdhul's real family, because I was too involved in my own struggle for survival. And now I was being punished.

But what if Brenda had been Abdhul's real mother? He was much better off with me, and if I had spent my own time and money to place him with her—or called foster services and gotten him into foster care—chances were conditions for him would have been much worse. Who wanted to be a foster child? Unless he was very lucky, he would have been sent to some family interested only in obtaining the monthly benefit from city or state. I did love him, in my own way, even though some might have said I was a lousy mother.

I felt like an amputee. Something had been violently ripped from me, my head, or my arm, or my legs. He wasn't here with me, in the room. I would do anything to get him back. I didn't want anybody else, only him. If I only had some drug—a sleeping pill, a tranquilizer—but there was nothing and it was too late to get a drink, the bar was closed. Hours passed, while the miserable Dalgleish snoozed peacefully, snoring. Now I cursed Abdhul, that he had the power to make me feel so bad, worse than any boyfriend had ever made me feel, worse than when my parents got divorced, and then I cried out of fear for what might be happening to him. Finally it was morning and through the slit in the diapered window I could see the sun beginning to come up.

I sat paralyzed in bed for several more hours. Around eight the manager knocked on the door—a different man from the night before, he must have gone off duty—and said that dogs and pets weren't permitted in the hotel, either I would have to get rid of the dog or I would have to leave. I guess the maid had seen Dalgleish and reported me. Initially I thought of hanging around for a few more days in the event that Abdhul might mysteriously return, but now I saw it was hopeless, and I told the manager I would check out by noon.

At last I went downstairs and managed to get my mother on the phone; she said she had accidentally kicked the plug out of the wall the night before. I explained to her that Abdhul was gone and my car needed repair.

Now that I wasn't worried about Abdhul, there was no reason for me not to use my credit cards; she would wire money into my New York bank account and in the meantime would call American Express and arrange to pay what was due today, so that I wouldn't be overdrawn on the account. I said after I got the car fixed I'd come to stay with her for a while, but she said that wasn't a good idea, that she was in the middle of teaching and expecting houseguests. "Go back to New York, find an apartment—I'll loan you the money. Find a decent job that you like," she said. "I'll look after Abdhul; he'll be better off with me. You knew he was only temporary at best. I know you feel bad, but if you want a kid why don't you get pregnant or find one to adopt? They had single men and women on one of those talk shows yesterday who had adopted some very cute Samoan babies."

"I don't want a Samoan baby," I said. "I want Abdhul. What are you talking about, you'll look after him? Don't you understand, *I don't have him!*" I lashed out at her because I had no one else to take the abuse. Maybe she knew I would be surly, and that was why she hadn't wanted me to come. All the women I knew sulked when they went home to visit their parents, even if they were forty years old. It was something to do with the secret, inner feeling that one was not in charge of one's life—and it was Mom's fault. For the most part men didn't get this feeling. More than ever I wished I had been born a man. If I had been a man, Abdhul would never have gotten into someone else's car; later I could have written a book about my life with my foundling son, and gone on all the TV talk shows. If I did so as a woman, I would only come across as a deranged, lunatic thief of children.

I hung up the phone and searched through the local Yellow Pages until I found an AAA garage. My mouth was dry and furry, my heart pounding as if I had swallowed a hamster that had taken up residence inside my chest, gnawing and nibbling a comfortable nest for itself. I would have done anything to obliterate this frantic, twitching pain. And yet the hamster within was too alive and throbbing for me to kill it; I wouldn't have wanted to hurt a living creature, even if the creature was me, who I despised.

I rang a gas station and they said they would send over a mechanic within the hour. In the meantime I went back to the room and collected my things. I should feed Dalgleish and take him out, but grabbing Abdhul's things from where they were strewn across the floor—the little T-shirts and blue jeans lined with flannel plaid—I was too nauseated to think of food for myself or even the dog. The tiny moronic—as Abdhul would have said, monronic—things he had loved so much, broken metal cars, brightly enameled canary-yellow and vermilion; the black plastic palm-size box with a button that when pressed emitted the sound of machine guns; his rock collection in a box, some of which he had found himself and others that came wired onto a cardboard, each specimen titled beneath: *Oolitic Limestone, Gypsum, Pyrite (Fool's Gold), Feldspar,* twinkling black crystals and mica chips, and categorized on various sheets according to their igneous, metamorphic, or sedimentary ways. Just junky things—but couldn't the woman have had the decency to let him come upstairs, say good-bye, and collect the toys he loved? I would have permitted him to take Dalgleish, too, not that the dog seemed to notice he was gone. I shoved everything into the bags and, dragging Dalgleish by the leash (he slunk behind, afraid of getting conked over the head by the corner of one of the bags), I went downstairs and waited outside for the car mechanic to arrive.

I inserted the key in the trunk, forgetting momentarily that it had ceased to be openable; but it had miraculously healed itself, and I threw the suitcases in. A man in a towtruck pulled up into the lot; I waved and he pulled over. Without saying a word he opened the driver's door to my car, slid in, and popped open the hood. Then getting out, he began eagerly, lovingly, to palpate the organs and projectiles of the engine. A prod, a squeeze, perimeters of a polyp examined, a raise of the dipstick, his fingers swimming down some automotive keyboard; I stood alongside to watch while Dalgleish inspected some fragrant stain on the front left tire, lifted his leg for the first time, and then once more began to nose the richly soiled spot. At last muttering something indecipherable, the mechanic said he would have to tow the car to the garage; the damage was minor, but would take several hours to repair. In the meantime I could come along, or could remain at the hotel and he would bring the car back later on.

I opted to go with him to the garage. I was too tired to keep up my personal level of anxiety and it was amazing how different I felt now that it was gone. The worst had happened to me, although I had never known that Abdhul's disappearance was going to be the worst thing to endure. Why had no one ever told me that once the worst had happened there was nothing more they could do to you?

It took some time for the mechanic to hook his chains to the twisted front bumper; I climbed in the front of the towtruck with the dog and at last we drove off, the car rattling its shackles behind. The mechanic looked over nervously out of the corner of his eye. "Say, what kind of animal is that, anyway?" he said.

"It's a dog," I said. "An affenpinscher."

"Oh, it's a dog," he said, letting out a short breath. "I figured it was probably a dog, but I thought at first maybe it was some kind of monkey."

"No, it's a dog," I said again.

"It's one weird-looking animal," he said. "I bet a lot of people think it's a monkey. How much would one like that cost?"

"Anywhere from four hundred to a thousand dollars," I said.

For the rest of the trip we didn't speak. At the gas station the mechanic explained it would be several hours before he could work on my car; he was the only one there on duty that day, there was another car he had to do a lube job on first, and I might as well leave and come back later. Through a glass window on one side I could see an office, with a pay phone and a vending machine; I went in and purchased a lukewarm paper cup of some coffee-substitute, watery brown and sweet, with clumps of artificial whitener bobbing on top. Using the credit card I made a call to the Rent-A-Wreck Company in New York and explained that I would be returning the car a tiny bit later than originally stated. And that was that. There were no threats of lawsuits for neglecting to return it so long ago, no accusations that I had stolen it or that the car's absence had been reported to the police. It was possible the phone was answered by someone who just didn't understand, but somehow I doubted it. Perhaps it was simply that now that I was no longer afraid, nothing was going to happen to me.

On the corner was a cash machine in a booth. On a lark I stuck my credit card in and to my amazement the machine didn't take my card away from me but spewed out quantities of money. So I dragged Dalgleish to the convenience store across the street. I bought a tunafish-size can of Happy Pup—flip-top, Steak and Veg. dinner—a small container of orange juice, and a prewrapped manufactured cheese sandwich from the cooler.

On a low cement bench bedecked with cherry pop stains, particles of cheese nachos, wrappers from Kit-Kat bars, and discarded instant lottery tickets, the two of us sat and ate our meal. Dalgleish had his straight from the can after I had checked to make sure there were no sharp edges. The sandwich was dry, with only one thin slice of Swiss cheese, but I washed down the thick bread with swigs of orange juice.

Abdhul was in New York, I was certain. Maybe it was a psychic impulse. But I knew I had to go back and find him. He had been discovered by somebody I knew—perhaps Amber, perhaps Alby. The thing was, how could I show up in Manhattan without landing in a lot of trouble? By now Daniel Loomis's body might have been discovered in the crawl space, for which I would be blamed. And there was the bomb threat, and—I couldn't even remember all that I had allegedly done. Then I realized: *as long as they didn't know that I was me, I couldn't be blamed.*

A few doors down was a Hair 2000; once a small town would have had its local barbershop for men and beauty salon for women, but now these things were gone, replaced by "unisex" chains with pulsing music and blowdryers. I went in, pulling Dalgleish. Magazines were stacked by the door, the sort I knew depicted various hairstyles long out of date. There were two women, one occupied with a man at the far end, the other who came over and asked if she could help. Her hair was cut in an Early American Heavy Metal rock style. The back was long, wispy tin-blond, while the top part was cropped short. Perhaps the two stylists experimented on one another? I picked up a magazine and pointed to a male model whose hair had been coiffed in a fey, somewhat English style, with an effete fetlock. "Cut my hair like that," I said.

"That's a man's haircut," she said.

"I'm aware of that," I said. "Are you capable?"

"Yes," she snapped in the same voice as my own.

In the changing room I took off my shirt, put on a robe, and then sat in one of the chairs with Dalgleish on my lap. He was trembling as if some operation were about to be performed on him. "All right, just calm down," I told him. "Nothing's going to happen to you." The other hairdresser finished brushing off the man and he stood. He had a soft, puffy face and his hair had been shaped into a little cap like a bird's nest. "Thanks a lot, Terry," he said, sweeping past with a strong gust of aftershave. Aftershave always made me think of a man masturbating alone in a hotel room.

The other stylist came over to my side. "I'll take the little pup," she said kindly. My stylist lifted up hanks of my dry hair. "Are you sure you want it just like the picture?" she said.

"That's right," I said, following her to the basin. "Make it just like the picture. Only less feminine."

Suddenly I was overcome with a longing to call my mother and ask if I was doing the right thing. How juvenile that was, to want to call one's mother and obtain permission to get a haircut. And yet, that was my current state of fragility. Without her I felt there was no one to corroborate my world-view of reality. Was it normal to spend the time and money to get my hair cut off under such circumstances? My father, my brothers, any man I had ever gone out with—would simply have shrugged if questioned about his opinion as to whether or not I should get a haircut. A girlfriend, if I had had one, would have pretended interest. Only my mother would have weighed the pros and the cons with as much involvement as if it were her own appearance at stake. But perhaps it was time to grow up, to make decisions on my own. The stylist wrapped my dripping head in a towel and

I sat back down in front of the mirror. Time slowed; it had become some caustic substance: already I felt as if I had been sitting in that chair for days or even years, and though I had no desire to speak I was sorry I had snapped at her—maybe she would take it out on my hair—and now I tried to make up for it by asking her a few questions. Her words dripped over me, I could only catch one or two here, a string there—her husband was an electrician, they had two children seven and two years old, she had gone back to work when the smallest was a year old—but all the time she spoke I kept thinking *Where is he?* Tiny movielike fragments floated on the mirror, Abdhul eating a hamburger with ketchup covering his chin; Abdhul bursting in the door to the house and yelling "Imbimbo!" at the top of his lungs; the time I woke him up in the middle of the night when I heard a noise and we went out to look at a scavenging skunk and his eyes were bright as cherries.

At last she brushed me off. The floor around the chair was thick with clumps of hair. I could hardly bring myself to look in the mirror. It was quite remarkable, but really I might have passed for a rather effeminate man. She unsnapped the plastic tarp and I stood. Maybe for a man I was a little dumpy around the hips, a little slumped around the shoulders—but then, so was Daniel Loomis. Involuntarily I stroked the few dark hairs above my lip. The stylist looked stricken. "Now that it's so short we could dye it blond," she chirped, and then hastily added, "But I think it looks very nice."

"This is fine," I said, and paying her I collected Dalgleish, who was happily gnawing on Terry's wristwatch strap as she held him on her lap by the front door. "Oh!" she said, and recovering herself went on. "This little dog is just so cute! I'd just love to play with him all day."

"I wish you could too," I said, my voice somehow coming out deeper than normal.

Women I knew who had gone from being brunette to blond said their lives had changed, that they felt different and men really had started paying a lot more attention to them. There was no reason I shouldn't feel different going from long hair to short. I didn't want to be a lesbian, I just wanted to see briefly how the other half lived. When bad things happened to men they just picked up the pieces and got on with their lives. Even if their wives left them, taking the kids, they met new women, had more kids, and hardly seemed to notice there had been a change in personnel. I stopped in a Speedy Specs and in one hour had a pair of black industrial-style glasses made up for me. Now I looked vaguely like an artistic type of guy who hung out in downtown Manhattan bars. My features were not good—my nose too broad, my mouth too thin, my chin a bit too pointed—but they were better features for a man than a woman. I was five eight, maybe a little on the short side but well within the range of average men's height. Certainly I wasn't really thinking about anything I was doing. I went back to pick up the car. The mechanic was sitting out in front, puffing on a cigarette, near a little pool of gasoline or some other liquid on the ground by his feet. "My car ready?" I said, gesturing toward it. "What's that?" he said, letting out a little yelp and flicking the cigarette behind his back as if he had been caught doing something illicit. My eyes followed the butt as it rolled toward the pool on the ground and then stopped, still lit, a foot away. "Oh yeah, yeah, your car," he said, giving me a puzzled look. "I wouldn't have recognized you, except for your dog!" He began to chuckle in a mirthless voice. "Your car's all ready, heh-heh. Got your hair cut while you were waiting, huh? I wouldn't have recognized you. Thought for a minute there you were some—" He stopped himself, and I suddenly envisioned him arriving home to find his wife or girlfriend sobbing passionately over a too-tight permanent wave or a dye job gone green. "You're from New York, right?" he blabbered. "I guess you'll fit right in with the latest fashion . . . in New York."

This, then, was what the women's movement had accomplished in the twenty-odd years since its inception. It had created a car mechanic attuned to women's fashions in hair-styles. After he had explained to me at great length what had gone wrong with the car—some kind of kink in the ignition electrical wiring, or maybe the spark plugs were dead—I got in, put Dalgleish on the front seat next to me, strapped him in with the shoulder seatbelt, and drove off.

A few exists down the highway were signs for Crank's Big Boy, and here I pulled off. Leaving Dalgleish in the car—the sun was hot, but in the back of the lot I found some shade, and unrolled the windows partway down—I bought a local paper from the machine in the front entrance and, sitting down at the counter, ordered a cup of coffee and began to peruse the local help-wanted ads. I wasn't sure exactly what I had in mind. I knew I was hungry, in fact I was ravenous, even though I had eaten the cheese sandwich not long ago, and I was about to ask the waitress who had brought me the cup of coffee for a menu when I realized she was staring at me intently. "If I could have a menu—" I said.

"Oh!" she said and flushed shell-pink. "I'm real sorry about that, I don't know what I was thinking of." It wasn't that big a deal, to be a few seconds slow with a menu; I guess my appearance needed some work. To resemble a manly lesbian wasn't my intention, no offense to manly lesbians intended; it was just that if I had any interest in becoming a lesbian, which I had not, I certainly couldn't see the point in trying to look masculine. It seemed to me the whole point of being a lesbian would be in not having to bother with sexual stereotypes, but to rid oneself of male and female attributes altogether. But as for myself, I was interested in sexual stereotypes. When I had gone along with being female, I had worn lots of makeup, although I admit this was mostly in order that people not scream when they saw me on the street. Now I wanted the power that seemed to be a given in the male sex; if I had to acquire male attributes in order to obtain that power, then so be it. Gingerly I stroked my chin. There was no other solution, I would have to shave my face. I was too wrinkled around the eyes to resemble a downy-faced adolescent; I supposed I could dye my facial hairs a darker hue, but how to dye one's facial hair without actually tinting the skin? And even if I could figure it out, it would only be grotesquely wispy. Oh, how awful to touch my face and feel stubble, I didn't see how I could bring myself to do this. Maybe it would be best just to acquire a wig until my insanity left me.

"Let me have a cup of corn chowder, a medium rare hamburger, and the fries," I said. The waitress, still fixed in her trance, twittered, and, snatching the menu from my hands, ran off, looking back at me with a slanty smile. Hey, maybe it wouldn't be so bad being a man after all. Maybe I had some peculiar chemical aura that made me very attractive to women, an aura that all this time had been subverted. My mother once had a very plain friend who was amazingly attractive to men, despite her years and rather kangaroolike face. Men seemed to follow her down the street as if she were exuding some sexual pheromone, and even though my mother begged her for the name of the perfume she wore and we both went out and bought it, it obviously wasn't that drugstore scent. If only I had one of those names that could be easily circumcised, like if I were Georgina I could call myself George, or Antonia, Tony. Pamela—there were no male versions of that. Paul—at least that began with the same letter, but what a mushy, mealy name it was, reminding me of a bowl of cold cereal or the mouth of a gun dog carrying a limp duck. If I really could be a man I would have to use Pamela's credit cards and hope that no one questioned me, though if they did I guessed I could say Pamela was my sister and I had taken her card by mistake.

I skipped through the classifieds. What a pitiful assortment of jobs were available in the area. Men to work the night shift unloading parts at some local corporation, an equal opportunity employer. A trainee at a fast-food restaurant that could eventually lead to a managerial position. Part-time employment at a souvenir concession at the local sports arena. A job in sales at the video store in the shopping mall, experience required. Were such pursuits supposed to occupy a person for the rest of their life? And the salaries—sixteen thousand dollars a year, some medical benefits—who could live on that kind of money? Who would want to stay here? Winter in this part of the world was endless, the trees without leaves, the sky gray and overcast, the remaining farmland only thin strips, divided and cut by endless highways and discount factory outlets. Already as a man I wanted more.

The waitress brought my corn chowder, the silly grin still affixed to her face. "Hope you like it!" she said and winked. What a face—swollen and buttery, with puffy, sexual lips and a vegetable expression that made me want to fuck the hell out of her.

Oh my God, what was I thinking? I jumped up from my stool and ran to the toilets. Men's or Ladies'? The problem was, Pamela with her vagina did not want to have sex with a waitress—but Paul and his nonexistent penis was plenty ready. On the other hand, I wasn't sure whether my manly appearance was something that only I alone saw. Jeans, T-shirts, and sneakers were a modern costume worn by either sex. Forty years ago females couldn't even go out of the house without wearing stockings and a little hat. Still, it would make matters worse to stand for too long in front of the toilet doors, obviously debating the issue. I pushed open the door to the men's room and quickly locked it behind. Ha! There in the mirror I was greeted by the face of my uncle Pigham Bernstein—a younger version. Pigham Bernstein was my half-Jewish uncle whose gentile mother had named him Pigham as an act of revenge on her promiscuous husband. He had the same slitty, wily features I saw before me now. How lucky I had never bothered to pluck my eyebrows. If placed alongside Ralph and Mitchell, I definitely would have been the prettiest of the three brothers, although it occurred to me a big jacket of some sort was in order, to cover up what in a woman was a flat chest but in a man was unbecoming projectiles.

But what sort of jacket to acquire? A motorcycle jacket would have been a bit of a swaggering cliché, although it would have done much to compensate for my lack of shoulders. A denim jacket? But I was already wearing blue jeans, it was a bit too much to be all in denim. Ah, this was stupid, real men didn't stand around men's rooms worrying about what to wear, although actually this probably wasn't true, since all the men I knew in New York disappeared into the men's rooms for great lengths of time and, if there was more than one of them, often returned to discussing their wardrobes with the other fellows.

Luckily there was a normal toilet in a stall besides the three urinals, and I closed the door to practice urinating backward while standing up, so that in future I could take my place with the other men. Luckily I had that quantity of pubic hair to hide the paucity, nay, the absence, of penis—but I hoped there would be no cause for closer inspection and discovery of my microcephalic condition. Men did come in all sizes after all, and in the past during my survey of the male sex I had been startled to come across one who had a mere nubbin, so minute as to be impenetrable; many years later I ran across this same man, now happily married and starring on a hit TV show, so length was not really a measure of success. And what about that famous case in which a rather well known jazz musician, living in Oregon or Washington State, married and with two adopted children, had upon his death been discovered to be a woman? Early on he had explained to his wife that some sort of accident (perhaps it was a bicycle accident, I never understood why bikes for men had that dangerous crossbar between seat and handlebars) had rendered him impotent.

Anyway, I had no intention of keeping up this charade for long; only until I found my son. I unlocked the door and went back out into the hall. A man was lurking; he gave me an irritated look and pushed his way inside.

I slapped the last of my liquid assets alongside the now gray, greasy patty of meat; the waitress rushed over, murmuring dismay, and offered to return the hamburger to the kitchen and obtain a fresh one for me. I explained I had forgotten an appointment and had to leave. "In that case, let me take it off your bill," she said. "I'm not supposed to, really, but I hate to see you pay for something you couldn't eat."

"Oh, that's nice of you," I said. "Thanks." If I had had more cash I might not have accepted her offer. She gave me an intimate look. I hoped she didn't expect me to put out after this. It did make me feel kind of good, to have a fuss made over me by a waitress. So this was what it was like to be a man! Or maybe it was just the Trowel genes at work, for on many occasions I had watched women coo and giggle at my father. But the whole thing was too preposterous for words.

I found a Salvage Discount Factory Outlet. Unfortunately everything smelled like mildew, but here I found a plaid suit, possibly dating from the 1970s, with bell-bottom trousers. There was also, after some searching, an oversize cap in plush fawn velour. There were two pairs of shoes that fit: brown, with platform soles, and a pair of rather pointy red-and-gray wing tips. I changed in the dressing room—I'd pay on the way out—and the completed effect was not bad, though I couldn't decide if I looked as if I was dressed by an extremely modern French designer, or simply looked like a pimp. The suit jacket compensated for my shoulders. I got the cashier to snip off the price tags as she rang up the items, asking her for directions back to New York while trying to gauge her response to me. She chattered amiably for a bit, a soft look in her water-buffalo eyes, telling me to make a left and go straight ahead, then turn right, etc. She likes me! I thought, startled.

After a few minutes drive I didn't feel any different than ever. After all, most of the time I didn't sit around thinking, I am female, I am female. No, I was thinking about what to cook for dinner, or trying to analyze and figure out different people I had met, or examining a leaf that had fallen onto the pavement. It wasn't even as if I had suddenly been freed from a corset; after all, these were modern times, I could have easily bought a very similar outfit in the women's department, only a few details were different. I didn't even need to change my actions in any way. In college there was a stunning black girl who lived on my floor, nearly six feet tall, who wore sheer stockings and tiny dresses and platform shoes—but despite her appearance she didn't act demure or feminine or flirtatious, but swaggered around and spoke in a gruff voice. And then there were many men I had met, who spoke softly and offered a soft, moist paw by way of greeting and nobody ever thought to question them. As for "lockerroom talk"—well, were I to find myself in a lockerroom, although I couldn't see how or why, I was certain the conversation would be no different than when a group of particularly outspoken women got together at a baby shower. Only the names of the genitalia would be changed, I hoped.

Anyway, all I had to do was find Abdhul and we could get out of the city and I could go back to normal.

Four hours later Dalgleish and I were in Manhattan. I dropped the almost completely trashed car off in front of the Rent-A-Wreck. Luckily the place had already closed for the night, so I was able to put the keys back in the folder and stick it through the letter slot in the door; what a little surprise they would find in the morning!

Nearby was a fifth-rate residence hotel, and there was a room free, they didn't mind dogs, and so I checked us in. I was uncertain of my plans; but I knew if I stuck around Abdhul would return to me. He was a smart kid, he was street-wise, and if he had been put into foster care or returned to Brenda, it was only a matter of time before he would come looking for me.

Lying on the lumpy bed in the peeling, drunken room scarcely wider than the bed, I decided that in the morning I would go back to my old apartment and ask the new tenants if any little kids had been hanging around. I might post signs for him, telling him where I could be found. At present it seemed best to maintain my manly disguise. There were too many people in New York who were mad at me. Then, too, as Pamela, probably my reputation preceded me, the magazine world was quite small. As Paul I might be able to forge some letters of recommendation from an imaginary, now-defunct magazine located on the West Coast and perhaps land myself an entry position at some other publication.

I will now say the following: as a man I was no better than other men, but I was blessed with two qualities I had, as a woman, always found supremely desirable in the male sex. The combination, irresistible to my-self, proved to be irresistible to other women as well. The first was, that unlike the majority of men, I was a supreme listener. The second factor was my aloofness—due to my fear of discovery. But why was it that the men who didn't ask one out on dates, who were always busy, who didn't return your phone calls, were so much more exciting than the dull plodders who regularly rang to ask you out to the movies?

No matter that my job at *Bride-to-Be* was a lowly one; the receptionist, Dalma, quivered at the sound of my step. My boss, Sylvana, was only a few years older than I was: she took me out to lunch (as editor-in-chief, she said laughingly, she could do as she pleased) and there spoke, only three days after my arrival, of her dissatisfaction with the current director of advertis-ing, Emily Grossman, and her plans to eventually get rid of her—"And then we will see about putting you there in her place, Paul." I quickly downed another scotch-and-soda; although drinking at lunch in New York was at present a sign of mental weakness and lassitude, I found it brought out the manly side of me, which helped in my little charade. "But tell me about yourself, Paul," she said while we perused the menu. "You appeared so suddenly, out of nowhere—surely I might have heard about you, or bumped into you somewhere before?"

Pink, pink, the restaurant was pink and coral, with dewy pink recessed lighting that flushed the air, and chunky brown leather banquettes to balance the yin and yang of the place. Pasta laced with squid ink, at thirty-five dollars a plate, grilled chunks of tuna, opalescent oysters carried on beds of shaved ice across the room by snappy waiters neat as silver minnows—it was like being under water, Atlantis resurfaced in luxe Man-hattan!

"Oh, I'd much rather hear about you," I assured the overheated Sylvana. "You're so young, and already editor-in-chief of a national maga-zine!"

"Oh, well then," she said, gazing at me across our little table for six (table number 10, no Siberia for this girl) with eyes of misty myopia, "it is like this—"

Sylvana was French, with black, soigné hair, that lilting accent (exaggerated slightly, I believe, for my benefit) and that manner of making a man feel desirable that only a French woman can have. Little did she suspect the squalid drug-addict hotel I inhabited and even worse, that—as Paul—I had forged my letters of recommendation from an imaginary, now-defunct magazine located on the West Coast, with which I landed the entry position at *Bride-to-Be*.

". . . from Lyon, I went to Paris, and for a time I modeled, although this, you know, was to me a bit silly. And, though my father"—(this was pronounced fazzer)—"was a Communist, and hoped perhaps for me to become Simone Weil, I would not; as a Jewish girl I continued to believe that secretly I had been adopted and was really the child of a prince, who would arrive on a white horse, with his nose of velvet and cream—"

"The horse, or your father?" I interrupted.

"Yes, yes," Sylvana said impatiently. "The horse, not the prince." (pranze) "And the horse, drawing behind him a red coach, covered with little bells, and on top a huge egg of rubies and emeralds. From the carriage the prince emerge: 'Sylvana, Sylvana!' he say. 'Here I am!' " She paused momentarily for effect, although I was not quite sure what response was expected from me. "And you? What is the mysterious secret lurking within your eyes? You are married? You have a lurid past?"

"A bit lurid," I admitted.

"Aha! You are blushing. But this is a charming attribute. One day you will tell me, Sylvana, everything, for I find it impossible to resist a secret."

"I have a little dog—" I began.

"Oh, no! Do not tell me. I cannot abide a sad story about an animal."

"No, no," I said. "It's just that it's hard to leave him alone at home all day."

"But you must bring him to work with you," she said. "Unless he makes the pee-pee upon the floor, or if he barks—otherwise, there will be no problem."

Of her meal she consumed little (translucent pink sheets of smoked salmon, triangles of brown bread, a half-lemon in a snood of cheesecloth), but sucked thoughtfully on her smallest finger while watching me devour a hearty meal of grilled Hawaiian mahi-mahi and a tangled nest of indescribably thin french-fried potatoes, curled crisp fringes. At last I was finished; Sylvana excused herself to go to the toilet, and while I waited I heard—

coming from behind me—a familiar, piercingly nasal voice. "They had to reset my arm twice," the voice was saying. "And I thought I was going to need plastic surgery for the scar on my leg, but thank God it seems to be going away."

"But how did it happen?" the voice's companion responded.

"I fired an employee who tried to kill me," the voice said.

"How terrifying," said the other. "What will you do? Can you sue?"

"At the moment nobody can locate her."

What was perpendicular became horizontal, as if the walls of the room had been knocked askew by some wrecker's ball. I pretended to look around the room for the waiter. There in profile was Amber MacPherson, her arm still thickly swathed in chalky plaster and held up by her short neck in a sling. In what was rather a charming touch she had had the cast embedded with large paste jewels, topaz and tourmaline, although perhaps the jewels weren't paste but real, which I didn't think was such a good idea in Manhattan—what if a mugger took an ax to her arm, hoping to acquire the valuable merchandise? Far be it from me however to point such possibilities out to her. At that moment Sylvana reappeared.

The waiter recited a string of delicacies—lemon tart, frozen white-and-dark chocolate mousse cake, crème brulée, and raspberry sorbet. Sylvana waited for me to order first. "I'll have the crème brulée and a cup of coffee," I muttered.

"Very good," Sylvana said. "But now, I must be leaving you."

"Hi, Sylvana," Amber whined from behind.

"Oh, gee, I wouldn't have ordered if I thought we were going."

"No, no, no," she said. "You must stay and have the dessert. I have already signed for the bill. I have a fashion show I must attend at two thirty, I am meeting Emily there, but I will see you in a little while back at the office." She turned to the table at her side. "Hello, Amber!" she said. "Have you met Paul Trowel?" Idiot! I should have changed my last name, though luckily due to her French accent it came out as True-elle.

"No, I haven't," Amber said. "Hi, Paul. What do you do?"

"I just started at *Bride-to-Be,*" I croaked. Sylvana was collecting her things from beneath the table, and I rose to my feet. With a flurry of pitty-pat kisses and French perfume she said good-bye and left the room. I sat hunched at the table, my back to Amber, wondering how long I should wait to leave to avoid bumping into Sylvana at the coat-check out front or trying to get a taxi. "Did Sylvana leave you all alone here, Paul?" The voice of Amber addressed my back. "Did you order dessert? Come over and join us, we have room."

I rose to my feet again, a saggy smile pasted above my jaw, and stumbled over to her table. "Sit down," Amber commanded, an amused twinkle in her eyes. "Paul, this is Pimmi Stimples, from Carson Steenburge." Carson Steenburge was either a multinational investment corporation or a famous law firm, I couldn't remember. I supposed things could have been worse: Amber could have been lunching with Virginia, or Debbie, or somebody else. Pimmi Stimples had an expensive face and brown chin-length hair; from her ears dangled uvula-shaped pearls. I couldn't seem to rid my face of the fixed smile. "Where were you before *Bride-to-Be,* Paul?" Amber said suddenly—a bit suspiciously, I thought. At that moment the waiter appeared with my crème brulée, and I nearly shouted, "Los Angeles!" plunged my spoon into the thin, crackling skin that covered the little custard pot, and rudely began to eat. How crisp the topping of caramelized sugar, like the fried head of a baby, and how dense the custard beneath: it was as if I had spooned Pond's cold cream into my mouth, I was unable to swallow and practically gagged. Amber had really aged a great deal. Maybe she was just having a bad day. And yet there was something tasty about her—if the WASP, sunny, field-hockey style of woman was your type. "What do you do, Amber?" I said, my mouth half full.

"I'm the editor of *Hunter's World,*" Amber said. I nodded appreciatively. As a woman I would have said, "Oh, wow—terrific!" or some more enthusiastic and phony note of praise. Men, however, were not so caught up in such public rituals of admiration. Over the next ten minutes Amber attempted to grill me: where I had gone to college, my father's background and business, where I attended prep school—and though I simply pieced together bits of information stolen from this person and that, apparently my answers met with her approval, although I was a lousy liar and would never remember later what I had said. But she suggested, in an aside to Pimmi, that Pimmi invite me to a party she was hosting that evening—it was a dinner for ten in a restaurant whose name sounded vaguely familiar—to celebrate Pimmi's twenty-seventh birthday. Another male guest had dropped out at the last minute. I must have still been very frightened of Amber. I found myself saying that I would attend. The check arrived—I prayed Amber wouldn't expect me to pick up their tab—and quickly rising I said good-bye and that I would see them that evening at eight. Then I went off to the men's room; in a sophisticated restaurant such as this, the toilets were not assigned to sex, but rather there were simply two separate, private tiled rooms, and I darted into one and quickly locked the door. My behavior with Pimmi and Amber had been rude—disinterested, coarse, there was no doubt about it—but they hadn't seemed to notice. Perhaps

Amber was competing with Sylvana; perhaps Pimmi was single and looking for a mate; or maybe that was just how men behaved. In any event, it was much pleasanter to be a man about town than it had ever been to be a woman. An invitation to a dinner party, after only three days in the city! I had been in New York for years before this, and couldn't remember when there had been an invitation for which I wasn't expected to pay. As I left they were standing with their backs to the room by the coat-check, and I overheard Pimmi saying, "Do you think he's gay?"

"Actually, I think he's kind of dorky," Amber said, a bit cruelly, though whether it was cruelty directed at me or Pimmi I couldn't be certain. After all, if Pimmi was interested in me, it spoiled things a bit if I had already been categorized as a dork. "Bye-bye, girls!" I said, brushing past.

"Bye, Paul!" Amber said, crinkling the corners of her little eyes.

In the evening, walking Dalgleish, I returned to my former apartment and knocked on the door. The previous two nights the lights in the basement had been off; maybe the occupants were away. But now I rang the bell, which had been fixed, and the front door opened. A woman peered up at me through the metal security gate at the bottom of the stairs. She looked like me. "I, uh—" I said.

"Yes?" the woman said. Long frizzy curly black hair, a manly, plain face . . . Put on some lipstick! I wanted to say. I know what it's like to live alone in this apartment, I almost told her—it's located above an Indian graveyard, or under some horrible interplanetary conjunction! Get out while you have the chance, before the gelatin in the bathroom crawls out and strangles you while you sleep, or some little boy appears on your doorstep and wrecks your life! The woman looked at me impatiently, yet with a sympathetic stare. Perhaps she, like me, wished to find a man on her doorstep to come into her life, no strings attached. "I, uh—" I said again, nervously. "There used to be a little boy who lived here, and I wondered if maybe he's been around, looking for me."

"Oh," the woman said, puzzled. "A little boy? No." She looked a bit disappointed.

"Listen, if he shows up, tell him I—tell him Pamela is waiting for him, at the Belleclaire Hotel. I don't have a phone in my—Pamela doesn't have a telephone. Actually, Pamela sent me here to look for him—Abdhul—in case he shows up."

"I haven't seen any kids around," the woman said sluggishly. Dalgleish, on the end of his leash, suddenly emitted a pained cry of delight, as if he had just recognized her, and began to throw himself against the bars of the grate, slurping. "What a cute little dog," she said. "I'm thinking about getting one—this apartment would be great for a dog, it could go out in the garden in back." The fact that I had a dog seemed to dissipate some of her nervousness, that I might be a fast-talking rapist who would hypnotize her into letting me in.

"But if you do see a little kid, walking around looking lost, or who knocks at your door, could you tell him Pamela's at the Belleclaire? It's only a few blocks away, he'll know."

"Well, sure," the woman said. "But—" and here she seemed to give a little shudder and collect herself, as if dimly remembering one of those one-night courses at an Adult Education Center on Making Friends in the City. "What's your name?"

"I'm Paul," I said. "Paul True-elle."

She looked up through the bars. "I'm Marjorie Morgenstern," she said. "I haven't seen any little kids—but do you want to stop back in a couple of days, in case I have?" She poked her fingers through the bars to pat Dalgleish on his pate.

"Okay," I said. Now she was going to go call her mother or a girlfriend and relay the adventure of the evening. "It's good you didn't let this person into your apartment," they would tell her. "But why didn't you offer to meet him for a drink up the street?" But what if she was lying and had already found Abdhul, and he was watching TV in the bedroom inside? I grabbed onto the bars and tried to peer around through the open door within. She gave a little thrilled scream and took a step back. "Sorry, Marjorie," I said. "A good place to do chin-ups, ha-ha! I'll see you later, bye-bye."

I passed a newsstand. Big signs were plastered all over it, advertising the latest issue of *Hunter's World,* and I bought a copy and leafed through it while I walked back to the hotel. Here was something funny: on the masthead, Virginia Loomis's name was printed as editor-in-chief, while below Amber had been reduced to managing editor; why, she had out-and-out lied to me, earlier that day, when she told me she was editor-in-chief. Apparently in the weeks since I left, Virginia had usurped her position. Nor was there any mention of Bronc Newman as art director, so perhaps he had lost interest and returned to whatever it was he was doing before he accidentally got an electric shock in the bathroom of the magazine. On the other hand, Daniel Loomis wasn't on the masthead either, so maybe Alby's arrow had hit its mark. But, my God, what had happened to this magazine? If before it had been contemptible, it was now more so, in a truly insidious way. The cover featured a famous movie star in an erotic pose; accompanying this was a puff piece about her while she espoused her Philosophy of Acting. I was so distracted I didn't realize the elevator was out of order; finally, after ten minutes I took the stairs and sat down to look over the rest of the issue. A vicious piece about a struggling writer, and a rave review of a fashion designer who previously had best been known for his theft of other designers' designs but who had now (perhaps with the help of ten pages of purchased advertising) suddenly had a breakthrough and become an original. Pages and pages of English Society reports; a famous chef opening his own restaurant was here modeling leather motorcycle gear. A ten-page report of an heiress who had OD'd, and to round out the issue under the heading of Politics was a story about the first female prime minister of a small Asian country and a list of the men she had allegedly slept with while at Oxford before entering purdah.

Suddenly I had a sort of mental shudder, perhaps similar to the one Watson had experienced while gazing at a church spire and realizing the double helix structure of DNA. What if Amber had been the one to follow me and steal Abdhul? She had come to my apartment, those many weeks ago, and found Abdhul alone in the house. The magazine now appeared to have been strongly influenced by a ten-year-old. Oh, I admit it was far-fetched—but no more so than the English Society reports. I put the magazine down on the bed, feeling sick, and changed my clothes for Pimmi's party. Some sort of birthday present would have to be obtained on my way over.

I tried not to think about my revelation. But if I didn't permit myself to think about Abdhul, the only other things to think about were just as bad. Did no one aside from me see how contemptible and puerile *Hunter's World* had become? At least, before, it was honest in its disgustingness. But now, every article—whether positive or negative—had an underlying tone of cattiness. It was just generally bitchy, and also ladylike, in a way that ladies were supposed to be back in the 1930s, ladies who had their hair done and were interested only in the most trivial, juvenile aspects of existence. Probably Virginia was at this very moment the toast of New York. Damn! Now I was late, and I had forgotten to Xerox my scribbled sign to Abdhul, telling him to look for Pamela at the Belleclaire, that I intended to Scotch-tape to the street lamps and in the park. Maybe I would ask Emily Grossman for a half day off tomorrow, so I could put up the signs and buy myself something apart from this one ridiculous outfit. Of course, even to be dressed this way wasn't as bad as being a woman. If I were a woman, there would be other women in sequined cocktail dresses, much nicer than anything I would have, and in the bathroom they would be arranging their breasts and complaining about their perfect hair, and then catching a glimpse of me behind in the mirror, I would see them thinking with relief that things could always be worse—at least they didn't look like *me*. But as a man—as a straight man, which I hoped I was—I was oblivious to such things. Plus, previously I would have felt sick after looking at Virginia's magazine—all those glossy ads for overstuffed furniture covered in blue chintz, wallpaper and fabric that cost a hundred dollars the square inch, the models wearing magic makeup that apparently turned the user into a flawless being, the sporty ads for convertible automobiles that brought, magically, upon purchase, endless joy, joy I could never afford.

Maybe this type of bombardment didn't work on men; or at least it wasn't working on me, to make me feel my life was lacking. Just up the street was a Korean grocery store with bunches of flowers in buckets outside, and here I paused to examine the tottering sunflowers, heavy heads drooping, the thick crumpled and folded velvet of cockscomb, waxen purple orchids swathed in sheets of clear plastic, yellow fresias pinioned to green stems in girlish, fragrant clouds, drowsy, vagina-pink roses. I couldn't remember when I had last bought flowers for a girl—not as a man, anyway. Finally I selected a bunch of medicinal-smelling chrysanthemums, orange and yellow, certainly the most hideous and hateful of everything on display. Most definitely my choice would be proof to Pimmi, once and for all, that I was heterosexual. Men who were not ambiguous had lousy taste in floral arrangements.

I got to the restaurant late but nobody else had even arrived. I was told by the maîtresse d' to wait at the bar. A guy came in and sat down next to me and without thinking I looked over and said, "Hey, Bronc." A dim look came over his big horse-head and he nodded and said, "How ya doing?" though it was obvious he didn't have the slightest idea who I was, though perhaps some of his memory was gone after being electrocuted. Unfortunately, though, it was coming back to *me* that the reason this restaurant had previously sounded familiar was because I had been here before: the Pony Bar and Grill, how could I have forgotten! Only—what had happened to me here? Anyway at this point, it was beside the point. Something, though, *had* changed—something was different, but like the dim fly embalmed so long ago in the ear wax in my head, I could not quite figure out what that thing was. "You, uh, here for Pimmi's party?"

Bronc looked relieved. "You're a friend of Pimmi's—?" he said. "I met you before with—?"

I nodded. "I'm Paul," I said.

"I can't stand these fucking dinners," Bronc confided, eying the woman bartender. "I just came in for a drink to say hi: then I'm taking off when my friend Lee gets here"—he looked at his watch—"at nine fifteen. He's going to come in and say there's an emergency at the office."

"Ah," I said. "So who do you think's going to make it to the World . . . Series?"

"Orioles against the Dodgers," he said. "What are you drinking?"

"Jack Daniel's on the rocks," I said, catching the bartender's eye. My God, what an unattractive bartender-woman. She slithered over and expertly milked the tap. "My name is Makona," she said, and leaning forward said rather loudly in my direction, "I'll be having the operation in June!"

"I . . . think it's going to be the Orioles against the Pirates," I said, struggling. "The, uh, the Pirate—"

"Pitching?" Bronc said.

"Yeah, the Pirate pitching is very—"

"Strong."

I nodded. "They can usually score a few . . . runs!" I said triumphantly.

"I don't know," Bronc said. "I still take the Dodgers because they had a really hot September and a better record against Pittsburgh through the regular season. Let me have a vodka, sweetheart."

"Uh-huh," I said. I slurped my Jack Daniel's and Bronc quickly downed his vodka. "Tell me something," I said when Makona's back was turned away. "What did she mean—her operation?"

"Ya ever been in here before?" Bronc said. "This place has changed." He looked at me with eyes of love. "So what are you doing later?" he said. "You going to stick around for this shit?"

"Yeah, I guess so," I said.

"Me and Lee are going down to the Big Bottom Lounge for a burger," Bronc said. "You want to come?"

It was so mean, all the men skipping out of Pimmi's party. It was also confusing—Bronc being so friendly to me. Previously my relationship with Bronc hadn't been a success; but maybe now things would go better. "Well, I feel kind of mean, leaving the party, ya know?" I said. Bronc raised his eyebrows contemptuously. "Whatever," he said. "What a roll those Giants are on, huh? Three and O—they've really been dominating the opposition."

"That's for sure!" I said with a chortle. He really was so awfully cute, with his big boot head, and that tough manner of speech that didn't seem exactly real. Just then Amber swept in, followed by Martin, my ex-psychiatrist, and the four of us went to the table to await the others. By the time we sat down I had already slurped the rest of my drink, and I ordered another. Surely of the three, one of them would recognize me. I forgot why I had ever come in the first place. Was it some sort of trap? At any moment Bronc was going to rip my clothes off; the police would arrive and produce a pair of handcuffs; with a flourish Martin would sign a piece of paper sending me to involuntary confinement in a psychiatric hospital. I thought briefly about running to the pay phone and calling my mother. But the strange thing was, I no longer had that same need, that craving to call her up as often as I formerly had. This perhaps was a true symbol of how manly I had internally become.

Martin introduced himself to me and sat down. He looked over at the dripping, wilted bouquet wrapped in paper in my clenched hand. "Oh, jeez, you brought flowers, huh?" he said. "I forgot it was supposed to be a birthday party."

"What do you do, Marty?" I said, trying to pry my left hand free of the bouquet with my right.

"I'm a shrink," he said.

"Oh, really?" I said, looking at him intently. He gave a pleased nod, but there was no sign of recognition in his eyes. A tiny scuffle broke out to my right as Bronc and Pimmi attempted to sit next to me at the same time. "Bronc, it's boy-girl-boy-girl, and I want to sit next to Paul," Pimmi said.

"Yes, well, I'm going to move them apart when Amber gets here," Pimmi said and, addressing me, added, "Amber and I went to Smith together." That perhaps explained Pimmi's zombie-like lack of facial expression; any Smith College girl I had ever met had apparently taken a course in facial immobility, and they all seemed to be wearing invisible gloves and hats with little veils. Probably it was required reading to study Sylvia Plath, too. Pimmi's eyes were quite wooden and I wondered if she were a patient of Martin's. But I could have told her that her only problem was it was no longer the 1950s—at least then she could have married a doctor or her already-married professor, straight out of college, and then learned to bake bread and have children in between trips in and out of the mental hospital. "For you," I said, thrusting the soggy heap of chrysanthemums at her.

"Thank you," she said blankly as Amber came into the room. "This is my friend Amber MacPherson."

"I know," I said.

"Oh?" Pimmi said.

"I met you through her earlier, remember?" Pimmi looked dismayed, even startled.

"It was going to be my present, Pimmi's birthday dinner," Amber bawled, "but I forgot my credit cards." She sat down opposite me and gave me a meaningful look. "We can all chip in. I'm in the middle of breaking up with my husband, you understand. I do hope he doesn't burst in here and cause a scene." She glanced over her shoulder toward the door. Oh, come now, Amber, I wanted to say, there's not a man left in New York who would bother to make a scene because some woman broke up with him. Believe me, your ex-husband is either a throwback to some primitive time—perhaps your 1950s—or else he's already out with some new girlfriend. In fact, he probably behaved badly to you simply in order to incite you to get rid of him. Just then a large group of people swept into the room and all sat down at a nearby table. "Look," Martin said. "That's Ian Franklin. Can you believe how many blondes with big tits he has hanging all over him? Unless—those are men. Which one's he with?" Martin looked wistful.

"Who's Ian Franklin?" I said. "And who's that older woman next to him?"

"His mother," Martin said. "He never goes out without her. He's in denial."

Oh, it was good to be home, in a way. There really *was* no place like home, and it made me realize I had missed it all, the endless bits of useless information, the hustling and jousting, the electrically charged air produced by insignificant, desperate people whose minds were preoccupied primarily by themselves. But they were all alive, virulently alive, were they not, and each individual seemed ready to burst in an orgy of nonsexual replication, so desperate for love and attention were they. If only I didn't have this constant and steady worry over Abdhul. Once I had carefully baked a fruitcake, though I no longer remember why, and after taking it from the oven I wrapped it in aluminum foil. This fruitcake must have cost ten or twelve dollars; by the time I was finished purchasing the dried apricots, cubes of pineapple, soapy lumps of Brazil nuts, I really would have been better off buying a fruitcake, and in the morning when I got up to admire my handiwork a mouse or a rat had come during the night and gnawed straight through the aluminum foil and carved out a fairly good-size hole in the middle. The whole cake was spoiled, and this was how I felt now, gnawed and spoiled, only the mouse or rat was still within, growing plumper, choosing the choicest cherries and rum-soaked heart. What if Amber was keeping Abdhul in her basement, tied up and subject to sexual molestation? I didn't really think this was the case, but it *was* a woman who had picked him up, and it must have been someone he knew. He had met Amber. I had told him over and over again not to get into any cars or go off with strangers. Now I thought I would have been content to stay here in New York, boyfriendless, friendless, without a real career, if only I could have had him back. I wouldn't mind being an observer, on the sidelines. The endless hunger of the others—the hunger of ambition, of wanting bigger apartments, fame, money, better jobs with more power—was gone from me, at least temporarily. The fact that others had more no longer bothered me. It was replaced by my need for Abdhul. Of course, maybe if he had come back, my old miseries would have returned, but somehow I didn't think so. Life was short, one couldn't keep up the hormonal storms of rage and desire forever, the body simply stopped producing these impulses.

Martin leaned over to me; I thought he was about to confide some psychiatric revelation about the evening's gathering, an ironic word on the exchange of discourse and ideas. "You like to fish?" he said. "I just came back from a week in the Baja; I caught a seven-hundred-pound marlin. Here, let me show you a picture." From his wallet he removed a photo of a large, dead fish.

"Magnificent," I said, squinting.

He looked disappointed and took the photo away. His upper lip curled in a sneer. Had I said something wrong? I snatched the picture back again. "That's some fucking fish," I said.

"Yeah, well," Martin said, but his lip returned to its normal contour. Don't look at me like I'm a fucking fag, you indiscreet psychiatrist, I wanted to say, and realized I was somewhat drunk. Where the hell was the food in this place? What kind of dinner was this, anyway. The gaunt, sickly waitress looked far more like a waiter and never stopped to question if there was something someone at our table might want. "I want another Jack, on the rocks, when you get a chance," I suddenly bellowed. Then I turned to Martin. "Ever been frog hunting?" I said. "I was just out with my kid."

"Yeah?" Martin said. "What do you catch them with, your hands?"

"Naw, a BB gun," I said. Bronc leaned over Pimmi and said, "That sounds pretty cool. I have a BMW, but I'm getting a Porsche. Want to go some time?"

"We should do a story about frog hunting with a kid and Paul," Amber said. "It could be very French. Or English, with the right clothes. I have a very sexy little kid staying with—"

"What'd you say you use?" Bronc said. "A BB gun? We could try it with one of my Purdys."

"Great," I said, talking out of the side of my mouth. "We could use a, uh, Purdy." I hoped I was giving the appearance of a certain regular-guy insouciance. "You know, there are several ways to prepare frog's legs. The one I prefer is from the *Joy of Cooking*. Cut the legs in three or four pieces, cover with boiling water—or a light stock—add two slices lemon, some onion and pepper. You sauté your mushrooms—" Apparently I had failed in some way, for Bronc and Martin now began to talk across me. Amber, however, leaned forward and said, in a titillating voice, "Ever open an oyster and put lime-juice on it while it's still alive? All of a sudden it starts to squirm. I just noticed this in Palm Beach, last weekend. Don't you have a house in Palm Beach, Paul?"

"You make me sick," Pimmi said to Amber while smiling at me. "I don't even eat lobsters anymore."

"Pimmi thinks that lobsters are probably very intelligent," Amber said. "She's convinced me that lobsters might very well be a higher life form that we're not aware of. Thanks to Pimmi I like lobsters but I don't eat them any longer." She tossed her hair as if to say *Isn't Pimmi silly, but aren't I a good friend?*

"What—what's happened to you?" I said. "Did you say you had a kid?"

Just then she suddenly turned around, caught the attention of the waiter, crooked her little finger, and, when he came over, she said, "What sort of vegetables do you have this evening?"

"Vegetables?" the waiter said. "There's spinach, and squash."

"Do you have any potatoes?"

"No, I'm afraid there are no potatoes tonight," he—or she—said.

"You don't have any potatoes?" Amber said. "You have no potatoes?" Her voice rose.

"No, there's no potatoes," it said, "except mashed potatoes."

"That's what I wanted!" Amber shrieked in the most vicious tone possible. "Don't tell me you don't have any potatoes when you have the mashed potatoes!" *I wouldn't speak to a dog in that tone of voice,* I thought, *don't tell me about your great love of lobsters.* Still, I felt somewhat relieved that she hadn't undergone a complete transformation of personality. She seemed to hear my thoughts; she suddenly said in a calmer, though still superior voice, "Please bring me spinach." Then, addressing me, she said, "No, I don't have a child."

"But you said—"

"I understand, Paul, that you're from the True-elle fortune family?"

"The True-elle fortune?" What the hell was she talking about? Then it came back to me, I, too, like so many others, had studied the annual magazine listing of the 100 wealthiest families in the United States. Mr.

Truell was some old geezer listed around number four. I believe he was in the hardware business and still lived with his wife in a tiny ranch house outside Cleveland and drove an old truck and by dint of never spending one single penny, had at age seventy-eight amassed billions (two sons, one daughter, only the three grandkids, Robert, Susan, and . . . Paul! There, so much for my lack of memory, I remembered every trivial, useless detail, the various wives of Eddie Fisher, Liza Minelli's miscarriages and former drug addiction). "Ah, no, that has nothing to do with me," I said.

"And is it true you're thinking of buying *Bride-to-Be?*" Amber said. It seemed impossible to believe she really didn't recognize me; lucky for me she really did not see very well and was too vain to wear glasses. "Why don't you start up a new book? I'd happily leave *Hunter's World,* if there was a magazine I could really be involved with from the ground up."

"I'll get back to you on that," I said.

"Shall I call you?" Amber said. "What about lunch? I'll call you in the morning, to see what your schedule looks like. You know, you have a very strange face—it's ugly, yet pretty in a familiar way. I've always gone wild over men with glasses. I bet all the women are just crazy about you."

"Just lately," I said.

"Ha!" Amber said and squeezed me coyly on my thigh. "You're a funny one. Now, let me tell you a little secret: the magazine I'd like to start is called *For the Love of Our Animals.* Whenever I have a free minute, I'm out there raising money to educate people about our animals—it's beautiful, and sad. Already I'm organizing a benefit for the spring. Would you like to be head of the Junior Committee, Paul?"

"The magazine I'm interested in starting would be primarily about disease and other strange phenomena: a long profile of a couple of Siamese twins, for example, an interview with one of the remaining lepers, a story on the psychology of a dentist who rapes his patients while they're passed out."

"You're a riot!" She threw back her head in a silent laugh. "Have you ever thought about doing stand-up comedy?" She thought I was kidding, but I was not: my idea was a brilliant one, after all, and I dreamily finished off someone else's glass of white wine at the minute Virginia Loomis walked in with a tall, handsome man in his fifties. Oy gevalt. Maybe Amber hadn't yet recognized me, nor Bronc (which might in their cases be due to the electroshock they had received by my hands) nor Martin; but I had the feeling that Virginia was just a little too perceptive. She hadn't gotten where she was, after all, by being stupid, just unethical and socially ambitious.

"Hello!" Virginia said, waving grandly at the assembled. "We can't stay. We've just been to a preview of Dirk's latest play. It was fabulous."

"I'm shattered," said the man she was with, who I presumed was Dirk. He had a shock of white hair and the appearance of a long-billed crane.

"Waitperson!" Amber snarled. The waitperson, poor gentle hyena, slunk across the room.

"What are you drinking, darling?" Dirk addressed Virginia.

"Just a glass of soy milk," Virginia said.

"I'd like a champagne cocktail," Dirk said.

"Could I have another Jack Daniel's on the rocks?" I said, though it was obvious at this moment it wasn't my place to order. Virginia was staring at me intently. "Say, uh, what's your play about?"

"Oh, it's just something I dashed off over the summer," Dirk said.

"Dirk, how can you say that?" Virginia said, distracted for the moment. "It's brilliant, a work of genius."

The waiter returned with drinks for the table, and Dirk raised his champagne cocktail to Virginia. "Tell me, whose birthday are we celebrating?" he said. "Are you the birthday girl?" He looked at Pimmi—he obviously *knew* it was her birthday. "Stand up, and let me examine you and your wonderful dress." Pimmi eagerly rose to her feet; she was wearing a scaly, sequined sheath, covered with large green reptile disks that gave her the appearance of a freakish half-human snake in the process of molting. "Now turn around," Dirk commanded. Shyly Pimmi twirled. "Why, you're looking very shapely, my dear," he said lasciviously, though his eyes were on the rest of the table.

"We really have to get going, Dirk," Virginia said, still staring at me. "We promised not to be late for Milos'."

"If you'll excuse me," I said, pushing back my chair. I left the table as Dirk was regaling his comatose audience with a tale—told in strictest confidentiality—of his recent trip to Rome, during which his old friend Gore had urinated in the sink in the middle of a public bar. He was one of those men, I thought on my way to the men's room, who deliberately acts very fey and effeminate as a means of proving that a straight man need not act macho; women flocked to him, assuring one another that he was indeed heterosexual. But the entire act was really a cover-up for the fact that underneath he was gay. It didn't make much sense, but there you had it. Actually I think there was some play by Shakespeare, where a guy acted gay so he could have an affair with somebody's wife without them suspecting; probably Dirk had gotten the idea from this. It came back to me that Dirk was married to Alyona Kirsov, a famous actress, and in a *House and Garden* profile of this magical couple were photographs of their two apartments—Dirk's being on the East Side, and Alyona's on the West.

I was pondering the complexities of human nature while I stood in one of the toilet stalls in the men's room—the door didn't have a lock, not the front door nor the stall door—well, not exactly standing but half-squatting with my back to the door, and wondering how I could make my escape from the dinner party as innocuously as possible before one or the other of them ripped me from my soft, fragile shell. Surely Virginia was questioning Pimmi about me—and where was Amber? Their unified brain might operate more swiftly than when they were apart. If only Bronc's friend Lee arrived, I could exit under the protection of the two men. And in a way I still longed to be with Bronc; maybe I just wanted to prove I could get him to like me, but I wanted to give it one more shot.

I pulled up my panties just as the door of the stall smashed into me from behind. "Oh!" I said, lurching forward and toppling into the wall, my blue jeans around my knees.

"Oh, Christ, sorry," Martin's voice said behind me. At least my back was to him; I simultaneously cowered and tried to pull up my pants. Was there no privacy to be found in Manhattan? In the midst of my struggle I glanced over my shoulder and glared at him. He showed no signs of moving, just stood with the door half open. "It wasn't locked," he said vaguely, his eyes lowered.

"There was no lock!" I said, scrambling to button my fly.

"Excuse me if I just say one thing," Martin said. "I wonder if you might be interested in joining my male cross-dresser support group."

"What?" I said. Oh, for heaven's sake—my bikini panties! Why hadn't I thought to purchase an assortment of boxer shorts emblazoned with patterns of hamburgers or cactus? Or at least those plain white jockeys? But I had always enjoyed my pretty panties, certainly it didn't occur to me to discard them, after all, who was going to take a peek? And these I had on were pale lavender, tied at the sides with glossy purple ribbon, and fringed in back with tawdry lace. True they weren't in the greatest condition. They were clean, however, it wasn't that they were dirty, but I never should have machine-washed them.

Martin misunderstood my response. "Believe me, I don't think there's anything wrong with wanting to wear women's clothing," he said. "It's a male cross-dresser *support* group. It's just that it gives everyone a chance to come to terms with their feelings—some people feel guilty, or maladjusted—and we trade tips . . ." With an intimate look that caused me to back into the far corner he began to unbutton his shirt, revealing a dark red corset. His pectorals bulged gently, uplifted by the top of the garment. "See?" he said. "Of course, I wear this because of my bad back—but I thought there was no harm in having something soft against my skin, and it makes the patients in the group feel more relaxed."

In a defiant gesture of manliness I stuck my index finger up my nose and cleaned out my right nostril. "What's it cost?" I said in a sullen voice. I tried to push out past him but he blocked my way.

"You come the first time for free, and if you like it, we can work out something with your insurance to cover half the cost," Martin said.

"Yeah, well," I said, "I don't have any insurance." Martin was not going to move. What if in an abrupt, friendly gesture he gave my shirt a tug—as if playfully expecting to reveal a bra—and exposed my breasts instead? Get me out of here! "I'm leaving now, to go and lead the group," he said. "Why don't you come with me? If you don't like it, you don't have to stay."

"And will you help me leave the restaurant?" I said. "I don't want to . . . have to talk to anyone, on the way out."

"Of course, of course," Martin said. "I understand. You're embarrassed, right, that I saw your panties." He gave me a playful punch on the shoulder. "Come on, Halloween's coming up—you can be free to be yourself!"

"Well, um—" I said. He was not going to budge until I gave him a definite response. "What about—I have some other problems in my life, that I'm going through. Could your group help with that?"

"Of course!" Martin said. He backed away, permitting me to leave the toilet stall. As we left the room he slung his arm around my shoulder. "Let me tell you about some of the others you'll be meeting. There's Toby, sixty-two years old, happily married for twenty years, his wife has always been very understanding, maybe you saw him last week on TV—"

We walked back through the dining room, Martin murmuring gently in my ear. "I don't want to see the others!" I bawled.

"Of course, of course," Martin said. "You go and stand by the bar, wait for me, I'll make the excuses."

I lurked by the front of the restaurant. My plan was that when Martin's back was to me I would sneak out the door and go home. Unfortunately at that moment Virginia was wending her way to the door, Dirk in tow. "You're leaving too?" Virginia said regally. "You're not going to the same dinner party we are, are you? Milos is having a few people to his place in Hampshire House . . ." She peered at me curiously—perhaps she was too vain to get glasses or contacts—and seemed about to say something further, when Dirk joined in. "You have an extraordinary face!" he said. "Without being insulting, I've been mesmerized looking at you all evening—you have the perfect face of a drag queen. What did you say your name was?"

"This is Paul Truell, Dirk," Virginia said. "Hardware."

"Oh, yes?" Dirk said, his steel glasses sliding down on his nose. "How nice to meet you."

"We've met before," Virginia explained firmly. "I'm glad you've finally moved to New York, Paul! You must come to dinner next week, I'll give you a call . . ." Involuntarily I curtsied as she offered me her hand, and so to compensate I gave it a kiss. What a strange sensation that was, to kiss the back of a person's hand, the dry skin against my own wet mouth, and without thinking I gave my lips a wipe as they left.

"I hope he wasn't offended by my comment," Dirk said as they went out the door. "But it really is extraordinary, to come from Cleveland and have a face like that. Do you think perhaps there was some mix-up at the hospital? Why, this might become my next play . . ." His voice carried even as the door shut.

Over at the table Martin was arguing with the others, I guess about dragging me away. Amber had joined the group, and when she saw me she gave a flirtatious wave as the waitperson approached with a few cups of coffee on a tray. "Oh, Paul, don't go!" she called. "Want a cup of coffee? I bet you'd really scream if I poured it on you."

I smiled weakly. Bronc was apparently leaving as well; as he passed he took my hand in his, which was bandaged. I hadn't noticed this before, nor that when he walked he had a rather stunted limp. "Hey listen, man," he said, "it was really, really great to meet you." He pumped my hand avidly in his. "Let's get together really soon, okay? I have a feeling we have a lot to talk about."

"By the way, what happened to your hand?" I said.

"Ah, this?" He held up the trembling bandaged object. "Freak electrical burn—months ago."

"Oh, my God, I'm really sorry," I said.

He looked surprised. "It's nothing. I was making a citizen's arrest."

"Oh, really?" I said. "You weren't injured watching a pig have sex?"

"What are you talking about?" he said, as I walked out on the street. It would be only a matter of time before they found out I was no Truell. *Let them,* I thought defiantly. I had never insinuated I was rich. Anyway, there were plenty of poor boys who had come to the city and made good. One twenty-year-old guy had, only the year before, married and divorced a famous choreographer, some twenty-five years his senior. Now she had to pay him quantities of alimony, to enable him to finish his education. Something similar might happen to me; at the very least, having a wife, especially one with money, would enable me to fight for Abdhul in the courts, and I would be able to prove I was part of a happy, secure family.

"People in New York are graded," Martin explained solemnly as the empty crosstown bus rattled through the park. "And for your first few weeks here in Manhattan, everything you do will contribute toward your grade. Naturally your family background happily assures you of a seventy-five-point start, perhaps even more. But the rest is up to you: the people you meet, the people you choose to associate with, all this will help everyone to categorize you—permanently. Personally, if I were you, I wouldn't have been so quick to go to work at *Bride-to-Be,* even if you do want to learn the magazine business from the ground up. But I think my male cross-dresser support group will help you in more ways than you thought possible."

The group met in the upstairs classroom of a West Side junior high. Entering the dingy front hall, with its musty, rank smell of glue, pencil shavings, mimeograph fluid, the remains of pubescent sweat, instantly returned me to my own days in grammar school and public high, endless caged days that by now I had almost completely blanked from my mind.

An obese, girlish figure was dragging the chair-and-desk combos from their neat rows and arranging them in a semicircle in front of the room. Emitting a final grunt (as I discovered upon attempting to move one farther away from the circle, the chair-and-desk units were quite heavy, with a slanted flap-top that when opened released a gust of rotten-banana odor) the man beseeched Martin to have a private word with him. Martin smiled apologetically and gestured to him to sit down. From the hall the voice of the fat man floated in to me. "I don't have anything to wear to the Grand Librarian's ball," he said. "I don't know what to do; I'm flying up next weekend, and—"

A new character now slithered in the door, sticking close by the wall, and plopped himself in the desk opposite me. "Don Worth," he said gruffly. "We're not supposed to tell our full names in here, but I'm not really part of the group. I just want to make it clear, because I'm gathering material for my new novel—although probably you've recognized me anyway: I got the Oscar last year for best screenplay, a script based on my novel for which I got a tidy seven hundred fifty thousand dollars. I like to be upfront with new members of the group." His right hand had been buttoned, Napoleonic style, into his rather offensively cheap jacket, and he now removed it, clutching a little vial. "You want a sniff, before Martin gets back?" he said. "One of my students up at Columbia just gave it to me."

"Gee, thanks, Don," I said. "Maybe another time." Boy, did I feel sick. Somehow I had never gotten dinner; the alcohol, oily and oaken—maybe from being cured in aged barrels in Tennessee—lay in my stomach like a pool of mosquito repellent. "Let me add, however, that I'm sincerely impressed."

Don licked his fingers with a modest expression. "Ah, well. Just got back from St. Tropez, where I go every year, only this time it was with the BBC film crew doing a story on me—so I must say, I'm anxious to get back to work." He gave a little snuffle as Martin returned with the obese figure whom he introduced as Herman.

Then the others arrived and were introduced. There was Rice, a bland, oatmealy man in his fifties, wearing an expensive suit; Toby, who Martin had mentioned previously, sixty-two, handsome, resembling an aging game-show host; Sergei, an angelic boy in his twenties with a faint Russian accent; a stunning transvestite or transsexual, a gold turban wrapped around his head, a long leather Marlene Dietrich coat, and beauty mark below pouting Tallulah Bankhead lips, who introduced himself as "Gorgeous"; and lastly, to my horror, my old friend Moe. He really looked ghastly, an absolute shattered wreck: one lens of his glasses was smashed, he had wrapped them around his head with tape, his eyes were vacuous, and he had lost a great deal of weight. "My God, what happened to you?" I blurted.

"Moe, what's happened?" Martin said, luckily too absorbed with Moe's devastation to question how I knew him.

"I finally got a girlfriend," Moe said, almost bawling. "But it didn't work out."

"Tell us about it, Moe," Martin said.

"Do you promise what I say won't go any further than this room?"

A general twitter softly arose. "Oh, yes, yes." "Of course." "That's what we're here for."

"I spent all my time at the Pony Bar and Grill," Moe said. "But things weren't working out for me in New York. . . . I went away for a while . . ." I held my breath as Moe glanced around at the assembled intently. "When I returned, I reverted to my old ways; every day I went to the bar with my Scrabble set, it was my only social life. But something had changed—it was now a very popular place, with many beautiful women, who were friendly to me, oh, so friendly. One voluptuous lady became very intimate with me—to show her affection she did something very unusual. With her mouth—"

"Don't you know the Pony Bar is the most fashionable drag queen club in New York now?" Gorgeous said in a disgusted voice.

"Oh," Moe said. "I wondered why my new girlfriend wouldn't take her clothes off."

A dim aura of despair swamped the room. Poor guy, he really was brain damaged, but I suppose in one sense this was a positive thing in that he obviously had no memory of me. "Well, I guess that's everybody who's coming this week," Martin said. "Herm, we ended last time just as you were telling us about work. Do you want to begin? But let me reiterate: we're not here to judge, but in order to provide constructive criticism."

"I'm frightened about losing my job," Herman said. "Everybody's getting fired at the studio, and I heard this morning that the library staff is going to be the next to go. I got so nervous that at lunchtime I bought a chocolate cake and ate the entire thing."

"Oh, for God's sake, Herman," Rice said. "It's always the same problem with you, can't you come up with a more exciting story? I'm in real trouble: when I got home last night I had been burglarized, and all my neo-Gothic furniture was stolen."

"I'm heterosexual," Toby said. "But I happen to like the feel of silk against my legs, and the scent of perfume on my body. My wife has always been very old-fashioned, but over the years—"

"We all know about you and your dowdy wife, Toby," Herman said vituperatively. "You haven't fucked her in years, and you've beat her into submission by humiliation, not that she doesn't deserve it. If it weren't for the fact that she's blind—"

Rice interrupted, fixing me with his raisin eyes. "Who's the new boy? Tell us why you're here, Paul."

I hadn't been paying much attention to the various monologues. That Sergei really was very cute. He had a waiflike, antiquated face, as if his head had at some point been placed in a vise and gently flattened. "I'm uncertain of my sexuality," I suddenly blurted.

"Oh, so what else is new?" Rice whined.

"No, no, you don't understand," I said. "I don't like girls."

"Then what's your problem?" Gorgeous said seductively.

I couldn't explain it, but there really was a problem: no straight guy was going to go out with me in my present condition. Maybe there were plenty of gay guys who would be interested in me at first, but at some point they would want to consummate our relationship, and while because of AIDS things might be postponed for a time, eventually there was going to be a peculiarly ghastly scene, the shock of which might lead to some poor man's demise, similar to the depraved state in which Moe now appeared to exist.

"I'd go out with a real woman, if I could find the right one," Rice said. "There's someone now who's interested in me—blond, very attractive, she dresses seductively and acts aggressive, which frightens me."

"She acts aggressive because a) she's very insecure," I said, "and b) she probably has a drinking problem."

"Do you think?" Rice said cheerfully. "Paul, what are you doing after group? Do you want to come and have dinner with me at my club? She said she'd be there later; then you could see her in person and tell me more."

Before I could answer, Martin interrupted. "I caught Paul in the men's room, wearing purple panties. How did that make you feel, Paul?"

"Nervous," I said.

"Why don't you come out with it, Paul?" Gorgeous said.

"What?" I said. "With what?"

"Oh, come now—you don't have to be so secretive here."

"I'm not hiding anything!" I said. "I have only one problem, my little boy is gone, I want to get him back."

"You don't like women, you dress up in women's clothing, but you're ashamed of being gay."

"I'm not ashamed of being gay!" I said. "I'm not gay!"

"You hate your own kind," Gorgeous said. "I know somebody who could blow your face up on a giant poster and put it around town—"

"You want to think of yourself as a big, macho, tough guy, don't you, Paul?" Toby said. "But why don't you own up, admit to the soft *female* within you—"

"You think you're a good parent?" Don suddenly jumped in. "Hey, if I had a kid, and I was you, and they took him from me, I'd say it was for the best. I have nothing against homosexuality, but I do have something against liars and fakes and mendicants—"

"I'm not lying or hiding!" I said.

"Then tell me," Martin said, "why do you sound so defensive?"

Finally I spoke. "Maybe you're right," I said. "There is something."

"Yes?"

"Earlier this summer I found a head in the road, and I kept trying to bury it rather than turn it in, for fear of having my little boy taken from me."

Martin rose and went to the blackboard. "You found a head in the road," he repeated.

"That's right."

"When Paul tells us he found a head in the road—" Martin now addressed the others, "he is not talking about a real head, but rather a mnemonic device, an objective correlative, a *symbol* for the Freudian id or unconscious. He tells us, 'I kept trying to bury it.' This so-called head is his Jungian *animus*—the female inside him, which is trying to escape. Paul's fear is not of having his child taken from him—but of being *found out*. It is the feminine part inside him that Paul is trying to murder; and this makes him feel guilty. But even as we speak—remember the pretty purple panties—this female part will take control and revolt."

"That's what I said before," Toby said, tossing his head.

Now I, too, got to my feet. "The feminine part!" I said. "The feminine part! I'm not concerned with that—it's the masculine part that's revolting!" The group looked puzzled but pleased that they had gotten a rise out of me. "Don't you see—" I began, just as Martin announced, "And now, I think it is time for us to take our five-minute break."

I stood for a moment and then went into the hall, where the others had collected in a little group. "Hey, Paul, where are you going?" Herman called. "You want a sip of my Coke?"

"Back in a minute," I said, and continued toward the stairs.

I had only gone a little way when I had the sensation of padded, foxy feet creeping up behind. "Pavel, Pavel," a voice said softly. "Excuse me." I turned and stopped. It was the angelic Sergei. "You are leaving, I think?"

"It got late," I said. "I had another appointment."

"I am going with you, I think," Sergei said. "May I accompany you some distance?"

"Well—" I said, looking back up the stairs to make sure the rest of the group wasn't also coming along. "Let's get out of here." On the street he wrapped his arm affectionately through mine; maybe this was something guys did in Russia, but instinctively I recoiled. "So, are there a lot of guys in Russia who like to cross-dress?" I said.

"Hmm?" he said. "Excuse me?"

"You like to wear women's clothing in Russia?" I said, a bit loudly.

"To wear the women's clothing?" he said.

"You were at the cross-dressers' support group," I said.

"And what does this mean, cross-dress support?" he said.

"For men who like to wear women's clothes!" I said angrily.

Something seemed to change in his eyes, as if the focusing lens of a camera was being adjusted. "Ahh," he said. "Yes, I am wondering, why these men are so interested in shoes."

"But what did you think it was?" I said.

"Support," he said. "For the learning of English and the making of new friends. This man Rice has befriended me and offered me a job as houseboy. Now he will be angry that we have not accompanied him to the nightclub."

"You go ahead," I said. "I'm looking for somebody."

"I understand," he said. "I will help."

For hours we prowled the streets, traversing Manhattan. It was all so silly, to think I would find Abdhul on a street corner, or crouched in the stairwell of the back entrance to the Port Authority bus terminal. Sergei talked all the while, muttering in his soft, unintelligible voice.

On Eighth Avenue I thought for a second I saw him. A little kid, wild hair, trundling along in baggy, too-long pants and walking with a peculiar kind of hop that indicated to me he was trying to step on the cracks, or trying *not* to step on the cracks. "Hurry up!" I said to Sergei, and began to run. But when I got closer I saw it was not Abdhul but some other child, mean-faced and wizened, out at night too late by himself and already broken by whatever it was life had to offer.

But I couldn't stop my restless search. And why was this Sergei so insistent on keeping up with my aimless steps? It was as if a sapling had pulled itself up from the forest, thin branches entwined in mine, thin trunk side-by-side with my stouter one. "Temporarily," he said. "I reside with other Russkies in Brighton Beach, you know this place?"

"Yeah, yeah sure," I said.

"It is only a question of time, however, before I am acquiring a New York gallery and a penthouse. I am artist, you understand, without modesty I must say I am great artist."

When I casually asked him to describe his work, he said—batting his tender lashes up at me—that he had photographs and slides in his valise, if there was only a place to sit down then he would show me . . .

It was late, my search was futile, my feet were growing tired. We went into a sleazy, still-open bar. The place was empty; I bought two beers and carried them over to Sergei at a table in the back. From his plastic briefcase he removed a series of photographs in which was featured a reproduction of a painting by Caravaggio, altered in various ways.

In one, the woman's face had been daubed with a mustache; on another the entire canvas splattered with paint; one was plain but hung upside down. "You see, this is called *After Marcel Duchamp,*" he said. "This one is called *After George Baselitz*. This one, *After Jackson Pollock.*"

"Very interesting indeed," I said. After all, I was no art critic, though I suppose I had hoped for more from the depths of a Russian soul. It was just as bad as the current American art, where artists made a fortune out of painting scenes showing their latest trip to India, or taking endless pictures of themselves, or gluing a lot of junk down on a big canvas. "Listen, I have to get going. I'm tired, I don't know how it got to be so late."

"Excuse me, Pasha," Sergei said. "I am now staying in Brighton, and will arrive after two hours. Would you mind if I stayed with you?"

"I live in one room," I said.

"This is no problem, I can stay on the floor. In the morning, I will see if Rice has room."

Perhaps half of me didn't want to be alone. In a not very gracious tone I said okay, he could sleep on the floor. Oh, gee, I felt mean: the bed was lumpy, it was uncomfortable, but it was a double bed, and there was room for two, it was more comfortable than the lone blanket I had tossed to Sergei in the tiny space between the bed and wall. "This is stupid," I said, when I came out of the bathroom, dressed in a pair of too-large pajamas that had belonged to my dad. "You can sleep in the bed, on the inside," I said. "I have to get up a lot in the night to pee."

He was so very sweet and boyish, stripped down to his underpants; it was nice to have another body in the bed. A faint smell of mackerel, of cloves, of raspberry jam and sweat, billowed up from time to time as I adjusted the sheets.

I hadn't lost my old knack for picking out gay men, that was for sure. But Paul turned out to be quite a devil in bed, sexually, that is. Sergei's artificial breathing suggested he was feigning sleep. He lay on his stomach, tender, scrawny, the palm of his hand upturned. Just give me some human contact! Even the gorilla or baboon lowest on the social scale spent more time grooming and being groomed than I ever did. I slipped my hand into his. It was dry, firm, the fingers did not draw away. What did it matter that we had nothing, really, to say to one another, that he didn't understand my English, when our hands could arrange themselves in such intimate fashion? A nerve, a ganglia, connected my brain to my wrist, my hand to his, and his to his head; it was a union as intense, or more intense, as any other.

I should have left well enough alone. But no, my other hand slithered beneath the sheets and, as if unconnected, began a spider's dance across his chest. He was naked except for underpants. He tensed, let out a sigh, and lay perfectly still. Still his right hand patiently, childishly, clutched my own; half-propped on my side my free left hand patted, stroked, touched in the dark. The tips of my fingers felt sandpapered. Here the tense sinew from neck to clavicle, the thin web of skin below the Adam's apple above the trachea, the nipples rimmed with sparse hairs, rubbery erasers. A pip of navel. Balking at the elastic pants line, my hand returned up. The shell-like ear, cartilaginous edge, fat flesh lobe. Now our tongues met, blind as flatworms, how sweet his breath tasted, gold, fermented dandelions. He took my hand and pushed it down inside his underpants. Animal heat wafted up and out. My hand rummaged down . . . Sergei was now trying to strip me of my sweatpants, luckily I had tied the string around my waist very tight, with a double knot. "No, no," I murmured, "I can't do anything, I'm afraid. It's too dangerous. I don't know you."

"Just help me," he whispered. "Please, hold him in your hand, like so—" He fixed his hand around mine, pulling it up and down across the sleek shaft, his mouth fixed firmly, jellyfish-fashion, onto mine. "Oh, it's so good," he said. "It feels so nice. I have a condom, I have a condom, just let me put it in for a minute. I'll be careful."

"Is it a Russian condom?" I said.

"What?" he said. "No, no. American, extra-large."

"Where is it?" I whispered.

"I'll get it," he said.

"No!" I said. "I don't want you to turn on the lights—I, I don't want you to look at me."

"Oh, I understand," Sergei said. "My darling, you're shy. Don't be shy with me."

"I don't want you to see me," I said.

"It's just on the floor, in my wallet, in my jeans. I can find it in the dark. Take these off." He gave a little tug at my sweatpants.

"You can put it in, but I don't want you to touch me." The sheets and tangled blankets had fallen to the floor. I sat up and slipped out of my pants, then I turned and lay on my stomach. His cool hand touched my bottom. "I said, don't touch me!" I said. It would be a simple matter, after all, once he had on a condom, for me to see that things found the right orifice—the one intended by nature for reproductive and mictorative process.

"Yes, yes, Paul," Sergei said. "But it's beautiful." In the dark he slid off the bed and stood. There was a ferocious scream: first from the floor and then from Sergei. Then a sort of demonic yowl and growl, the sound of snapping jaws, I had the sensation that Sergei had gone skyrocketing up. Next a shrill yip-yip-yip. Without thinking I turned over, shirt bunched around my neck. "What's happening?" I yelled. "Jesus, you stepped on the dog!"

"Aaaagghhh!" Sergei yelped, drowning out my words. "What is this?" He leapt across the room, smashing into the chair and toppling a metal wastebasket; then flicked on the goose-neck lamp. Illuminated it resembled a skinny horse, throwing up his neck and whinnying. The screeching

Dalgleish, teeth sunk into Sergei's calf, now let go and came running to me, tail tucked between his legs, and hopped into bed. Sergei had stepped on him in the dark. "Why, look at that," I said. "You don't have any problems jumping onto the bed when you want to; you were just pretending you couldn't."

Sergei stood transfixed and limp by the lamp. "Oh my God, Paul," he said. "Oh my God. Paul. What is wrong with you? You are not a man, Paul. You are not a man. You are a woman."

Looking down, I realized he was referring to the fact my pants were off.

Obviously if I wasn't a man then I was a woman. Generally speaking, there were only two choices for that sort of thing, though I suppose if I had been a hermaphrodite my feelings would really have been hurt by his look of horror. Or even worse, what if I hadn't had any exterior genitalia whatsoever: think of how bad he would have made me feel then. My mother always liked to give me updates on what she had seen on the latest afternoon TV talk shows, and one of the most memorable was a program about this person who had been born without any exterior genitals, and my mother said that the person seemed very sweet, but one minute it was like looking at a man and the next like looking at a woman, and it was confusing.

The person didn't have any sexual feelings whatsoever—or so It said— and even though the doctors had told it that it could decide and then they could create superficial organs, the person said it didn't want to. But It had led a very lonely existence, until It got a dog. I wanted to know how it went to the bathroom, and my mother said she thought It did have a urethra; the other thing I thought of was that if this person was walking down a deserted street late at night and a rapist came along, It would really give the attacker the shock of a lifetime.

Sergei was busy scrambling into his pants while I cuddled the whimpering Dalgleish. He seemed to be muttering in Russian. Frankly, I couldn't make out a word of it. "You, you're sick," he finally said. "You are a crazy person." I didn't think it was very nice that he was leaving me in an unsatisfied condition. Still muttering in Russian, he put on his socks and, carrying his shoes, he left, slamming the door. "Das vedanya!" I said.

In the morning I felt no guilt, no loneliness, no female within whining, "Will he call me again?" Still, getting dressed, I did have a dim foreshadowing of unease.

I went to work, carrying Dalgleish. I utilized the office Xerox machine to make two hundred copies of a sign telling Abdhul to look for Pamela at the Belleclaire. I got Sylvana to agree to my getting my first paycheck in advance, which I was able to cash at the bank with a special Employee I.D.

I asked Emily Grossman if I could take the day off—I would return in the late afternoon, I said, but it was hard to get organized moving to a new city and immediately starting a job. "Fine," she said. "But I think you should come back to check in later."

"Definitely," I said. I left Dalgleish in the company of the receptionist, and then I went down to Centre Street, where after entering four successive buildings I at last found the Division of Children's Aid. I had to wait on one line to fill out a form; I was then told to sit and wait until a social worker was free. Two hours later my name was at last announced. Mrs. Dinmore's office was a glass booth filled with old papers and a metal desk, in the middle of a row with similar metal desks stretching in both directions.

At first hesitantly, and then more bluntly, I confessed the entire story.

"What do you want me to do?" Mrs. Dinmore said when I was finished.

"What do I want you to do?" I said. "Find him!"

"What's his name?" she said.

"Abdhul."

"And his last name?" She was busy filling out a form, this seemed to me to be a positive sign. Some attempt to trace him would be made.

"I don't know," I said.

She put down her pen. "I don't know what to say," she said. "Your story really doesn't make any sense. Are you interested in applying to be a foster family? It's very difficult, as a single, to get approval; although there are many children who need to be placed in foster care, they really prefer married couples. It's unlikely you'd be judged suitable. Anyway, it takes them at least a year to decide."

"I don't want to have a foster child!" I said. This sounded a bit churlish; I added, quickly, "I mean, not right now, although it might be a very good thing to do at some point. I want to find out what happened to Abdhul. Doesn't anybody care?"

"Of course I care," Mrs. Dinmore said. "If you don't know the child's name, perhaps you have a picture of him that I can circulate in the department?"

"I never thought—I didn't—I don't have a camera," I said.

"Mr. Truell," Mrs. Dinmore said. "I want to make it quite clear that it's people like you who waste the taxpayer's money. I look at you and I see a person with the attitude 'the world owes me a living.' Part of my training as a social worker was to be a good listener. But unlike a psychiatrist, a social worker is also trained with the skill to provide concrete, specific advice. Perhaps you've been able to make something of a financial success in life; I don't know."

"Not really," I said.

"But success is not about making money. Until last year I worked with the retarded, and I put forty-two thousand miles a year on my car. Then I worked with cancer patients. Do you see this bandage across my throat? I had a thyroid operation, and I'm on a great deal of medication."

"Oh, gee, I'm sorry about that," I said.

She nodded dismissively. "When you sit down here in my office, do you stop to think it might be polite to say, 'How are you today? It must be rather uncomfortable to be wearing those bandages?' "

"Well, I—" I said.

"I can't tell you how many people sit down here, and stop to take the time to look around and then say, 'Oh, Juliet—what a lovely name.' " She pointed to a plastic nameplate set into a wooden holder that read JULIET DINMORE. "Just last week I had a man and his little boy in here—they stopped by to say hello, and we got to talking about birds. It turned out we had both been to the same preserve in Belize, and he came back earlier in the week to give me a record of Audubon bird calls."

"I'm interested in birds," I said.

"To come in here—to sit without waiting to be asked, to speak with a rather surly, superior, and dismissive air—believe me, I've worked with a great many young men from middle-class, college-educated backgrounds, and I can only think that your mother indulged you in every way possible." Tears came into my eyes. Mrs. Dinmore looked pleased. Oh, she was right; I was spoiled and surly, her words stung. "If you're interested in coming to see me on a private consultation basis, my fee is sixty dollars an hour." From the top drawer of her desk she slipped me a card. "Otherwise, feel free to return when you have more information about the child. If you can provide me with a name, or a photograph . . ." My eyes blurred; I stood and left. Everything was crumbs, crumbs and ashes, I was a miserable human being. All I wanted was to find Abdhul; now I wished I was dead. Probably what I needed was sleep, a good meal, some vitamin pills. But try as I might I couldn't build my life into something meaningful, and how quickly it was passing me by.

When I returned to the office a message was waiting for me from Virginia Loomis. I gave her a call. She was in a meeting, but Debbie (I thought it must be Debbie, the high-pitched voice was all too familiar, and I felt a momentary pang of nostalgia) asked for my name and then put me on hold. Finally Virginia came on the line. "Oh, hello, Paul," she said coolly. "Listen, I'm just in a meeting, but I wanted to see if you were free tonight. I'm organizing a rather impromptu dinner at home, and thought perhaps you'd like to come by."

"Oh," I said. "Yeah, yeah—great. Sure, I'd love to." It didn't take much to restore me—an invitation from Virginia Loomis, to dine in her home! This is what an alcoholic hangover can do to a person's judgment. I really wanted to see Daniel; though it didn't seem polite to ask on the phone if he was going to be there, I assumed he would. And if I got a chance, over dinner, to tell the story of how I had found and lost Abdhul, perhaps Virginia would be motivated to run a story about it in *Hunter's World,* and somebody would spot him and call.

When I got home I had a few shots of bourbon, and then at the designated hour set off, determined to walk across town to Virginia's. With my rounded shoulders and tendency toward stomach, it really was important for me to try and keep up appearances, and I thought of maybe taking up racquetball. In the meantime a couple miles walk through the park wouldn't hurt. The night air hung crisp and expectantly around me. New York air was often like that, imbued with its own personality and viscosity, possibly from having been inhaled and exhaled so many millions of times by people.

The crunchy leaves swished angrily overhead. Probably it was not a good idea to cross Central Park at night but I stuck to the main paths and tried to stay alongside the traffic. Suddenly I had the idea that somebody or something was following me. This made me nervous, as I didn't want to be bludgeoned over the head, mugged, and left bleeding, although my grandmother might have thought the less of me for admitting such fear. Still, my grandmother need never know, need she? If I were to be raped, too, by a male rapist in search of what he thought was a lone male in the park to handcuff, sodomize, torture, then kill and prepare into soup to be generously served to the homeless, *this, too, I would not want to happen to me,* particularly when the attacker found out that I was not a male but a female, which might really make him mad.

I increased my pace and the loathsome footsteps behind me increased too. A kind of musical soundtrack throbbed in my head; probably I shouldn't have had those swigs of bourbon. Maybe, as my mother might have pointed out, some kind of alien civilization was trying to get in touch with me to warn me. It sounded suspiciously similar to the theme from *Dr. Zhivago,* the one that went "Somewhere, My Love," and was known as

"Lara's Theme." I wondered if this meant I was looking forward to seeing Virginia. Perhaps I had always been more interested in Virginia than in Daniel.

At last I got through the park. Virginia and Daniel's townhouse was only a block off Fifth Avenue. If my molester was planning to attack, he had lost his—or her—chance. I turned and wheeled forcefully. "What do you want?" I said, darting up the mansion's steps at the same time. For a brief second as I turned I half-expected to see the body of my head—the head I had found with Abdhul on the road—staggering up to me with out-stretched hands.

Then I saw it was Alby. I let out a squeak and started to ring Virginia's bell. "Excuse me," Alby said.

"What do you want?" I said.

"I—I don't know," he said slowly. "There's something—I started following you, I thought I knew you."

I gave him a look of contempt and he cringed; obviously he didn't want to be thought of as a gay guy. I almost felt sorry for him at that moment, as he shuffled off into the gloom. Maybe he really had been genuinely in love with me, but was so inarticulate that the only way he could express it was to display his penis. Maybe his love for me had been based on some intangible chemical reaction like mixing ammonia and bleach together, or sulfuric acid and ketchup.

But in that case, if it was so elemental and involuntary as a chemical event, there was no reason for me to feel sorry for him, staggering off, stricken, since it had nothing to do with me—his love for me was an external event that was unconnected with my self or my personality.

I rang the doorbell again and Virginia opened the door, pouncing shyly yet aggressively at the air on either side of my cheeks. "Paul," she cooed, "come in, come in."

I followed her down the hall. Since my last visit they had apparently acquired a new selection of artworks—Egyptian mummy cases. For a brief second I had the sensation that one of them contained the corpse of John Lennon—certainly Virginia and Daniel were rich enough—but, while this might have been a true psychic perception, I hesitated to ask. A wave of ferocious jealousy swept over me, envy that I would never be able to afford a bunch of moldy sarcophagi. God help me, in all this time why had I not come to some sort of spiritual understanding in life? I had fought so hard for my salvation, struggling to read badly written books about the lives of saints in the hope that it would make me a less trivial person.

I trudged behind Virginia, past the Roman atrium with its lap pool;

briefly I noticed the floor, tiled with Byzantine mosaic. Even though I knew she was no better than anybody else, watching her little backside switch, there was something about Virginia that radiated purity, as if she had stepped out of the pages of an English novel in which a large family gathers for a breakfast of kippers and kedgeree in the morning room.

I couldn't believe she hadn't had her nose fixed, it was so tiny. If only fashion would all of the sudden change and big noses become "in"! And she would have to rush to get her nose enlarged. "I was a little nervous when I opened the door," she was saying. "Our TV intercom is out of order. I'm going to have to hire a security guard."

"Butler?" I suggested.

"This might sound silly, but I have a butler phobia, due to a childhood trauma. The thing is, there was a horrible incident at the magazine a few months ago, and since then I've been a bit on edge."

"Oh?" I said. "What sort of horrible incident?"

"My husband was attacked by a crazed employee; she destroyed the toilets and threatened to bomb the place on Christmas Eve; then she disappeared."

"Good God," I said. "Was he badly hurt?"

"We don't talk about it," she said softly and looked at me with a gaze so piercing I felt I was diving into all of Mother Russia, although her appearance was more like one of the Scandinavian countries. Perhaps Virginia was not so lightweight as I had thought—or perhaps even a superficial person has deeper aspects of themselves simply waiting to be plumbed, with a range of internal activities clanging and lighting up like a pinball machine. "Will you be happy with champagne?" Virginia said as we went into the living room. "I've got the Cristal all chilled and waiting." She gestured for me to take a chair: it resembled a little fish, covered in very pale billowing fabric, set on trembling golden legs. I sat down. It was very uncomfortable, in a way I admired. "I love that little chair," Virginia said, seeing me stroke the seat. "It belonged to Josephine. They say Napoleon used to sit on her lap." What a lot of exquisite furniture they had, lemony yellow Agra silk carpet on the floor, everything all minty pale green and gold and white velvet.

I truly had terrific sharp pains in my stomach. Even were I to win the lottery I would never be able to exist this way, not with today's standard-of-living index (whatever that was) and the fact that I would probably select the wrong interior decorator.

"So," Virginia said, taking a bottle of champagne from a silver bucket and pouring, "how do you like working for *Bride-to-Be?* What's Sylvana really like to work for?"

"Oh, gee," I said. "She's all right." I spread my legs a little wider apart, as men sitting on chairs or the subway were wont to do. *Wont*—what a beautiful and almost useless word that was, and so difficult to work into a sentence. I was still badly shaken by my encounter with Alby, his nice white shirt and pleated trousers. How he resembled a South American playboy of the 1950s. Was I right to throw his love away, when I might never experience such pure love again?

Just then Daniel came into the room and I leapt up, but was so stricken by my stomachache I had to sit right down again. My precious darling, he was in a wheelchair, reduced to a little brown, bug-eyed mouse of twisted quiverings. What could I have ever seen in him? "My God," I said. "What—what's happened to you?" and added, hastily, "I don't mean to be rude. Maybe you've always been this way." I really felt obligated to protect him; after all, what if Virginia had plans—or was in the process of—slowly poisoning him in order to do away with him, hardly an original concept. "You look very familiar," Daniel said, ignoring my question.

"Hello!" I said brightly. "I'm—"

"I thought you had gone to bed," Virginia said. "This is Paul. Daniel, Paul Truell."

"Hello," Daniel said, and to Virginia, "I couldn't sleep. It's not even nine o'clock."

"Take a sleeping pill," Virginia said.

"You know, a lot of people say I look familiar!" I said. "I guess I'm just one of those people who look like everybody else!"

"Truell hardware family, Daniel," Virginia said, and Daniel gave me an imperceptible nod of acceptance. There really was no point in spoiling things for my new friends, I thought. "Virginia tells me you were recently in an accident?" I said.

"I've been reading one of your *Human Sexuality* magazines, Virginia," Daniel said, and explained to me, "We're thinking of buying *Human Sexuality* and *Diseases of the Skin* for our publishing group. Listen to this," and he began to read, holding up the magazine. " 'The psychiatric literature on female genital self-mutilators may be misleading in that it consists of only a few case reports that emphasize the rarity of the behavior and link it with eating disorders and histrionic behavior. The term Caenis Syndrome was proposed for this triad of symptoms. In Greek mythology, Caenis was a beautiful girl who rejected marriage. After raping her, Poseidon offered to give Caenis whatever she wanted. Her wish was to become a man. After—' "★

"If Caenis was raped and because of that her wish was to become a man, what the hell does that have to do with genital self-mutilation and eating disorders?" I said.

"Oh, that's enough," Virginia said, ferociously guzzling her champagne. "Did you find out anything about men who hurt themselves spying on women in the ladies' room? Men who go from one tiny, sordid love affair to the next, manipulating the hearts of moronic women?"

"Oh, come now," I said, and began to say, "Not *moronic,*" when the doorbell rang and I doubled over with my stomachache.

"Daniel, please go and see who's at the door," Virginia said.

It seemed a shame to make him wheel himself down the hall and stairs, but my stomach hurt so much I couldn't offer to go myself. "Why we can't get a butler . . ." Daniel muttered, spinning his wheelchair around as he left.

"He knows I hate butlers," Virginia said. "There was an incident from childhood, when a butler frightened me very badly."

"How?" I said.

"I found him dead with a paper bag over his head."

"Can you die from a paper bag?" I said.

"There was a plastic bag underneath. Oh, Paul, Paul, I'm so unhappy." She leapt up as I grabbed my legs around my knees in pain. Could the champagne have been poisoned? "There's something I liked about you almost at once. I can't put my finger on it, but . . ." She opened a cabinet—it appeared to be a sort of gilded hutch snatched from the back of a Venetian gondola—and took a postcard from a drawer. "Read this," she said, handing it to me. "My husband's been fooling around."

"Dear Daniel," I read aloud, "I will always remember that in bed you were the best. Love Pamela." I turned over the card: a photograph of several limp pancakes lying on a bed of blue syrup. I couldn't remember having written it; however, it was the sort of thing my mother probably told me to write, insisting that if I dashed off such a missive to him, Daniel would never be able to forget me. "Pamela, Pamela," I said, gingerly fingering the postcard.

"A desperate hustler," she said. "It's rather sweet, that he would fall for such pitiful manipulations."

"She was no desperate hustler!" I said. "I doubt she even slept with him."

---

*★Human Sexuality, May 1991.*

"Why?" Virginia said. "How do you know? Do you know her?"

"Who do you think that could be at the door?" I said. "Are others expected for dinner?"

"Of course, from the beginning our marriage was one of convenience," she said. "I know it's a bit of a cliché, but my husband had his heroin, and I had . . . my children, and a few times a year a little trip abroad to see one boyfriend or another. I don't want you to think me shallow or superficial, Paul. You know what it's like, having this much money—our lives are different."

"Yes, we're richer," I said, trying to remember the original quote.

Virginia nodded. "For some reason I feel I can talk to you as if you're a friend. The thing is, something changed for me when I found this letter to Daniel from Pamela. I suppose, in a way, I was jealous."

"Of Pamela?" I said, astonished.

"You know, she wasn't much to look at. And she dressed terribly—as if she were wearing my discards from last year. But there was a certain . . . oh, I don't know, a certain *life* to her, as if she were a real person, she was very alive—"

"Miserably so," I said.

"Oh, probably, but that didn't stop me from somehow wishing I were she."

"Well," I said. There wasn't anything I could say. How could it be, that Virginia, who had looks and money and a husband and children and any sort of career she wanted, was jealous of me, who had nothing? Was it possible that this anguish I felt was an expression of reality that was enviable? That she felt more unworthy, lifeless, and less interesting than I? Now I liked her very much. I was just about to lean forward and whisper this to her when Daniel—no longer in his wheelchair—came into the room, followed by Alby. "Oh, no!" I shouted, leaping up.

"He says don't call the police," Daniel said.

"That's right," Alby said. "Don't call the police."

"He forced his way in," Daniel said.

"This is one of the terrorists who destroyed our magazine office," Virginia began to explain to me. At that moment I glanced down over where I had been sitting. The seat of the chair of the Empress Josephine was covered with blood. In fact, I now noticed a terrible stickiness between my thighs. My God, I had been having cramps! I was getting my period, after all this time. It really was a shock. I suppose, somehow, I had secretly had thoughts from time to time that I was pregnant—perhaps some kind of immaculate conception. Because after all I hadn't really had sex with anyone, nothing had actually been consummated, and yet I had stopped having my period, something I hadn't wanted to think about. Before anyone could notice the blood all over the pale green fabric I quickly flung myself back down onto the seat.

"Don't call the police," Alby said. "I quite honestly couldn't help myself, it's this person over here." He came a few steps toward me. "I don't know what's come over me, I saw him on the street and I'm like a crazed person. I tried to stop myself, I tried to go away, but I saw him come in here and I had to see him once more." He leaned down and came very close to me, inhaling deep breaths. Was he trying to identify me by my smell? Was that it, my personal Pamela pheromones had driven him crazy? Plus, what had happened to his antiquated gangster accent? Now he sounded just like a regular college student, loud and uneducated.

Then I had an idea: I leapt straight up, knocking him aside, and began to shout, "Help, help! He's stabbed me!" I jumped off the seat and toppled onto the ground.

"Oh my God, my chair!" Virginia screamed. "My beautiful chair is covered in blood."

"I don't have a knife!" Alby shouted, flinging up his hands. "I don't have a knife!"

"He doesn't have his knife!" Daniel yelled. "Quick, find his knife, it must have dropped on the ground!" He fell to his knees and began to fumble about on the floor.

I lay on the rug on my side, clutching my stomach, while Daniel crawled around. "Jesus," he said, running his fingers along the floor behind my back, "he's cut you down here! Between your legs! Oh, oh, oh!" He let out a keening whimper. "This is bringing back such terrible memories!"

"Wait a minute!" Virginia shouted. "Something's not right here. You're bleeding all over my carpet." Carpet—was that an upper-class terminology? I wasn't certain. It might have been the equivalent of people who try to sound fancy by saying draperies, when in fact they should have said drapes—or vice versa. "No, something's not right!" Alby joined in, bending over my prostrate torso. "I don't have a knife, I don't have a knife! Take his clothes off!"

Before I could stop them or do anything, Virginia and Alby, one on either side, were unbuttoning my trousers, unzipping my fly, and pulling down my pants. "There's blood everywhere," Alby said, tugging the elastic of my undershorts. "Let me do it, I've had first-aid train . . ." His voice dwindled as it became apparent, to one and all, that I was not a man. No, not a man.

"Listen, I'm very sorry about the carpet," I said, taking advantage of the silence to pull my panties back on and zip up my fly. "And the chair belonging to the Empress Josephine. Please feel free to send me any dry-cleaning bills. I can find my own way out."

In the morning a black car was parked in front of the Belleclaire. A man was standing alongside; I was practically past when he yelled, "Excuse me! Mr. Truell? Are you Mr. Paul Truell?"

"Yes," I said, and stopped.

"Mr. Truell, I'm from the Transatlantic Car Service, here with your car."

"I didn't call for any car service," I said.

"I don't know," he shrugged. "They told me to come and pick you up."

"Who called?" I said.

"I don't know," he said.

Maybe Sylvana had sent a car from the office—I knew she used a car service on a daily basis. That was nice of her, I thought, and I got in. Or maybe, I thought, as we headed downtown, maybe Virginia was truly smitten with me, and sent a car to save me the awfulness of riding on the subway. But the car didn't stop at the magazine offices. I tapped on the glass. "Driver!" I said. "Excuse me, driver?"

"Yes, passenger?" he said.

"Are you taking me to my office?" I said, and gave the address.

"No, no," he said. "They told me to take you over to Bellevue Hospital, they'll meet you there. That's all I know."

Now I ask myself why I didn't wait until we were stopped at a red light and jump out. And the answer is, I don't know. Maybe I thought we were going to a charity benefit: things like this go on in the city all day. Maybe I thought it was a surprise party for me. Soon we pulled up in front of Bellevue, on the far east side of town. I got out. A small crowd had gathered in front. "How nice of you all to come!" I said, looking at the faces. Amber, Sylvana, Martin, Alby, Daniel, even Angela and my dad, that they had all come such a distance, and interrupted their daily routine—that was unusual.

"Is that her?" one of the policemen said. "Him?" He looked suspiciously like my old acquaintance Officer Berlino, although surely there were other police officers in this city. Amber squinted and leaning forward gave me a jab in the stomach. Then she let out a squawk. "My God, it *is* you, Pamela. I hope they arrest you and put you in jail forever. You need treatment."

"I'm Theodore Grasse, of Grasse, Cravatch and Weimar. I represent the Loomis family," said a strange man, stepping forward. He turned to Daniel. "Is this the one who made the bomb threats?" Daniel nodded weakly, although I noticed at least he was out of his wheelchair. "Oh God, I'm so unhappy," he said. "If only you hadn't put it in writing, Pamela, my dad would never have insisted we prosecute."

"You burned down our house," Angela whined. "You've always been jealous of my relationship with your father."

It was too much to take, all at once. "You want to know why I only bought a two-pound bag of flour at a time, rather than the more economical large size?" I snapped. "Apart from the fact that I've never had any storage space—and let me remind you I've never tried to borrow money from you, despite the fact that you're rich—read Adelle Davis! She says anything more than a small quantity quickly loses nutritional value." Angela gave my father a look—in fact everybody gave each other a look—and for the third time in thirty-six hours I sensed I was being judged and found wanting. "Okay," I said hastily, "maybe the flour isn't really the issue here. But let me tell you something—"

"Oh God," Angela said, "you'll never change."

"No," I said, "*you* cannot change—you're rigid. Whatever I do, you see me the way you want. You have a preset idea of what you think I'm like. And therefore anything I do, you adapt to your own reality. You've always wanted to believe I'm surly and unpleasant—so what I do makes no difference."

There was a silence. "She's crazy," Amber said at last.

"She's always been crazy," my dad said. It was strange to see him after thinking him dead. "I should never have let her mother have custody. But I was afraid her mother would kill herself if I didn't."

"Oh, what nonsense!" I said. "Because I haven't obeyed your rules, you attack—because you imagine it's the only way you can stop me from attacking first!"

Now Alby came forward, I hadn't noticed him in with the others before. "You must see how insane it looks, for you to disguise yourself as a man," he said. "You're very attractive, as a woman."

"You've all made up your own story for what you think is happening!" I said. "You all think you're better than me, superior to me, but you don't even have the slightest idea of who I am."

"Are you Miz Pamela Trowel?" the policeman I thought of as Officer Berlino asked. I nodded. "Will you come this way, please?" he said.

"Where are you taking me?"

"Is this man your psychiatrist?" the cop said, indicating Martin.

"That's a trick question," I said. "If I say no, you'll say I'm crazy again. If I say he is, I'll have to associate with him."

"I've arranged for you to go to Bellevue," Martin said sympathetically. "If you agree, that is. Your other choice is to be arrested. You can get out on bail, I suppose, but as it's Grasse, Cravatch prosecuting, the bail will probably be very high and . . ."

"I'll go to Bellevue," I said.

They left me with a security guard at the emergency entrance. There was a long L-shaped room with several overstuffed chairs—all of which were occupied by dozing patients, or perhaps visitors—and a row of less-comfortable-looking metal benches, where a nurse told me to take a seat. Nearby was a man tied onto a stretcher. Then two security guards came in, escorting a huge woman, a giantess really, who was wrapped in a blanket but stark naked beneath. After a minute a nurse appeared, gave her a jab, and she was quickly led off through a door.

There were ten or twelve people in the room; some did seem crazy, but no more insane than most people I saw on the street. There were two people sitting and talking; at first I didn't know which was the patient and which the visitor until one said, in loud disbelief, "You were going to jump off the Brooklyn Bridge and *you bought a new outfit to do it in?*"

"When Nora finds out, she's gonna kill me," the other man said.

Nobody paid me the slightest bit of attention. A man—I assumed he was a doctor—came out from a hall door and I said, "Excuse me."

"Not *now,*" he said furiously. "Don't bother me *now.*"

"But when?" I said.

"Tuesday," he said.

"Not till Tuesday?" I said. At that moment Martin came in, carrying a bunch of chrysanthemums, and the doctor who had been scurrying off stopped. ". . . borderline-borderline personality," the doctor said, or so I thought. Martin had that humble, submissive look a dog gets when it meets a more dominant one on the street. When they saw I was looking intently at them they stopped talking and the hospital doctor hurried out. Martin handed me the bunch of chrysanthemums. "The others wanted to stay," he said. "But I told them it would be better to leave you alone for a few days. They're a little angry. Unfortunately, I've spoken to the admitting physician, and he doesn't know when they'll be able to get you into a bed upstairs. They're completely full, and with the long holiday weekend it may be you'll have to stay in Emergency until Tuesday. It's unfortunate that you don't have any insurance—"

"I do have insurance," I said. "My mom took it out for me, through her university."

"Oh?" Martin said. "I didn't know. This could change things. In that case, I might try to see about getting you moved over to Oakdale. By the way," he added, "I forgot to tell you that your mother wanted me to tell you that the little boy is okay."

"Abdhul's okay?" I said. "Why didn't you tell me before?"

"For one thing, you already knew, didn't you? Your mom says she picked him up when you were staying in the motel in Massachusetts. But she told you that. She said you agreed that he was too much for you to handle."

"She never told me," I said. Betrayed! Oh, well, the only real betrayal in life could come from someone you trust, and she had been the only person—apart from Abdhul, and he was just a child—who had meant anything to me.

But how could I see myself as abnormal, in a world where there were no normal people left? Abnormality was the norm. In college there was a guy who liked me and was interested in having an exclusive relationship. Later he became a urologist and moved to Minnesota. That had probably been my one chance to stay out of trouble.

They let me out after twenty-one days. I wish I could say I was schizophrenic, or manic-depressive, or even a psychopath, which is currently known among psychiatrists as an "amoral personality." There seemed to be some argument, in that one doctor said I had a "narcissistic personality disorder," while another, unofficially, said he didn't believe so, but that I was probably "borderline-borderline." That they couldn't brand me with a term—or perhaps there was one, and they decided not to tell me—didn't really seem to matter.

I went home to my mother's until I could get on my feet again. "Where's Abdhul?" I said as soon as I got off the plane.

"You'll see him later," my mother said. "He's at his riding lesson. I've been keeping him very busy." Somehow we didn't have much to say. My mother thought I looked tired and sent me to her room to take a nap. By the time I woke up it was after six; from the living room I could hear the sound of someone playing the piano. I got up and washed my face. When I went into the other room, Abdhul was practicing. I was about to go over and say hello, but my mother stopped me. "Wait until he's finished," she whispered, so I turned around and went back to the bedroom. After a while the sounds of Für Elise stopped, and Abdhul came in. "Hi, Pamela," he said.

"Hi, honey," I said. "Boy, you really look like you've grown."

He shrugged. "Where's Dalgleish?" he said.

"There was a girl at work who wanted him," I said. "Do you want me to see if I can get him back?"

"That's okay," Abdhul said. "Mom said we'd get a golden retriever. A big dog is better for a person like me."

"Mom?" I said. "Abdhul, just tell me one thing, quickly, before she comes in: how come you got in the car with her, at the motel, when I told you not to go with any strangers?"

"Mom's not a stranger," Abdhul said. "I mean, Grandma. I knew who she was. You showed me her picture. And you have to admit, that was no kind of life we were leading, not for a small boy."

"Yes," I said.

"Anyway, she said you'd be here in a little while—and here you are!" He let out a little belch. "Mom!" he suddenly bellowed. "When's dinner? I'm hungry!"

I was happy for him, that he was the sort of person who could bond so easily with people. Life would be much easier for him that way. Once I read the memoirs of a famous dog anthropologist who raised chow-chows. These dogs were so loyal that if their owner went away they would starve to death. That was no way for a dog to live. People, too. If you lived in this day and age, the ones who survived were the ones who could adjust.

My mother signed him up for golf lessons with a really nice guy from the country club. It wasn't a fancy place; anyone could join, and use the tennis courts or take a boat out on the lake. Sometimes Frank, the instructor, came over with his wife, Melba—she was with the National Guard, in some sort of administrative capacity, and I liked her a lot, too. They had a little boy approximately Abdhul's age, and two children who were younger, and gradually Abdhul started spending more and more time over at their house. They didn't live far away, and in the summer childish voices could be heard floating over the backyards from their above-ground swimming pool, across to my mother's apartment, calling, "Marco!" "Polo!" "Marco!" "Polo!" I never actually knew what the game was.

A short time later I had four cysts removed from my ovaries; then my mother suggested I get pregnant, since time was running out and Abdhul was anxious for a little brother or sister. There are sperm banks for that sort of thing; my mother began to look into it. Of course, we didn't want me to end up with sperm that my brother sold. If not the sperm bank, my mother had a graduate student she liked—Italian, visiting from Milan, doing research into dowsing, who she wanted to invite to dinner. She thought he might be a vegetarian. I wanted to make red lentils and Brussels sprouts on rice, a recipe I clipped from a magazine. My mother planned to wear a waitress outfit and serve the meal. Abdhul said he'd be the bartender. He practiced on us every night, trying different things: rob roys, gimlets, tom and jerry, maiden's prayer.

## Tom and Jerry

*Take any number of egg whites. Beat to a stiff froth. Add 1½ bar spoons sugar to each egg. Beat yolks separately. Then beat well together to a stiff batter. Add to this a pinch of bicarbonate of soda. Stir up frequently so eggs do not settle or separate. Use large bowl. To Serve: Put 1 tablespoon of batter into Tom and Jerry mug, add 1 jigger rum and brandy, mixed. Fill up with boiling water or milk. Stir with spoon, grate nutmeg on top and serve at once.*

## Maiden's Prayer

*⅛ orange juice*                    *⅜ Cointreau*
*⅛ lemon juice*                     *⅜ Dry Gin*

After a few weeks at home I found a job at Woolworth's. I didn't want to keep taking my mother's money, although she said she didn't mind. I never could add or subtract, but the new cash-register system meant I didn't have to, just run each product over a magnetic plate of some sort and then watch the numbers appear in front of me on the screen. *Dried Jerky Strips, Jergen's Baby Lotion, Pepsi, Macadamia nuts, plant kelp fertilizer* . . . At lunch I would have a grilled cheese sandwich in the coffee shop and eavesdrop on the elderly ladies who came in for hot fudge sundaes and meatloaf. I don't know how long I might have gone on in this fashion. Probably a long time. But then, thanks to my mother, I got a job in Admissions at the university. It pays twenty-four thousand dollars a year, not a lot to live on, but with our combined salaries we were able to buy a small house. It was a little farther away from where Frank and Melba live, but Abdhul still rode his bike over.

One night Frank and Melba invited us over for drinks and said they wanted to adopt him. "You know," Frank said, "this kid is so talented at golf—I don't want him to know—but I can see him easily getting a scholarship somewhere, or possibly even turning pro. If he's with us, it'll give me more time with him."

"What does Abdhul say?" I said.

"He wants to," Melba said. "But he doesn't want to hurt your feelings and he wanted us to talk to you."

My mother and I looked at each other. "Of course," I said at last. "If that's what he wants." They called him in from the driveway, where he was playing basketball with Ted. "After all," Frank said, while we waited, "it's not like he'll never see you."

Abdhul came in, wearing baggy blue jeans and a shirt with tails sticking out; that was what boys his age dressed in. He looked at Melba and Frank. "They say it's okay," Frank said.

"Great!" Abdhul said. Then he looked over at my mother and me. "I'll come visit," he said. "It's not like anything will be any different."

"And this means there's a scholarship fund at the country club he'll be eligible for," Frank explained. "In the event that the golf doesn't work out."

"Now," Melba said, "why don't you stay and have dinner with us? We're barbecuing some steaks in the backyard, to celebrate."

"All right, Mom!" Abdhul said, and then looked sheepish.

"Oh, thanks," my mother said. "But . . ." She gave me a questioning glance. "We have to get going," I said. "I, uh, have some things I have to do at home. Abdhul, come over on Saturday, if you have time and you want me to show you how to bake bread."

"Pick me up after school tomorrow instead!" he said and we left.

Over dinner—frozen Budget Lo-Cal Gourmet, mine was Indian Lamb Curry, my mother's Chicken Divan—we discussed environment versus heredity, but in the end could come to no conclusion. "But on TV, and in the news," my mother said, "you always hear the social workers saying kids available for adoption can only be with families of the same racial background. So maybe he'll be happier with Melba and Frank."

I went to get him after school and took him to Buttermilk Park. How old could he have been by then? Nine? Ten? Eleven? "I feel strange today," he said, as we sat at the picnic bench near the waterfall. "But I don't know whether I feel sad, anxious, or embarrassed."

"Oh?" I said and was about to ask him why, when he went on. "I guess I feel embarrassed," he said. "There's this girl I like at school—her name's

Rachel—and her best friend, Anya, knows I like Rachel, and she must have told her. Because today, in front of a whole lot of people Rachel said, 'I know you like me, Abdhul!' And now, I don't know what to do."

I hesitated, not certain what advice to offer. But he didn't wait for my response. "I guess," he said, "I'll ask her out to lunch."

The elementary school was located right next to a mini-shopping mall, and the little kids—if they had a letter of permission from their parents—were allowed to eat lunch at the various restaurants there, something we certainly wouldn't have been permitted when I went to school. "I just don't know where to take her, though," he said. "There's McDonald's, Wendy's, Roy Rogers, and Louie's Pizza."

"That sounds like a good idea," I said. "Invite her for pizza. She must like you, Abdhul, if she said that in front of all those people."

He attempted a wink—more of a twitch, actually—and grinned. "So?" he said. "Maybe I'll get lucky. Anyway, I'll take her someplace cheap, that's for sure."

"How come?" I said.

"Because, I'm saving my money!"

"For what?" I said.

He looked irritated. "To buy a car! So you don't have to keep borrowing your mother's car, and then we can get out of here! Frank's going to get me a job as a caddy at the golf course, and then I can work after school and on weekends. You get good tips. How much do you think a decent used car will cost?"

"But, Abdhul," I said, "what about college, and Melba and Frank, and a professional career in golf?"

"Oh, come on, Pamela," he said. "What's happened to you? That's not like us. You don't want to get too conventional, do you?"

In this state, he can get his license when he turns sixteen. At the moment, that's our plan.